"Carachel! Come face challenge!"

"I am here." Carachel stepped out of the trees. He held up a hand, and the serpent ring flashed on his finger. "Who are you?"

"I am Wengarth of the Guild of Mages," the large man replied, "and my apprentice is named Laznyr."

"And what do you want of me?" Carachel's voice was almost a chant, and Jermain realized that he was watching a ritual as formal as a coronation.

"I come to challenge you to the combat sorcerous for the wrongs you have done to all wizards, to the Guild of Mages, and to me," Wengarth replied.

"I accept your challenge. Let the circle be drawn."

THE SEVEN TOWERS

PATRICIA C. WREDE

ACE FANTASY BOOKS
NEW YORK

THE SEVEN TOWERS

An Ace Fantasy Book / published by arrangement with
the author and the author's agent, Valerie Smith

PRINTING HISTORY
Ace Original / March 1984

ISBN: 0-441-75973-4

Ace Fantasy Books are published by The Berkley Publishing Group,
200 Madison Avenue, New York, New York 10016.
PRINTED IN THE UNITED STATES OF AMERICA

For Joel and Beth, who listened with great patience to many improbable ideas, and for Nate, Pam, Steve, Kara, Will and Emma, who wouldn't let me get away with any of them.

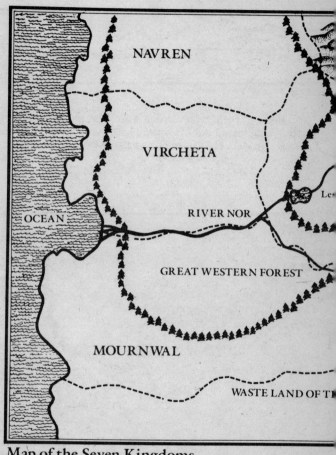

Map of the Seven Kingdoms

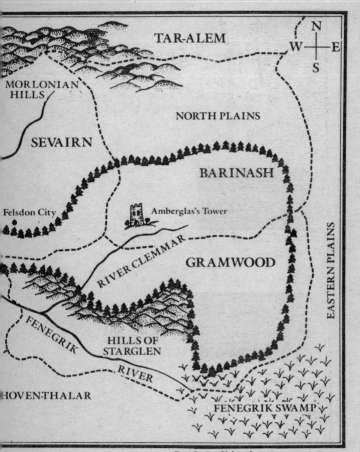

TAR-ALEM

N
W   E
S

MORLONIAN
HILLS

NORTH PLAINS

SEVAIRN

BARINASH

Felsdon City

Amberglas's Tower

RIVER CLEMMAR

GRAMWOOD

EASTERN PLAINS

FENEGRIK

HILLS OF
STARGLEN

RIVER

HOVEN-THALAR

FENEGRIK SWAMP

Borders of kingdoms – – – – – – –
Hills
Forest 🌲🌲
Swamp ᴠ ᴠ ᴠ

Chapter One

Jermain crouched low on his horse's neck as he urged the animal to greater speed. Small branches stung his face as they whipped past, but he barely felt them. He could hear the sounds of his pursuers crashing through the brush behind him. Too close, they were much too close; he didn't know this forest well enough to lose them. He shut the thought out of his mind and concentrated on escape.

The trees were becoming larger; good. He might be able to gain some ground once his horse was clear of this little bushy stuff. He dug his heels into Blackflame's sides. The horse responded at once. Jermain felt the lengthening stride and knew a moment's hope. No one in the Border Guard had a horse to match Blackflame. Perhaps he could get away from them before blood loss forced him to stop.

Expertly he guided his mount through the trees. He could feel himself weakening, but he could not spare a hand to staunch the blood. Desperately he spurred the horse once more. His eyes searched the forest for a shelf of rock, a stream, something he could use to hide his trail. He found nothing.

His vision blurred, but he did not dare to stop. He clamped his right arm against his side, clenching his teeth against the pain. The pressure might slow down the bleeding, or it might not, but the pain would keep him conscious a little longer. He could make it yet. The shouts and horns were fainter; he had gained a little ground.

The forest seemed to be thinning ahead; perhaps he could gain a little more time. He guided Blackflame toward the place where the trees grew farthest apart. A moment later, they broke into a large clearing. Jermain had just time to see the slight, startled figure standing in Blackflame's path; then the horse planted its forefeet and stopped, so abruptly that it was forced back almost on its haunches. Jermain was flung forward out of the saddle and fell heavily to the ground.

Darkness and pain surged over him. Jermain forced them back. He couldn't pass out now; he would lose too much time. "Dear me," a voice said somewhere above him. "That was a rough stop. Are you hurt?"

Jermain opened his eyes and blinked in disbelief. A woman stood a few feet away, her back toward him. A heavy mass of steel-colored hair fell to the waist of her pale blue gown. Blackflame stood in front of her, trembling from exertion. The woman had one hand out, stroking Blackflame's nose. She was talking to the horse.

To the *horse?* Jermain blinked again. He tried to roll onto his side so he could see more clearly, and a fresh wave of pain made him gasp. Apparently he had broken a rib or two in that fall. The noise attracted the woman's attention; she turned and looked at Jermain. She was young; not a damsel of sixteen, certainly, but no more than thirty, and obviously a lady.

"It's quite all right," she said vaguely, "I will be there in a minute. Of course, you're here, so it really doesn't matter, but most people seem to feel better if I explain about these things." She turned back to the horse, and her head tilted to one side in critical examination.

For a moment, Jermain lay motionless. He would have cursed, but he had no energy for it. He tried again to get to his feet; he made it to his knees. The woman turned around again.

"You really shouldn't do that, especially if you're not feeling well, which I can see you aren't, what with that hole in your side and so on. I assume you realize that, though one can never tell. People can be so very odd. There was a man I used to know, who always wore his boots on the wrong feet for one day out of every month. So I thought I'd mention it, in case you didn't."

"I have to get out of here," Jermain croaked, ignoring her jumbled speech. She had to help him, or he was finished for certain.

"No, you'll be much better off staying here," the woman said. "Well, not here precisely, at least not for very long. No, certainly not long; you would be very uncomfortable, I am sure, and the damp would get into your wound, which would probably give you a fever, though sometimes it doesn't.''

Jermain ignored her completely this time. He was having trouble balancing on his knees, and he knew that if he fell over now he wouldn't be able to get up again. He thought about it for a minute and decided to crawl. That, he could manage. He dropped to his hands and knees, and began working his way slowly toward Blackflame, trying not to think about the pain in his chest. The woman made no move to help or hinder him. "Really, you are being very silly," she said kindly.

The sound of shouts and hoofbeats came clearly to Jermain, growing quickly louder. With the last of his strength, Jermain lunged for Blackflame's stirrup. He missed and sprawled painfully on the ground, fighting to remain conscious. The woman walked over and knelt beside him; he felt gentle fingers on his injured side. "If you stop jumping about like that, you probably won't bleed to death," the woman said, and six horsemen broke into the clearing.

For a brief, nightmarish moment, Jermain was certain he would be trampled. He did not even have enough strength left to try to roll aside; somehow the horses missed him anyway. The Border Guards pulled their mounts to a halt, forming a circle around Jermain and the woman who knelt at his side. The woman blinked at them.

"Dear me," she murmured. "Such a lot of people."

The leader of the group, a burly man with a Captain's braid on the front of his faded jacket, looked at the woman in surprise. Evidently he came to the same conclusion Jermain had, for he bowed respectfully before he said briskly, "Lady, I am Captain Morenar of the King's Border Guard. This man is a dangerous criminal. You will, of course, oblige us by retiring at once. I would not wish to distress you by executing him in your presence, and we can't risk letting him escape."

The woman looked critically down at Jermain, then back at the Captain. "Not at all," she said firmly. "He does not look in the least dangerous. I'm quite willing to believe he is extremely foolish, but a great many people are, and I have never heard of anyone being executed for it, though I couldn't say for sure that it's never happened. Of course, if he continues to run about with that wound bleeding all over everything and making such a mess you won't have to.''

Morenar frowned and tried again. "Lady, we have been chasing this man for four hours; I assure you there is no mistake."

"Well, it is certainly rude of you to contradict me, and I don't believe you at all," the woman said flatly. "At least, I believe you have been chasing him, but not for four hours, and certainly he's not a criminal. Though I can understand why you say so; it would probably be very awkward for you to explain. So many things are; awkward, I mean. Large kettles, for instance, and carrying three brooms at once, and those fat brown birds with the red wings whose name I can't remember just at present. They waddle."

"Lady," Morenar said, "we have not made a mistake."

"I didn't say you had. You obviously weren't paying attention. Why are you chasing him?" the woman said.

"We are under orders direct from Leshiya," Morenar replied, obviously relieved that the woman seemed to be making sense at last.

"But Leshiya is the capital of Sevairn," the woman said gently. "And, of course, you're not in Sevairn just now, and neither am I; but then, there are a great many places that aren't—in Sevairn, I mean—so perhaps you hadn't noticed. The border is back that way." She pointed.

The Captain stared at her for a moment. "We have wasted enough time," he said abruptly. "Alver, Rusalk, escort the lady elsewhere, at once."

Two of the soldiers swung down from their horses and started forward. Jermain tensed, wondering whether he was strong enough to get away while they were attending to the woman. He didn't think so; he seriously doubted whether he could even get himself upright again, much less stay there. Beside him, the woman rose to her feet. She looked at the two soldiers, then at Morenar. "This is not wise of you," she said softly. "Not wise at all."

"Take her," Morenar said, and the men reached out.

"Well, if you won't listen," the woman said, and made a swift throwing motion with both hands.

The two soldiers went stumbling backward into a brownish-grey fog that Jermain was certain had not been there a moment ago. One of them screamed; then the brown cloud billowed upward, hiding them, and the rest of the Border Guards, from Jermain. Only a small area around Jermain was free of the fog; Blackflame and the woman and a little grass were the only things he could see. Even they were whirling; Jermain felt a stab of fear. A face bent over him, framed in steel-colored hair.

"Don't worry," the woman said as he slipped into unconsciousness. "I will see to things."

That, thought Jermain with the last of his awareness, is what I am afraid of.

Eltiron leaned outward. The stone of the tower battlements was cool and smooth beneath his hands; nearly all of Leshiya was visible below him in living miniature. This must be the way birds see us when they fly, he thought. I wish I were a bird. He leaned farther, as if the motion would bring him closer to the sky. Somewhere below him a bell chimed.

Startled, Eltiron straightened. A brief wind ruffled his brown hair as he stood concentrating. Three, no, four chimes; he was late again. His shoulders slumped. No matter how much he hurried now, Terrel would still be certain to point out his irresponsibility to everyone when he finally arrived at the King's Council. There was no point in rushing. Eltiron took a last look upward, then turned and started back into the castle.

Inside the tower Eltiron paused. It wasn't as if anything important was ever discussed at the Councils anymore; Eltiron's father and Terrel made most of the decisions in advance. Reluctantly, Eltiron started down the stairs. No, he couldn't justify missing the meeting completely, even if it only gave Terrel another chance to sneer at him. Eltiron reached the bottom of the stairs and turned down the corridor that led to the Council chambers. His steps slowed as he neared the door. With a sigh he straightened his shoulders and went in.

The two men at the far end of the Council table looked up as Eltiron entered. "It's about time," said the large man wearing the gold crown.

Eltiron bowed with deep respect. "Father." He nodded briefly to the second figure, a handsome blond man in red. "My Lord Terrel."

"Your Highness." Terrel's bow was a hair too shallow and a fraction too brief; no one but Eltiron would have noticed. He looks more like a Prince than I do, Eltiron thought resentfully as Terrel resumed his seat. Though Eltiron was tall, Terrel was nearly two fingers' width taller, and, in addition to his

striking good looks, he moved with a practiced grace Eltiron
could not seem to imitate, however hard he tried.

"Sit down, sit down," the King said, waving at an empty
chair. "There's no reason for you to stand around keeping us
waiting."

Eltiron looked around and realized suddenly that there was
no one else in the chamber. "I was not told of any change in
the time of the Council," he said as he took a chair. Inwardly,
he winced. Practically the first thing he said, and already he
sounded apologetic.

"Of course you weren't," his father said. "Half the time no
one can find you, and the other half you aren't interested
anyway. What I've done to deserve a son like you I don't
know."

Eltiron felt his face grow hot. The King glared at him for a
moment, then went on in a milder tone, "The truth is, this
time it wasn't your fault. I'd forgotten until Terrel mentioned
it, but you couldn't very well be present while we discussed
your marriage. So I changed the time of the meeting."

Another one of Terrel's bright ideas for undermining me,
Eltiron thought. Then the rest of the sentence penetrated.
"Marriage?"

"Of course, marriage," his father said irritably. "Didn't I
just say that? We settled it all this morning. You're going to
marry the King of Barinash's daughter—what's her name
again, Terrel?"

"The Princess Crystalorn," Terrel said. He smiled. "The
marriage will cement the alliance between Sevairn and
Barinash; it is an excellent move."

"But I don't want to get married yet, sir," Eltiron said,
finding his voice at last.

"Yet? What do you mean, yet?" the King demanded.
"You're nearly twenty; how long do you expect to wait? Or
did you think I was going to leave things to chance?"

"No, sir," Eltiron said hastily. "But this is very sudden."

"Oh, you'll have at least a month to get used to the idea,"
his father said, waving away the objection. "It'll take that
long to make the rest of the arrangements and get the girl
here."

"The rest of the arrangements?" Eltiron said bitterly. "I
see. I am to have no say in the matter. How long has this been
under consideration?"

"I think Terrel mentioned it about six months ago," the King said. "Not that it makes any difference."

"Six months? For six months you've been planning to marry me to this Princess I've never met, and you never thought to ask me about it?" Humiliation and anger together left Eltiron speechless.

The King frowned. "It's a fine marriage; it will tie Barinash firmly to Sevairn. You have nothing to complain about."

"Nothing to complain about!" Eltiron was shocked out of his normal reserve. "Six months ago you never would have considered such an alliance! Before Jermain left, you—"

"Jermain!" The King's hand slammed down on the arm of his chair. "I told you I never wanted to hear that traitor's name again! Yet every time I see you, it's Jermain this and Jermain that, until I wonder whether you know any other name in the world. Enough of Jermain!"

"Prince Eltiron was close to Jermain," Terrel said. "It is natural that he would wish to defend his friend."

"It should not be natural for my son to defend a traitor!" the King roared.

Eltiron winced. "Father, I—"

"Silence! You will marry whom I tell you to, and you will make alliances where I say you will, and if you mention Jermain to me again I will have you imprisoned for treason yourself! Is that clear?"

"But—"

"No more arguments! You may go. Go watch the birds, or write a poem for your bride, or whatever it is you do with your time! Go!"

"Yes, Father." Eltiron's shoulders slumped. As he turned to leave, he saw the gleam of satisfaction in Terrel's eyes; it was almost more than he could stand. He bit back a half-formed comment and left the room. The door closed silently behind him, but he could still feel Terrel's eyes on his back, as if the man could see through wood and stone. He shivered and walked rapidly away.

Chapter Two

As soon as he realized that he was awake, Jermain opened his
eyes. He was lying in a narrow bed near one wall of a large,
rather cluttered, circular room that smelled of cloves and
honey. Directly across from him was a solid wooden door;
beside it a flight of stone stairs led upward, curving part-
way around the wall of the room to vanish into an opening in
the ceiling, just above the foot of the bed. A rough-hewn table
occupied the center of the floor. Three mismatched chairs
stood around it, and a large black bird was perched on the
back of the tallest, preening. A squirrel sat on a window ledge
nearby, scolding noisily.

Someone had bandaged Jermain's side while he'd slept; he
could feel the tautness of the linen as he breathed. His side still
ached, but the pain was no longer insistent. Perhaps he had
only bruised his ribs after all, not broken them. Jermain sat up
carefully. He was considering what to do next when the door
swung open.

"Be quiet, Garren," said a female voice, and the squirrel
stopped chattering at once. An instant later, the woman who
had rescued Jermain from the guards appeared in the doorway. She went straight to the table without bothering to shut
the door behind her. She set down the armload of plants she
was carrying, then turned to observe the air in Jermain's general vicinity.

"I'm so glad you're feeling better," she said. "That is, if
you are. You haven't said anything about it, so perhaps you
aren't, which wouldn't be at all surprising, what with losing all
that blood and breaking a rib and so on, though possibly

you'd rather I didn't go into detail. Still, I do think it's a mistake not to talk about unpleasant things, even if people are sensitive; after all, if one worried all the time about offending people, one would never say anything, which in some cases would be a very good thing."

"I am glad of the chance to thank you for your timely rescue, lady," Jermain said. He rose and bowed, wincing. "My name is Jermain Trevannon."

"How nice for you," the woman said. "Mine is Amberglas. Do sit down again; you really aren't recovered yet, and it would be inconvenient for me to have to put you back together again."

The bed creaked as Jermain sat down. The squirrel made a disapproving noise. Amberglas pulled out one of the chairs and seated herself at the table. She picked up one of the plants she had brought in and blinked at it, then set it aside and took another.

"Lemon verbena is quite out of season," she said. "Still, it ought to be good for something, if I can only think what; nearly everything is. Except skunk weed. If you can think of a use for a skunk weed plant, you may have the one growing at the edge of my garden. I can't imagine why I leave it there, but if you take it, then of course I'll know. Whyever were all those unpleasant people chasing you?"

Jermain hesitated. "I'm an outlaw," he said at last. He was surprised by the bitterness in his voice; he'd thought he was used to it by now.

"That has nothing to do with it," Amberglas said firmly. "There are a great many outlaws in the mountains, and the Sevairn Border Guards never bother with any of them, which is extremely shortsighted, but quite understandable since most of the outlaws are far better at fighting than the guardsmen. It really reflects rather poorly on King Marreth's training program, but perhaps he doesn't care about outlaws."

"Well, he cares about this one," Jermain said shortly.

"Yes, I know. Or at least, I'd know if you would tell me, which isn't the same thing at all, but is actually quite close, if you think about it." Amberglas was still sorting plants, seemingly at random. "Why?"

Jermain studied the woman. Her questions seemed innocent enough, but experience made him reluctant to be too trusting. On the other hand, he had no reason to believe that Amberglas would suddenly hand him over to the very people she had helped him escape. Furthermore, he owed her some explanation; however much he would prefer not to answer, the woman had a right to know whom she had rescued. "King Marreth fears I may return to Leshiya," Jermain said at last.

"Yes, of course," Amberglas said to the black bird. "If he didn't, he wouldn't send guards after you. Although it does seem a little unusual for a King to be afraid of an outlaw, but then, I haven't known very many outlaws, so perhaps it's more common than I'd thought."

"Most outlaws don't come from the King's court in Leshiya."

"No, that's quite true. At least, I think it is. I knew a thief once who was from the capital of Tar-Alem, and there are quite a few murderers who come from good families, but that isn't exactly the same thing. Still, a great many things turn up precisely where one doesn't want them—rats in bakeries, for instance, and those large green worms on cabbages—so I suppose it's quite possible for a King's court to have outlaws. What were you before you were an outlaw?"

"I served King Marreth," Jermain said. "I was his Chief Adviser for six years."

"You must be very good at giving advice." Amberglas dropped a small blue-flowered plant on a pile of middle-sized red flowers and looked up. "Why did you become an outlaw?"

"I had very little choice," Jermain said. "Between Terrel and Eltiron, I never had a chance. You talk of outlaws at the King's court; well, Terrel Lassond fits the description. He's the sort who would sacrifice the whole country if it would help him get what he wanted. I wish Marreth joy of his new adviser."

"He doesn't sound pleasant," Amberglas agreed. "I don't suppose there's any chance of Marreth's discovering this for himself?"

"Oh, he'll find out, all right," Jermain said with renewed bitterness. "When it's too late. Marreth deserves what he's going to get. He's made his stew, now he can eat it. For all I care, he can boil in it." Jermain stopped. For six months he had schooled himself not to think of Leshiya, Marreth, Terrel, or Eltiron; the violence of his reaction to Amberglas's questions shocked him.

"I see." Amberglas studied one of the plants she was holding. "I don't suppose you would be inclined to explain just what it was that all these people did? Because you haven't, yet. You may not have realized it, so I thought I would point it out to you."

Jermain snorted. "Terrel and His Royal Highness Prince Eltiron convinced Marreth that I was guilty of treason. As a result, Marreth stripped me of my lands and position and awarded them to Terrel. Isn't that enough?"

"I do see that you might think so," Amberglas said. "Were you?"

"Was I what?"

"Were you guilty? Of treason, I mean; there are a great many other things you could be guilty of, but since you weren't accused of any of them, they don't really matter. Well, no, they do matter, certainly, but I'm not particularly interested in them at the moment, though if you happen to think of anything else you want to mention, it's quite all right with me."

"I am no traitor," Jermain said stiffly.

"I didn't think so. But of course, you could still be guilty of treason. That's why I asked about it," Amberglas said.

"No, I was not guilty," Jermain said after a moment. "Unless it's treason to believe an old friend's warning, and counsel that preparation be made." Absently, he fingered the place where the short scar on his left arm was hidden by his sleeve.

"That doesn't sound much like treason," Amberglas said. "Of course, it would depend on the friend. And the warning. Telling someone that his dinner is burning isn't treason, at least not in most places, though I couldn't say for certain about Navren. The King there has made such extremely peculiar laws that one never knows what is treason in Navren. Or what isn't," she added thoughtfully and looked at Jermain.

For a moment Jermain hesitated, then he nodded. He had no reason to remain silent. If safety was his main concern, he had already told Amberglas more than was wise; finishing the tale would make no difference. Besides, there was always the chance, however slim, that she might be willing to help him.

"Judge for yourself," he said. "Ranlyn is one of the Hoven-Thalar, who roam the wasteland between Mournwal and the South Marnish Desert. He . . . owes me a debt, and among his people debts are a grave matter. So when he came to Leshiya seven months ago with the news that his people were beginning to move north, I believed him. I told Marreth, and advised him to prepare the army, and to send messengers to Gramwood, Mournwal, and Tar-Alem as well. Marreth refused to believe me. Terrel and Eltiron made it seem that Ranlyn lied, and that I wanted war only to serve my own ambition.''

"How very sad," Amberglas said absently. "Did you?"

"No!" Jermain almost shouted. "If Sevairn doesn't join Mournwal, the Hoven-Thalar will sweep right over it, and Sevairn will be next! Even with Gramwood and Tar-Alem to help, it would take luck to stop a determined movement north. And the Hoven-Thalar are determined, believe me. I've spent the past six months in the south with Ranlyn, to see for myself. Does that sound like personal ambition?"

"Not precisely, though sometimes it's hard to tell," said Amberglas, even more absently than before. She tilted her head to one side. "You're quite certain Marreth won't change his mind?"

Jermain's lips tightened. He shook his head, and his voice was harsh as he said, "You saw those men. Marreth couldn't quite justify killing me publicly, but now that I'm safely forgotten, he's willing to send his men to murder me in secret. Marreth can't bear to be wrong; he won't change."

"Dear me. He must not like you at all." Amberglas rose from her chair and began gathering up the piles of plants. "I suppose it is entirely possible that you are mistaken, although I must admit it doesn't seem like it. But then, of course, it wouldn't. People who are very sure of themselves never sound as if they are mistaken. I met a girl once who insisted that she was the Queen of the Thieves. Really, she was very bad at stealing. But very good at making up stories. She was quite convincing, if you didn't know better."

"Who was she?" Jermain asked, half from curiosity and half from a desire to turn the conversation in a new direction.

"The Princess of Barinash," Amberglas said. "But she promised not to do it anymore—tell people she was a thief, I mean—so it's quite all right now, though not exactly the same as being mistaken, now that I come to think of it."

Amberglas finished gathering up the plants and started for

the stairs. She stopped at the bottom step to look back at
Jermain. "I really do think you had better lie down and rest a
little more. That was quite a bad wound in your side; in fact, it
still is, though I've seen worse, but only on people who had
been in battles, and I don't believe you can call a fight with
Sevairn's Border Guard a battle. At least, you could call it
that, but it wouldn't really be proper."

Depression and weariness swept over Jermain in a sudden
wave. "Perhaps you shouldn't have stopped them," he said.

"If you mean that I should have let them kill you, you are
being exceedingly silly," Amberglas said. "I certainly should
not, which ought to be plain even if you are feverish. Though I
had rather hoped you wouldn't be; still, it's not surprising
considering the blood loss and the damp ground and those extremely rude people."

Jermain shook his head. Amberglas frowned in his direction. "I have no intention of allowing you to die here," she
said severely. "If you really want to, you'll simply have to do
it somewhere else, which of course you can't until you are well
enough to leave. So you had very much better stop this
foolishness and rest instead."

Amberglas started up the stairs. Jermain lay back, watching her with weary bewilderment. She moves with grace, he
thought. Marreth's ladies would envy her. Who is she, and
why is she helping me? Amberglas's silent tread upon the
stone stairs gave him no answer, and presently he slept.

The next two days brought Jermain no closer to understanding Amberglas's motives. He found it hard to believe that she
could be a sorceress, but how else could she have saved him
from the Border Guard? Jermain was certain he had not imagined the brown fog which had come from nowhere to engulf
Morenar and his men. He tried, once, to ask her about it, but
Amberglas's answer—which involved mist, the River Nor,
rowan trees, smoke, and a woman with two dogs who might
have been taken for a witch if the dogs had been cats—so
thoroughly confused him that he did not bring the subject up a
second time.

Jermain was also worried about Blackflame, in spite of
Amberglas's confused assurances. The horse was practically
the only thing Jermain had been able to bring out of Sevairn,
and Jermain prized him highly. And what, really, could
Amberglas know about caring for a war horse? Jermain was

not reassured until Amberglas took him out to a small building just outside the house and showed him where Blackflame was stabled.

To his surprise, Jermain found the horse comfortable, clean, and well provided for. His saddle and bridle had been cleaned and polished; they hung on a peg just inside the door. Jermain examined everything carefully, partly from habit, partly to justify his earlier concern, but he found nothing to complain of. Finally he looked up from beside Blackflame. Amberglas was watching the horse. Jermain rose.

"I think I owe you an apology," he said. "You were quite right; you need no advice from me. The King's stables could do no better."

"Well, I don't suppose you could have known that," Amberglass said as they started toward the stable door. "It is rather difficult to be sure of such things when you can't see them, which of course you couldn't since you were lying in bed most of the time. Actually, you really should go back; this is the first time you have been up—not counting meals, of course, which is quite reasonable, though not strictly accurate —and you really shouldn't do too much just at present. So of course you were concerned about your horse."

"I do feel a little—" Jermain broke off in midsentence and froze in the center of the open stable door.

"Dear me," said Amberglas from slightly behind him. "Whatever is the matter?"

Jermain hardly heard her. He was staring incredulously at the building in front of him. Amberglas's home was no house, but a tower; and line for line, stone for stone, it was an exact duplicate of the Tower of Judgment in Leshiya. The Tower of Judgment, where King Marreth's Council met. The Tower of Judgment, where Jermain had been sentenced to disgrace and exile.

A hand touched his arm lightly. Jermain swung around and found himself blinking at Amberglas. "You do seem quite upset," Amberglas said. "I don't suppose you would care to answer my question after all?"

Slowly, Jermain forced himself to relax. This was not Leshiya; no castle rose behind the tower, and he was surrounded by trees, not a city. "I am sorry," he said at last. "I had not really looked at your tower before, and it brought back—unpleasant memories."

"The tower? Why?"

The woman's voice was almost sharp, and Jermain's head turned in surprise. A slight shock went through him as he realized that Amberglas was looking, not past him or through him, but at him. Her gaze was clear and intense, and highly unsettling. Suddenly Jermain had no difficulty at all in believing she was a sorceress.

"Ah, it reminds me of a place in Leshiya," Jermain said.

"What place?"

"The Tower of Judgment."

"I see," Amberglas said. She smiled, and her eyes took on the same slightly out of focus look that they had had before. "Under the circumstances, that would be quite unnerving, though this isn't Leshiya, of course, or even Sevairn, which I think is quite a good thing. But then, some people think I have peculiar taste."

Jermain was still too unnerved to think of an adequate answer. Amberglas, however, did not appear to require one. In silence, they crossed the open space between the stable and the tower.

Amberglas did not mention Sevairn, Marreth, or the tower again. Jermain was puzzled, but he remembered that odd, intense gaze too well to bring the subject up himself. He spent an uneasy night, and he awoke early. He was sitting at the table, watching the squirrel eat nuts on the back of one of the chairs and trying to decide whether to take his leave of Amberglas and the tower, when he heard a shout outside.

Almost at once, Jermain was out of his chair heading for his sword. The shout came again, more clearly this time. "Amberglas!"

Jermain slowed. The voice sounded too young to be a real threat. Still, he picked up the sword and fastened it in place before he took his seat again. A moment later the door banged open and a small, windblown figure burst into the room.

"Amberglas! Where are you? You won't believe—" The girl stopped, staring at Jermain from inside an incredible mass of tangled brown hair. Her eyes were a dark, vivid blue. "Who are you?" she demanded. "And where's Amberglas?"

"My name is Trevannon," Jermain said. He rose and bowed slightly. "Will you honor me with yours?"

"Crystalorn," the girl said a trifle less hostilely. "Would you tell me where Amberglas is, please?"

Jermain blinked, thinking he must certainly have heard wrong. The girl's clothes were rich enough, and surely there was a suggestion of court training in her mannerisms, but what would the Princess of Barinash be doing alone in the middle of a forest? He realized that she was still waiting for an answer and opened his mouth to reply.

"I'm right here," said Amberglas's voice from behind him, "which of course doesn't really say much, but as long as you are, too, it can't matter a great deal." Crystalorn and Jermain both started and turned to find her standing at the bottom of the stairs.

"Amberglas! I'm so glad I found you. I have to—" Crystalorn stopped again and looked at Jermain. "Amberglas, can you come outside where we can talk? I have to decide what to do, and they'll find out I'm missing before too long."

"That's quite all right, dear," Amberglas said vaguely. "Do sit down and explain. It's really much more comfortable in here, if you'll only persuade Garren to take a different chair. Not that the other one isn't quite as comfortable, but—"

"Oh, Amberglas, do you have to run on like that right now?" Crystalorn said. "This is important!"

"Well, of course it is, or you wouldn't have come to see me this way," Amberglas said. "Now, sit down and tell me about it."

Crystalorn looked at Jermain uncertainly, then turned back to Amberglas. "You're sure it's all right?"

"Whyever not?"

"All right, then." Crystalorn flopped into the nearest chair. The squirrel chattered at her and went back to cracking nuts. Crystalorn ignored it. "Father wants me to marry the Prince of Sevairn," she said.

Jermain caught his breath. Had Marreth gone mad? Relations between Sevairn and Barinash had been strained ever since Barinash's brief, abortive attempt at invasion eight years before; most of the nobility still believed that Barinash was simply waiting for the right opportunity to try again. If Marreth wasn't careful, the nobles would revolt, and . . . Jermain shut off the thought. He was no longer Marreth's adviser; there was nothing he could do.

"How interesting," Amberglas murmured. "Marriage is quite a good thing; at least, most people seem to think so. I really couldn't say, since I've never been married myself, but a great many other people have done it quite successfully. Though of course, that doesn't always follow."

"But I don't want to get married," Crystalorn said, leaning forward. "And it isn't even Father's idea. Salentor talked him into it."

"Dear me," said Amberglas. "That seems a little strange. Are you quite certain?"

"Of course I am," Crystalorn said impatiently. "I knew they were going to be talking about me, so I hid in the next room and listened. And now they're taking me to Sevairn, and I'm to be married to this Eltiron person in less than a month, and they didn't even ask me about it. I'm seventeen; Father should have at least asked me. So I ran away to see you."

"I quite understand," said Amberglas. "At least, I believe I do. It is very annoying to be made to do something one doesn't at all wish to do. It's rather like washing socks; most unpleasant."

"It's not at all like washing socks!" Crystalorn said. "And you aren't really helping. What am I going to do?"

"I suppose you are quite sure you don't wish to marry Prince Eltiron? He is rather well spoken of. By most people," Amberglas said, gazing at the air about three feet to the left of Jermain's head. "Though of course it would be exceedingly surprising if no one had anything bad to say about him. I believe I knew someone like that once. You wouldn't have liked him at all; he was very dull."

"I don't even *know* Eltiron!" Crystalorn said.

"Then perhaps you should go to Sevairn and meet him before you make up your mind whether to marry him," Amberglas said. "On the other hand, perhaps you would rather go to Gramwood and meet him; it's fairly close, and it has quite a good Princess to distract him if you should decide you don't want to marry him after all. Of course, Prince Eltiron isn't *in* Gramwood just at present, so it would take longer, but some people think good things are worth waiting for, so perhaps you wouldn't mind."

"If I wait until I get to Sevairn, I'll never be able to get away from all the guards," Crystalorn objected. "Castles are hard to sneak out of."

"You didn't seem to have any trouble in Mournwal," said Amberglas. "Or was it Navren? No, Navren is the place with the extremely unpleasant King I haven't been to. Or is it the place with the rain? Not that I mind rain—it's quite useful— but too much of it can be very dreary, and it does seem to have a depressing effect on the people who live there all the time, which isn't at all surprising, what with water dripping down the back of one's neck every time one goes outside. But then, there are a great many places I haven't been to, so I tend to mix them up occasionally."

Crystalorn didn't seem to be listening. "Maybe I should meet him first," she said thoughtfully. "I wonder what Sevairn is like?"

Jermain fought down an impulse to answer. Crystalorn had not been addressing him, and he had no right to involve this lovely child in the intrigue that surrounded Marreth's court. Still, the thought of having someone in Leshiya who believed him was extremely tempting—assuming that she would believe him. And the court might well be safer for her if she knew who was not to be trusted. Terrel Lassond, for example. . . .

"I believe Jermain could answer that question," Amberglas said calmly. "Of course, he isn't likely to tell you anything at all unless you ask him, which is quite proper but rather inconvenient, because you wouldn't know what to ask unless he told you he knew, which of course he won't. So I am, instead."

Crystalorn turned toward Jermain, a questioning look on her face. "You know about Sevairn?"

"I was born there, Your Highness," Jermain said carefully, "and I lived in Leshiya until . . . recently."

"That's wonderful!" Crystalorn said enthusiastically. "If you've lived there, you ought to know something about the court. What's Prince Eltiron like?"

"I'm sorry, but I don't think I ought to discuss Prince Eltiron with you, Your Highness," Jermain said after a moment. "I have personal reasons to dislike him, and anything I could tell you would be biased."

"Oh, I see," Crystalorn said. Curiosity struggled with courtesy in her face; courtesy won by a hair, and she went on, "Then can you tell me about the rest of the court?"

"I can if you wish it, Your Highness," Jermain said.

"Please."

Jermain nodded and began describing the members of Marreth's court. He started with Terrel, and was working his way down when he was interrupted by a knock at the tower door.

Crystalorn's head turned. "What's that?"

"I believe someone is at the door," Amberglas said, rising. "That's what knocking usually means, particularly knocking on a door, though not always. Unless of course you meant to ask who's outside, in which case you really ought to learn to say what you mean. Or mean what you say, which isn't at all the same, but frequently has the same effect."

Amberglas reached the door as she finished speaking and opened it. A man in the full dress uniform of a Barinash captain stood on the doorstep; behind him, Jermain could see several mounted guardsmen. "Such a lot of visitors today," Amberglas murmured. "Do come in."

Chapter Three

Eltiron stared morosely out the narrow window of his chambers. In the two hours since his father had told him of his proposed marriage, he had made and discarded one plan after another for escaping his predicament. He had considered killing Terrel Lassond in a duel; unfortunately, Terrel was unquestionably a better swordsman than Eltiron. Besides, killing Terrel, though it would certainly be satisfying, would do nothing to stop the wedding.

He had also considered, briefly, killing himself instead of Terrel, which would certainly stop the wedding but which had no other advantages as far as Eltiron could see. Killing the Princess would also stop the wedding, but Eltiron couldn't bring himself to seriously consider it.

Running away might help, but Eltiron had nowhere to go and no way of earning a living, even if he could escape the inevitable search. He might insult his prospective bride so badly that she would refuse to have him, but since the marriage was a political one her father would probably force the girl to marry him anyway, and Eltiron had no desire to have a wife who hated him. Eltiron had even considered marrying someone else secretly, then announcing the fact at the last minute, but he could think of no one he wanted to marry, and it would be foolish to exchange one unknown and unwanted girl for another.

A knock at the door interrupted Eltiron's thoughts. He turned and started across the room, then hesitated. He did not really wish to see anyone; perhaps if he did not respond, whoever it was would go away. The knocking came again, and with a sigh Eltiron moved forward.

He had taken two steps toward the door when a voice on the other side said clearly, "You call that knocking? Out of the way, feather-fingers, and let me do it." An instant later the door shook under a series of blows that sounded as if someone were hitting the wood with a very large hammer. "Eltiron! Open it up before I knock it down!"

Eltiron unfroze abruptly and sprang forward. "Vandi!" he shouted as he flung the door open. "If I'd known it was you, I wouldn't have taken so long."

The woman in the hallway turned a pair of penetrating grey eyes on him for a moment, then snorted. She threw back one side of her cloak and began ostentatiously dusting splinters off the pommel of her sword. "Fine welcome for a traveler. I could have ruined the whole hilt on this while you dawdled."

"If it comes to that, you did ruin my door," Eltiron said. "It wasn't meant for pounding swords on."

"How else was I going to get your attention?" the woman demanded. She stopped brushing at the sword hilt and ran her fingers through her greying blond hair. "If you think I have nothing to do but— Here! What do you think you're doing?" The last sentence was addressed to the slightly flustered guard who was edging between her and Eltiron.

"My, um, lady, you're wearing a sword," the guard said.

"No, I'm holding it. What does that have to do with you?"

"I'm afraid you can't carry a sword in the presence of the Prince," the guard said apologetically.

The woman made an elaborate show of returning the sword to its sheath. "All right, I'm not carrying it. Now, get out of the way."

"I'm afraid that isn't quite enough, my, ah, lady," the guard said, even more apologetically than before. "You'll have to give it to me."

"You want it, come take it, squirrel-brain."

"That's ridiculous!" Eltiron said to the guard. "Vandaris is my father's *sister*; do you think she's going to murder me?"

"No, Your Highness," the guard said, not moving, "but I have orders."

"Oh, go lose yourself," Vandaris said in disgust.

"Orders are orders."

"Look, mush-mind, just go back to your post, and if anyone asks, tell 'em the orders were changed."

"Who's going to change them?" the guard demanded.

"I am," Vandaris said cheerfully. "And before you tell me I can't, you'd better think a little about who you're talking to. Blood and fire, but it's a poor state of affairs when two members of the royal family have to persuade some guard that it's all right for them to talk to each other." She pushed the dumbfounded guard aside and strode through the doorway.

With a small sigh of relief, Eltiron closed the door on the guard's belated protests and turned. Vandaris was standing in the center of the room, watching him. Eltiron cleared his throat. "It's good to see you again."

"No need to sound so apologetic," Vandaris said. "What's it been, three years? No, more like five; you weren't here last time I was in Sevairn." She eyed him critically. "You've gotten taller. And I thought you'd finished growing when you were fifteen!"

"Not quite," Eltiron said with a grin. "See what you miss when you're gone so long?"

Vandaris shook her head. "You've grown up better-looking than I expected, too, and you seem to have some sense. More than Marreth, I think, unless he's changed a lot since the last time I was here."

"He hasn't," Eltiron said gloomily. He had briefly forgotten his uncomfortable situation, but mention of his father brought it back with a rush. Vandaris gave him a sharp look.

"I thought you looked a bit off temper," she said. She glanced around the room again, then walked unerringly to the most comfortable chair in it. She dropped her cloak carelessly across it, seated herself, and leaned back, stretching her long legs out in front of her. "Want to tell me, or would you rather talk about something else?"

Eltiron hesitated, then started talking. He told Vandaris everything that had happened at the non-Council meeting, ending with, "And even if I could back out now, it would probably cause a war."

"That," said Vandaris, "is Marreth's problem. There's no reason why you should get married just to keep *him* out of trouble. What gave Marreth this idiotic idea in the first place?"

"I think Terrel did. He can talk Father into anything, and it would be like him."

"Who's Terrel?"

Eltiron stared. "Don't you know?"

"Look, fur-brain, if I knew, would I ask?"

"You might," Eltiron said with a brief grin. "I was just surprised. Whenever you come home, I forget you've ever been away. Terrel Lassond has only been Father's Chief Adviser for the last six months, but it seems as if he's been around a lot longer."

"Chief Adviser? What happened to Trevannon?"

Eltiron winced. "Six months ago he was convicted of treason and exiled. It doesn't make any sense, but Father won't listen to anything I say; I can't even mention Jermain's name without getting into trouble."

"Really." Vandaris looked thoughtful. "I think I'm going to be very glad I came to see you before I went to Marreth. If I'm going to get into trouble, I like to see it coming. What else has changed since I was here last?"

"Lord Danivor was killed in a duel about a year ago," Eltiron said, trying to remember who had been at court three years before. "Lady Rivalna was caught with a Navren stableboy last summer; the boy was hanged for a spy and she was exiled. Her husband went with her. Parrane and Iverly got into debt; they're still around somewhere, but they don't have much influence anymore. And you already know about Jermain."

Vandaris looked startled. "So many!" Her eyes narrowed. "And all of them people with strong opinions. I don't like this at all; it's worse than the Guild of Mages."

"What's wrong with the Guild?"

"They've been losing members by the score for the past five years or so. Not that it matters in Sevairn. Is Anareme still in charge of the army?"

"So far," Eltiron said. "Terrel's been trying to get Father to replace her, but it hasn't worked yet."

"I'm going to have to meet Terrel," Vandaris said thoughtfully. "What's his family again?"

"Lassond."

"Lassond, Lassond, Terrel Lassond," Vandaris said. Suddenly she looked up. "Not that gorgeous blond idiot from Miranet City? The one all the unattached women were after?"

Eltiron nodded glumly. "The women are still draped all over him, but I wouldn't call him an idiot," he said.

"No? Well, he may have changed." Vandaris stared off into space for a few minutes, then grinned. "This visit may be a lot more fun than I'd thought."

"How long will you be here?" Eltiron asked.

"I hadn't planned on long, but I may change my mind," Vandaris said. "Don't look so gloomy; I'll stay through your wedding, at least. That is, if you have one. We'll have to see about that."

Eltiron smiled in some relief. He was more at home with his aunt than with anyone else at court, and he had not realized how much he had needed someone to talk to since Jermain's exile. "Will you go to the King now? You really ought to; he's sure to be angry if he finds out you came here first."

"Marreth will be angry as soon as he finds out I'm back, for all the good it does him. I have other things to attend to first. Are my rooms still empty, or has Marreth moved them?"

"They're empty; he couldn't convince Orvel Seravis that they were needed for anything else. Every time he tried to put someone in them, Orvel found somewhere much better, and finally he gave up."

Vandaris grinned. "Rooms in an inconvenient corner and a castle steward who likes me. Handy combination, that; I'll have to remember it for the future. Remind me to thank Orvel."

"If you aren't going to see Father, what are you going to do?" Eltiron said. He felt a little uneasy; if Marreth discovered his sister's breach of custom and courtesy, he would not hesitate to blame Eltiron, however little Eltiron could have done to prevent it.

"I'm going to get my sword-squire and my goods and move into my rooms before Marreth has a chance to think of some reason why I can't," Vandaris said. "Not that he could stop me, but it'll be easier on everyone if he doesn't have a chance to try. I'll see him when I'm finished."

"Your sword-squire? Father won't like that at all."

Vandaris grinned again. "She's only fourteen; it would take the worst gossip in Sevairn to make anything of it."

Eltiron felt his face grow hot. He had indeed assumed Vandaris's squire to be a man, and somewhat older than fourteen, someone whose duties could be supposed to include more than cleaning swords and grooming horses. Knowing that his aunt had guessed his thoughts didn't help his state of mind; what would she think of him now? "I'm sorry," he said wretchedly. "I didn't mean . . ."

"What's the matter with you?" Vandaris said, frowning. "Every other time you open your mouth, you're apologizing for something. Morada's smile, man, it's not that important!"

"I'm sorry, I—" Eltiron stopped short in midsentence and grinned reluctantly. "I see what you mean."

Vandaris looked at him sharply, but let the subject drop. "Come down with me and meet my sword-squire," she suggested, rising. "I left her taking care of the horses, but I ought to get her installed in the castle before Marreth has a chance to object."

Eltiron nodded. Vandaris picked up her cloak, and the two left the room, heading for the stables.

The sword-squire was sitting cross-legged outside one of the stalls at the far end of the stable when Vandaris and Eltiron entered. She was a tiny, brown-haired girl who looked closer to twelve than fourteen, and she was industriously polishing the brass rivets on a worn leather bridle. She looked up as they drew near, and she brightened.

"Vandi! Wait till you hear—" She stopped and her brown eyes narrowed suspiciously. "Who's he?"

"He's my nephew, Eltiron, and he happens to be Prince of Sevairn," Vandaris said. "If you expect to live in this castle for any length of time, you'd better learn a few more manners."

"Well, he doesn't *look* like a Prince," the girl said in the tones of one paying a high compliment.

"Tari . . ." Vandaris said warningly.

The girl looked at Eltiron. "Was that the wrong thing to say? I'm sorry; I didn't realize. I'm Tarilane Corriel."

Eltiron nodded. He had no idea what he ought to say; squires, in his experience, were seldom seen and never heard. He noticed Vandaris watching him unusually closely, which made him even more nervous. "Um, I'm glad to know you," he said finally.

"Huh," Tarilane said. She sounded skeptical, but not unfriendly. "What are we going to do next, Vandi?"

"Haul the bags up to my rooms before Marreth gets wind that I'm here," Vandaris said. "Come on, brat; we don't have all day."

Tarilane gave Vandaris an odd look. "You sure you want to stay here that long?"

Vandaris was already halfway inside the stall. "Why not?" she replied over her shoulder.

"Oh, reasons," Tarilane said, looking warily at Eltiron. "I heard some people talking."

There was a muffled sneeze from the interior of the stall, and a moment later Vandaris stuck her head back out into the aisle. "Tari, in this castle you listen to people talking in order to find out what they're trying to hide and who they're planning to back-knife. You don't *believe* any of them. What'd you hear?"

Tarilane made a quick survey of the stable, glanced at Eltiron, shrugged, and said, "They said he isn't to be trusted."

"Eltiron?" Vandaris said in surprise. "That's interesting. Why?"

"Something to do with somebody important who got killed or something a couple of months ago. They said it was the Prince's fault."

"Who?" Eltiron burst out. "Who was it?"

"Why do you want to know?" Tarilane demanded.

"If I'm being accused of killing someone, I want to know who I'm supposed to have killed!"

"Oh, *that* who," Tarilane said. "I thought you meant who did I overhear. I didn't catch the name, but I'd recognize it if I heard it again."

"Was it Jermain?"

"That's it!" Tarilane looked at Eltiron suspiciously. "How'd you know?"

"That's something you can find out later, elephant-ears," Vandaris said. "You going to stand there all day, or could I maybe get some help?"

Tarilane scowled at Eltiron and ducked into the stall. Vandaris looked at Eltiron.

"You heard anything about this?"

"No, I—" Eltiron swallowed hard. "Jermain was my friend; I thought everyone knew that. How could anyone think I—" He stopped abruptly, not knowing how to finish the sentence and afraid his voice would fail him before he could do so.

Vandaris studied Eltiron intently for a few moments, then nodded. "This visit gets more interesting by the minute, and it's hardly started. I wonder what Marreth's got under his belt to surprise me with?"

Eltiron did not reply. His aunt shook her head. "Do you always take gossip this hard? Or is there something in it?"

"No!" Eltiron's shout echoed through the stable; the horses shifted nervously in their stalls.

"Calm down," Vandaris said mildly. "I was only asking. Look, I'm in a better positon to hear things than you are. Would it help if I listened around for a few days and told you about it later? It'll give you some idea of what's being said, anyway."

"Could you?"

"Dragon's teeth, man, would I have said it if I couldn't? I'll talk to you about it in a day or two, after I'm a bit more settled." Vandaris slung one of the saddlebags across her shoulder, gave her sword-squire a cheerful cuff, and started toward the door of the stable.

Eltiron did not see his aunt at all the following day. Terrel had arranged a seemingly endless series of meetings, during which Eltiron sat and listened to the royal tailors argue about wedding garments, the court secretaries argue about protocol, the castle stewards argue about menus and supplies, and all the lords and ladies in the city argue about precedence. At least that was what it seemed like to Eltiron, who hated the whole business with a passion he had no time to indulge.

The meetings went on into a second day, followed closely by another brief and painful interview with Marreth, but somehow Eltiron found enough time to send Vandaris a message. Vandaris responded in a scrawled note, the gist of which was that she would meet him the next day at the top of the Tower of Judgment.

The Tower of Judgment was the oldest and tallest of the three castle towers, and Eltiron had haunted its top for years. Because of its height, he could see much farther than from either of the other two; sometimes it seemed to him that he could see more clearly as well. In addition, the top of the Tower of Judgment was one of the few thoroughly private places in the castle. Hardly any of the servants or courtiers ever took the time to climb the long, spiral staircase to the tower-top, and Eltiron had come to think of it as his own. It was therefore a shock when, on the third day following Vandaris's arrival, Eltiron arrived at the door at the top of the Tower of Judgment and heard voices on the other side.

He paused uncertainly. Had Vandaris brought someone with her? He set one hand to the door, and a fragment of the conversation came clearly to him.

". . . overstepped yourself. Did you think I would not learn of it?"

"I never doubted it, my lord."

Eltiron started and pulled his hand away from the door as if he had suddenly discovered that it was made of live snakes. Neither of the speakers was Vandaris. Eltiron did not recognize the first voice at all; the second was Terrel Lassond's. But who would Terrel call "my lord" besides Marreth?

"Then you were a fool to try," the first voice said. "It is fortunate for you that your attempt did not succeed. My plans for Jermain Trevannon do not include his death."

Eltiron started again and missed Terrel's reply. He still could not place the other speaker, but the mention of Jermain was enough to make Eltiron abandon all thought of not listening further to the conversation.

"And the other matters?" said the first voice.

"I expect no trouble about the marriage," Terrel said. "The party from Barinash should arrive in another week, and the wedding will be at the end of the month. Marreth is being . . . intractable about other things."

"Persuade him if you can," the first voice said. "Otherwise we must wait until after the Prince's wedding. I want nothing to interfere with that."

"I understand. You know, of course, that the lady Vandaris has returned to Sevairn?"

There was a moment's pause. "No, I had not known." There was another brief silence. "For now, proceed as we had planned. I will let you know if there is a need for any change."

"As you wish. But I would not like to underestimate her. I haven't met her myself, but from what I hear she could be a dangerous opponent."

"I will keep your advice in mind, should I feel a need for it.

Now, I believe there is one more thing." Behind the tower
door, Eltiron shivered at the sudden, smooth menace in the
unknown voice.

"Yes?" Terrel's voice was expressionless.

"The little matter of Jermain Trevannon. I have no use for
unreliable assistants; too much depends on our success. You
appear to have forgotten that. Allow me to remind you."

Eltiron heard a choking cry, quickly muffled. "Fare you
well, my Lord Terrel, and remember, in the future, not to
cross me," the unfamiliar voice said over the sound.

Suddenly Eltiron realized that the conversation was at an
end; in another moment, someone would come through the
door and find him. He pulled back and looked desperately
around. The top landing of the Tower of Judgment was small
and bare, and there was nowhere he could hope to hide if he
remained. He turned and plunged down the stairs, hoping to
get out of sight around the curve before the door opened.

Three quarters of the way down the first spiral of stairs,
Eltiron paused, listening. He heard the tower door open and
close again, and realized that he might still be seen descending
the stairs, or crossing the courtyard outside the tower. Besides,
he still had to meet Vandaris. On the other hand, neither Terrel nor his companion would think it strange to meet Eltiron
coming up the stairs; his liking for the tower-top was well
known. Without stopping to think further, Eltiron turned and
began to climb.

He had retraced over half his steps before he finally saw
Terrel coming slowly downward. The Chief Adviser's face was
white, and when he saw Eltiron his smile was strained as well
as faintly mocking. He hesitated just long enough for Eltiron
to notice, then stepped aside to let him pass. "Your Highness," he said.

Eltiron nodded without stopping. "I hope you enjoyed the
view, Lord Terrel," he said with cold politeness as he went
past.

Terrel's eyes narrowed, but he did not reply, and after a moment Eltiron heard the echoes of his footsteps fading gradually as he descended the tower. Eltiron sighed in relief; now
there was only Terrel's unknown companion to get past. The
tower door reappeared around the curve of the stairs above
him. Eltiron's steps slowed; when he reached the top landing,
he stopped completely. This is ridiculous, he told himself.

You're a Prince; you have every right to be here if you want to be, and there's no way he can guess that you heard anything. Eltiron took a deep breath and opened the door.

His first reaction was a strong feeling of relief; there was no one on the tower-top at all. Eltiron relaxed a little and stepped out onto the flat roof of the tower, pulling the door shut behind him. As he did, the impossibility hit him like a blow: There was no one on top of the tower. He had heard two voices, but only one man had passed him on the stairs, and there was no other way to get down from the tower-top. There *had* to be someone there.

There was no one. Eltiron paced the entire surface of the tower-top and peered over the battlements, but he found nothing. After two circuits of the tower-top, Eltiron sat down with his back to the stone of the parapet and his face toward the tower door, hoping fervently that Vandaris would not take much longer to arrive.

Chapter Four

Jermain rose and moved away from the table as the Captain entered. As soon as he had room to draw his sword without hindrance should he need to, Jermain stopped and studied the newcomer. The Captain moved with the confident ease of an experienced fighting man. He's good, thought Jermain, and he must have either birth or brains as well, or he wouldn't have been made a Captain so young.

"Your Highness," said the Captain, bowing deeply to Crystalorn. He gave Jermain a brief, appraising look, then turned and bowed politely to Amberglas. "My lady."

"Not yours, exactly," Amberglas said. "Fortunately, it doesn't matter; but then, a great many things don't—what color wind is, for instance, or how far rain falls, or whether the fourth King of Gramwood's mother-in-law served soup in a Dangil china bowl or an Ilmar tureen. That is, if she bothered to serve soup, which some people don't. So perhaps I shouldn't have mentioned it."

The Captain blinked. "I agree," he said after a barely perceptible pause. "I hope I have not offended you."

Amberglas smiled. "Not at all. Why are you here?"

"I have come to conduct the Princess Crystalorn back to her retinue," the Captain replied.

"That's obvious," Crystalorn said, eyeing the Captain with disfavor. "It *would* have to be you."

"I don't think so," said Amberglas to one of the chairs. "There's no reason why he couldn't have been someone else, except, of course, that he isn't, which is a very good thing for him. Being someone else is very difficult for most people because, you see, they aren't used to it, particularly if they aren't sure who they are to begin with. It makes things difficult for other people, too, because they don't know whom they're talking to, which tends to be confusing. Do you know whom we're talking to?''

"Oh, I'm sorry, Amberglas," Crystalorn said. "This is Captain Balandare Forrain." She scowled at him briefly, then apparently decided to continue the introductions. "Balandare, this is Amberglas, and his name's Trevannon. He was just telling me about Sevairn when you interrupted."

Balandare gave Jermain a sharp look as Crystalorn finished. "I apologize for cutting short your conversation," he said slowly.

Crystalorn answered before Jermain could reply. "Well, you ought to. I thought Salentor would send Kayth to bring me back; I could have talked for hours before he would have found me. Why'd they have to pick you instead?"

"As far as I know, Lord Salentor has never willingly chosen me for anything," Balandare said.

"Then what are you doing here?" Crystalorn demanded. "Didn't he send you after me?"

"I believe Lord Salentor is not yet aware that you have left the caravan, Your Highness," Balandare said quietly. "Should he ask, Torfil will tell him you are out riding, with myself and a suitable escort."

Crystalorn looked at him speculatively. "That was very nice of you, but are you sure Salentor will believe it?"

"Why should he doubt it, when he sees you return with us, Your Highness?"

"But—" Crystalorn stopped short and looked at the Captain for a long moment. Then she smiled reluctantly. "All right, you win. I can't let you get into trouble for trying to keep me out of it."

"I am relieved to hear you say so, Your Highness," Balandare said, smiling.

"Ha! You planned it!" Crystalorn said. "Sometimes I wish I had someone stupid in charge of my personal guard; it would be a lot easier for me to do what I want."

"Of course, Your Highness; I'll see to it as soon as we get back to the caravan. Would Captain Kayth be satisfactory? I'm sure Lord Salentor would be willing to reassign him if you wished it."

"Yes, and I'm sure I'd stick a knife in him within two days. I can't stand Kayth, and you know it. And I don't want anyone else in charge of my guard, and you know that, too, so stop teasing."

"As you command," Balandare said, bowing deeply, and Crystalorn giggled. "Now, shall we go, Your Highness?"

"I suppose I must," Crystalorn said with a sigh. She looked at Amberglas, who had been observing the interchange with an air of vague interest, and sighed. "Good-bye, Amberglas. I hope I can come back soon, but if I really do get married to this Prince I don't know whether I'll be able to. Leshiya is a long way away."

"It is, isn't it?" Amberglas said. "Though one can't always tell from descriptions, and a great many places are closer than most people think. Still, I haven't been anywhere in a long time, and perhaps things have changed, though they don't usually, at least not much. That is, I've been here, which is obviously somewhere, but isn't anywhere else. At least I think it isn't. So I shall quite enjoy it, I'm sure."

"Amberglas, what are you talking about?" Crystalorn said.

"Visiting Sevairn," said Amberglas. "I thought I explained that. I'm coming with you."

Balandare looked startled; Crystalorn's face lit up. "You are? Amberglas, that's wonderful! I won't mind going nearly as much if you're going to be there for me to talk to. Will you stay for the wedding?"

"I would rather expect to, though it's hard to be quite positive. So many things can happen, particularly when one isn't expecting them."

"Oh, wonderful." Crystalorn turned to Jermain. "Will you come, too? I still want to hear about Sevairn."

For a moment, Jermain was tempted; then he shook his head. "I fear I cannot accept your invitation, Your Highness. I am not welcome in Sevairn, and I have no wish to cause trouble between you and Prince Eltiron."

Crystalorn looked puzzled, but Balandare nodded. "Then you are Lord Jermain Trevannon, King Marreth's adviser," he said. "I wondered, when I heard the name."

"I once held the position you name," Jermain admitted. "As matters now are, I can only ask that you do not mention my whereabouts when you reach Leshiya; it is not my advice Marreth wants now."

"I understand," Balandare said, "and I will not volunteer the information." He smiled slightly. "Nor am I likely to be asked. Kings and Princes normally do not question foreign guards."

"Thank you," Jermain said. He turned to Amberglas. "And thank you also, for your hospitality." He noticed a faint line between her eyebrows as she gazed in his direction, and he went on, "I was intending to leave today in any case; I have already taken advantage of your kindness for too long."

"Not at all," Amberglas said, still frowning faintly. "It's just that I'm not certain— But then, one hardly ever is, except about things like rocks and flowerpots and boots, which either are there or aren't there, but are never almost there. I don't suppose you'd care to reconsider?"

"Reconsider?" Jermain said.

"Yes, do!" Crystalorn said. "You could at least ride with us until we get to the border tomorrow, even if you won't go on into Sevairn."

Jermain felt an uneasy twinge at the enthusiasm in her voice. Not that she was unattractive; quite the contrary. But she was a Princess, and much too young, and she was promised in marriage to a man who had been Jermain's friend. Still, a day's travel in her company would certainly be pleasant. . . . A day? He'd thought the border was closer than that! Jermain looked at Amberglas just as Balandare cleared his throat and began speaking.

"I'm afraid that Lord Trevannon's presence would cause complications, Your Highness," he said. "It would be difficult to explain his presence to Lord Salentor, for one thing. And I'm sure you're aware of the political implications if anyone in Sevairn heard that you'd been associating with a man King Marreth exiled. I wouldn't trust all of the caravaners to keep silent about it if they see him."

From the look on Crystalorn's face, that aspect of the situation had not occurred to her. "I suppose you're right again," she said after a moment. "But we'll have to explain Amberglas to Salentor anyway, won't we? It shouldn't be any harder to explain two people than one."

"Not necessarily," said Amberglas. "You haven't answered my question."

"Question?" Crystalorn looked bewildered.

"About reconsidering," Amberglas explained gently.

Jermain blinked, then shook his head. "I beg your pardon, but no, I can't. It would be foolish for me to go back now, and it would only bring trouble to you as well."

"People can be so inconsistent," Amberglas said, smiling vaguely at him. "I knew a man once who wore half a mustache because he couldn't make up his mind whether he liked mustaches or not. I believe it was the left half, though it wasn't precisely inconsistent, now that I think of it. So perhaps it didn't seem foolish to you to be in Sevairn three days ago."

"If it hadn't been a foolish thing to try, the Border Guard wouldn't have come so close to killing me," Jermain said, struggling to keep his temper. "In any case, I won't go back until I know how they learned where I was so quickly. Do not try to persuade me."

"Very well, I won't," said Amberglas.

Crystalorn was staring at Jermain with wide eyes. "You mean the Border Guard was ready to kill you just for going back into Sevairn? What did you *do*, anyway?"

Jermain shifted uncomfortably without speaking. Crystalorn opened her mouth to speak again, then stopped abruptly. Her eyes narrowed, and she turned to Balandare.

"Why haven't I heard anything about this, whatever it is? Salentor was supposed to teach me everything important that's happened in Sevairn in the past ten years, but he never mentioned anyone named Trevannon."

"Perhaps Lord Salentor did not consider Lord Jermain's dismissal important," Balandare said. "Though I will admit, I am surprised."

"When a King's Adviser does something bad enough that he gets thrown out of the kingdom, it's important," Crystalorn said flatly. "Particularly if it happened recently. Salentor should have told me."

"I agree, Your Highness," Balandare said. "But no doubt Lord Salentor has good reasons."

Jermain suppressed a snort. Lord Salentor Parel had spent two years as Barinash's ambassador to Sevairn, just after Barinash's abortive attempt at invasion. Jermain remembered him well, liked him little, and trusted him not at all. He was greedy, ambitious, and without conscience; Jermain found himself wondering suddenly just why Salentor was so interested in the marriage between Eltiron and Crystalorn. And why *hadn't* the man mentioned Jermain's exile? There was a pattern in this somewhere, there must be.

"People generally do," Amberglas said, breaking Jermain's concentration. "Or at least, they think they do, though quite often other people disagree, which isn't at all surprising when you think of what odd ideas some people have. I wonder what Salentor's odd ideas are?"

"Well, I'm going to ask him about his reasons when we get back," Crystalorn said. "And they'd better be good ones."

"Then, Your Highness, I believe we should start back soon," Balandare said. "Or Lord Salentor may be more interested in asking questions than in answering them. Torfil cannot make excuses for us forever."

"Oh, all right," Crystalorn said. "Amberglas, are you ready to leave? You haven't packed anything."

"I think perhaps you had better start without me," Amberglas said. "A great many things do—start without someone, I mean—and it makes very little difference to most of them. In fact, I believe the seventh Queen of Mournwal's coronation started without her, though one can't always be certain that the historians are correct about things. Of course, it would be rather difficult to *finish* a coronation without someone to crown, but that is an entirely different thing, and there are always a great many people willing to be crowned if one can't find the proper person at the right moment. Still, it would be rather awkward. So you had better go on, and I will join you in a little while."

Crystalorn attempted to argue, but Balandare's diplomatic insistence and Amberglas's rambling refusals were more than she could handle at the same time. Finally she abandoned the effort, and in a few minutes more, she and Balandare took their leave. Amberglas watched from the doorway until the sound of the horses' hooves had died away. Then she turned back to look at Jermain.

Jermain bowed. "Once again, I thank you for your hospitality and bid you farewell."

He stepped forward, then stopped. Amberglas had not moved out of the doorway. "That's quite unnecessary, though of course very courteous; still, it would be far more helpful if you would tell me whom to speak to in Sevairn."

"Speak to?"

"Certainly. How can I deliver a message for you if I don't

speak to someone? Unless you write it down, which is perfectly possible; at least it would be if I had anything for you to write on. Unfortunately, I don't have anything just at the moment, which is very inconvenient, unless of course you don't wish to write your message, in which case it doesn't matter."

With an effort, Jermain fought down a sudden, wild hope and forced himself to think clearly. A moment later, he shook his head. "Lady, I know King Marreth well, and I suspect that the mere mention of my name at court is now cause for suspicion of treason. Delivering a message for me . . . I cannot ask you to take such a risk."

"You didn't ask me," Amberglas said. "I dare say you've forgotten, or else you didn't notice, though I don't see how you managed to be a King's Adviser for six years if your memory is as bad as that."

"This has nothing to do with my memory!" Jermain said. "Don't you realize how dangerous it could be?"

"Do you think so?" said Amberglas, looking faintly interested. "But then, a great many things can be dangerous, especially if one is careless, and some of them are quite ordinary. Walking down wet stairs, for instance, or chopping carrots, or juggling someone else's Dangil china cups. So it won't necessarily be particularly exciting."

"Exciting!" Jermain took two deliberately slow breaths. "No. I can't. I won't. Marreth's been executing spies; one mistake and he'd have your head. Not to mention exiling whomever he caught you talking to."

Amberglas blinked at him. "Dear me. Perhaps you had better write it down after all."

"I am not," Jermain said carefully, "going to give you a message."

"Well, I suppose I will have to manage without one, then. Still, it's a pity; mistakes can be so very awkward."

For a moment, Jermain stood staring, utterly taken aback. Amberglas could not possibly mean to deliver a nonexistent message from Jermain to some unknown person in Leshiya. He looked at her again and changed his mind; that was exactly what she meant to do, and the only way he could prevent her was to give her a real message. Either way, she would be taking a grave risk. Unless . . . There was one person in Leshiya who would not be penalized for receiving a message from Jermain; Marreth could hardly exile his own son.

"I'll give you a message, then," Jermain said in a voice he barely recognized as his own. "Tell Prince Eltiron that all his dissembling will not keep the Hoven-Thalar from overrunning Sevairn. And tell him . . . tell him I will not forget what he and Terrel did."

"I will tell him." Amberglas remained where she was, regarding Jermain with an air of great preoccupation. "I don't suppose you've decided where you're going next?"

"To Gramwood, and then to Mournwal," Jermain said. "They have little hope of withstanding such a horde as the Hoven-Thalar can raise, but I must at least warn them."

Amberglas nodded, looking, if possible, even more preoccupied than before. "Yes, I see, though I can't think what good it will do you there; but then, things are often useful in the most peculiar places. I knew a man in Tar-Alem who used his mother's sword for hoeing cabbages, though Tar-Alem isn't really much more peculiar than other places, so perhaps it isn't the same at all. Of course, it wasn't intended to be particularly useful, but one never knows, and I do hope you'll take it anyway."

"What? What are you—" Jermain caught himself just before the words "babbling about" slipped out. Amberglas did not seem to notice.

"The medallion I'm going to give you," she said. She reached into the pocket of her skirt, pulled out a small package, and held it out to Jermain.

Jermain hesitated, then reached out and took the package. The wrappings were slightly dusty; he pulled them away and was absurdly relieved to find only a heavy brass medallion on a chain, the kind used by professional messengers for identification and safe-conduct. With a slight shock, Jermain realized that he had been half-afraid the package would contain some sort of magic amulet, and he almost laughed aloud. What had made him think that any sorceress, however absentminded, would give something like that to a chance acquaintance? Still, he was glad that the gift was relatively ordinary; he had no wish to become involved in affairs of sorcery.

He looked up and found Amberglas watching him. "Thank you," he said. "This will be very useful."

"I thought it might be," Amberglas said with some satisfaction. "Useful to you, I mean; it isn't likely to be useful to me, except as a paperweight, though one can't always tell. Par-

ticularly since you've been exiled, which can make traveling
very difficult because so many places have guards who ask a
great many unpleasant questions and insist on knowing who
one is before they will let one in. Or out. Which can be extremely inconvenient, though sometimes it isn't.''

Jermain nodded. Briefly, he wondered how Amberglas had
come by the medallion, then dismissed the question; it was no
concern of his. He slipped the chain over his head and adjusted it, then bowed and thanked her again. She murmured
something polite but rather vague and at last stepped out of
the doorway and let him by. Jermain made a somewhat hasty
farewell and left the tower.

When he reached the stable, he found Blackflame's saddle
and bridle hanging by the door of the stall. On the floor below
them were Jermain's saddlebags, which seemed considerably
fuller than he remembered. Uneasily, he wondered how she
had known he would be leaving today; she certainly had had
no time to replenish them since he'd announced his departure.
He shrugged; if Amberglas was determined to provide him
with supplies, he would certainly not throw them away.

Jermain saddled Blackflame and led him out of the stable.
The tower door was open, but Jermain saw no sign of Amberglas. Feeling slightly disappointed, he glanced about the clearing to check his directions, then turned to Blackflame. The
medallion swung against his chest as he mounted, and after
a moment's thought Jermain lifted it and dropped it down the
neck of his tunic. Few messengers displayed the medallions
openly without need; he would attract less attention with it out
of sight. He shrugged twice to get the chain in a comfortable
position, and rode out of the clearing.

The weather was warm, hovering between late spring and
early summer, and Jermain made good time. His side
bothered him not at all, and by nightfall he was well south of
the tower. The following day he reached the River Clemmar.
He turned Blackflame east along the river's bank, looking for
a place where he could ford it. This part of the Clemmar ran
narrow, swift, and deep, and he could not risk Blackflame being injured in the crossing. One stumble, or one rock flung too
forcefully by the current, and Jermain might lose days waiting
for the horse to heal.

At last Jermain found a spot that suited him, and, after
checking the fastenings on the saddlebags, he urged Black-

flame into the water. The crossing was uneventful, though twice the horse had to swim when the river grew too deep. They reached the opposite bank in soaking safety, and Jermain stopped at once and built a fire to dry his clothes and Blackflame's gear. While his tunic and cloak steamed on a rock beside the fire, Jermain gave his horse a thorough rub-down.

By the time Jermain finished, his tunic was dry enough to wear. He put it on and made sure Amberglas's medallion was concealed beneath it, then examined the cloak. The heavy wool was still too damp for comfort. Jermain was trying to decide whether to continue once the cloak was dry or simply camp where he was, when he heard a rustling from the woods behind him.

Jermain was on his feet in an instant. Three strides put the fire between him and the source of the noise. As he loosened his sword in its sheath, he saw a dark-haired man on a bay stallion riding slowly through the trees toward him.

The rider stopped just within speaking distance. He looked about forty, and he was dressed in dark blue velvet and a cloak of grey wool. His eyes were black and intelligent, and he had an air of decisiveness about him that Jermain liked. Jermain noted with surprise that he wore a dagger at his belt in place of a sword. *Either he is very brave, or he is very foolish,* Jermain thought. *Possibly both, though he looks more like a warrior than a fool.*

"I crave your pardon for this intrusion," said the horseman after a moment, "but I have been traveling for some time and your fire was too inviting to resist. May I join you for a while?"

Jermain did not reply at once. He was well aware that his own appearance was barely respectable, and he wondered why a lone traveler would risk approaching him. Still, Jermain did not wish to refuse hospitality merely because of a few doubts, particularly when talking to the horseman was probably the only way he could ever learn the answers to his questions. He let his hand rest on the hilt of his sword with deceptive casualness. "You are welcome, sir."

"I thank you." The horseman dismounted and tethered the bay, then seated himself by the fire. "May I know your name?"

"Trevannon."

"Ah." The satisfaction in the man's voice was unmistakable. "Then you are the man I have been looking for these past six months."

Jermain tensed. "Indeed?" he said, trying to sound casual. "I'm afraid I don't see why."

"You have information I need and skills I want," the man said promptly. He smiled. "It's a common enough reason, I'm afraid, but true nonetheless."

"Perhaps." Jermain allowed his skepticism to creep into his tone. He was not the only man in the Seven Kingdoms to possess experience or skills of swordplay, and he doubted that anyone would risk a King's enmity for such common abilities. That left three possibilities: his knowledge of Sevairn, his knowledge of the Hoven-Thalar, or his presumed treason. "What skills do you need, and why do you come to me to find them?"

"I know your reputation. I've been looking for you since I heard of your exile, but you went south too quickly for me."

"I won't betray Sevairn," Jermain said abruptly.

The traveler raised an eyebrow, but all he said was, "I have little interest in Sevairn at present, but I will bear that in mind."

Jermain felt himself flushing. "Why should you want a man who has been convicted of treason? How do you know I won't 'betray' *you*?"

"Because you didn't betray Marreth," the man said flatly.

Jermain's eyes narrowed in surprise. The man looked at him sharply and went on, "You were exiled for giving unpopular advice, no matter what name Marreth chose to put on it. What difference should that make to me, as long as the advice was good as well as unpopular? And the advice was certainly good."

"How do you know?" Jermain said.

"You told Marreth to arm Sevairn because the nomads will move north this summer, did you not? I have my own sources in the south, and I do not think you are wrong. If I had known in time, I might have . . . But it is far too late for that now. Still, I think I can use your services, if you are willing to join me."

"Who are you?" Jermain demanded.

The man hesitated an instant, then looked straight at Jermain. "My name is Carachel."

Jermain felt his eyes widening. "The Wizard-King of Tar-Alem!"

Carachel nodded. "Some call me that."

"Then I fail to see, my lord, what use you may have for my services," Jermain said. "Who can advise a wizard?"

"I am more interested in your other skills," Carachel said. "The Hoven-Thalar move northward this summer, and I want you to command my army against them. Will you?"

Chapter Five

By the time Vandaris finally arrived, Eltiron was beginning to think he had imagined the whole conversation between Terrel and the unknown man. He had almost decided not to mention it, but Vandaris saw the way he started when she opened the tower door, and she demanded an explanation.

"It was Terrel," Eltiron said reluctantly. "He was out here with someone when I got here; at least, I think he was."

"So you're afraid enough of Terrel Lassond that you jump when a door opens? Fire and sand-snakes, what's the man done to earn that kind of reaction? Now, if you'd said it was me you were worried about, I'd believe you had reason."

"If it were only Terrel, I wouldn't have been so tense," Eltiron said, stung.

"Well, explain, then, and convince me."

"You'll think I'm crazy."

"Try me, squash-head. I've seen a lot more strange things outside Sevairn than you'll ever know about."

Eltiron sighed inwardly and explained. To his surprise, Vandaris seemed to believe him. She listened without interrupting until he finished his tale, then shook her head.

"So Lassond is taking orders from someone. I wonder what they're after? I think I must make a point of allowing him to meet me sometime soon."

"You haven't seen him yet? But you've been here nearly three days! Terrel must be busier than usual; he hardly ever waits that long before he calls on guests."

Vandaris smiled nastily. "He isn't waiting by choice; I've been stalling him. Fortunately for him, he's finally starting to

45

sound interesting. Now, about this person Lassond was talking to. Are you sure he couldn't have hidden on the stairs while you went by?"

"There's no place for anyone to hide. If there were, I'd have used it myself. And I only heard the tower door open and close once."

"And there was no one here when you came up. Hmmph. Stay here a minute; I want to look around."

"What for?" Eltiron said irritably as Vandaris began slowly circling the tower. "There's nothing around; you can see that from here. Besides, I already looked."

"Not very hard," Vandaris said from one of the battlements on the south side of the tower.

"What?" Eltiron went to join her, and she nodded toward the flat surface of the wall. In the center of the parapet was a patch of something wet and red, about the size of Eltiron's hand. Eltiron stared in disbelief, and his skin crawled.

"It wasn't here before!" he said. "It can't have been! I'm sure I looked through all of these."

"Well, it didn't come out of nowhere," Vandaris said mildly. She eyed the red patch briefly, then drew her dagger and leaned forward as if to touch the spot with the dagger's point.

Without thinking, Eltiron grabbed her wrist. "Don't touch it."

Vandaris's eyes narrowed, and Eltiron hastily let go of her. "I-I'm sorry, I don't know why I did that, I didn't mean—"

"I don't want an apology, dragon-bait," Vandaris said, not moving. Sunlight glinted on the dagger she held. "I want an explanation."

"I don't *have* an explanation," Eltiron said almost desperately. "I just— just did it, that's all, and I'm sorry."

"You have singularly dangerous impulses, then." Vandaris sheathed her weapon and turned away, and Eltiron felt as if a door had closed in his face. Then he realized that Vandaris was staring down at the stone parapet, and his eyes followed hers.

The red patch was barely half the size it had been a moment before. As Eltiron watched in disbelief, it shrank even further, like a living thing drawing back hastily from something painful. Then it was gone completely, leaving no trace on the stone.

Hesitantly, Eltiron reached forward and touched the place where the redness had been. He felt a brief warmth, and for an instant his hand tingled as if it were asleep, and then there was only the cool, familiar stone of the battlement beneath his hand. Slowly, he drew his hand back and looked at Vandaris.

"Morada's sword!" she said softly, still staring at the stone. Then she looked at Eltiron. "I apologize. Whatever that was, you were right to keep me from touching it."

"But what was it?"

"Sorcery," Vandaris said matter-of-factly.

"*Here?*" Eltiron jerked away from the parapet and almost lost his balance. "How do you know? Are you sure?"

"Of course I'm sure. I told you, I've seen strange things outside Sevairn; I should have realized earlier."

"Why would anyone want to—to put a patch of blood on top of one of the towers of Leshiya Castle?"

"What makes you think it was blood?"

Eltiron blinked. "Wasn't it?"

"No."

"Then what *was* it? And what was it for?"

"Maybe some sorcerer in Navren was trying out a new long-distance spell, or maybe it was a side effect of something else entirely. Who knows what magic is for?"

"I thought you said—" Eltiron stopped short, trying to find a tactful way of finishing the sentence.

Vandaris snorted. "You think I'm a magician, cloud-head? I can't even tell you what kind of sorcery that was; I can recognize magic when my dagger hits it hard enough, that's all. Come on, let's see if there are any more."

Eltiron swallowed, but he did not reply as he turned to follow Vandaris. The idea of sorcery unnerved him, though he knew that there were places where magic was not as rare as it was in Sevairn. Still, he was relieved when they found nothing else unusual, though it took two turns around the tower before Vandaris was satisfied.

"No reason to spend any more time here," she said finally. She frowned. "Is Lassond coming to Marreth's dinner tomorrow?"

"He shows up at all the court functions," Eltiron said. "He doesn't—he couldn't be responsible for that, that *thing* you found, could he?"

"I don't know, but I intend to find out. Besides, it's been a

long time since I attended one of Marreth's fancy dinners; I
think I need a reminder of how boring they really are.''

"Are you sure it's wise? I don't think Father expects you to
be there.''

"So much the better! Marreth needs stirring up a little, and
no one else around here seems inclined to do it.''

"After what Father did to Jermain, no one wants to take
chances.''

"Why not?'' Vandaris demanded. "A lot of things are
worse than being exiled from a court as dull as this one.''

"Some people don't think so,'' Eltiron muttered.

Vandaris looked at him for a moment. "If it comes to that,
Marreth isn't the only one in this castle who needs stirring up.
Let's go. If there's sorcery about, this is nowhere to stand
talking.''

Eltiron agreed with alacrity, and they started down the
stairs. Vandaris maintained a thoughtful silence, for which
Eltiron was grateful. He was uncomfortably aware that he had
displeased Vandaris, and the idea depressed him. I never seem
to be able to do anything right, he thought. He was so absorbed that they had almost reached the bottom of the tower
stairs before he remembered why he had arranged to meet
Vandaris there in the first place.

"Vandaris?'' he said tentatively.

Vandaris jerked around as if she had been stung. "Dragon's
teeth, man, don't use that tone of voice with me! You sound
as if you expect me to cut your fingernails off at the elbow if
you so much as glance in the wrong direction. Star's breath
and shadow-fire, you're a Prince; you don't have to worry
about things like that.''

"Maybe.''

"What do you mean, maybe? You're Marreth's heir; no
one's going to make you an example of anything.''

"Father might. He's already threatened to have me locked
up for treason, and I think he meant it.''

"He *what?*'' Vandaris's foot almost missed the last step as
she turned to stare at Eltiron. "What for?''

"For talking about Jermain. At least, that's what he said
the last time.''

"For talking about— That's absurd. Even Marreth couldn't
be that stupid.''

"He doesn't want his son defending a traitor,'' Eltiron explained. He scuffed a boot along the stone floor, then looked up. "Jermain isn't a traitor, I don't believe it, but Father won't listen to me and I suppose I couldn't prove it even if he would, but . . . Vandi, what are people saying about Jermain? And me?"

Vandaris looked thoughtful. "Lots of things, and none of them in loud voices. Two of the stories I heard say you and Trevannon were selling information to the nomads; in one version, you got scared and betrayed him, and in the other you were both caught and you blamed everything on Jermain. According to another tale, the charges were completely false. Supposedly you arranged the whole trial from evidence to exile, but nobody knows why. There's also a story that you used your friendship with Trevannon to spy on him, and one— I don't see any point in repeating all of them. The only thing they agree on is that you are the person responsible for Trevannon's exile or death or whatever."

"But I didn't—Jermain is my friend!"

"He was. Which is one reason why you seem to have very few others just now. No one wants to risk being accused of treason, or perhaps a worse crime. One that means beheading, for instance."

Eltiron sat down heavily on the stairs. He had expected the gossip to be bad, but he had never thought that everyone might be believing it. He felt as if someone had just dropped him off the top of the Tower of Judgment and he hadn't hit the ground yet. "I don't understand."

"I'm not sure I do, either, but I have lots of guesses." Vandaris paused and leaned back against the wall. "It might help if you told me what really did happen."

"I've already told you what happened. Jermain told Father to start building up the army because the Hoven-Thalar were going to come north this summer. Father said no, and Jermain insisted, and finally Father had him exiled."

Vandaris shook her head. "I know that much, squirrel-brain. I want details. What happened at the trial?"

"I don't know; I wasn't there. No one was, except Father and Terrel and Lord Corteslan."

"I'm surprised Marreth was intelligent enough to give Trevannon a private trial," Vandaris said, frowning. "Still, I suppose he can't do everything wrong. How did Trevannon find out about the Hoven-Thalar, anyway?"

"Jermain has a friend in one of the Hoven-Thalar caravans; I used to see them talking whenever the wagons came to Leshiya."

"I see. And Trevannon went to Marreth as soon as this friend told him what to expect?"

"No, he waited until the caravan was gone. I think he was afraid Father would arrest everyone in it or something."

"Well, Marreth's reaction to bad news always has been to knife the messenger. What happened when Trevannon finally talked to him?"

"Father got angry. He wanted to know how Jermain knew anything about the Hoven-Thalar, and Jermain wouldn't tell him. Terrel said—"

"Lassond was there? Didn't Trevannon talk to Marreth privately?"

"No, he brought it up before the Council."

Vandaris whistled. "That was a mistake. Marreth doesn't like surprises at Council meetings; Trevannon should have known better. Well, go on."

"Terrel started hinting about unknown informers being nonexistent as well. Jermain didn't say anything at first, but finally he told Terrel not everyone was anxious to be the power behind the throne. Terrel said, 'Oh, you want the throne itself!' and Jermain got so mad he got up and left in the middle of the Council."

"Marreth wouldn't like that, either. I think I'm beginning to understand. Then what?"

"As soon as Jermain was gone, Terrel started talking about how many army commanders have overthrown Kings and how useful a false rumor of invasion could be and things like that. I told Terrel that Anareme was the commander of the army, and anyway Jermain wouldn't start false rumors. Terrel said, 'Then why won't he tell us who he heard it from?' I got angry and said I knew Jermain had a friend in the Hoven-Thalar caravan and he probably didn't want to get him in trouble. Terrel didn't say anything, he just looked smug, and Father called the end of the Council. The next day, Jermain tried to bring it up again, and Father had him arrested."

Vandaris shook her head. "I don't believe it. I thought you and Trevannon had some sense, but between the two of you, you've managed to make the most miserable tangle of a straightforward affair I've ever seen."

"What? What do you mean?"

"First Trevannon springs a major decision on Marreth at a
Council meeting. Then he refuses to say how he found out
about it, and *then* he loses his temper. That would have been
bad enough, but you start being helpful and explain all about
how Jermain knows a Hoven-Thalar caravaner. Dragon's
blood, didn't you know that would make Marreth even more
suspicious? Marreth would be sure Trevannon was plotting
with the Hoven-Thalar, especially after all the hints Lassond
seems to have been dropping. Of course Trevannon was arrested as soon as he brought the subject up again!"

"Then it really is my fault that Jermain was exiled," Eltiron
said miserably.

"Oh, stuff it in a rat-hole and leave it there. It's as much
Trevannon's fault as it is yours, and it's much too late to do
anything about it."

"I suppose so." Knowing that he couldn't repair the
damage he had done did not make Eltiron feel any better, but
he didn't think he could explain that to Vandaris.

"Then stop sulking. We still have to think of some way to
convince Marreth to double the size of the army in a hurry."

"We do?"

"Of course! Do you want to be killed by the Hoven-Thalar
three months from now?"

"No, but—"

"Well, how else are we going to stop them? They *are* moving north, you realize."

"How do you know?"

Vandaris snorted. "Trevannon isn't the only one with
sources in the south; I've heard rumors from other places as
well. Mournwal is arming already."

"Have you told Father?"

"You think I'm stupid? Another day won't matter, and I
have to know what's going on here first. Besides, Anareme
isn't nearly as stubborn as Marreth, and she can do a lot
without official word. Now, come on; we've wasted too much
time here already, and I have things to do before tomorrow
night."

Eltiron spent the remainder of the day being measured for
what seemed an endless series of betrothal and wedding
garments. At first he was glad to have time to think about his

conversation with Vandaris, but he quickly found that his thoughts only made him more unhappy. He went over the Council meeting again and again in his mind, seeing more and more clearly every mistake he had made and wishing he could go back and do it differently. Vandaris was right; he should have seen what could happen.

It occurred to him suddenly to wonder what things Vandaris might want to do before Marreth's dinner. The thought was unsettling, but at least it did not make him feel any more wretched than he already was. Eltiron began worrying about Vandaris instead of Jermain. When the tailors finally left, he went straight to Vandaris's rooms, but neither she nor her sword-squire were there. Eltiron found that even more disquieting.

He spent much of the next day speculating worriedly about Vandaris's plans. Several times he tried to find her, without success. By the time he entered the Great Hall that evening, Eltiron was nervous as well as worried. He was so busy looking for Vandaris among the assembled guests that he did not see Terrel approaching until it was too late to avoid him.

As soon as he was within speaking distance, Terrel stopped and bowed. "I am delighted to see you here, and in good health, Your Highness," he said.

"I thank you, Lord Lassond," Eltiron said warily.

"The preparations for the wedding are going well, I trust?"

"Quite well," Eltiron said as coldly as he dared.

A faint, amused smile flickered on Terrel's lips, then vanished. "I notice that you still have time to visit the castle towers."

"Occasionally."

"I am glad for you, Your Highness. I thought perhaps your additional duties might prove too . . . arduous to allow for your normal pastimes."

"It doesn't take *that* much time," Eltiron said, stung more by Terrel's tone than his words. The man might as well come out and say he thought Eltiron too stupid to handle protocol properly.

"Ah. Then you will have time for our match tomorrow morning." Terrel smiled in satisfaction. "I had feared you might be so busy with your other duties that you would cancel it."

"Our match?"

"Kaliarth has graciously allowed me to take his place for a few days as your instructor in swordcraft. I thought to use tomorrow's lesson to demonstrate your skills publicly; it will be excellent practice for the sword-games at the wedding, Your Highness."

Eltiron felt trapped. Terrel was by far the better swordsman; if Eltiron fought him in public, the match would be a humiliating farce. Canceling the match would be nearly as bad. Terrel would make sure that everyone in the castle was told of the entire conversation, and Eltiron would appear a braggart or a coward sheltering behind feeble excuses.

Eltiron was trying to decide whether it would be worse to cancel the match or hold it, when a voice behind him said, "Too bad, lizard-legs. Prince Eltiron has a prior engagement. With me."

"Vandi!" Eltiron said in relief. He turned to greet her, and swallowed in surprise and dawning apprehension. Vandaris wore the full-dress uniform of a mercenary Captain. Silver buttons shone against the deep green velvet, and a decorative knife sheath swung on silver chains from her belt. She stood out against the artistic fragility of Marreth's women and the dignified formality of the court ladies like a panther in a flock of peacocks. Eltiron was sure Marreth would not be pleased.

"You expected the White Beast of Mithum? Introduce me, or we'll be standing here all night."

"Oh, of course. Vandi, this is Lord Terrel Lassond, Father's Chief Adviser. Lord Lassond, this is my aunt, Vandaris."

"I am charmed," Terrel said, bowing deeply. "And, of course, it will give me great pleasure to relinquish my match with Prince Eltiron to you."

"Pity you can't, then," Vandaris said.

"I beg your pardon?"

"Work it out for yourself, slow-skull. If Eltiron has an engagement with me, he can't have one with you, so you haven't got anything to relinquish."

For an instant, Terrel looked taken aback; then he bowed again. "As you say. I hope you will not be disappointed in Prince Eltiron's skill."

"Why should I be? Never mind; I'm not that interested."

"Prince Eltiron is not devoted to swordcraft," Terrel said, smiling in a way that set Eltiron's teeth on edge.

"Well, it's about time someone in this castle had more brains than brawn," Vandaris said. "The last time I was here, Trevannon was the only one with sense."

"It is sad that one so gifted should have been proved a traitor," Terrel replied.

"Very sad," Vandaris said dryly. "And even sadder that nothing has happened in the past six months to give the castle gossips something more interesting to talk about."

Terrel raised an eyebrow. "I trust you do not include me among them."

"Did I say that? I must be getting careless."

"I find that difficult to imagine."

"Well, some people have limited imaginations." Vandaris grinned cheerfully at the shocked expression on Terrel's face and turned to Eltiron. "I think I ought to be moving on; Marreth seems to like everyone to speak to everyone else at his dinner parties, and it would be a shame to disappoint him. Will you join me, Eltiron?"

"Certainly," Eltiron responded immediately. "I'm sure you'll excuse me, Lord Lassond; good evening to you." He nodded in Terrel's direction as he turned away, thoroughly relieved to have come through the encounter as well as he had.

Vandaris chuckled softly as they walked away. "Not bad," she said when they were out of earshot. "The tone of voice could have been better, but the little nod as you left was just right."

"Just right for what?" Eltiron said, puzzled.

"Just right to make Terrel look a little foolish—no, don't look back, numb-wit! You want to spoil the effect? Right now about a quarter of the people in this room think they saw you casually dismiss Terrel Lassond, which is going to make them think better of you and worse of him, and neither one would be a bad idea."

"I can't say I would object, but I didn't do anything, really. You did all the talking."

"So? Nobody was close enough to overhear us. All anyone knows is what they saw, and what they saw was Lassond looking foolish. What's more, he knows it; if eyes shot arrows, you'd look like the straw dummy after target practice right now."

"Just because we walked away from him?"

"Every pebble helps. And people will remember it tomorrow, when Terrel has to explain why he isn't having his demonstration match with you, the way he's been telling people he would. Why else do you think he's so angry?"

Eltiron did not reply at once. He knew Vandaris was exaggerating the effects of the encounter to make him feel better, but he was more interested in his own sudden comprehension of one possible reason for some of Terrel's behavior. Terrel had always been the one who bowed and walked away from a conversation, leaving Eltiron standing awkwardly and uncomfortably in the middle of the floor. It was one of the things Eltiron disliked about Terrel, but he had never thought that it might be a deliberate attempt to make him look foolish.

"Eltiron!"

Vandaris's whisper interrupted his train of thought, and he looked up with a jerk. "What?"

"Look awake; the fun's just starting." Vandaris nodded at something to her right. Eltiron turned his head and suddenly found himself wishing he were somewhere else. Marreth was bearing down on them, and he did not appear to be in the best of tempers.

"Vandaris!" Marreth's roar stopped conversations all over the Great Hall. "What do you think you're doing here?"

"Enjoying myself," Vandaris said imperturbably. "Isn't that what you're supposed to do at parties?"

"You were not asked to attend this dinner!"

"So? In case you've forgotten, I'm your sister."

"You're a disgrace to the throne of Sevairn!"

"That depends who's sitting on it. Most people think joining the mercenaries is fairly respectable."

"I am not most people—"

"Thank Viran the Wise for that," Vandaris muttered.

"—and I consider your conduct disgraceful. It's embarrassing to have a member of the royal family of Sevairn serving as a common soldier!"

"Oh, never that."

"What?" Marreth stopped short and stared at his sister.

Vandaris smiled sweetly. "I am never common. And you'll notice that I'm a Captain now."

Marreth snorted. "Why you refused to buy a position suitable to your rank at the very beginning, I'll never understand."

"No, I don't suppose you will. What bothers you more, the

fact that I didn't take any help from you to start with, or that I was made a Captain anyway?''

"Enough of this! I have lost my patience."

"I noticed."

Marreth turned a darker shade of purple. "Leave! At once!"

"Oh, strap it down and sit on it," Vandaris advised. "You can't exile me, you can't throw me out, and you can't have me imprisoned or beheaded without evidence, so stop trying to chop ironwood with a kitchen knife. We have more important things to discuss."

Marreth's eyes narrowed. "Such as?"

"A little matter of treason and injustice. I have some new information regarding the affair of Jermain Trevannon."

Chapter Six

Jermain stared at Carachel for a long moment. "Before I answer you, I think you must explain a little more, my lord. Tar-Alem is far enough north that the Hoven-Thalar are unlikely to be a threat to you. Even if a few of them come that far, why would you not command your army in person?"

"I have other things that must occupy my time."

"Such as? If I do choose to serve you in this, I will need to know more than that."

"You cannot—" Carachel stopped. "No, you are right. If I am to trust you in one thing, I must trust you in the rest."

The wizard stopped again and stared into the fire. Finally he shook his head. "It comes back to the Hoven-Thalar. Do you know why they are moving north this year?"

"The southern wells are going bad. The clans from the southern waste have already come north, and there isn't enough food or water to support them as well as the clans that normally live there. By midsummer they'll have to move north again, into Mournwal."

"They will move long before midsummer," Carachel said. His lips tightened and he struck a fist against his leg. "If I only had more time! Another year, or even six months, would be enough."

"Enough for what?"

There was a long pause. "I need time to be sure I will be strong enough to win this war completely. I cannot afford a partial victory; none of us can."

Jermain frowned. "You would destroy the Hoven-Thalar?"

Carachel hesitated briefly, eyeing Jermain. "The Hoven-Thalar are not the only ones who move northward," he said finally. "The Matholych comes behind them, and that is not something which can be dealt with by a mere army."

"What is a Matholych?"

"It is a creature of sorcery; I doubt that I can explain any better than that. The Hoven-Thalar call it the Red Plague."

"I have just come from four and a half months with the Hoven-Thalar, and I heard no talk of such a thing," Jermain said skeptically.

"Had you stayed another month, I think you would have. I doubt that your friends knew the nature of the being poisoning their wells, but they soon will. Do you see why I need you? No man can do two things at once and do them well. I cannot command an army and still discover how to keep the Matholych from wreaking destruction on what little the Hoven-Thalar will leave behind them."

"You expect to find your answer alone?"

"I must." Carachel looked suddenly tired. "This is a thing only sorcery can manage, and the others would not listen to my warning. Indeed, there are some who seek to stop me."

"Who, and why? If the danger is as great as you say . . ."

"It is greater! The Matholych will kill what it finds alive, and turn cities into ruin. It will smash the foundations of magic for years to come, and in its wake it will leave plague and famine. There is no protection from it; if it is to be stopped, it must be fought. And it must be stopped." Carachel stared into the fire with unseeing eyes, and his voice was almost a whisper. "Whatever the cost, it must be stopped."

"Why would anyone want to keep you from doing so?"

Carachel started as if he had forgotten Jermain's existence for a moment. "Wizards are no more reasonable than other men. Stopping the Matholych will require more power than any single wizard has amassed in centuries, and since the Guild would not take my advice I must try alone. Many see the power I am gathering as a threat. If they had believed my warning, we could have worked together, but it is too late for that now."

"But when this Matholych thing arrives in the southern kingdoms, some of them will have to believe you."

"If common sorcery could prevail against the Matholych, you would be right to think that that would make a difference.

But even if the wizards were willing to help, I have not time to teach what it has taken me years to learn."

"Years? How long have you known about this?"

"Fifteen years." Old anger and bitterness colored Carachel's voice. "Fifteen years ago I went to the seven wizards who headed the Guild of Mages and told them what little I knew of the Matholych. I told them it would come north in sixteen or seventeen years, and I begged them to search the records for more information if they would not believe me. They refused, and when I persisted they barred me from the Guild."

For a moment, there was silence; then Carachel looked up from the fire with a slightly strained smile. "So you see, we are both outcasts. Will you help me?"

Jermain did not reply at once. It was impossible to overlook the similarity between Carachel's experience and his own, and it shook him to the core. He was no longer alone; this man, too, had been disregarded and unjustly punished. Even their goals were similar.

"I would be honored to assist you in any way I can, my lord," Jermain said at last.

The strain left Carachel's face. "Thank you. That is a great relief to me."

"However, there is one thing I should tell you before you accept my service. I do not believe that Marreth is content to let me live in exile; I think he is trying to kill me. Six of his Border Guard nearly succeeded a few days ago. If he hears word of where I am and send an assassin . . ."

"I doubt that any assassin would succeed. I have ways of protecting those who serve me; after all, I *am* a wizard."

"You mistake me, my lord," Jermain said. "I have no doubt that you can do what you say; my intention was to let you know of Marreth's hostility before you let me join you. If he discovers that you have aided me, it may be awkward for you."

"If Marreth is foolish enough to try meddling in the affairs of Tar-Alem, he will regret it, be sure."

"Then I offer you my service." Jermain drew his sword and held it out, hilt forward.

Carachel drew the dagger from his belt and touched the hilt of Jermain's sword, first with the point of the dagger and then with its hilt. "I accept your offer."

The two men sheathed their weapons, and Carachel rose. "I suggest that we leave for Tar-Alem at once, if you are agreeable," he said.

Jermain blinked. "Will an hour or two of travel make so great a difference?"

"It can, if you do not fear sorcery. But I am more interested in getting away from the river; we are too easily found here."

"Found?"

"Certain types of magic are weakened by running water, particularly protective spells. The Guild of Mages is far more likely to locate me if we remain near the river than if we move."

"Then let's go," Jermain said, rising. "Fighting sorcery is not my idea of a pleasant evening."

Carachel laughed and went to untie his horse, while Jermain kicked dirt over the fire to smother it. In a few moments, both men were mounted and ready to leave. Carachel looked at Jermain.

"Can you keep your horse controlled under . . . unpleasant circumstances?"

Jermain felt a flash of anger that anyone would question Blackflame's abilities. "He is battle-trained."

"Very well. Follow me closely, and do nothing to distract me."

Jermain nodded and reached forward to pat his horse's neck reassuringly. Blackflame snorted and tossed his head, and Carachel turned away. For a moment, the wizard fumbled at his breast, then he slipped something on his finger and raised his arms.

A pale, hard light formed like a ball of mist around his right hand, growing gradually clearer but not brighter. Carachel swept his arm down in a wide circle, and all around the two horsemen the forest and river grew suddenly dark and quiet. In another moment, the color had leached out of the trees and grass and water, leaving only a picture in smoke and shadow against a background of charcoal.

Carachel lifted his reins in his left hand. A faint light still clung to his right, and he held it out in front of him like a beacon as his horse began to move. Mindful of his instructions, Jermain urged Blackflame into motion.

As the horse stepped forward, the shadowy forest twisted

and blurred into a nightmare of constantly shifting black fingers. Jermain's stomach lurched, and he transferred his attention hastily to his horse. The animal had begun to tremble, and it took all Jermain's skill to keep him moving. Jermain was almost glad to have a task to occupy his mind, but no matter how he concentrated he could not shut out the darkness dancing around the corners of his eyes.

For what seemed like days, Carachel's bay moved steadily onward into darkness and deadly quiet. Jermain sat tensely in the saddle, trying not to look around as he spoke soothingly to his horse. Abruptly, the shadows steadied and grew darker. Jermain looked up and felt a moment of panic when he did not see Carachel's light ahead of him. Then he realized that he could hear the wind and the small noises of night insects. Jermain blinked, and around him was an ordinary, night-shrouded forest.

Carachel turned in the saddle. "I think this is far enough for one night, and it is not a bad place to camp. I suggest you tend to your horse first; we have a long way to go tomorrow."

Jermain nodded without speaking. Carachel swung out of his saddle and tethered the bay. Rather stiffly, Jermain followed his example, then went to unsaddle his mount. He felt weak and light-headed, and his legs and shoulders were tense and sore. Blackflame's condition was no better; the horse was trembling and covered with sweat, as if he had been ridden at top speed all day instead of at a slow walk. Jermain had to spend some time calming and rubbing down the exhausted animal before he could attend to his own needs. When he finally turned to seat himself by the fire Carachel had just finished building, he found that his legs were so weak that they nearly collapsed under him.

"I am afraid that sorcerous travel is very wearing at first," Carachel said apologetically. "But you will soon become accustomed to it."

"You plan to keep traveling like that tomorrow?" Jermain said, repressing a shudder.

"For part of the day, at least. I have no wish to spend a month or more away from my troops when we can be there in five or six more days."

Jermain swallowed hard and nodded. "Of course, my lord." And I was the man who didn't want to get involved with sorcery, he thought wryly. Ah, well, if the real threat comes from sorcery, I could not have kept from it. Better to know what I will face before I must face it.

"You are not comfortable with magic?" Carachel said, echoing Jermain's thoughts with uncomfortable accuracy.

"I admit that I lack knowledge," Jermain retorted. "But is anyone truly comfortable with magic?"

Carachel laughed. "Even wizards are not always at ease with their craft. Forgive me." But his expression as he watched Jermain held a hint of worry, and after a moment he went on, "You have had no previous experience with magic, then? So many men carry amulets or talismans that I had assumed you knew at least a little."

"Such things are not common in Sevairn, and I have never carried any of them. If there is anything you wish me to know, I fear you must teach me from the beginning."

"But since you left Sevairn?"

"I have spent most of my time with the Hoven-Thalar, and they do not use amulets either. Is it so important?"

"No, no, I was only wondering." Carachel hesitated, then seemed to realize that some additional explanation was needed. "The spells I cast could not find you at first, and I thought perhaps you carried a protective charm. Something similar to the one I use to prevent the Guild of Mages from finding me. When I found you near a river, I was sure of it; such spells are weaker there."

"I am afraid you were wrong, my lord; I carry no such talisman."

"Well, perhaps it is natural talent, then." Carachel gave Jermain a speculative look.

"Natural talent? I did not know sorcery could be acquired except through study."

"For the most part, that is true, but like anything else some people have greater ability than others. Normally, it develops in persons who have spent much of their lives surrounded by magic; I would be surprised to find it in someone from Sevairn. I suppose you have never been tested for such talent?"

"No, my lord," Jermain replied. "And I must admit, I have no great wish to be. But if you think it will be of help to you, I am willing."

Carachel nodded thoughtfully, watching Jermain. "It may come to that. For now, however, there is no need." He looked at Jermain a moment longer, then smiled reassuringly. "Put it out of your mind now, and rest. I will take the first watch."

Jermain was too tired to argue; he wrapped his cloak around him and lay down where he was. In a few moments, he was asleep.

He awoke abruptly to the sound of birds in a dim, predawn light. The fire was a bed of glowing embers; of Carachel there was no sign. Jermain sat up and shook the last wisps of uneasy dreams from his mind. "My Lord Carachel?"

"Here." Carachel's voice came from behind him. Jermain turned and saw the wizard walking out of the shadows, carrying an armload of wood. "I'm sorry if I alarmed you, but the fire was getting low and I thought it best to get a little more fuel before it died completely."

"So I see. Why didn't you wake me?"

"There was no need. I am accustomed to little sleep, and we shall travel farther today if you are completely recovered from yesterday when we start."

Reluctantly, Jermain nodded. He could not argue with the logic of it, but he had agreed to serve Carachel and he felt strange letting Carachel bear the brunt of the work. He started to rise, intending to assist Carachel with the fire, but the wizard motioned him back.

"Stay; I will not be long with this." Carachel bent to set the wood beside the remains of the fire, and something flashed on the middle finger of his right hand.

Jermain blinked and looked more closely. He saw it clearly for an instant as Carachel laid a stick on the embers. It was a ring, made in the shape of two serpents, one of polished gold and the other of black iron, twisting around each other. Jermain opened his lips to comment on it, then stopped and turned the gesture into a yawn. He suspected rather strongly that the ring had something to do with Carachel's magic, and he was sure Carachel would not welcome questions that pried into matters of wizardry. Carachel might be willing to answer such questions anyway, but Jermain did not want to strain their brief fellowship by making rude or awkward inquiries. "I will take the next watch," he said instead.

Carachel looked up from the wood. "I told you I am accustomed to little sleep. That is not necessary."

"Little sleep is not the same as no sleep at all, my lord. Do you plan to travel in the same manner as we did last night?"

"Yes, of course. I thought I had made that clear."

"Then I would most respectfully urge you to sleep, and let me watch until sunup. My reasons are somewhat selfish, I admit; I have never heard that magic is safe, and I can't say I like the idea of being enchanted by a tired wizard."

For a moment Carachel stared at Jermain, then he began to laugh. "You are right, of course," he said at last. "Very well, I will rest." He rose and walked a little way from the fire. For a moment, he fumbled with the clasp of his cloak; then he wrapped it around himself and lay down while Jermain busied himself with the fire.

When the flames were burning steadily once more, Jermain sat back to consider his situation. The abrupt change from fugitive to nobleman required some adjustment. Carachel's sorcery made him uncomfortable; still, Jermain reflected, he had served Marreth for years, and Marreth had done many things that made Jermain far more uncomfortable than Carachel's magic.

Not that he had seriously considered refusing Carachel's offer. His other alternatives were unpleasant enough to make the wizard's proposal seem like a gift straight from Arlayne, though Jermain was more likely to attract the attention of the War Goddess Morada than the Lord of Mercy. But even under happier circumstances Jermain suspected that he would have accepted Carachel's offer, and not merely out of ambition, though serving the Wizard-King of Tar-Alem was undeniably prestigious. I like Carachel, Jermain thought, and that is more important than prestige or magic.

The remainder of the night passed swiftly. Shortly after dawn, Jermain woke Carachel, and as soon as they had eaten they saddled their horses. Jermain noticed that the wizard's right hand was bare, and he was therefore not greatly surprised when Carachel informed him that they would travel most of the morning without sorcerous assistance.

They rode until noon, when they stopped to eat again and rest their horses. At midafternoon they mounted once more, and this time Carachel worked his spell. Jermain was quick enough to see the serpent ring on Carachel's upraised hand before he entered the shadow-world, and then he was too occupied with Blackflame to notice anything at all.

It was night when they stopped at last, and Jermain felt as if he had been riding for a week without sleep, food, or water.

He forced himself to see to Blackflame and swallow a few gulps of water before he slept, but he was too tired to eat. Carachel woke him up after a few hours. The wizard seemed more tired than he had the previous day, and Jermain took the watch without complaint.

The next three days fell into the same pattern. The two men rode slowly during the morning, then stopped to eat and rest. At midafternoon Carachel cast his enchantment, and for endless hours they would travel in the shifting grey world of the spell. By the time they stopped for the night, Jermain and his horse would be exhausted.

The terrain changed rapidly. By the second evening they were in the middle of the North Plains, and on the fourth morning they reached the Morlonian Hills. Jermain was amazed at the effectiveness of Carachel's sorcery; they had made nearly a month's journey in four days. He was also glad that the trip was nearly over. Despite Carachel's assurances, Jermain had never become accustomed to the wizardry that had brought them so far so quickly, and he was looking forward to the time when he would not be utterly weary at the end of the day.

Late in the evening of the fifth day they arrived at the place where Carachel's army was camped, just inside Tar-Alem on the opposite side of the Morlonian Hills. Carachel had used his traveling spell for only a brief time that afternoon, so Jermain was not as tired as he had been on the preceding days. Still, he was glad to see the flickering dots of the watchfires ahead, signaling the journey's end.

Carachel answered the sentry's hail with a flare of light that announced to everyone in the camp precisely who had arrived. The sentry stammered apologies as he bowed and let them past. Ahead, Jermain saw messengers speeding between the rows of tents, shouting that the King had returned. Jermain and Carachel rode slowly on through a steadily increasing confusion.

The center of the camp was occupied by a circle of decorative pavilions, and the two men rode into it and stopped. A boy in black-and-gold livery leaped to take their horses as they dismounted, and, after a moment of irrational reluctance, Jermain let him have Blackflame's rein. He watched the boy until he vanished among the soldiers, then turned to Carachel.

"Will you do me the honor of joining me for dinner this

night, my lord?'' Caracehel said before Jermain could speak.

A murmur of surprise rippled through those bystanders close enough to hear the exchange, and Jermain knew it would be recounted throughout the army by the following morning. He felt a wave of appreciation for Caracehel's public demonstration of esteem; it would make the task of taking charge of the army much easier. ''I am at Your Lordship's service,'' he replied, bowing.

Caracehel nodded and turned away. Jermain followed him to the central pavilion, which was painted gold with a black curtain for the door. As they approached, a hand reached out of the curtain and pulled it aside. Jermain stopped in surprise. The figure in the doorway was a woman.

She was tall, and almost too slender to be considered attractive. Once, perhaps, she had been beautiful; now the stubborn pride in her bearing only served to emphasize the faded weariness of her face. She wore a cream-colored gown, and her long blond hair was held in place by a circlet of gold. ''Welcome home, my lord,'' she said in a low voice.

Caracehel bowed to kiss her hand, then drew her forward. ''My lady, this is Lord Jermain Trevannon, lately of Sevairn, who has agreed to command our army. Lord Trevannon, this is my wife, Elsane.''

''Your Majesty,'' Jermain said, bowing low. He was surprised to find her with the army instead of in Tar-Alem's capital; as he remembered, she had no reputation as a warrior. In fact, she had very little reputation for anything. Only child of the old King of Tar-Alem, she had married the younger son of the King of Vircheta thirteen years ago. On her father's death a few years later, she had immediately handed the kingdom over to her husband, and since then had played no real part in the politics of the Seven Kingdoms. Except, of course, to provide an heir to the throne; if Jermain's memory served him correctly, the child was now nearly three.

''Welcome, Lord Trevannon. I am glad my husband's errand prospered,'' said the lady, without any particular pleasure.

''Has there been any trouble while I was gone?'' Caracehel asked.

''No, my lord,'' she said in the same neutral tone. Jermain had a sudden memory of his first conversation with Caracehel, and abruptly he understood. If the wizards of the Guild of

Mages were trying to stop Carachel, they might well attack his wife and son. No wonder he kept Elsane with the army! Jermain was surprised that Carachel had left her long enough to find him and bring him here.

"I am glad," said Carachel. "Now, shall we dine, my lady?"

"Of course, my lord." She swept a curtsey, and led the way into the pavilion. Jermain thought he saw Carachel's lips tighten briefly, but the expression vanished so quickly that he was not certain, and the two men followed Elsane in.

Dinner was as formal a function as could be expected in a temporary camp. Jermain thought it strange that Carachel had not even taken time to brush the dust of travel from his clothes, but he had little chance to speculate on Carachel's reasons. Carachel was apparently accustomed to dining with his Captains and Chief Advisers, and his first action was to introduce Jermain to all of them.

Elsane took little part in the conversation that followed. The talk was mainly of military matters, in which she seemed to have no interest: how many of the newly levied soldiers would have finished training by the end of the month, how many weapons would be needed to supply them, and whether the latest levies from the northern part of the kingdom would arrive before the main army began to move.

"I think they will make it," a grey-haired commander said. "Kird is a good Captain; he knows when to force his men."

"I don't disagree, but he isn't dealing with trained soldiers, remember," said a short, brown-haired woman who had been introduced to Jermain as one of Carachel's advisers. "Even Kird can't do much with raw peasants."

"If we have another week of good weather, he'll be here," the commander said stubbornly.

"I am afraid you are wrong, Suris," Carachel said, looking up from his own conversation with a stiff little man in red. "Kird and his men will not reach us in time."

"What?" Commander Suris jerked his head in Carachel's direction.

"Kird will not reach us before we begin to move," Carachel repeated.

"Why not, my lord?"

"Because I cannot wait any longer. We march south tomorrow."

Chapter Seven

Marreth's face grew even darker. "New information? Ridiculous! You weren't even here when Trevannon was exiled."

"Pity about that; I might have been able to keep you from getting into this mess," Vandaris said. "Not that you'd ever listen to me."

"Trevannon was plotting against me!"

Eltiron opened his mouth to protest, then stopped. Vandaris must have some reason for baiting Marreth so deliberately, and he doubted that an outburst from him would help any. At the edge of his vision, he saw Terrel moving toward the argument, and he shifted position slightly so he could watch Terrel without being too noticeable.

Marreth was still bellowing at Vandaris in a voice that shook the crystal goblets on the tables behind him. ". . . a traitor, and he's been exiled, and that's the end of it!"

"Not if you're wrong, lard-brain."

Marreth stopped short and stared at Vandaris through narrowed eyes. "What do you mean?"

Eltiron saw a startled expression cross Terrel's face, and then Vandaris said, "You really want to talk about it here?"

Marreth shook his head. "I'll see you tomorrow. And you'd better be able to explain, or I'll send you after Trevannon!"

"I can think of worse things that could happen. Getting fat and out of shape, for instance."

"I've had enough of your insults! You've had your say; now leave."

"Did I say anything about you? I didn't think I had. Let's see." Vandaris looked Marreth over critically and shook her

head. "Now that you mention it, you don't look particularly
well. You really ought to do something about yourself, Marreth, or you'll collapse in the middle of a Council someday,
the way old Carawn did. Darinhal is a better physician than
the one Carawn had, but there are limits."

"Out! Get out of this room at once! *Now!*"

"And miss dinner? Of course not! *I* don't have to worry
about eating too much."

"Vandaris! . . ."

Vandaris smiled and sketched a bow. "Until tomorrow,
then." Without even glancing at Marreth's outraged face, she
turned and strolled toward the tables. Eltiron nearly followed
her, but prudence kept him standing where he was. Following
Vandaris would only irritate Marreth further, and besides,
there would be little likelihood of talking to her privately until
the dinner was over.

Eltiron's reflections were interrupted by Marreth, demanding that the steward have dinner served at once. The castle
servitors responded quickly, and soon the long tables were full
of rich food and nervous courtiers. Marreth spent most of the
meal glowering down the length of the table at his sister; he
barely noticed the ornamental woman who had joined him at
the head of the table. Terrel, for once, did not make Eltiron
the object of his barbed comments. He, too, was watching
Vandaris, with an odd, speculative look that Eltiron disliked
intensely.

As a result of Terrel's preoccupation, Eltiron had no need
to make conversation during the meal. He was glad to be
spared the effort; he was determined to talk to Vandaris privately, and he spent much of dinner planning the best way of
doing so. When the meal was over, he watched carefully until
he saw Vandaris leave, then quickly made his excuses to the
bald nobleman he had been talking to and hurried after her.

He almost ran over her in the hall outside; she was walking
more slowly than he'd expected. Eltiron stammered an
apology, and Vandaris shook her head.

"If you make a habit of charging through the castle like a
dragon in heat, I hope you're good enough with a sword to
win all the duels you'll get into. It's a good thing I'm tolerant,
not to mention a relative. What's away?"

"I want to talk to you," Eltiron said as he fell into step

beside her. "Where have you been?"

Vandaris grinned. "Planning for trouble. Which means I've been busy, and it will probably get worse. If you want to talk, you'd better do it now."

"All right. Why didn't you tell me you knew something more about Jermain?"

"Not here, crack-skull! It's too easy for conversations to be overheard in these halls. This way."

Vandaris started down a side passage, and Eltiron followed. She proceeded to lead him, by a more circuitous route than he had ever imagined possible in Leshiya Castle, to her chambers. Tarilane was sitting at a table inside, frowning intently at a large, leather-bound book lying open in front of her. She looked up as they entered.

"Vandi! Did it—" She stopped abruptly as she saw Eltiron behind Vandaris.

"Did it work, you mean? Yes and no." Vandaris dropped into a chair with a sigh, and motioned Eltiron to sit down.

Tarilane looked from Vandaris to Eltiron, closed the book, and stood up. "I suppose I should leave?"

"No, so you can stop getting ready to sulk and sit down. I want to know what luck you've been having, among other things, but we'll get to that in a minute," Vandaris said.

Tarilane nodded and sat down, her eyes shining with excitement and her back very straight. Vandaris turned to Eltiron. "Now, you wanted to ask me something?"

"What have you found out about Jermain?"

"Nothing at all."

Eltiron stared. "But you told Father—"

"I lied," Vandaris said cheerfully.

"*Why?*"

"I want to know who has a guilty conscience. The easiest way for me to find out is to convince whoever-it-is that it's a good idea to worry about me, which I have now done. I hope."

"Do you really think someone will fall for that old trick?"

"Who cares if it's an old trick, as long as it works? And even if it doesn't, I managed to get through one of Marreth's dinners without being bored, and that's something."

"What if someone sends an assassin after you, or a spell, or something?"

"I've taken care of assassins before, and I don't expect anyone to use magic in Sevairn," Vandaris said uncommunicatively.

"Someone already has," Eltiron said, remembering the red thing they had found on the tower.

"Really?" Tarilane looked at Vandaris. "You didn't tell me."

"There are lots of things I don't tell you, sponge-brain. You're too nosy, and you talk too much."

"I do not!"

"You're talking too much right now," Vandaris said pointedly.

Tarilane subsided. Eltiron looked at Vandaris. "Are you sure—"

"Would I be risking my neck if I weren't? Quit worrying; it's too late to do anything about it anyway, and I have quite a few tricks you don't know about."

Eltiron shook his head. "As long as you're sure it's all right. But if you don't really know anything about Jermain, what are you going to tell Father tomorrow?"

"That Mournwal's arming. That'll make him forget about Jermain in a hurry, believe me."

"But Father doesn't believe the Hoven-Thalar are coming north; why would he believe Mournwal's getting ready for them?"

"He doesn't have to. As long as he thinks the King of Mournwal is planning to invade Sevairn, he'll call up the army and start it moving south, and that's all we really want him to do."

"You're going to tell him Mournwal is planning to invade Sevairn?"

"I won't have to; he'll jump on the idea himself as soon as I mention armies in Mournwal." Vandaris grinned. "By the time the Hoven-Thalar get to the border, he'll think he planned the whole thing right from the beginning. I can handle Marreth."

"I hope so," Eltiron said. "But he can be awfully irritable."

"I'll admit his mood's gotten worse since I was here last. How long has he been like that?"

"Like what?"

"The way he was tonight, lead-skull. He's always had a lousy temper, but I didn't expect him to explode before I even said anything. He acted worse than a dreamsmoke addict."

"He's not a dreamsmoker!" Eltiron said, shocked. "He can't be! He isn't—I mean, he doesn't—I mean, he has too many . . ."

"Women? I know, and you're right, he couldn't keep any of them happy if he were a dreamsmoker." Vandaris grinned maliciously. "Though I'd like to point out that I never said he was."

Eltiron felt himself turning red, and said hastily, "Then what *did* you mean?"

"His temper, for one thing. And he's lost what little sense he had, not to mention being even more suspicious than he used to be. Furthermore, when he's in a rage he looks as if he were going to die of apoplexy any minute. How long has this been going on?"

"I don't know." Eltiron frowned. "I don't think I could give you a date even if I tried; he's just gotten more and more irritable."

"Maybe his brain's ossifying from age. Tari, has anyone else noticed anything unusual about Marreth or Lassond?"

Tarilane grinned, and gave a short and highly uncomplimentary account of Marreth's doings that left Eltiron amazed by the number of things she appeared to have overheard. She had less information about Terrel, due mainly to the fact that he had brought his own manservant with him when he moved into the castle. "He doesn't gossip, and as far as I could find out, no one goes inside Terrel's rooms except him and Terrel, so nobody knows much," Tarilane finished.

"Hmmmm. Wonder what Lassond's hiding in there," Vandaris said, leaning back in her chair with a thoughtful expression.

"I thought you'd want to know," Tarilane said. "So I tried to sneak in while you were at dinner."

"You did *what?*" Vandaris jerked upright and stared at Tarilane.

"I tried to sneak into Terrel's rooms," Tarilane repeated smugly. "I didn't make it, though; he's done something to the lock."

"What about the guards?" Eltiron said, fascinated.

"Oh, *them*. They were no problem. I dressed up like an ash-girl and got a bucket from one of the spare rooms. They didn't notice me at all."

"Tarilane." Vandaris's voice was almost expressionless.

Tarilane's head turned, and her face took on a stubborn expression. "Yes?"

"I told you to mix with the servants and tell me what you could overhear about Marreth and Lassond. I did *not* tell you to try to play Hanstall the Spy all over the castle, or to sneak past the guards and break into Lassond's room."

Tarilane raised her chin. "I thought you'd want me to."

"Oh?"

After a moment, Tarilane's eyes dropped. "No."

"I thought you were intelligent enough not to pull tricks like this. Were you looking for a quick tour of Marreth's dungeons, or were you just homesick?"

"You wouldn't really send me back, would you? Please don't, Vandi! I won't do it again, I promise."

Vandaris sighed. "I brought you along because I thought you needed some exposure to Leshiya's court life, and you certainly won't get it if I send you back to Tindalen. Just don't try anything like that again."

Tarilane nodded, somewhat subdued. Vandaris looked at her for a moment, then turned to Eltiron. "I think we have a few other things to worry about at the moment. Arranging our match tomorrow, for one."

"You're really going to do it? I thought you were just saying that to confuse Terrel."

"No, I meant it. Where do you usually practice?"

"The south ring."

"We'll use the north ring, then. It'll take Lassond longer to find us if he gets nosy, and you'll work harder if the ground is a little unfamiliar."

"If you're going to fight with swords, can I watch?" Tarilane asked eagerly.

Vandaris laughed. "You'll watch, all right, and bring the practice swords down, and made sure the ring is smooth before we start, and clean up when we're done. What else do I have a sword-squire for?"

"Oh." Tarilane's expression changed from anticipation to distaste.

Vandaris laughed again. "Cheer up, slow-bones; if you do a good job, I might let you take a turn in the ring."

Tarilane's face lit up. "I'll do everything perfectly!" she promised.

"Are you sure it would be wise to let her fight?" Eltiron asked Vandaris. "It's bound to make people talk."

"I've been causing gossip for more years than you remember, pigeon-wit. Tari's my sword-squire, and I'll see her trained properly no matter how much talk there is about it."

Eltiron nodded. He spent a few more minutes with Vandaris and her sword-squire, then returned to his own chambers. He sat staring out the window for some time, thinking about the events of the evening. He did not come to any startling conclusions, and eventually he went to bed. Just as he was falling asleep, he remembered that he had not told Vandaris about Terrel's odd behavior at dinner, and he resolved to mention it to her in the morning.

The following day, he did not see his aunt until the beginning of their match. He spent the early part of the morning listening to the castle steward explain the room arrangements for the guests, then went to the first fitting of the clothes he had been measured for the previous day. He was extremely glad when Tarilane tapped at the door and announced to the startled tailor, "I'm here to conduct Prince Eltiron to his appointment with Her Royal Highness the Lady Vandaris."

"That was exactly the right thing to say," Eltiron told Tarilane as they headed toward the practice rings. "Ayrl likes formality."

"I know," the sword-squire said, grinning. "Vandi told me. Hurry up; she's down there already, and she gets grouchy when she has to wait for people."

When they arrived at the practice ring, Vandaris was making passes in the air with one of the wooden practice swords. "Tari, are these the best you could find?" she demanded as they came up.

"The armorer said they were the ones Prince Eltiron and his teacher usually use," Tarilane said defensively.

"What's wrong with them?" Eltiron asked.

"They're too light; no wonder you've been having trouble learning swordcraft! We'll have to use real ones. Don't worry," she said as she saw the look on his face. "I won't touch you, and if you manage to slice me, it'll be no more than I deserve. Let's get started.''

"Uh, Vandi?" Tarilane said nervously.

"What is it?"

"I met Lady Anareme on my way to get him"—she jerked her head at Eltiron—"and she sent a message."

"You going to tell me what it was, or just stand there?"

"She said she's found two more men you can send out, if you want them, but you'll have to let her know right away."

"Did anyone notice the first two?"

Tarilane shook her head. "No. I watched. And no one's said anything since they left."

"Good. Nobody saw you watching, I hope?"

"Of course not!" Tarilane looked faintly indignant. "I know how to be careful!"

"Not that I'd noticed," Vandaris said dryly.

"What men?" Eltiron broke in.

Vandaris hesitated. "I suppose you might as well know. I sent a couple of messengers out after Trevannon; they left two days ago."

"You did? Why didn't you tell me? Where is he?"

"I don't know where Trevannon is; that's why I sent two men instead of one."

"Then it could be months before one of them finds him."

"Maybe, but I think I'm a better guesser than that. Trevannon knows about the Hoven-Thalar, and he won't give up on stopping them just because Marreth threw him out of Sevairn. Knowing the way his mind works, I'd bet he's already in Mournwal or Gramwood, getting ready to fight when the Hoven-Thalar come north."

"What will you do if he isn't?"

"The men I sent to look for him will come back, and I'll think of something else. Trevannon's a good strategist and he knows the Hoven-Thalar, but he doesn't *have* to be around when the fight starts."

Eltiron nodded without much conviction. He could hear the worry behind his aunt's confident remarks, and it made his own preoccupation with Jermain seem childish and self-centered. Until Vandaris arrived, he had not really thought much about the impending invasion of the Hoven-Thalar. His reasons for wanting to see Jermain again were purely personal, and he had not even tried to send anyone to look for the

man he called his friend. Eltiron began to feel foolish as well
as childish; even if Terrel had been watching him constantly,
he could have *tried* to do something.

"You going to stand there all day, cloud-brain, or are we
going to have a match?" said Vandaris, and Eltiron shook
himself and stepped into the ring.

The match went well. Eltiron performed much better than
he did when he practiced with Kaliarth. Then, too, Eltiron was
more comfortable with Vandaris as an instructor. Her acid
comments caught every mistake and sloppy move, but they
were easier to accept than Kaliarth's reluctant, deferential cor-
rections, and when Vandaris complimented a maneuver, she
meant it. When they finished, Vandaris announced that she
would repeat the exercise every day, as long as she was in
Leshiya.

"I need the practice as much as you do; at my age, it's entirely too easy to go stale," she told Eltiron. "I'll settle it with
Kaliarth." She grinned. "And it'll keep Lassond from trying
any more of his tricks for a while."

"What about me?" Tarilane demanded.

"That's right, I promised you a turn in the ring, too, didn't
I? You can use one of the wooden swords, and . . ." Vandaris
stopped and her head turned.

Eltiron glanced in the same direction, and saw a movement
in the shadow of the entrance gate. A moment later, the
shadow resolved into a man wearing a long cloak and a shapeless, dusty hat that hid most of his face. He seemed familiar,
but Eltiron was not sure why. The man made a small circling
gesture with his hand, and waited.

"You'll have to wait a minute, Tari. This shouldn't take
long; you can get the ring ready for another match while I'm
busy." Vandaris started in the direction of the gate.

Eltiron hesitated, then started after her, but Vandaris waved
him back and went on alone. He watched until Vandaris
reached the cloaked man, then turned thoughtfully to help
Tarilane rake the practice ring. He had caught a glimpse of
cream-colored robes and a crimson sash beneath the cloak,
and he knew now why the man seemed familiar. He was a
Hoven-Thalar, the same one Eltiron had seen once before,
talking to Jermain.

Vandaris returned a few moments later. Eltiron started to
ask about the exchange, but Vandaris shot him such a fierce

look that he changed subjects in midsentence and ended up
with a confused tangle that seemed to have something to do
with Terrel. He straightened it out by explaining that he'd
noticed Terrel watching Vandaris at Marreth's dinner and had
nearly forgotten to mention it. Vandaris seemed unconcerned,
and went on to her practice with Tarilane. Eltiron watched for
a few moments, then went off to his next meeting, wishing as
he did that he could ignore his obligations and go to the tower
and think. He had too many things he wanted to sort out, and
no time for any of them.

For the next four days, Eltiron's every waking minute
seemed occupied with preparations for either his wedding or a
war with Mournwal. Vandaris's interview with Marreth had
gone just as she had expected, and Sevairn was arming at last,
albeit to face the wrong enemy. Curiously, Terrel did not object to the resulting military activity; on the contrary, he
seemed almost relieved. Eltiron added that to the growing list
of things he wanted time to think about and went doggedly on
with his duties. He stood for endless fittings of wedding
clothes, attended Council meetings to discuss the war, enter-
tained various minor diplomats and nobility, and had daily
practice sessions with Vandaris, wishing all the time that he
could get away.

When he finally did manage to slip up to the top of the
Tower of Judgment, his first act was to check every inch of the
parapet for odd-looking red patches. He found none, and with
some relief he seated himself on the eastern side of the tower-
top, his back to the stone parapet, and tried to relax.

Too many things had happened in the last ten days. There
was Terrel; who had he been talking to on the tower, and what
were they trying to do? For some reason, Eltiron's marriage
seemed to be mixed up in it, unless he had imagined the whole
conversation, and so was Jermain. And from the way Terrel
had been eyeing Vandaris since Marreth's dinner party, he had
plans for her, too.

Then there was Vandaris. She refused to tell anyone
whether she had gotten any results from her performance at
the party; Eltiron had to take Tarilane's word that there had,
at least, been no assassination attempts. She likewise refused
to discuss whatever she had learned in her conversation with
the Hoven-Thalar at the first practice session. Still, she had
promised to let Eltiron know if she heard any news of Jer-

main, and she was practically the only person in the castle who took Eltiron seriously.

Finally, there was the impending war with the Hoven-Thalar. If what Vandaris said was true, the war could make everything else unimportant by comparison. Eltiron shifted uncomfortably. In spite of Vandaris's arguments and persuasion, he didn't like leading Marreth to believe that Mournwal was planning to attack Sevairn.

At least the preparations for battle had kept Eltiron from brooding on his coming marriage, and that was something. On the other hand, he would have to think about it soon; the Princess of Barinash and her escort should be arriving tomorrow. Eltiron shifted again and realized suddenly that his back was tingling where it touched the tower stone.

In a single bound, he was on his feet and a sword-length away from the parapet. He stood panting for a moment, more from fright than exertion. Nothing unusual seemed to be happening, so he moved cautiously forward, scanning the parapet as he came for red patches or anything else that might explain the odd sensation he had felt. He found nothing. Hesitantly, he put out his hand and touched the parapet just above where he had been leaning against it.

The stone was warm beneath his hand, but he felt no other strangeness. Eltiron sighed, wondering if it was all his imagination. A little gingerly, he leaned against the stone, looking out across Leshiya to the fields beyond. A small caravan was moving down the eastern road toward the city. Eltiron glanced at it, then stiffened abruptly as a brief gust of wind unfurled the banners at the head of the column. The banners were green and silver, the colors of Barinash.

Evidently, Eltiron's prospective bride was arriving early.

Chapter Eight

Jermain blinked in surprise at Carachel's announcement. The army was moving so soon? He looked around quickly to see how the others at the table were reacting. The brown-haired woman was looking thoughtfully at Jermain, while the rest of Carachel's advisers sat staring with the carefully blank looks of those who have been trained not to let their thoughts show. The military commanders were frowning, and some were muttering angrily. Only Elsane seemed unaffected by the news; she continued eating with the same calm disinterest she had shown toward the rest of the conversation.

"My lord, I must object," Commander Suris said after a moment. "Whoever has advised this course has not thought of all the problems it will cause." He glanced at Jermain as he spoke.

"You are wrong again, Suris," Carachel said. "This decision is mine; Lord Trevannon has heard nothing of it until now."

"That may well be so, my lord. But no matter how skillful he is, your new Commander-General will require time to become familiar with the men and what they can do, and prudence indicates that he should do so before he commands them in a battle."

"Lord Trevannon must learn as we march. Our time is running out. The Hoven-Thalar have already begun to move from the southern plains."

Jermain saw several of the military men and advisers exchange glances; apparently some of them had doubts about the threat of the nomads. He made a mental note of their faces as Suris said slowly, "Even so, we have time to reach the southern kingdoms before they do. A straight march should not take more than six weeks at most, and it has been done in less."

"We do not make a straight march, however. We will go east, around the Morlonian Hills into Barinash, and then south to Gramwood."

Suris frowned. "I do not wish to question you, my lord, but—"

"Enough." Carachel's voice was quiet and cold. "We go to Barinash because King Urhelds has agreed to send half his army south with us. We do not take the shorter route through Sevairn because King Marreth still refuses to consider my warnings seriously. Does that content you?"

"As you say, my lord."

"Then all of you may go as soon as you have finished your meal. I think preparing for the march will give you tasks enough to keep you occupied."

The councillors nodded, and several rose and took their leave at once. The others finished eating quickly and followed, leaving Jermain alone with Carachel and Elsane. Jermain cleared his throat.

"My lord, if you will tell me whom to see about quarters, I, too, will leave you."

Carachel looked up, his expression unreadable. "I suppose you think I was too harsh with them."

"You know your commanders better than I, my lord." Privately, Jermain thought that the Wizard-King had been more abrupt than necessary, but he did not feel ready to criticize Carachel directly. There was too much he did not know about Carachel and his advisers, councillors, and commanders, and he had no desire to make a mistake in judgment through ignorance.

"Yes." Carachel sighed. "They follow my orders because I am their King, but most of them do not really believe in me."

"Why not?"

"For nearly ten years I have been trying to prepare Tar-Alem to meet the nomads and . . . what comes behind them, and for ten years they have wondered and doubted. It is not easy for them to change their thinking, even when the proof is here."

Elsane rose abruptly. "My lord is correct, as always. If I may be excused?"

"My lady needs no permission from me." Carachel watched Elsane intently as he spoke, but she avoided his eyes, curtsied formally, and went out. Carachel sat looking after her with an expression of mingled pain and frustration. Jermain took one brief glance at the wizard's face, then became absorbed in the contemplation of a candle flame.

"You are discreet," Carachel said after a moment.

"Discretion is frequently necessary in a King's Adviser," Jermain said, without taking his eyes from the candle flame. He heard Carachel sigh.

"You had better know. My lady Elsane has . . . regrets. She gave Tar-Alem into my keeping, and now that it is years too late to change, she doubts the wisdom of that decision."

"Indeed, my lord."

"Elsane believes that I will beggar Tar-Alem in this war, and that Sevairn or Navren will destroy us once we have spent our army against the Hoven-Thalar. Do you wonder that she has come to resent me?"

"But surely you are not leaving Tar-Alem defenseless?"

"Very nearly."

Jermain frowned in surprise. "Then perhaps the lady's fears are justified."

"Yet what else can I do?" Carachel said, half to himself. "Should I let the nomads make a ruin of the southern kingdoms? And even if it were possible, how could I allow the Matholych to suck the life and the magic from every kingdom except Tar-Alem? That would be as bad as what my lady fears; even if so many deaths meant nothing, Tar-Alem depends on trade with the other six kingdoms. No, I have no choice."

Jermain pressed his lips together to avoid a too hasty reply. From what he had seen, he doubted that Elsane's reserve was due solely to a disagreement with her husband over the disposition of the army. Furthermore, he was certain Carachel was not telling him everything; but whatever stood between Carachel and Elsane, investigating it was certainly no part of his duties. Jermain cleared his throat.

"Just what does the Matholych do, my lord?" he said.

Carachel's head came around abruptly. "Why do you ask?"

"If it follows the Hoven-Thalar closely, it is possible that it will have some influence on the way I command your army," Jermain said, trying to keep his voice from becoming sarcastic. What seemed obvious to him might not be to Carachel; a wizard was not likely to have the same outlook as a warrior.

There was a long pause. "We can discuss it tomorrow," Carachel said at last.

"As you wish, my lord."

Carachel studied him a moment longer. "See Estrik about your quarters and a uniform, and come here tomorrow morning. Good eve to you."

Jermain rose and bowed, then left the pavilion. A few questions to one of the soldiers produced directions to Estrik's tent. Estrik proved to be a thin, black-haired man with the perpetually sour look common to every army quartermaster Jermain had ever seen. Jermain explained his business, and Estrik scowled.

"You want a uniform? I'll have to take something from stores; there's no time to make one, not if we're moving tomorrow."

"Whatever you have will be fine," Jermain told him.

Estrik looked at him critically. "Hmmph. You're Carachel's new commander? You'll want dark grey and gold, then. As if I kept officer's uniforms just lying around. Bah! I knew Carachel was going to replace Suris, but he might have told me when."

Still grumbling, Estrik turned and began rummaging among the stacks of bundles at the rear of the tent. After a moment he handed one of them to Jermain. "There. It'll have to do you till we get to Barinash; I can't possibly have one made before then, so don't ask."

"I won't. What makes you think I'm replacing Suris?"

"Every man with a brain knows, which means about six in the whole camp. Suris is a good soldier, but he's too stupid for King Carachel." The quartermaster's lip curled slightly. "So was the one before him. You won't last, either."

"Indeed." Jermain's eyes narrowed. "Why not?"

Estrik smiled thinly. "You're too smart. And I talk too much. I put up a tent for you in the corner when I saw you arrive with Carachel; I'll show you where it is."

Jermain spent the brief walk to the tent puzzling over Estrik's cryptic statements. Some of the quartermaster's ill-

natured remarks could be attributed to the man's obviously
sour disposition, but Jermain knew better than to dismiss
them all as one man's bad temper. Tomorrow, thought Jermain, I will have to talk to some of the men, and find out what
they think about Suris and Carachel. And me.

His reflections were cut short as they reached the tent. Jermain stifled a gesture of surprise and pleasure. His ac-
commodations consisted of a relatively private tent furnished
with a cot and a folding table: certainly more than he had expected, and far more than he had become accustomed to in recent months. Estrik provided him with blankets, towels, and
wash water, then left him to himself.

As the tent flap closed behind his escort, Jermain sighed in
relief and began stripping off his grimy clothing. He knew
better than to expect a hot bath from an army camped in the
field, but even the inadequate sponging he could manage with
the washbasin would be welcome. The medallion Amberglas
had given him swung against his chest as he turned toward the
table. Jermain smiled, remembering the confusing, bewilder-
ing sorceress. His smile faded after a moment, and he frowned
as he reached for the water pitcher.

Why hadn't he mentioned Amberglas to Carachel? He had
considered it several times during their journey to the army,
but he had never quite been able to bring himself to do so. The
three days he had spent at Amberglas's tower were among the
few pleasant memories that were unshadowed by his life in
Sevairn, and he was unwilling to share them even with Carachel. Of course, the Wizard-King did not seem particularly interested in talking about other magicians; under the circumstances, that was quite understandable.

Jermain shrugged and picked up a towel. If an opportunity
arose, perhaps he would say something to Carachel about the
sorceress, but suddenly it did not really seem important. He
finished drying himself, then wrapped one of the blankets
around his shoulders and lay down on the cot. He fell asleep
fingering the medallion and thinking of Amberglas.

Jermain had no chance to speak to Carachel the following
day. The wizard was busy with preparations for the march; he
sent Jermain a note expressing his regrets and canceling their
appointment. Jermain was too busy to be either angry or concerned. Though the army did not actually begin to move that

day, the preparations occupied the entire camp, and everyone
who was able was pressed into service.

To his surprise, Jermain discovered that the officers seemed
to expect him to direct the move. Apparently Carachel's comments on their arrival were sufficient guarantee of his author-
ity. Everyone from Estrik to Suris came to Jermain with their
questions, and he dealt with them as best he could. By the
following morning the army was ready at last, and soon a long
column began moving slowly along the edge of the hills.

Jermain continued to wear Amberglas's medallion under his
tunic, though he could not have explained why he wore it or
why he kept it hidden. It certainly was no longer of any use to
him. Most of the time he did not even remember that he had it;
he was too busy with the officers and the moving column of
soldiers.

At the end of his second day with the army, Jermain felt
almost comfortable in his role as commander. The men and
the other commanders accepted him without comment or
challenge, which served to impress him more with Carachel's
control of the soldiers than with his own ability to handle
them. Evidently Carachel's orders were thoroughly respected;
if Carachel said Jermain was the commander, no one in the
army would question Jermain's right to command, not even in
the small testings that were usually the lot of a new officer.

Carachel sent for Jermain as soon as the army had made
camp. When Jermain presented himself at Carachel's quarters, the Wizard-King was seated at a long table covered with
maps and scrolls, frowning. Jermain waited for a moment,
then said, "You sent for me, my lord?"

"Yes, of course," Carachel said, looking up. "Come in and
sit down. We have more to discuss than you may think."

Jermain took a seat opposite Carachel and waited expectantly.

The wizard hesitated, then slid a large map out from under
three smaller ones and spread it out in front of him. "We have
a month and a half, perhaps two, before we will actually face
the Hoven-Thalar, but I wish you to know my plans. This is
the route we will take."

Carachel's forefinger traced a curving line from the eastern
end of the Morlonian Hills into Barinash, and paused. "Here
we meet King Urhelds's army, if he has not changed his mind.
I do not think he will." The finger continued south into Gram-

wood, then west until it paused again at the border between Mournwal and Gramwood. "The armies of Mournwal and Gramwood will meet us here. I expect Vircheta to send some troops as well. Once they arrive, we will have little to do except wait for the Hoven-Thalar. And the Matholych."

"My lord, I am impressed. Combining the armies of five of the Seven Kingdoms is an accomplishment indeed."

Carachel sighed. "I had hoped for all seven. But the King of Navren listens too closely to his wizards, and Sevairn refuses to listen to a wizard at all."

"How did you persuade the others?"

"Mournwal and Gramwood know what they will face; they were glad to join me in return for a promise of aid. Vircheta, too, has a border close to the wastelands, and my brother rules there now. He was not unwilling to lend me some troops, once he was assured that I would be with the army." Carachel's smile was slightly twisted. "Barlistene has no objection to supporting a war that may remove his nearest possible rival for his throne, nor would he die of grief if the same stroke gave him the opportunity to become regent of Tar-Alem until my son comes of age."

Jermain nodded. Mournwal stood between Vircheta and the Hoven-Thalar, but Mournwal was neither large nor strong. Vircheta's King would hardly object to sending a few troops south on the chance of keeping the nomads from reaching his borders, and if he saw a chance that the war would rid him of a brother he disliked, so much the better. Jermain began to think Carachel was singularly unlucky in his family. "And Barinash?"

"The King of Barinash is ruled by his Chief Adviser, a man called Salentor Parel. I see you know him. I managed to . . . persuade Salentor to cooperate."

"You asked Salentor for help? And he agreed?" Jermain was shocked. "My lord, Salentor Parel is only interested in ways of enhancing his own power, and he is not particular as to the means he uses. Whatever promises he made, you cannot trust him to keep them."

"I know what he is, but I think the bribe I offered will be sufficient."

"You know what he is, and you dealt with him anyway?"

Carachel's face tightened. "I do what I must."

"Must! I don't believe it; surely there was some other way."

"If I knew one, I would use it. But Barinash's soldiers will be desperately needed when we face the Hoven-Thalar, and this was the only way to get them in time." Carachel's eyes caught Jermain's and held them. "We will need every man we can find. If the same methods would win Sevairn's support, or Navren's, I would not hesitate to use them again. If you can neither understand nor accept, you may leave my service when you will."

For a long moment, Jermain hesitated. He knew what the Hoven-Thalar would do to the southern kingdoms if they were allowed to move north, but he could not quite believe that the combined armies of Gramwood, Mournwal, Tar-Alem, and Vircheta would be insufficient to stop them.

"If it were only the Hoven-Thalar, I would not need Barinash so badly," said Carachel, answering Jermain's thoughts with uncanny accuracy. "Because if the Hoven-Thalar had simply decided to move north, some of the clans would undoubtedly prefer to remain in the wasteland. But this is not their choice; the Matholych is forcing them northward, and none of the clans will stay behind to face it. We will have to hold the entire strength of the Hoven-Thalar until I can defeat the Matholych."

"Hold them!" Jermain frowned. "My lord, I know the Hoven-Thalar, and it will be nearly impossible to hold them. They can move more quickly than any army; if we don't defeat them at our first meeting, they'll simply circle us and go on."

"We must hold them," Carachel repeated firmly, "and with as little loss of life on both sides as possible. That is why I need someone of your skill." He smiled. "You see, I am one of the few who know that you directed the men who threw back Barinash when they tried to invade Sevairn eight years ago."

"I thank you for your confidence, my lord, but what you are seeking would take a miracle!"

"Not for a large-enough army and a skilled commander."

The argument continued for some time. Jermain drew on all his knowledge of the Hoven-Thalar in his attempt to explain why it would be impossible to keep them penned in the area Carachel indicated, but Carachel refused to accept any change in his strategy. Finally Jermain left, taking with him several of the maps to study in more detail. In spite of his frustration, he had to admit to a grudging admiration for Carachel's position; he had never before met any commander who expressed the slightest concern for the lives of an enemy army.

Jermain spent much of the night studying the maps and returned to Carachel at the end of the next day's march with a proposal of his own. A little to the southeast of the battleground Carachel had chosen, the River Clemmar passed through the Hills of Starglen, forming a natural barrier. If the Hoven-Thalar could be driven toward the hills, it might be possible to hold them as Carachel wished.

Carachel studied the plan only briefly, then shook his head. Jermain argued in vain. At first, Carachel refused even to explain why the plan was unacceptable, but at last he sighed and said, "It is too far south."

"My lord," Jermain said, clinging firmly to the last shreds of his patience, "I thought you would find that an advantage. The Hoven-Thalar would not come nearly as far into Gramwood and Mournwal before we engage them."

"That is precisely the problem. We must meet them as close to the Sevairn border as we can, or we shall defeat the Hoven-Thalar only to lose against the Matholych."

"I am afraid I do not understand, my lord."

Carachel sighed. "The Matholych draws life and magic out of the land it passes over, and leaves behind a barren waste. Life can return to the land, in time, but to replenish magic takes far longer. The last time the Matholych came north—"

"The last time? This has happened before?"

"Several times. Each time it returns, it is stronger, and it moves deeper into the Seven Kingdoms. The last time was several centuries ago, and it came nearly to the northern border of Sevairn. That is why Sevairn and the two southern kingdoms have so little use for magic; magic has less power where the Matholych has passed."

"I thought you said no one knew about this thing, but if it has come north before . . ."

"Do not your histories speak of an invasion of the Hoven-Thalar, one that destroyed Gramwood, Mournwal, and much of Sevairn? The Matholych was more to blame than the nomads for that destruction."

Jermain nodded. He recognized the tale of the invasion; it was one that had come forcibly to mind when he first learned that the Hoven-Thalar planned to move north soon. The story

made no mention of anything like the Matholych, however.
"How did you learn of it, my lord?"

"Of the Matholych?" Carachel hesitated. "Some I learned
before the Guild cast me out, but most of what I know has
come from the library of Tar-Alem. There were a few wizards
at the time of the last invasion who kept their records there,
rather than at the Guild."

"With your permission, my lord, I would like to examine
those records; they may contain information I will need."

This time Carachel's hesitation was even more marked. "I
have only a few of them with me," he said at last, "and it will
take me some time to sort them out of this confusion. I will
send them to you tomorrow."

Jermain nodded again, wondering a little at Carachel's obvious reluctance. The conversation turned back to determining
an acceptable strategy for facing the Hoven-Thalar, and soon
after Jermain left. No progress had been made, and Jermain
found himself wondering whether any could be. Whatever his
reasons, Carachel was obviously determined to allow his army
to kill as few of the nomads as possible.

The scrolls were delivered next day, four stained and ancient
documents describing in obscure language the coming of the
Matholych. Jermain studied them with interest. Apparently
the Matholych grew weaker as it came farther north; the
records noted it repeatedly, but gave no clue as to why. The
scrolls contained no physical description of the monster, but
they were eloquent indeed on the subject of its power. Jermain
began to wonder how big the Matholych was, and how far its
power extended. Something that could suck three kingdoms
nearly dry of magic for hundreds of years . . .

Abruptly, Jermain set down the scroll he was reading and
spread out one of his maps. He looked at it for a long moment, then began carefully going through the scroll, noting the
places it mentioned as having been destroyed by the Matholych, along with the dates of their destruction. When he
finished, he did the same for the other records Carachel had
given him. He sat back and looked at the map.

He saw the pattern at once, a giant wedge forced into the
middle of the Seven Kingdoms. There were a series of circles in
northern Mournwal and another series in Gramwood, slanting
upward through Sevairn almost to the Morlonian Hills. The
northernmost point of the pattern of destruction was directly

north of the site Carachel had chosen for the battle. Jermain traced the line absently, noting with a twinge of apprehension that Leshiya lay almost exactly halfway between the battleground and the edge of the Matholych's destruction.

Shaking his head, he turned back to his study of the scrolls. The Matholych, after all, was Carachel's to deal with; a human army could do nothing, unless it were an army of wizards. He put the thought out of his mind, and began searching for references to the Hoven-Thalar.

When Jermain finally finished with the four scrolls, he thought he understood Carachel's insistence on the location of the battlefield, and he was more than a little apprehensive. In the last invasion, the path of the Hoven-Thalar followed a straight line north from the wasteland, but the path of the Matholych moved forward more like a wave, surging up on either side of the nomads' trail. The Matholych, if it was a single being, must be enormous; villages in western Mournwal and northern Gramwood had been destroyed at virtually the same time. Or perhaps it was not impossibly large, but simply was not limited by distance. Jermain remembered Carachel's spell of traveling, and shivered.

Firmly, he turned his mind back to the plans in front of him. If this invasion followed the same pattern as the last one, the destruction that marked the path of the Matholych would at first move northward faster at the eastern border of Gramwood and the western border of Mournwal. In the center, where the Hoven-Thalar would be riding north, the Matholych would move more slowly, forming an arc of ruin around an untouched center. Eventually, the center began moving forward more quickly, reaching halfway to the northern border of Sevairn in a single sudden wave.

Jermain could understand why Carachel did not want to explain his battle plan in great detail. It looked very much as if Carachel's army would be facing the Hoven-Thalar in the center of the arc, with the Matholych spreading northward on either side. And if the center of the Matholych moved forward too quickly, or sooner than Carachel expected . . .

Carefully, Jermain rolled the crumbling scrolls and stacked them on the edge of the table. He put out the lamp and lay down on his cot, but it was a long time before he slept.

Chapter Nine

By the time Eltiron reached the bottom of the tower, the courtyard was full of hurrying people. Eltiron picked his way among them, wondering who had brought word to the castle and whether the Princess really was with the caravan. He had covered barely a quarter of the distance from the tower to the main entrance of the castle when he was hailed with relief by the harried castle steward, who informed him that the Princess of Barinash would be arriving within an hour. Eltiron, said the steward, was commanded by the King to prepare himself to formally receive his bride; the Princess and her escort would be brought directly to the Grey Hall and everyone must be there to meet her, and why was Eltiron just standing there? Eltiron left hurriedly.

An hour and a half later, Eltiron stood beside Marreth at the center of the Grey Hall, waiting. He was uncomfortably aware of the way the courtiers were eyeing him, and he found himself wishing he could talk to Jermain, or Vandaris. But Jermain was in exile, Vandaris was somewhere among the mass of people lining the walls in hopes of witnessing the Princess's arrival, and Eltiron did not feel up to starting a conversation with his father. He waited in silence.

Terrel stood on Marreth's other side, looking as calm and at ease as if he had not dressed as hastily as everyone else in the room. He wore a red silk shirt, heavily embroidered with gold, which suited his blond coloration perfectly, and he seemed cool and comfortable in spite of the room's warmth. The crowd of courtiers had been waiting for nearly an hour, and the Grey Hall had quickly become overheated despite its size.

Silently, Eltiron cursed the man who had decided that pale

blue velvet would be appropriate for the Prince of Sevairn to wear to meet his bride. The clothes were hot and uncomfortable as well as unbecoming; once again, Terrel looked more the Prince than Eltiron. Eltiron felt a bead of sweat trickle down his back. Mentally, he cursed again and wished he had the courage to tell the tailors what he thought of this wonderful idea. His collar was making his neck itch. He put up a hand to ease it, and the horns outside blew to announce the arrival of the Princess.

A moment later, the doors swung open and the Princess of Barinash and her escort entered the room. First came the guards, resplendent in green-and-silver uniforms, and Eltiron had time to wonder how they managed to look so fresh after two or three weeks of traveling. A short, unpleasant-looking man followed; Eltiron had a vague memory of his having been an ambassador or something several years before. Behind him came the Princess and two of her ladies.

The short man began a rambling speech of introduction, none of which Eltiron heard. As the Princess entered, Eltiron's face grew hot, and he dropped his eyes in an attempt to regain some of his composure. Why hadn't anyone told him that the Princess Crystalorn was beautiful? At least, he thought it was the Princess he'd seen. He looked up, and his stomach knotted. The Princess hadn't even noticed him. She was watching Terrel.

Swallowing disappointment, Eltiron forced himself to look at the Princess's companions. She doesn't know yet who I am, he thought. Underneath the thought was the hurt of knowing that he was right, that he did not look like a Prince, that when she did learn who he was she would be disappointed. He didn't want to think about disappointing her, because there was no way he could prevent it. In a few minutes, she would be formally presented to him, and she would know.

Abruptly, Eltiron realized that he was staring at one of the Princess's ladies, a tall woman with hair the color of unpolished steel. She was regarding him with a direct and rather disconcerting gaze, and Eltiron blinked apologetically. The woman smiled warmly, and Eltiron felt himself smiling in return. As she looked away, Eltiron noticed with unreasonable satisfaction that her gaze swept by Terrel without pausing. At least there was someone among the Princess's escort whom Terrel did not impress.

"Eltiron!" Marreth's voice was low, but it held an angry warning. Eltiron came back to the present with a jerk and a sick, sinking feeling. He had not noticed when the unpleasant little man had finished his speech and the Princess had come forward. Now Marreth was facing Eltiron, the Princess Crystalorn at his side.

"My son," Marreth said in a louder voice, "I present to you the Princess Crystalorn Halaget, daughter of King Urhelds of Barinash."

"I give you greeting, my lady." Eltiron gave the formal response automatically.

"I thank you for your welcome, Prince Eltiron," the Princess said.

Eltiron was uncomfortably aware of the sweat on his palms but unable to do anything about it. As he took the Princess's hand and bowed over it, the room erupted into cheering. He straightened and found himself looking down into a pair of impossibly blue eyes framed in waves of thick brown hair. The eyes were studying him with a speculative frown, but before their owner could say anything, Marreth raised his hand and the courtiers quieted.

"We welcome the Princess of Barinash and her companions to our court, and we hope . . ." Marreth began the speech he always gave when someone of importance arrived in Leshiya, and Eltiron stopped listening. Instead, he watched the Princess watching him.

The Princess's scrutiny did not last much longer. When Marreth was about three sentences into his speech, she gave her head a tiny shake and gently disengaged her hand from Eltiron's. She turned slightly, so that she faced Marreth once more, and Eltiron thought he saw her sigh.

Marreth's speech seemed to last hours. When he finally finished, Terrel announced that the welcoming feast would be held in two days' time, to give the Princess and her escort time to recover from their journey. Then the horns blew again, and the formal welcome was officially over. The delegation from Barinash was shown to the rooms that had been prepared for them, the courtiers dispersed, and Eltiron, his head still whirling from his brief encounter with his prospective bride, went to look for Vandaris.

He found her in the gardens, shaving long curls of wood from a rough staff. She looked up as he approached and raised an eyebrow. "Well, now that you've met her, what do you think of her?"

"The Princess Crystalorn? She's . . . she's very pretty."

"Sweet snakes, man, is that all you want in a bride? I thought you had more sense!"

"Well, I don't know anything else about her; I've hardly talked to her at all," Eltiron said defensively.

"So arrange to talk to her! It shouldn't be that hard."

"What difference would it make? Terrel was the one she was looking at. Didn't you notice?"

"I think you are underestimating yourself rather badly," Vandaris said with uncharacteristic gentleness. "And I think you're underestimating Crystalorn as well. As for Terrel Lassond . . ." She frowned. "I wish I knew for certain what he's doing and how he's doing it."

"What do you mean?"

"Didn't you see the way he and Parel were eyeing each other?"

"Parel?"

"Salentor Parel, molasses-mind. He's the Barinash ambassador who brought Crystalorn. You can't have missed him; his speech went on forever."

Eltiron felt his face grow warm. "I'm afraid I didn't notice."

"I see," Vandaris said dryly. "Well, the two of them looked like a pair of cats watching the same mouse-hole —cooperating, but not too pleased about it, if you see what I mean. It makes me wonder." She sighed. "I wish Trevannon were here; I could use some of his sources."

"I thought you already were."

"What?" Vandaris sat up sharply. "What are you talking about?"

"The Hoven-Thalar you were talking to the day of our first practice match. Wasn't he the same one Jermain used to talk to? I was sure I recognized him."

Vandaris stared at him for a moment. "You're sure?"

"I think so. I've seen Jermain with him several times. You mean you didn't know?"

Instead of answering, Vandaris began cursing quietly. Eltiron listened for several minutes before he finally tried to interrupt. "Vandaris?"

"—and next time I see that lizard-livered nomad, I'm going

to feed him his own feet unless he tells the truth. All of it. That lockjawed idiot knows where Trevannon is, and he didn't say a word about it!''

"He does? How do you know?"

"I don't,'' Vandaris admitted, "but I'd still bet diamonds against dragon dung that I'm right. You didn't see the way he reacted when I said I was looking for Trevannon. And the worst of it is, he left nearly a week ago; he could be anywhere by now. We'll just have to hope he has sense enough to let Trevannon know what I told him.''

They talked for a few minutes more before Eltiron left to attend to his duties. He spent the rest of that day and most of the next running from one not-quite-finished thing to the next and wondering why no one had made any arrangements for the possibility of the Princess arriving early. Everyone had discussed at great length what to do if she arrived later than expected, but no one had been prepared for her to appear a day sooner.

In his few spare moments, Eltiron worried about the welcoming feast. Terrel's wit was always more pointed when he had a large audience, and he had arranged to be seated on the other side of the Princess from Eltiron. And how would the Princess Crystalorn react when she saw Marreth walk in with one of his "ladies"? Eltiron wished fervently that he could speak to her privately before the feast, even for a little while, but there was no way he could arrange it.

The feast was even worse than he expected. Marreth was unusually loud and irritable, and the entertainers were nervous. Terrel monopolized the Princess's attention for most of the meal, pointing out the important members of Marreth's court and making occasional verbal jabs at Eltiron. By the time the uncomfortable evening ended, Eltiron was more than glad to escape to his rooms.

After an hour of brooding on all the things he might have said in response to Terrel, Eltiron could stand the silence no longer, and he went out to pace the halls of the castle. The hour was late enough that hardly anyone was stirring; he passed an occasional guard, but that was all. He was tempted to visit Vandaris, but he doubted that she was still awake. Besides, he couldn't just keep running to her every time something went wrong; sooner or later he would have to do something. The question was, what?

Scowling in frustration, Eltiron kicked at an imaginary wrinkle in the carpeting. This was getting him no closer to solving his problems with Terrel; he might as well go back to his chambers and get some sleep. He glanced up to see where his rambles had brought him and saw a dim light spilling through a half-open doorway at the end of the hall.

Eltiron hesitated, wondering whether to investigate. Whoever was inside the room would think it very odd to be interrupted by the Prince of Sevairn in the middle of the night. Still, it was far more likely that someone had simply left a lamp burning and forgotten it. Much more likely. Eltiron walked down to the door and pushed it open.

At first he was surprised to find the room unlit; then he realized that this was the first of a series of rooms that might have been originally intended as guest chambers. There were several such odd arrangements in the castle, and as a child Eltiron had spent hours playing in them. The light was coming from the next room in the chain. Eltiron looked at the open doorway for a moment, then shrugged and walked across the room.

The second room was smaller than the one that opened into the hall. It had been furnished with a table and two slightly battered chairs; at the far end of the table, a small lamp was burning brightly. Just opposite Eltiron, another door led into the third and last room of the series. The door was closed, and a small, brown-haired figure crouched in front of it, listening intently.

Eltiron shook his head. "Tarilane, what are you—" The figure turned abruptly, and Eltiron's jaw dropped. *"Crystalorn?"*

"Shhhhhhh!" hissed the Princess. "They'll hear you!"

"Who?" Eltiron whispered. "And what are you—"

"Quiet! I want to hear this."

Crystalorn put her ear back to the door. Eltiron watched in utter bewilderment, wondering what he ought to do. Tarilane was the only other person he could imagine finding in a situation like this, and he couldn't treat a Princess the way he would treat Vandaris's sword-squire.

Abruptly, Crystalorn rose. "They're almost finished," she whispered as she took the lamp from the table. "Come on, or they'll catch us."

Eltiron hesitated, then stepped aside to let Crystalorn come through the doorway. As he did, he heard someone fumbling with the latch of the closed door. Crystalorn muttered something too softly for him to catch it and ducked around the edge of the door frame, out of sight of anyone in the room she had just left. Eltiron followed, and Crystalorn put out the lamp. An instant later, he felt her tug at his arm. Carefully, the two began backing toward one of the dark corners of the room.

Light spilled suddenly through the doorway, and Eltiron heard a sharp voice say, ". . . quite safe. No one will be about at this hour, not after a feast."

"You may believe that if you will; I'll not risk this twice," said a second voice, and Eltiron stiffened.

Terrel again! His head turned involuntarily toward Crystalorn, who shook her head warningly and pulled him toward a long, high-backed seat. She squeezed into the shadows between it and the wall, and motioned Eltiron to follow.

Eltiron had barely reached this rather dubious hiding place when he saw Terrel step into the room, carrying a lamp. He was followed by the short, unpleasant man who had accompanied the Princess to Sevairn—Salentor, that was his name. Eltiron froze as Terrel turned and gestured to the smaller man.

"You may have the privilege of being first to go your way," Terrel said with a touch of mockery.

"You do not intend to accompany me?"

"On the contrary. I do not want even a guard to see us together at this hour. I have gone to a great deal of trouble to establish my position here; I don't intend to ruin everything now."

"As you wish, but I think you are being far more cautious than necessary." Salentor bowed and left the room.

"Fool!" muttered Terrel. He shook his head, then began to pace. The lamp he held sent shadows leaping around the room as he walked. Eltiron shivered, hoping Terrel would not notice him, and tried to shrink farther back without moving. He did not think he was being particularly successful.

Terrel paced for several minutes, then set the lamp on a small table near the door. Reaching up, he removed the heavy gold chain he was wearing. Eltiron noticed for the first time that the medallion hanging from it was not the seal of office that Terrel usually wore, but an intricate web of gold wire with a large amber stone set in its center. Terrel stared at it for a

moment, then wrapped the chain around the medallion and
put it in his pocket. Absently, he turned out the lamp, and a
moment later Eltiron heard him leave.

For several minutes, Eltiron remained where he was. When
he was sure that Terrel would not return, he squeezed out of
his hiding place and stood up. He heard a rustling as Crystalorn emerged behind him and discovered that he was not sure
whether to be annoyed or grateful. Crouching behind a bench
to eavesdrop on a pair of courtiers was not only uncomfortable, it was undignified. On the other hand, knowing about
Terrel and Salentor might be very useful.

Behind him he heard a clinking noise, and then a muffled
exclamation from Crystalorn. "What's the matter?" he
whispered.

"I've spilled most of the oil out of this lamp. Can you find
the other one?"

"It's right by the door." Eltiron waited another moment
while his eyes adjusted to the darkness, then walked across to
the table and picked up the lamp. He gave it to Crystalorn,
who pulled something from her pocket and bent over it.
Eltiron could not see how she intended to light it, but he
turned and closed the door just in case she could manage.
After all, it was the light coming through the door that had
drawn his attention to the room in the first place, and he certainly didn't want anyone else to come down the hall and find
him now.

As the door swung shut, the lamp lit with a fizzing noise and
a bright flare of light. Eltiron blinked and squinted. "How did
you do that?"

"Firesticks," Crystalorn said with satisfaction. "It's the
first time I've used them; they work very well, don't they?"

"Yes. What are they?"

"Sticks for lighting fires. Or lamps. And don't ask me how
they work; Amberglas didn't tell me."

"Amberglas?"

"You haven't met her yet? She came to Sevairn with me. I
thought she said something about wanting to talk to you, but I
must have been wrong. Which isn't hard, the way she says
things. She gave me the firesticks."

"Oh."

Crystalorn looked at him warily. "I think we should go
now," she said after a moment, and reached for the lamp.

"I think you should explain first, Your Highness," Eltiron said, trying to sound firm.

"I suppose so." Crystalorn sighed, then smiled reluctantly. "You aren't at all like what I expected, you know."

"Neither are you. Why were you following Terrel?"

"I wasn't following him; I was following Salentor. He's been twitchy all day, and I wanted to find out why. Besides, I wanted to—" Crystalorn hesitated.

"Wanted to what?"

"I wanted to see if I could." She looked at him for a moment, then gave him a mischievous grin that reminded him forcibly of Tarilane. "This is a wonderful castle for sneaking around in; I think I'm going to like it."

"I hope so. Do you do things like this often?"

"Sometimes. How else do you find out what's really going on?"

"What did you find out this time?"

"Not as much as I thought I would. Salentor and your Lord Terrel are involved in some sort of scheme, but they didn't talk much about it. Mostly they made snide remarks; I don't think they like each other much. If it weren't for—" Crystalorn broke off and turned toward the inner door of the room. "I'd almost forgotten! Where does the other door to that last room go?"

Eltiron stared at her with a sinking feeling. "If you mean the room you were listening at when I got here, it only has one door."

"That's impossible! Someone was in there with Terrel and Salentor. I heard him leave, and he didn't come this way so there must be another door."

Eltiron went cold. "You're sure there was someone besides Terrel and Salentor?"

"Of course I'm sure! I'd know both their voices even if your Lord Terrel hadn't spent the whole evening trying to make me fall in love with him."

"He's not *my* Lord Terrel. You mean you don't like him?"

"Ha! He's much too sure he's irresistible," Crystalorn said. "I don't like irresistible people; they make me want to shake them or slap them or something."

"If you ever want to slap Terrel, I won't object," Eltiron said absently. He stared at the door on the far side of the room. He was sure that there was no other way out of this chain of rooms. Either someone was still waiting in the last room, or . . . Eltiron remembered the tower-top and shivered. There was only one way to find out, and he had to know. "Excuse me, my lady; I have to check that last room."

"Oh, that's right; I almost forgot again. If we can find out where that other man went, maybe we can figure out who he is."

Eltiron picked up the lamp and started forward without replying. Crystalorn followed. When they reached the third room, Eltiron paused in the doorway. The room was empty, but he remained uneasy. The shadows pressed on him, and he thought he could feel a wrongness in the air. He told himself firmly not to be foolish; he was simply imagining things. He felt uneasy anyway.

An impatient finger tapped at his shoulder, and reluctantly he stepped aside to let Crystalorn pass. She looked around, frowning, then turned back to Eltiron. "All right, I'm sorry I didn't believe you when you said this room only had one door. But there *were* three people talking in here. There must be a secret passage or something."

"A secret passage?"

"How else could that other person have left? Come on, let's look."

"Wait a minute. There are a few things you need to know first."

Crystalorn looked at him doubtfully for a moment, then nodded. Eltiron stepped back into the second room of the chain and sat down. Crystalorn took the other chair and looked at him expectantly. Eltiron took a deep breath and began to tell her about his experience on the top of the Tower of Judgment.

Crystalorn listened intently. Eltiron soon discovered that he had to do a fair amount of explaining about Jermain in order for his story to make sense. The first time he mentioned the name, Crystalorn's eyes narrowed and she started to say something, then apparently changed her mind and motioned Eltiron to go on. Eltiron was suddenly certain that she'd heard some of the gossip about himself and Jermain; she'd been in the castle for two days, which was plenty of time to find out what everyone thought of everyone else. He paused briefly, wondering how best to tell her what had really happened, then gave up and favored her with a bald statement of the facts.

When he finished, Crystalorn stared silently at the lamp for a few minutes, then shook herself. "This is getting more complicated than I thought. Would you mind telling all this to Amberglas? I think she should know, and . . . there are other reasons, too."

"If you wish." Eltiron did not see what good it could do, but he doubted that it could do any harm, either.

"Good. Now let's go back and search that room."

"What? Why?"

"To see if there are any red things or secret passages. We have to at least check." She stood up, took the lamp, and started for the last room, leaving Eltiron no choice but to follow.

To Eltiron's relief, they found neither secret passages nor red patches. When they finished their search, they returned to the first room and talked for a long while. Eltiron discovered, to his surprise, that Crystalorn seemed to take him almost as seriously as Vandaris did. Crystalorn insisted on making plans for Eltiron to talk to her friend as soon as possible. After some thought, Eltiron realized that he would have no time at all on the following day, so they arranged the meeting for the afternoon of the day after that.

Finally Eltiron escorted Crystalorn back to her chambers. He made sure that they went past several guards on the way. The castle gossips would certainly have noticed Terrel's behavior toward Crystalorn at the feast, and they would be quick to conclude that the King's handsome adviser had made a conquest of Eltiron's betrothed. But if they heard that Eltiron and Crystalorn had been seen together, late at night, without one of the Princess's ladies in accompaniment . . . Eltiron grinned to himself. Terrel was not going to be pleased when he discovered that his latest attempt to make Eltiron look bad had failed.

The following day was even busier than Eltiron had expected. It was as much as he could do to snatch a few minutes with Vandaris to let her know the barest outline of the night's events. Vandaris looked extremely thoughtful, but they were interrupted before she had time to tell him why. He saw Crystalorn several times, but they were always surrounded by a web of protocol and formality, and he could not manage to talk to her privately. By the time he returned to his chambers that night, Eltiron was convinced that the sole pur-

pose of the pomp that surrounded royal weddings was to keep
the principals from seeing each other alone.

On the fourth morning after Crystalorn's arrival in Leshiya,
Eltiron awoke early. He dressed hurriedly and went down to
the castle garden, hoping for a chance to have a few minutes
of solitude. The gardens were empty when he arrived, and
with a sigh of relief he sat down on one of the benches to
think. If there were only some way he could guess what Terrel
was planning . . .

"Dear me," said a voice from behind him. "How very convenient that you should be here. That is, it's convenient for
me, but only because I happen to be in the same place; if I
were somewhere else at the moment, it wouldn't matter at all.
At least, I think it wouldn't."

Eltiron turned. A woman stood watching him with an air of
intense abstraction. He recognized her at once; she was one of
the Princess's ladies, the one who had seemed entirely unim-
pressed by Terrel Lassond during the formal welcoming. He
rose and bowed. "Good morning, my lady," he said with
more warmth than he had intended.

"Yes, it is, isn't it? Though of course it's quite possible that
it isn't nearly as good a morning elsewhere. Shula Mari, for
example; I believe it frequently rains in Shula Mari at this time
of year, which could be quite depressing, though perhaps it
isn't if one lives there all the time. But then, I haven't been
there yet so I'm not entirely certain."

"I've never been to Shula Mari either," Eltiron said,
fascinated.

"I believe there are a great many people who haven't. Been
to Shula Mari, I mean; it's always best to be specific about
these things, because there are so very many places for people
to not have been to, which makes them very easy to mix up,
though some of them are really quite different."

Eltiron blinked. He started to ask a question, then realized
that he still did not know the woman's name. He bowed again
and asked.

"Amberglas," said the woman. "And you, of course, are
Prince Eltiron Kenerach. I believe I have a message for you
from Jermain Trevannon."

Chapter Ten

The army moved slowly southward for several days. Jermain quickly became accustomed to his position as Commander-General, and began to learn more about the personalities of the men under him. He was a little surprised by what he found. Though all of Carachel's commanders were competent, most were uninterested in what they were doing and why. They reminded Jermain of mercenaries following orders for pay, without concerning themselves with personal loyalty to the man who paid them. Jermain thought he was beginning to understand why Carachel had seemed lonely.

He continued to dine with Carachel each evening, along with the King's other commanders and advisers. Elsane was no longer present; three days after the army broke camp, she ceased attending the evening meals. Jermain knew she was still with the army, for he had seen her once or twice from a distance, but he did not speak to her. Carachel's wife had little to do with the military, and Jermain had neither desire not reason to seek her out. He was, therefore, taken completely by surprise when he returned to his tent one evening and found her there, alone. When he entered, she was sitting at the table, twisting a long, narrow ribbon over and over in her hands. She looked up as he let the tent flap fall behind him.

Jermain bowed, effectively concealing his reaction. "Your Majesty."

Elsane flinched, and when she spoke her voice trembled slightly. "Please be seated, Lord Jermain."

"I thank you for your kindness, Your Majesty." Jermain saw her flinch again as he added the formal address. He

bowed again, and seated himself at the end of the table, where
he could observe her easily while still keeping the table between them.

"I—" Elsane hesitated, not looking at Jermain. "How go
the preparations for the war?"

"Quite well. Would you wish me to give you a complete
summary, or is there something in particular you would like to
hear of, Your Majesty?"

Elsane flinched again and shook her head. Jermain pre-
tended to interpret the gesture as permission to begin, and
launched immediately into a long and deliberately dull recita-
tion of the status of the various companies of the army. He
studied her as he talked, trying to guess the purpose behind her
visit. His first thought had been that she was there to seduce
him, but she seemed far too frightened for that. An attempt to
ruin his credit with Carachel, perhaps? No, not likely; he'd
had little time to make enemies, and such an attempt would be
better planned. But why else was she here?

He droned on, watching Elsane. She grew more and more
nervous, until finally her hands clenched around the ribbon.
"Stop! Stop it!"

"Certainly, Your Majesty."

"I—I didn't come here for that."

"Indeed. Then to what *do* I owe the honor of this . . . most
unusual visit?"

Elsane took a deep, uncertain breath. "I came to talk to you
about the war."

"Then perhaps I should continue my summary of our
preparations. The supplies for the—"

"Be still, and let me speak!" Anger made Elsane's tone
sharp and imperious, and for a moment Jermain saw a flash
of the regal spirit she must have had fifteen or twenty years
before. He inclined his head.

"As you wish, Your Majesty."

"I came to you because you have my—my husband's ear,
and you may be able to persuade him where I have failed. This
war must be stopped!"

"And you believe I can persuade King Carachel?"

"Carachel respects your opinions; I have heard him speak
of you, and I know. There is nothing else he cares for except
his sorcery." She looked down at her hands. "Nothing. Do
you see why I come to you?"

"I think you wrong your husband, Your Majesty," Jermain said gently.

"Do you think that after thirteen years I do not know him? I have . . . grown accustomed to his ways. I can live with it because I must, but I cannot let him destroy Tar-Alem and perhaps Mournwal and Gramwood as well just to preserve his cursed sorcery!"

"I do not believe I understand."

"Has he not told you of the Matholych and what it does?"

"He has told me."

"And you do not see? He is a wizard, but if he is to remain so, there must be power for him to draw on. He wishes to stop that creature because it drains the magic from the land, and for no other reason."

Jermain did not reply immediately. Elsane could be right; the lessening of magic would certainly be a powerful motive for a wizard to oppose the Matholych. But even if she were, did it matter? The Hoven-Thalar and the Matholych must be stopped, or between them they would ruin the Seven Kingdoms. Carachel was trying to stop them, whatever his reasons, and Jermain could not justify trying to make him give up his efforts because of Elsane's fears for her country. Besides, he knew Carachel, and he could not believe that the Wizard-King was acting solely from selfishness. He tried to explain, but Elsane would not let him finish.

"I am not a fool," she said quietly. "I can see that something must be done. But there must be another way! If he truly realized what he does . . . But I cannot make him see! He is too certain that only he can do this, and only in this way."

Jermain thought of a haunted face staring at a fire, and a voice whispering, "Whatever the cost, it must be stopped." He remembered the bitterness in Carachel's voice when he spoke of the wizards who refused to listen to him, and the frustrated pain in his eyes when he watched Elsane. "I think he knows the price, my lady, and I think he may already have paid a greater one than you believe."

Elsane stared at him for a moment. "Do you know what he intends?"

"We have discussed the plans for the battle."

"And you can still defend him?"

"He works for the good of all the people of the Seven Kingdoms, not merely for Tar-Alem. Even when we face the

Hoven-Thalar, we will not fight to kill them; he would not
give such an order if—''

"You do know, then!" Elsane looked at him as if he were a
snake. "You know how many deaths it means; how could you
consent to it?"

"I do not deny that it will be difficult," Jermain said,
somewhat puzzled by her reaction, "but with careful planning
we should lose no more men than we would with a more con-
ventional strategy, and perhaps less."

Elsane did not seem to hear him. Her shoulders sagged and
she seemed to fade and shrink as Jermain watched. "I have
lost, then," she said with quiet despair. "You were my last
hope, and I have lost. So I must watch him—watch him—"

Her voice broke and died, and her head bowed. Jermain did
not speak. After a moment her head lifted, and she rose. "I
bid you good eve, my lord," she said in a colorless tone. "I
shall not come again." She did not look at Jermain as she left
the tent.

Even though Jermain did not believe in Elsane's view, her
visit disturbed him. She knew Carachel, certainly much better
than Jermain, and yet she seemed to think that Carachel
meant to deliberately sacrifice his own troops in order to avoid
killing Hoven-Thalar. Jermain found himself going over the
plans for the battle, looking for some clue that might explain
Elsane's strange conviction.

He did not find one. The plans were clear and straightforward, and the strategy was sound, if a bit unusual. Jermain
spent much of the night poring over maps and diagrams, but
when morning came he still could see no reason why
Carachel's army should suffer unusual losses. Even so, he remained uneasy. The problem continued to worry him for the
next two days, until it was submerged in the rush of activity as
Carachel's army met King Urhelds's men.

Jermain was at first relieved when the scouts brought word
of the army camped near the meeting place in the upper part
of the North Plains. Despite Carachel's assurances, he had
not been entirely certain that the men would be there, for even
if Salentor was willing to keep his part of the bargain, Jermain
knew from experience that no one could be certain of persuading a King. He was glad that Carachel had not been
mistaken in his estimate of Salentor's influence.

When he came within sight of the army, Jermain's relief changed to worry. The Barinash troops were a sprawling, disorganized mass of men, and Jermain found himself wondering how he was ever going to combine them with the men from Tar-Alem. As he drew nearer, Jermain recognized some of the banners that flew above the central tents, and he frowned angrily. Salentor had sent the rawest and worst-trained troops in the Barinash army! No wonder they seemed so disorderly. Jermain went in search of Carachel to explain the situation.

To Jermain's surprise, Carachel was not disturbed by the poor quality of the troops Salentor had provided. "No man is a soldier until he has been in battle, no matter how well he has been trained," he said. "These men have a little more to learn, that is all."

"True," Jermain replied. "But may I remind you that your plans for this battle are a bit unusual, to say the least? It will be difficult to hold the Hoven-Thalar without killing many of them, even for experienced men. With these troops, it will be nearly impossible. Unless, of course, you have changed your plans?"

Carachel looked startled. "Not at all. Is it so bad, then?"

"I won't know for certain until I have a chance to talk to the Barinash commanders, but from what I've seen it may well be worse. I'd like to keep them separate from the rest of the men until I find out."

"Of course. Put them at the rear of the column. It will take some time for it to reach them, and they'll need the extra time to break camp."

It was Jermain's turn to be startled. "Wouldn't it be wiser to see the Barinash commanders first, my lord? After all, we don't know yet what their orders are."

"If they have not been ordered to place themselves entirely under my command, they are no use to me," Carachel said firmly. "Tell them to break camp and join the column or to go back to King Urhelds."

"Yes, Your Majesty."

Carachel smiled. "Do you know that you only call me 'my lord' or 'Your Majesty' in public or when you disapprove of what I am doing?"

"I meant no criticism," Jermain said stiffly.

"I'm not so sure of that. But this is no whim, though you may think it so. I do not want men I must persuade to the

proper course of action; we may have no time for explanation
and persuasion when the Matholych arrives. And we cannot
afford the time we would lose if we stopped now to talk with
them.''

"Then I had best go and tell them what you expect.''

As Jermain had anticipated, the commanders of the
Barinash army were not happy to be told to break camp immediately and fall in behind the column of men from Tar-
Alem. They had little choice, however, for their orders were
much as Carachel had described. Reluctantly, they gave the
necessary orders, and the Barinash troops hastily began
preparing to leave. The disorganized way the men went about
their preparations did nothing to improve Jermain's opinion
of them, but somehow they were ready when the end of the
Tar-Alem column finally moved past the camp.

The combined armies made good time for the rest of the
day, but by the time they pitched camp the Barinash troops
were in an unhappy frame of mind. Many resented being
forced to "eat dust" at the back of the army, and a number of
fights broke out between the men from Tar-Alem and those
from Barinash. Jermain spent several hours trying to pacify
irate Barinash officers, then remained awake late into the
night designing an order of march he hoped would be satisfactory to everyone.

The next day's march was easier, and in three more they had
crossed the North Plains. The two armies began to show signs
of merging; there was less grumbling and the fights practically
ceased. They continued to move faster than Jermain had expected, but Carachel grew more and more worried about their
speed. Finally, Jermain grew puzzled by Carachel's continued
anxiety. When the army camped for the night, Jermain went
to Carachel's tent and demanded to know the reason for his
concern.

"If I push the men too hard, they'll be in no condition to
fight when we reach Gramwood,'' he told Carachel. "I don't
want to do it without an explanation.''

"You'll follow my orders,'' Carachel snapped.

"Yes, Your Majesty,'' Jermain said with icy formality. He
stood and waited, stiff with anger.

Carachel lowered his head until his forehead rested on the
edge of his hand, covering his eyes. "I am sorry,'' he said after
a moment. "Of all the men who serve me, you deserve that the

least. I fear my temper is not the best these days.''

Jermain did not reply, but he relaxed a little. Carachel shook his head tiredly.

"You want an explanation; well, I cannot give you one. Only that I feel uneasy. . . . I do not know what is wrong, but I fear that someone has stirred the Matholych, that it moves sooner than I had thought.''

"But you are not sure?''

"My spells do not work well in the southern kingdoms, and messengers are too slow. I can sense the wrongness, but that is all. The only way for me to learn what is actually happening is for us to move south more quickly.''

Jermain frowned. "Are you certain it would do no good to send scouts farther ahead? They may not be as fast as sorcery, but they'll give us at least a day's notice of anything unusual.''

"Send them by all means, but do not expect too much. Your scouts have neither the ability nor the training to detect the first stirrings of the Matholych.''

"Then perhaps you could give them something that would assist them,'' Jermain said, his temper rising once more.

Carachel looked startled, then thoughtful. "Yes, that might be possible. It must be a simple spell, something that will use very little power, for I must hoard my strength to face the Matholych. Still, I think it can be managed. I will have them for you tomorrow morning.''

"Thank you, my lord.''

"Even so, we must move more quickly than we have been. If the Matholych is stirring—''

"What good will it do?'' Jermain demanded. "If sorcery alone can prevail against the Matholych, why should we weary the army with a forced march? If speed is your only concern, it would be better for you to ride ahead with a few men, since you are the only sorcerer among us.''

Carachel was silent for a few moments. "Perhaps I have been overly concerned; as yet, I know very little for a certainty. But if the Matholych is stirring, the Hoven-Thalar may also be moving earlier than we expected. And if we are too late to oppose them . . .''

"It will be just as bad if the men are too tired to fight when we arrive.'' Jermain was familiar with the effects of too fast and long a march, and he did not want to take men into battle whose reflexes were dulled by fatigue and lack of sleep.

"I do not think so. And we must be in time." Carachel rose and began to pace the length of the tent.

"We do not know that the Hoven-Thalar are moving yet," Jermain pointed out. "And even if they are, surely the armies of Gramwood and Mournwal will be able to hold them for a little while."

"A day; two at most. That is not long enough. I must have some time to . . . prepare for the Matholych. How quickly can we reach the battlefield, if you push your men?"

"We can be there in a week to ten days, if we must, but such a pace risks exhausting the men. We can, however, move somewhat faster than we have been. It would not take too much longer, and I would prefer not to try a forced march until we are certain of what the Hoven-Thalar plan."

"Very well," Carachel said reluctantly. "We will compromise for a few days, unless we learn more in the meantime."

"Thank you, my lord."

Next morning, Carachel gave Jermain the charms he had promised: six glass mirrors the size of a silver coin, each suspended from a thin gold chain. The mirrors were dark, but Carachel assured Jermain that at the first sign of the Matholych they would glow red. Jermain gave the mirrors to his scouts with a minimum of explanation; if any of them saw his mirror glowing, he was to note the place and return to camp at once, no matter what else he might wish to investigate.

The scouts received their orders somewhat nervously, and several threw dubious looks at the mirrors. Jermain was mildly surprised at their obvious discomfort; he had expected the men of Tar-Alem to be less fearful of magic than those of Sevairn, since magic was more common in the north. He watched the scouts depart, then turned back to prepare the army for the day's march.

The army continued to travel quickly, and by evening they were camped at the edge of the nameless forest that covered the southern part of Barinash and much of Gramwood. As soon as the men were settled, Jermain ordered extra sentries posted. He himself spent much of the night riding around the perimeter of the camp, for though he did not share Carachel's apprehension, he was restless.

The restlessness grew worse as the army moved on into the forest. Jermain spent more and more time near the front of the column, where the road before him was clear and he was not as conscious of the mass of men around him. Several times he went on ahead of the army, though he could not go too far without leaving his duties as Commander-General unfulfilled.

The trees along the road grew larger as the day wore on, providing the marchers with welcome shade. Unfortunately, thought Jermain, they also provided more than sufficient cover for anyone who might wish to follow the army unde- tected. He frowned, wondering what had made him think of that, then laughed a little at his own foolishness. The track left by the combined armies of Tar-Alem and Barinash was suffi- ciently obvious that no one would have any need to skulk in the woods to discover the direction of their march. Jermain shook his head and rode back toward the rear of the column.

When the army camped at last, Jermain was tired but still restive. He would once more have spent the night riding the perimeter of the camp, but he did not wish to tire Blackflame unnecessarily. He therefore contented himself with walking, and it was very late before he finally sought his bed.

The army's second day in the forest was worse than the first. The deep shadows along the path seemed ominous; in vain Jermain told himself that the forest was no different than it had been when he met Carachel a few weeks before. He began to urge the men to greater speed, and he found himself looking over his shoulder as he rode and periodically touching the place where Amberglas's medallion lay beneath his tunic.

By the end of the day, Jermain's uneasiness was disturb- ing Blackflame as well. The horse had become accustomed to being cared for by Carachel's grooms during the two weeks of the army's march, but when they stopped at last to set up camp he refused to allow any of the grooms near him. Jermain walked the horse for some time, talking soothingly in hopes of calming the animal enough for the grooms to take over, but to no avail. Finally he decided that it would take less time to groom Blackflame himself than to soothe him, and he led the horse around to the back of his tent.

Jermain's tent was near the edge of the camp, beside a small stand of trees and bushes. There were few other tents nearby. The trees were too large and too close together to permit the tents to be pitched in their normal orderly rows, and as a result the army was spread out far more than Jermain liked. He frowned as he replaced Blackflame's bridle with a halter and tethered the horse to one of the trees. Was it too early in the march to order the captains to increase the security around the edge of the camp?

Jermain was about to remove Blackflame's saddle when the horse shifted and pulled away from the trees. At the same time, Jermain heard a rustling among the branches. He stepped back and drew his sword. "Whoever is there, come out and declare yourself," he called.

A tall, hooded figure slid out of the shadows and stood beside Blackflame. "This is a poor greeting for a blood-bonded friend, Jerayan."

There was only one man Jermain could think of who would use the Hoven-Thalar version of his name. "*Ranlyn?* You fool, what are you doing here?"

Chapter Eleven

Eltiron stared. "You have a message from Jermain? But you came from Barinash, and he's somewhere in Gramwood or Mournwal! How can you—that is, I would appreciate it if you would explain, lady."

"Explanations are so useful," Amberglas said thoughtfully. "Though not quite so useful as kitchen knives and brooms and saddlebags, which are generally much more practical but not as interesting. Of course, one can put a great many interesting things *in* a saddlebag, but that's not quite the same thing. It's quite simple, really. He's in Barinash."

"He is? What's he doing there?"

"Several different things, though not all at the same time, which is quite sensible of him, since it's rather difficult to travel in two directions at once. Although there are a few things that can be done at the same time. Singing and washing turnips, for instance, or writing a letter and chopping wood. Of course, someone else has to chop the wood."

"Oh. May I see Jermain's letter, lady?"

"I'm afraid that's quite impossible."

"Why?" Eltiron said, bewildered.

"Because he didn't write a letter. I do hope it isn't inconvenient. Inconvenient for you, I mean; it wasn't particularly inconvenient for him because he didn't really want to write a message to anyone."

"It isn't inconvenient," Eltiron assured her. "But what did he say?"

Amberglas appeared to be studying the bushes immediately behind Eltiron's left ear. "He said, 'Tell Prince Eltiron that all his dissembling will not keep the Hoven-Thalar from overrunning Sevairn. And tell him I will not forget what he and Terrel did.' "

For a moment, Eltiron stared at her, trying to absorb what she had said; then he shut his eyes in pain. Ever since his talk with Vandaris he had known that Jermain, too, might think Eltiron had deliberately betrayed him. Now he could no longer convince himself that Jermain would understand the mistake. Jermain thought Eltiron had known exactly what he was doing. Worse yet, Jermain apparently thought Eltiron and Terrel had planned the whole thing. It hurt Eltiron that Jermain could so severely misjudge him, and disillusionment made the hurt worse. Didn't Jermain know him and trust him better than that?

Eltiron sighed and opened his eyes. Amberglas was watching him with a faint frown, and he shook his head. "It . . . was not quite like that, lady."

"I'm not entirely surprised, though of course he was quite positive; but then, people generally are positive even when they are quite wrong. And I don't think he was in the best of humor, which isn't at all amazing, what with that broken rib and losing a great deal of blood and so on. Not to mention making it worse by riding around the forest without attending to any of it, which was really very foolish of him."

Eltiron went cold. "Jermain was wounded? How? Is he all right?"

"Not precisely," the woman said vaguely. "Of course, it is frequently very difficult to be precise, but then, so many things are. Difficult, I mean. Climbing Dragon's Head Mountain in midwinter, for instance, or running from Leshiya to Miranet City in less than three days. Or being patient."

Eltiron closed his mouth on an angry reply and looked at her for a moment. "Please continue, lady," he said at last.

"Very good," Amberglas said approvingly. "I thought perhaps he was underestimating you, though of course it's quite easy to underestimate people, which may explain why it is done so frequently. Jermain Trevannon is quite well at the moment, though I really couldn't say how long it will last; people are so very unpredictable. And it's certainly no fault of those extremely impolite soldiers who were chasing him when we met."

"The Barinash guardsmen were chasing Jermain?"

"I don't believe so. They certainly weren't chasing him the last time I saw him, but of course, they may have been busy elsewhere, which would account for their not chasing him quite well. And the Barinash guardsmen are generally quite polite, rather like that Captain who came for Crystalorn, though of course you haven't met him yet so I don't believe you know."

"Then who *was* chasing Jermain, lady?" Eltiron asked, trying hard to be patient.

"The Sevairn Border Guards. Which was rather foolish of them, since they really don't belong in Barinash at all; but then, there are a great many things that the Sevairn guards aren't at all good at, and perhaps remembering where the border is is one of them." Amberglas tilted her head to one side and observed him with a preoccupied air. "While I realize that you can't do anything about it just at present, perhaps you can persuade them to be more civil once you are King of Sevairn. And of course their training is quite dreadful."

"Of—of course," Eltiron said, considerably startled. No one had ever been quite so matter-of-fact about his eventual assumption of the crown of Sevairn. "Do you know why they were chasing Jermain, lady?"

"It's really quite unnecessary for you to keep addressing me as 'lady,' and I would think their reasons were rather obvious, though of course you weren't there so perhaps you haven't realized yet. They were trying to kill him."

"They were *what?*"

"The Sevairn Border Guards were trying to kill Jermain Trevannon. They had a great many reasons for doing so, most of them extremely bad and not at all credible; but then, people frequently do things for odd reasons so perhaps it doesn't matter. I believe the real reason is that they were told to; the Captain mentioned getting orders directly from Leshiya, though he really shouldn't have told me that."

"Orders from Leshiya? But Father wouldn't have ordered Jermain killed, not after he'd decided to exile Jermain!"

"I didn't say he had, and neither did Captain Morenar, though I must admit that your friend Jermain made the same assumption. At least, it sounded like the same assumption. He said his orders came from Leshiya, and, of course, there are quite a few people in Leshiya just now besides King Marreth, and I would think that most of them were here a month ago as well. Though he never said exactly when his orders came from Leshiya, so it might have been longer."

"If it wasn't Father . . ." Eltiron frowned. Wendril Anareme could have given orders to the Border Guard, but she had no reason that Eltiron knew to want Jermain dead. Terrel was the logical person to have ordered Jermain killed, but Terrel wasn't supposed to be able to give orders to the Border Guard. Eltiron's frown grew deeper. There was something he should remember about Terrel and Jermain. . . .

Abruptly, it came to him: the conversation on the tower. Terrel and the other man had been discussing Jermain, and the strange voice had not been pleased with Terrel. What had he said? "It is fortunate that your attempt did not succeed. My plans for Jermain Trevannon do not include his death."

Eltiron looked up. "How long ago did you meet Jermain and these guards?"

"Two weeks ago."

"And it's been ten days since I heard Terrel on the tower-top. That *is* what they were talking about!"

Amberglas's gaze focused on Eltiron with disconcerting suddenness. "Which tower-top?"

"The Tower of Judgment," Eltiron said. "I'd forgotten; Crystalorn asked me to tell you about it."

Amberglas nodded, and Eltiron plunged into the same story he had told Crystalorn two nights before. Amberglas listened intently, then asked him in a rather roundabout fashion to give his version of what he had seen and heard when he'd found Crystalorn eavesdropping on Terrel and Salentor. When he finished, Amberglas looked extremely thoughtful.

"I believe I would like to look at this tower a bit more closely," she said.

Though he was a bit puzzled by the request, Eltiron agreed to take Amberglas to the Tower of Judgment. It was not possible for him to do so immediately, however; it was nearly time for him to go back to begin the meetings and formal receptions that had been scheduled for the day. He offered to have someone else show her the tower, but when it became clear that Amberglas wanted *him* to show her the tower and not someone else, he agreed to meet her early the following morning.

He left the gardens wondering why she was so anxious for his company, but he soon forgot his puzzlement in the rush of

the day's activities. First there was a long and uncomfortable
session of planning for the movement of the army. Marreth
was more unreasonable than usual, and, though Anareme,
Vandaris, and even Terrel urged him to send the army south at
once, he refused to allow it to be moved until after Eltiron's
wedding, two weeks away. When the meeting ended, Vandaris
and Eltiron went to their daily practice match, and after
that there was a series of lunches and receptions for various
groups of nobility who were interested in meeting Eltiron's
prospective bride. In the evening there was another feast
which jammed the banquet hall with courtiers and entertainers.

It was late when Eltiron finally reached his chambers, but he
lay awake for some time, thinking about Jermain. As a result,
he slept later than he had intended next morning. When he
awoke at last, he hurried to the garden to keep his appointment with Amberglas, but stopped short when he entered and
saw two figures waiting for him instead of one. He hesitated as
he realized that the second person was Crystalorn. In broad
daylight she did not seem much like the mischievous girl he
had found eavesdropping on Terrel Lassond, and he felt a
little shy.

Crystalorn looked up and saw him. "Prince Eltiron! Oh,
good; I was beginning to wonder whether I understood
Amberglas as well as I thought I did. Do you mind if I come to
see this tower, too?"

"Of course not," Eltiron said. "But I don't think it will be
very interesting. It's just a tower."

"Not necessarily," Amberglas said absently. "Besides,
people are frequently interested in very ordinary things like
candles and cartwheels and chimneys and eating. I don't
believe I've ever met anyone who wasn't interested in eating,
which is quite ordinary if you think about it, though perhaps
you haven't."

"Yes, of course," Eltiron said. "I mean, no, I haven't."

"I'd like to see your tower even if it is ordinary," Crystalorn said. "And if Amberglas is interested in it, it probably
isn't."

"What do you mean?" Eltiron asked as they started around
the castle toward the Tower of Judgment.

Crystalorn glanced warily at Amberglas, who responded
with an abstracted smile. Crystalorn shrugged and turned

back to Eltiron. "Amberglas is a sorceress."

Eltiron stared at Crystalorn for a moment, then looked at Amberglas with mingled disbelief and apprehension. "A sorceress?"

"Exactly," Amberglas said, and Eltiron jumped. Crystalorn looked at him sharply, but did not speak, and he mumbled an apology. They continued toward the Tower of Judgment in silence, while Eltiron tried to sort out his emotions.

The idea of someone so . . . so absentminded wielding magic power made Eltiron's shoulders twitch uncomfortably. Sorcery was rare in Sevairn, but Eltiron had seen and heard enough to give him a healthy respect for magical abilities of any sort. Still, Amberglas hadn't done anything unusual yet, and Crystalorn seemed to trust her completely. It occurred to him that it might be useful to have a friend who could work magic, particularly if Terrel or the other man he'd heard was using sorcery for something. But Amberglas?

By this time, they had reached the tower. The guard at the door stiffened to attention as he recognized Eltiron, then his eyes widened as he recognized Eltiron's companions. His lips twitched, as if he were suppressing a question or a knowing smile, and when he looked back at Eltiron he seemed somehow more respectful, even though he had not changed position. Eltiron wondered if the guard's reaction meant that he had heard about Crystalorn and Eltiron's late-night wanderings, and decided it did. Suddenly, Eltiron felt much better about everything.

Crystalorn and Amberglas entered the tower first, and Eltiron followed. Once inside the tower, his uneasiness returned. He tried to conceal it, though it was not really necessary; Crystalorn was well ahead of him on the staircase and Amberglas seemed to grow more preoccupied as they neared the tower's top. By the time he reached the last landing of the staircase, Eltiron had convinced himself that he was being foolish.

Amberglas and Crystalorn had already gone out onto the tower-top, and Eltiron hurried to follow them. As he stepped through the door, he felt a moment's dizziness and a sudden flash of heat, as if someone had rapidly opened and closed an oven door. He swung around in surprise and found himself facing Amberglas. "What are you *doing?*" he demanded.

"How very nice," Amberglas said. She sounded remarkably pleased about something. "I rather thought you might, though of course I wasn't sure, and I doubt that you realize it yourself yet, which is quite understandable since it isn't at all obvious. But then, even when things are exceedingly obvious, people frequently overlook them, which generally causes a great deal of difficulty for everyone."

"What are you two talking about?" Crystalorn said, looking from Eltiron to Amberglas and back again.

"I don't know!" Eltiron said. "I felt something when I came through the door, and if she's a sorceress it has to be her." He could still feel it, he realized suddenly. There was a warmth around him that had nothing to do with the weather, and his head felt strangely light.

"You are quite wrong, though I can see why you might think so," Amberglas said. "Magic is so very confusing for beginners, particularly when one doesn't know it."

Eltiron stared at her with a sinking feeling. "What are you talking about?"

"You and the tower, of course," Amberglas said.

"Amberglas, sometimes I could shake you," Crystalorn said in exasperation. "That doesn't explain anything! What does the Tower of Judgment have to do with Eltiron?"

"He has a link to it. Or rather, he has a link to the power within it, which isn't quite the same thing but is considerably closer than most people think."

"That's impossible!" Eltiron said. "Even if the Tower of Judgment *is* magical, I'd have to be a sorcerer to use it. And I don't know anything about sorcery."

"I'm afraid that's not true at all. Of course, most of what you know is quite wrong, which is perfectly understandable since you were born in Sevairn, though it wouldn't be if you had been born in Navren or even Vircheta. Still, I can't recommend it. It's so very difficult to change the place one was born in, and it's hardly ever worth the effort, particularly if you're considering Navren. I believe it's quite an unpleasant place."

"I meant that I haven't been trained to be a sorcerer," Eltiron said. "So how can I have a link with the tower?"

"That," said Amberglas, looking directly at him, "is something I intend to find out."

"What does this link feel like?" Crystalorn asked, eyeing Eltiron speculatively.

"It doesn't feel much like anything."

"It isn't like someone humming in the back of your head?"

"Dear me, why do you ask that?" Amberglas said.

"I've been feeling something like that off and on ever since we got up here," Crystalorn admitted, "and I was wondering if it was the same thing."

"Not at all, though I can see why you might think so. I don't suppose you've ever noticed it before?"

"No," Crystalorn said positively. "I'd remember."

"How very interesting," Amberglas said to the stone battlement just behind Crystalorn's head. Eltiron waited for her to continue, but she did not. After a moment, Crystalorn sighed.

"Well, then, if Eltiron has some sort of link with this tower, what can he do with it?" she asked. "Could he use it to find out what Salentor's up to?"

"I rather doubt it, since there is very little that can be done with any of the towers just at present," Amberglas said. "Though I expect that can be changed. Most things can, if one works at them hard enough; part of the difficulty in this case is that I believe most of the towers are not really suited to being deliberately controlled."

"Towers?" Crystalorn said. She peered over the parapet at the rest of Leshiya Castle. "How much of this castle is magic?"

"None of it, I'm afraid; the Tower of Judgment isn't really part of this castle. Of course, it would be much more convenient to have everything in one place, but it doesn't seem as though Galerinth was particularly interested in convenience, which is really quite like him now that I come to think of it."

"Then what other towers were you talking about?" Eltiron asked.

"And who's Galerinth?" Crystalorn put in.

"Galerinth is the sorcerer who built the towers," Amberglas said. "I believe there is at least one in each of the Seven Kingdoms, though it's rather difficult to be certain, since no one but Galerinth knew where they all were and he has been dead for a great many centuries. They are all identical—the towers, I mean, not the centuries, though of course they might *seem* quite similar after a while if one actually lived through them."

"How do you know the Tower of Judgment is one of Galerinth's towers?" Eltiron asked.

"It's exactly like mine, or rather, the tower I've lived in for the past several years. Which wouldn't matter at all, except that it is definitely one of the towers Galerinth built, so of course all the others are exactly like it.''

"What would a sorcerer want with a bunch of towers?'' Crystalorn asked.

"I'm afraid he didn't tell anyone, which is most inconvenient, though perhaps understandable since it turned out so very badly. I'm sure he was quite embarrassed, because no matter how good one's motives are it's awkward to have such a large project do so little. People with good motives frequently forget to pay proper attention to the way they intend to do something, though not always.''

"You mean they don't *work?*''

Amberglas nodded. ''And it's a great pity Galerinth didn't know more about sorcery than he thought he did when he put all that power into the towers. Though of course, no one then knew quite as much as we do now, what with a number of years in between, so it wasn't entirely his fault; still, he really should have known better.''

"What did he do wrong?'' Eltiron asked.

"He tried to make the towers perfectly good; I believe he wanted to make sure they could never be used for evil purposes, which was not at all wise, and he very nearly succeeded.''

"What's wrong with that?'' Eltiron said. ''It sounds like a good idea, especially if they're so powerful.''

"Nothing at all,'' Amberglas replied. ''Unfortunately, magic isn't particularly good or evil; one can use it either way, depending on how one feels at the moment. Rather like an ax, which one can use to chop wood or to chop people's heads off, though some people don't think chopping heads off is a bad thing unless it's their head, which is perhaps a little shortsighted of them. And of course it's quite impossible to make an ax that will chop wood but can't possibly be used to chop heads, so naturally they didn't work at all well.''

"The towers?''

"Exactly. They have a great deal of power, of course, but it's almost impossible to get at because half of it isn't there, which is most regrettable.''

"So the towers don't do whatever it is they're supposed to do because Galerinth took out all the power that he thought could do evil things,'' Crystalorn said. She frowned thoughtfully and began twisting one long strand of hair around her fingers. "But where'd he put it?"

"I really don't know, though it would make things a great deal easier if I did because what with the Matholych coming and so on it would be so very useful if the towers worked. Or even one of them."

"Amberglas!" Crystalorn said with irritation. "Every time I think I'm beginning to figure out what you're talking about, you bring up something new. What's a Matholych?"

The description that followed was extremely confused, but by the time Amberglas finished, both of her listeners were thoroughly alarmed. The Matholych was something very old and powerful, which destroyed people and animals wherever it moved. Only sorcery could fight it, though unfortunately no one seemed to know exactly what kind of sorcery. There were a great many different theories, but since the Matholych ate magic, testing them was apt to be rather awkward. . . .

"I thought you said the Matholych ate people," Crystalorn objected.

"Not at all," Amberglas replied. "It eats *magic,* and there is quite a large amount of magical power in killing people and animals. Of course, getting power that way is a bit unpleasant, which may explain why it is generally regarded as Black Sorcery by everyone who doesn't use it."

Eltiron shuddered. Somehow, killing people to get magic from their deaths seemed much worse than killing them for food. "And this thing is coming north?"

"Quite soon."

"I'm going to have to tell Vandi about this," Eltiron said. "She's been trying to get Father to do something about the Hoven-Thalar, but this sounds even worse."

"Vandi?" Crystalorn sounded puzzled.

"My father's sister, Vandaris." Eltiron did not feel capable of describing Vandaris in greater detail.

"I believe Vandaris is already aware of the problem," Amberglas said. "She's really been quite helpful."

"You know Vandaris?" Eltiron said.

"Quite well. I believe we met in Torrith, when that exceedingly silly Princess was trying to have the town conquered by Bar-Zienar so she could marry the King."

Eltiron remembered the incident, though it had taken place nearly ten years before; it was one of Vandaris's less successful

campaigns, and Marreth had taunted her with it for years.
Eltiron was rather surprised that Amberglas and Vandaris had
remained friends so long. His acerbic aunt seemed to him to
have little in common with Amberglas, particularly if this
rather vague woman really was a sorceress.

"That's nice, but what are we going to do about this
Matholych thing?" Crystalorn said.

"I'm afraid Galerinth's towers are the only thing I know of
that might be at all useful for doing anything to stop the
Matholych, which is a bit unfortunate though not exactly surprising."

"But you said the towers don't work properly! So how can
we get them to do anything at all?"

"That depends almost entirely on how willing Prince
Eltiron is to try strengthening his link with the Tower of Judgment."

Crystalorn's expression suddenly became very thoughtful,
and she fell silent. Eltiron looked down, trying to think. The
Hoven-Thalar were bad enough, but at least he knew what to
expect from them when they came north. The Matholych
seemed more like the stuff of nightmares—deadly, powerful,
and unpredictable. He did not want to even think about it. But
if Amberglas was right, he might be the only one who had a
chance of doing anything to stop it. "What do you want me to
do?" he said at last.

All Amberglas asked was that Eltiron spend a few minutes
each day with her at the top of the Tower of Judgment.
Eltiron agreed with some relief, and for the next twelve days
he made sure that he found the time she had requested. With
all the official meetings, parades, fittings, Councils, feasts,
sword-practices, and wedding preparations, this was no easy
task. He was not motivated entirely by fear of the Matholych;
on most mornings Crystalorn joined them, and Eltiron was
glad of the chance to see her without crowds of courtiers
around them. He was beginning to like his promised bride.

On the first morning Eltiron was nervous, not knowing
what to expect. Amberglas seemed a bit vaguer than usual, but
as far as Eltiron could tell she did nothing unusual, and the
time passed quickly in conversation. Though he was relieved
to find that she did not try to teach him spells, he occasionally
wondered just what she was trying to do. At last he asked her,

but her response was so extremely confusing that he decided
she did not want to explain. He did not ask again; he had plenty of other things to worry about.

Chief among Eltiron's other worries was Lord Terrel Lassond. After a few days, Terrel had ceased courting Crystalorn
in public, and at first Eltiron had been relieved. Then he noticed Terrel watching Vandaris at one of the receptions, and he
began to grow uneasy again. He started to watch Terrel and
realized that Terrel spent a good deal of his time studying Vandaris. Once he was sure, Eltiron tried to warn his aunt, but she
was unconcerned.

"Lassond is the least of my problems," she told Eltiron.
"Anareme can't get the army moving until Marreth gives the
orders, and he's being even more of an idiot than usual."

"I've noticed," Eltiron replied. That was another of the
things that were bothering him. Marreth had always been
stubborn and short-tempered, but since Crystalorn arrived he
had been harder to live with than ever before. Even Terrel
seemed to be on edge when Marreth was present. Fortunately,
Marreth did not seem to take much interest in the preparations
for Eltiron and Crystalorn's wedding, so Eltiron was spared
the worst of his father's temperament, at least until the wedding breakfast on the first day of the festivities.

Custom and tradition dictated that a royal groom begin the
three-day wedding festival with his family, so Eltiron broke
his fast with Marreth and Vandaris. It was almost amusing, in
a way. Vandaris and Marreth spent half the meal trading insults. The argument wandered over many subjects, and they
agreed on none of them. Marreth kept coming back to Vandaris's profession; he considered it an insult to his name that
she should be a mercenary. Finally Vandaris told him that it
was a good thing she, not he, was the one who had become a
mercenary. Marreth, she said, would have made a very poor
soldier.

"We'll see if you say the same when I've beaten you in the
sword-games this afternoon!" Marreth retorted.

Vandaris's eyebrows rose. "You're in the sword-games?
Are you sure you're up to it? Darinhal seemed to think you'd
be better off doing something . . . less strenuous."

"Darinhal forgets that he is merely the castle physician, not
the King!"

"Doesn't surprise me," Vandaris muttered. "But when did your name go on the lists? I didn't see it when I looked over the layout two days ago."

"Terrel arranged it for me yesterday," Marreth said with some satisfaction. "I'm taking Eltiron's place on the cards."

Chapter Twelve

The cloaked man bowed to Jermain. As he straightened, he swept the hood back from his dark hair and gave Jermain one of his rare smiles. "I came seeking for you," Ranlyn said. "As you see, I am successful."

"Yes, and how did you manage it?" Jermain demanded as he sheathed his sword. "You couldn't have known where I was going; I didn't know myself when I left you."

"A Hoven-Thalar can always find the friends of the heart."

Jermain nodded. Though the Hoven-Thalar were known as peerless trackers, few believed that a Hoven-Thalar could feel the object of his search as a magnet felt the pull of the north. During his six months with Ranlyn, however, Jermain had seen too many Hoven-Thalar move unerringly toward their prey to remain completely skeptical. Besides, he knew Ranlyn well enough to realize that he would get no further explanation. "Why didn't you stop when you saw the army? Didn't you realize what might happen if you were caught?"

"A well-trained army is of great value against another army, but a single man may easily avoid it. I have been following your soldiers since you entered the forest, waiting for a chance to speak with you. This night offered me my desire."

"I should have guessed," Jermain said, shaking his head. "No one else could get past the sentries without raising an alarm, even if he wanted to. And who else would take the risk?"

"One who in truth has a debt to pay."

"You've saved my life more times than I've saved yours. That debt is long paid."

Ranlyn shook his head. "Aid in battle is a debt any man owes his companions; it is one of the Twelve Lesser Obligations, and when battle is done the debt is finished. The Three Great Obligations are not paid so easily, and my debt to you unites all three—a debt of water, a debt of blood, and a debt of life."

"You'll be in no condition to pay debts to anyone if you stay here long," Jermain said roughly, abandoning the old argument. "Friend or no, I should have you arrested as a spy, and if you don't leave soon I'll have no choice."

Ranlyn smiled enigmatically. "Every man has choices; I have made some few of mine, and now the sands fall to your side of the wheel. The moment of choice is not always recognized, but it is always present."

"Ranlyn, please! I don't want to order you killed."

"And when did the generals of the north begin executing their own spies?"

Jermain winced. "I never asked you to betray your people. I couldn't refuse to use the information when you gave it to me, but I never asked for it!"

"I know." Ranlyn's face was impassive. "It is part of my life-debt, to you and to them."

For a moment, Jermain stood studying the other man. He would despise as a traitor anyone else who had done what Ranlyn had done, but he could not despise Ranlyn. Ranlyn lived by the Hoven-Thalar code, which put personal debts above the claims of people, clan, or clan-head; by his own code, he had done no wrong in serving Jermain's interests at the expense of his own people.

"I don't understand you," Jermain said at last, "but if you're going to be stubborn, at least come in where it's more comfortable." Jermain had not finished with Blackflame, but he wanted to get Ranlyn out of sight before someone else arrived and he was forced to claim him as a spy. It would not harm the horse to wear a saddle for a few more minutes.

"Your tent is mine," Ranlyn replied gravely.

Jermain suppressed a sigh of relief as he led the way into the tent. "Sit down and tell me what you have been doing since we parted."

"Traveling. Most recently in your homeland."

"Sevairn is no longer my home."

"The heart speaks more truly than the tongue. You have no

interest, then, in the presence of the King's sister at Leshiya's court?''

"Vandaris? So she's finally gotten home again. What's she doing?''

"Raising an army against my people and seeking you.''

Jermain hid his surprise. "Why is she looking for me? And how do you know?''

"I had speech with her before I left Leshiya, and she offered me gold to search for you. I regret that she did not share with me the reasons for her search.''

"Do you know how long she'd been in Leshiya before you talked to her?''

"Several days, I think, though she was not exact. She spoke of angering her brother at a dinner gathering the evening before.''

"Then she must have heard about . . . what happened seven months ago. And she was still looking for me?''

"As you say. She said that if I saw you I should tell you that she knows you are guiltless of treason.''

"And she's really gotten Marreth to raise an army?'' Jermain said after a moment. "I wouldn't have believed it possible.''

"I saw the beginnings of the preparations myself. She means to keep the Hoven-Thalar from Sevairn.''

Jermain's eyes narrowed suddenly. "Indeed? And how did the Lady Vandaris learn that the Hoven-Thalar were coming north?''

"I informed her of it,'' Ranlyn said calmly.

"I suppose you owe her a debt as well,'' Jermain said with angry sarcasm.

"Vandaris has no claim on me save that of any other warrior: courtesy, hospitality, aid to a companion, and a clean death to an enemy. No more.''

"Then how did she persuade you to betray your clan and the clans of the other Hoven-Thalar?''

"She did not persuade me. I offered her the information, as I offered it to you, and to Kilkaver of Mournwal, Santh of Gramwood, and others.''

"Ranlyn . . .'' Jermain did not want to believe what he had just heard. *"Why?"*

"That is what I have come to tell you,'' Ranlyn said. His face was somber as he looked at Jermain. "You gave the blood of your life to keep me from death; above all else I owe you truth. And that is a debt I have not paid."

"Then do so," Jermain said grimly.

"Truth is a harsh lord, and slippery as a swamp-eel. When I came to you last fall and told you that the Hoven-Thalar would ride north this summer, I spoke truth, but not the whole truth. I knew your position, and I made use of you for my own ends."

"How?"

"I warned you of only half the danger you faced, and that the lesser half. For whether the Hoven-Thalar ride or no, the Red Plague moves north this year."

"I have heard of the Red Plague, but by the name of Matholych."

"You have heard it, but not from me, and I doubt that you have heard all that you need to know. The Red Plague has been the scourge of your people and my own for centuries, but we remember more of it. Six times has it swept north out of the desert, and—"

"Six? I know of only three."

"The histories of the Hoven-Thalar speak of six, but the first two did not cross the wasteland. When it comes, it moves always northward, devouring what life and magic lie in its path. And as it eats, it grows weaker."

"Weaker? That doesn't make sense!"

"Nonetheless, it is true. The strong can outride the Red Plague; the weak lag behind and slow it further, until it has had its fill and returns to its place in the desert. And when it has fully absorbed all that it has taken, it comes forth again, stronger than before."

"What does this have to do with your . . . conduct?"

"The Red Plague will be stronger this time than it has ever been before. The last time it came north, it reached the edge of the Morlonian Hills before it was satisfied. How far will it come this time, and how fast? If my people ride north, I think few of them would survive."

"None of them will survive if you stay where you are!" Jermain exploded. "You can't go west into the ocean, and if speed is your concern, riding north is considerably faster than trying to get through Fenegrik Swamp."

"Under normal conditions we could travel more swiftly if we moved north. But if an army waited for us, to slow us and perhaps stop us? The Red Plague moves swiftly; even a small delay could be our death.''

"You knew that, and you still told me that the clans would ride north this summer?''

"I told you for their lives. I knew you, or someone else, would believe and prepare, and when the preparations began I brought word of them to the clan-council. When the clan-heads heard my story, they voted to change the path of the riding. The Hoven-Thalar ride east, through Fenegrik Swamp. The Lady of the Tower has promised us dry passage, and by the time the Red Plague reaches the end of the wastelands, the Hoven-Thalar will be well away from danger. This is the use I have made of you and your armies, and now my purpose is accomplished.''

Jermain stared at his friend for a long moment. "You mean—''

A horn sounded just outside the tent, cutting Jermain off in midsentence. A moment later, a loud voice cried, "Carachel! In the name of the Guild of Mages, come out and face challenge!''

Jermain jumped to his feet and pulled back the tent flap. He felt Ranlyn rise and follow, but most of his attention was concentrated on the scene outside. Two men stood a little in front of his tent. Several soldiers lay groaning on the ground behind them; scorched places on their uniforms bore witness to the way the two men had bypassed the sentries. If anyone else had been present when the wizards arrived, they had wisely taken themselves to their tents, for the clearing was otherwise empty except for Jermain, Ranlyn, and the new arrivals.

The two men stood facing the center of the army, with their backs toward Jermain. After a moment's hesitation, Jermain eased out of the tent and circled the clearing to get a better view of them. He was a little surprised by what he saw. The first was a large, brown-haired man in his prime; he looked more like a blacksmith than a wizard. The second man was a blond, gangling youth who sported two inches of scraggly fuzz on his chin as proof that he was old enough to grow a beard. Both men wore plain clothes and green cloaks. The large man wore a heavy silver ring set with a green stone on his left hand; the youth held a horn, and his hands were bare.

"Carachel!'' the large man called again. "Come face challenge!''

"I am here." Carachel stepped out of the trees in front of them. The golden vest he wore shone in the sun, making him for a moment a pillar of light. Carachel stopped and held up a hand, and the serpent ring flashed on his finger. At the edge of his vision, Jermain saw Ranlyn stiffen as Carachel went on. "Who are you?"

"I am Wengarth of the Guild of Mages," the large man replied, "and my apprentice is named Laznyr."

"And what do you want of me?" Carachel's voice was almost a chant, and Jermain realized suddenly that he was watching a ritual as formal as a coronation.

"I come to challenge you to the combat sorcerous for the wrongs you have done to all wizards, to the Guild of Mages, and to me," Wengarth replied.

"What are these wrongs which bring you here?"

"You have followed the ways of Black Sorcery, which must be the concern of all wizards. You have sought and killed two score of the mages of the Guild, taking their magic and their deaths to enhance yourself. And among those you murdered was my brother, Grinlown. Is this sufficient?"

"It is sufficient, and I accept your challenge."

"Will you answer the charges before we begin?"

For the first time, Carachel hesitated. His eyes flicked toward Jermain. "The charges are false. When I have killed, I have done so in defense of my life and to preserve the Seven Kingdoms from destruction."

Wengarth looked faintly surprised by Carachel's response, but he answered almost immediately. "Then there can be no agreement between us. Let the circle be drawn."

Carachel inclined his head and stepped forward to stand some twenty paces in front of the other wizard. Wengarth's apprentice stepped between the two men. From under his cloak he drew an ornate dagger. He offered it first to Carachel, who inspected it carefully before returning it, and then to Wengarth, who simply nodded. As he turned away, Jermain saw Wengarth lean forward very slightly and whisper something to the younger man.

The apprentice made no response, and Wengarth settled back into his position. Jermain watched narrowly as the apprentice raised the knife and bowed toward the north, then repeated the gesture to the east, south, and west. He drew a

complex pattern in the air, then bent and began scratching a
line on the ground. In a few minutes he had enclosed Carachel
and Wengarth in a rough circle. Jermain noticed that the apprentice was careful to make sure there were no breaks in the
line.

When the circle was complete, the apprentice stood. He
bowed once more to the north, west, south, and east, then
turned to face the two wizards. He raised the knife once more,
and said loudly, "The circle is drawn; let no man pass its
bounds until the combat is decided." He gestured with the
knife, and white light flared briefly from the line he had
drawn.

"The circle is completed; will you test it?" Wengarth asked
Carachel.

"I have seen the spell cast, and I am satisfied that no one
may pass the barrier without the aid of sorcery. I decline the
test."

This time Wengarth's surprise was more obvious, but after
a moment he nodded. "Then we begin."

The apprentice crouched at the edge of the circle, still
holding the knife. He looked very white, and he did not take
his eyes from Wengarth. The two wizards raised their hands.
Jermain saw the silver ring on Wengarth's finger shining, as if
it were gathering sunlight around itself. Involuntarily, Jermain's head turned toward Carachel. Light was gathering
around Carachel's hands as well, but the serpent ring was dark
on his finger.

For a long moment, the two men stood motionless. The
light spread and intensified until each of the wizards was
enclosed in a glowing sphere. Then Wengarth brought his left
hand down. A portion of the light surrounding Carachel died
abruptly, as if it had been split away. Carachel's face was impassive; he brought his own hands together and made a throwing motion. A globe of light went spinning toward Wengarth.
It hit the light surrounding him with a bright flare and a loud
crackling.

When the crackling dazzle stopped, Wengarth stood un-
moved. Carachel looked startled, and Wengarth grinned
mirthlessly. "I prepared carefully before I came, dark mage,"
he said as he brought his hand down again.

Another piece of Carachel's sphere split away and died.

"You see?" Wengarth said. "I will break your power back
into the pieces you stole from others. This time it will do you
no good."

"You know less than you think," Carachel said and
gestured.

The light around Carachel dimmed, then began to grow
again, brighter and more intense than before. Carachel
brought his hands up, and the serpent ring began to glow. The
sphere of light around Carachel expanded rapidly, and
Wengarth staggered as it struck his own globe. He recovered
quickly and raised his hands. A bright net of sparks appeared
where the two lights struck each other, a few feet in front of
Wengarth.

Jermain watched closely, feeling the beginnings of worry.
Wengarth's words had triggered an unwelcomed thought.
Only a few days before, Carachel had seemed worried about
conserving his power to face the Matholych. How far would
this duel drain him?

The boundary wavered between the two wizards for a moment, then crept with agonizing slowness toward Carachel.
Carachel frowned slightly, and the serpent ring grew brighter.
The net of sparks began to move more quickly, in little jerks
of an inch or more, but it did not change direction. Jermain's
jaw tightened, and he looked at Wengarth.

Great beads of sweat stood out on Wengarth's forehead,
and Jermain could see the fear in his face. Wengarth gestured
suddenly, and the bright border leapt nearly a foot back
toward him. Carachel's frown deepened. The serpent ring
blazed like a firebrand, and the boundary of light began moving toward Carachel once more.

With a sudden feeling of disorientation, Jermain realized
that the struggle was the exact opposite of what he had
assumed. Each of the wizards was pulling the net of light that
marked the separation of their power toward himself, not
forcing it back toward his opponent. And Carachel was winning the struggle.

Jermain relaxed fractionally as the boundary continued to
move toward Carachel. A movement on the other side of the
circle caught his eye, and he saw the apprentice rising to his
feet. Laznyr looked even whiter than he had before, and his
right hand was clenched on the hilt of the knife. Jermain
frowned and began edging around the circle toward the youth.

If Wengarth had intended some treachery . . . He glanced back toward the wizards in the center of the ring.

The border of light had almost reached Carachel. Wengarth's breath came in great gasps, and his face was twisted with effort. It was clear that he could not last much longer. As Jermain watched, he began to move forward, slowly and jerkily, like a puppet with molasses on its feet, until he and Carachel were two paces apart instead of twenty. Jermain looked back at the apprentice just as Wengarth gasped, "Laznyr! Your promise . . ."

The youth gestured, then raised the knife and plunged forward into the circle. Without thinking, Jermain dove after him. Light flared around him as he passed over the edge of the circle, and something slowed him, resisting his passage. Then he was sprawling on the ground inside the ring.

Laznyr was just ahead of him. Jermain rolled and managed to grab the other's ankle, tripping him before he could reach the two combatants. Laznyr cried out in shock, and dropped the knife as he fell on top of Jermain.

For a moment, the two men grappled on the ground, Laznyr struggling to regain the knife and Jermain to prevent him from reaching it. Suddenly Laznyr gave a cry of triumph. Jermain saw the knife glitter, swinging toward him, and he jerked backward. He was barely in time. The knife slashed though his tunic, grazing his chest, and Laznyr broke free.

Jermain scrambled to his feet and followed, but Laznyr was too quick. He ran toward the wizards, who seemed to have noticed nothing. Their eyes were locked; they were barely a sword-length apart. Laznyr slid toward them as Carachel's right hand, which bore the serpent ring, reached for Wengarth. "Laznyr!" Wengarth croaked, and his voice held desperation.

Laznyr raised the knife. Jermain stopped and jerked his own knife from his belt. With all his strength, he hurled it at Laznyr, just as the other man brought his arm down.

The ornate dagger plunged through the glowing light that surrounded the wizards and buried itself to the hilt in Wengarth's chest, just as Jermain's knife struck Laznyr. Wengarth opened his mouth in a soundless scream and collapsed. The light winked out like a snuffed candle. Carachel cried out and staggered backward, his right hand still outstretched and his face unpleasantly twisted.

Laznyr made a slow half turn to face Jermain. There was a look of surprise and relief in his eyes. "Thank you," he said in a ragged voice. "I thought you were with—" A coughing spasm shook him, and blood began to run down his chin into his beard. His knees buckled, and he fell heavily atop his master, Jermain's knife protruding from his side.

For an instant, Jermain stood stunned by the unexpected turn of events; then he swung around to face Carachel. "My lord? Are you well?"

Carachel was bent over, panting, but after a moment he looked up. His face was a mask of rage and frustration. He glared blindly in Jermain's direction without seeming to see anything. "You fool! I needed—I wanted them alive! What good are they to me now?"

"Who seeks the power in dying may forget the power of living," Ranlyn said from the other side of the circle. He stepped forward into the circle and stood looking at Carachel, his face unreadable.

"You!" Carachel straightened abruptly. He took a deep breath and made a visible effort to calm himself. "You come at a bad time, as you see. Still, I am always anxious for news of the Hoven-Thalar. How soon do you move north?"

Ranlyn did not answer. Jermain glanced from Ranlyn to Carachel, but though he knew Ranlyn's message, he did not speak. Ranlyn's arrival, his description of the Matholych and his news, Wengarth's charges and Carachel's answer to them, the wizards' duel and its unexpected end—all formed an unpleasant pattern. Jermain could not quite believe what he thought he saw, but he could not deny it, either. He waited, hoping for something that would refute his suspicions and not really expecting it.

"You have no need to fear me," Carachel said at last. "Come, what news do you bring?"

Ranlyn took a step forward, and his cloak swirled around him like a cloud. "Truly is it said that he who knows not his debts is cursed. My debt is now to the truth, and to my clans, and to my friends. What obligations are yours, wearer of the Ring of Two Serpents?"

"I do what I must." Carachel's voice was cold.

"So I have seen," Ranlyn said. "And I say to you that whatever debt you owe me, I renounce it. If I have a debt of water from you, I refuse it. If I have a debt of blood from you,

I relinquish it. If I have a debt of life from you, I repudiate it. For myself, if I owe you water, may it be ashes; if I owe you blood, may it be poison to you; if I owe you life, may it be your bane. And may all obligation be at an end between us."

Jermain stared at Ranlyn in shock. During his time with the Hoven-Thalar, he had seen ceremonies where one person had refused or relinquished an obligation, and once or twice he had heard rumors about men without debts or obligations, outcasts and renegades, but that was all. Ranlyn's formal words were a sweeping condemnation of a kind Jermain would never have expected from any Hoven-Thalar, much less his friend.

From the look on his face, Carachel, too, knew the implications of the denunciation. He hesitated briefly, then bowed. "If you will have it, then, let it be so," he said, and Jermain heard tiredness and frustration in his voice. "Yet I would like to know why, if you will tell me freely and without obligation."

"No man may owe obligation to a Servant of the Red Pague."

"No!" Jermain's involuntary cry made both of the other men turn sharply toward him. Carachel's expression was one of horror and repulsion at Ranlyn's accusation; Ranlyn's face was expressionless. Jermain's eyes sought Ranlyn's. "You are wrong, Ranlyn. My Lord Carachel seeks to destroy the Matholych, not to serve it."

"Wisdom rests in the mind and heart. I do not mean that this one owes obligation to the Red Plague. But he wears a Ring of Two Serpents, and those who wear that symbol gain their power from the deaths of men, even as the Red Plague does. Therefore among the Hoven-Thalar are such men called Servants of the Red Plague, though you in the north call such dealings Black Sorcery."

"You do not know what you say," Carachel said coldly.

"Why, then, did those who challenged you prefer death at their own hands to death at yours?"

"If my lord draws power from death, why has he commanded his armies to fight your people with as little loss of life as possible?" Jermain said angrily. "He intended a battle to hold the Hoven-Thalar, not a fight to the death."

Ranlyn's eyes widened briefly, then narrowed as he looked at Carachel. "And you wish to destroy the Red Plague."

"I will destroy it in spite of you and the Guild of Mages!" Carachel shouted. "I will not allow the Matholych to spread death and destruction through the Seven Kingdoms again!"

"And to keep the Red Plague from the lands of your people you would destroy mine. The Red Plague grows weaker as it eats, but only the magic of living men can feed it. You would not have your army kill the Hoven-Thalar, for dead we would be no use to you. How long would you have held us, while the Red Plague devoured us from behind? How many men would the Red Plague have taken before it was weak enough for your spells to defeat it?"

Chapter Thirteen

Eltiron stared at Marreth in utter disbelief. Being excluded from the sword-games would be far worse than making a poor showing, particularly when the games were supposed to be in his honor. Marreth did not have to take Eltiron's place if he wanted to participate; the marshals always left one or two cards empty to hold places for last-minute entries. "You're taking my place?"

"Are you missing ears as well as brains? I just said so, didn't I?" Marreth studied him for a moment, then gave a disgusted snort. "Just as well you won't be fighting, too; this way I won't have to worry about you making a spectacle of yourself in front of the whole court. Not that you'd care for a good fight anyway."

Vandaris slammed a hand down on the table, making Eltiron and all the dishes jump. "That's one of the stupidest ideas I've ever heard. Don't you realize what kind of an impression you'll be giving by replacing Eltiron? I'd be surprised if Barinash didn't take insult, and—"

"Nonsense," Eltiron interrupted firmly. The other two looked at him in surprise, and he went on, "Barinash can only be honored that my father chooses to compete in these sword-games, and I will be glad to give him my place if he wants it."

"Good!" Marreth settled back in his chair. "That's settled, then."

"I shall, of course, speak to the marshals immediately about taking one of the blank cards myself," Eltiron continued with more confidence than he felt. "It would not be

right for me to miss the games entirely, since they are in honor
of my wedding.''

Vandaris grinned openly at Eltiron. Marreth stared for a
moment, then burst into an unexpected roar of laughter. "So
you want to be in the games after all! First time you've done
anything sensible in years. Be sure you get Kaliarth to give you
some decent armor; wouldn't want you at the wedding tomorrow with a hole in your arm.''

Eltiron breathed a quiet sigh of relief. Marreth's sudden
shift to high good humor was disconcerting, but at least
Eltiron had succeeded in staying in the sword-games.

The remainder of the meal passed quickly, and when it was
finished Eltiron went to make arrangements with the marshals
of the games. They seemed a little surprised by Eltiron's request, but none of them commented aloud. Eltiron stayed
long enough to be certain that the blank card was inscribed
with his name and returned to its place on the table, then he
went back to his official activities for the day.

Eltiron spent most of the morning watching parades in
honor of himself and his bride. He sat on a platform in the
square outside the castle, waving at the marchers occasionally,
worrying about Terrel, and sneaking glances at Crystalorn out
of the corner of his eye. He thought she looked even more
beautiful than usual in the festival gown she wore, and she
seemed very different from the companion Eltiron had come
to know over the last few days. In his spare moments, he
worried about the kind of showing he would make in the
sword-games. What if his father were right about his sword
skill? It occurred to him that Crystalorn would be in the royal
box, watching him in the games. Suddenly Eltiron's anxiety
doubled.

The sword-games began at noon. The entire court and at
least half the city proceeded to the stands that had been
erected on Threehills Green. Seven circles had been laid out on
the ground in front of the stands, so that several matches
might take place at the same time. The crowd milled around
for a few moments, settling into seats or setting up betting
booths. Then the horns blew and the marshals picked up the
first two cards and announced the names. The contestants
marched onto the field, the crowd cheered wildly, and the
games began.

Eltiron's name was called for the fourth set of matches. As

he started to leave the royal box, he brushed by Crystalorn and felt her press something into his hand. He looked down to see a blue ribbon, the sort many of the men wore as a "favor" from their ladies. Eltiron closed his hand on it; all at once he felt much better about being in the games. Vandaris winked at him as he left the box, but no one else seemed to have noticed.

One of the marshals met Eltiron outside and escorted him to the edge of the field. Kaliarth, the castle swordkeeper, was waiting with a coat of chain and a selection of weighted wooden swords. Eltiron slipped into the coat and tied Crystalorn's ribbon around his left arm, then turned to choose a weapon. He tried not to hurry; the last match wasn't quite over, so he still had time to be careful. He tried to remember some of the advice Vandaris had given him, but the only thing that stuck in his mind was her voice shouting, "Keep moving, turtle-foot!"

Finally, Eltiron chose a sword a little lighter than the one he had been using in his practice sessions. He swung it a few times to get the feel of it. Satisfied that he would be able to manage it, he turned back to watch the end of the other match. As he did, he caught sight of Amberglas, wandering toward him along the edge of the field. In a few moments more, she reached him and they exchanged greetings.

"I hope you are enjoying the sword-games," Eltiron said.

"There seem to be rather a lot of them," Amberglas said, "though I understand that's quite normal. But practically anything is if it happens often enough, or at least people think so, so it doesn't necessarily mean anything. Still, I've been wondering, particularly since Vandaris mentioned that the King wanted to take your place, which wasn't exactly wise of him but perhaps is only what you would expect. So I decided to see you."

"I think Terrel suggested it; it's not the sort of thing Father would think of by himself. Why did you want to see me?"

"Because I thought I might want to give you this." Amberglas held out her hand, and Eltiron saw that she was holding a thin gold chain, hardly more than a thread, with a six-pointed star made of gold and silver dangling from it. Eltiron reached out and touched the star, very gently, without taking it.

"Is it magic?"

The crowd cheered and Amberglas tilted her head to one side. She studied Eltiron for a moment, then gave a little nod.

"Quite so. And of course it wouldn't be at all proper for you to wear it if it did anything to help you win your matches, but it doesn't, which is precisely what makes it so very useful in situations like this when one isn't entirely certain about things. Unless someone else does, but that's what it's meant for."

"Are you trying to tell me that you think someone is going to use magic in the sword-games?" Eltiron said incredulously.

"No, I'm trying very hard *not* to tell you that, but you're making it rather difficult." Amberglas gave him one of her sharp, disconcerting looks. "Still, I don't suppose it matters, which is extremely fortunate, though not exactly surprising."

"I'm afraid I don't understand."

"That's quite all right. At least, it is just now; it won't be later, but that can probably be managed without too much trouble. Wear it under your mail."

Reluctantly, Eltiron took the gold chain from Amberglas's hand and looped it over his head, then tucked the star out of sight beneath his armor. "Thank you. But are you sure—"

"Next match, Prince Eltiron Kenerach and Baron Gindreth Markon!" shouted a voice from the field.

Eltiron bid Amberglas a hasty farewell and went out to his first match. Though he trusted Amberglas, he was uneasy about the amulet, or whatever it was, that she had given him. As a result, he was unusually self-conscious during the beginning of the match; he was trying to watch for anything in his own behavior that might be due to some magical influence. Then Markon swung at his head, and Eltiron forgot about magic and concentrated on fighting.

He won his first match, thanks in large part to the things he had learned in his practice matches with Vandaris. He left the field with considerably more confidence; he would make a respectable showing in the games, no matter what his father thought! One of the marshals was waiting to tell him when to expect his next match. Eltiron was surprised to learn that he would be on the field again in three rounds of matches; normally contestants had at least five rounds to rest during the early stages of the games.

After a moment's thought, Eltiron decided not to bother returning to the royal box for such a brief interval. Instead, he retreated to the semi-shade under the stands while he waited for his next match. He was not alone; the sun was hot, and there were nearly as many people under the stands as on them.

Eltiron made his way to one of the huge wooden posts that
supported the top row of seats and leaned against it, watching
the crowd. Idly, he glanced in the direction of the royal box
and saw Marreth and Terrel, accompanied by one of Marreth's guards, coming in his direction.

Eltiron ducked his head, hoping they would not recognize
him in the crowd. He did not want to deal with Marreth just
then, whether his father was in a good humor or a bad one. He
was lucky; neither Marreth nor Terrel appeared to notice him,
though they passed close enough to touch him. They were
deep in conversation, and as they went by Eltiron caught part
of what Terrel was saying. ". . . your sister, Vandaris,
and . . ."

Without thinking, Eltiron slipped away from the post and
followed. The next few minutes were extremely frustrating.
Eltiron could not get close enough to hear what Terrel was
saying without being seen by Marreth or the guard. Bits of
sentences were all he could catch, and what he heard was not
reassuring. ". . . been patient long enough . . . feast tonight
. . . perfect time; she won't . . ."

"All right, then!" Marreth roared suddenly. "But my way,
and no more of your arguments! Go see to it."

Terrel bowed and turned away; Eltiron was barely able to
duck back into the crowd in time. He stared after Terrel until
he lost sight of him, then started toward the royal box, hoping
he would be able to get there and warn Vandaris before his
next match. With most of the afternoon left before the feast,
Vandaris might still have time to do something about whatever
Terrel was planning.

Unfortunately, Vandaris was not in the box when Eltiron
arrived. "She left for her first match a few minutes ago,"
Crystalorn told him in answer to his questions. "I think she's
fighting on the other side of the field. Why do you—"

The horns blew, announcing Eltiron's next match. Eltiron
cursed, apologized hastily to Crystalorn, promised to explain
as soon as he had time, and dashed back to take his place on
the field. He made it just in time to keep from forfeiting the
match.

Eltiron's second opponent was one of Terrel's supporters, a
minor lord named Badelian with a reputation as a poor
swordsman. Eltiron spent the first few moments of the match
in a series of moves intended to test his opponent's skill. The

results were much as he had expected; Badelian was very strong, but slow and rather clumsy. Eltiron frowned in puzzlement. Why had the man even bothered to enter the swordgames?

There was no sense in prolonging the match. Eltiron blocked one of Badelian's swings, then danced aside and aimed a blow at Badelian's head. As he started to move, he saw Badelian's sword come around in a sweeping overhead arc. He twisted to avoid it, and felt the wind of its passing. There was enough force behind the swing to break his shoulder if it connected. The sword reversed and swung back. It was moving fast, impossibly fast, no one could swing a sword that fast . . .

Coldness exploded at his chest, and Badelian's sword slowed to normal speed. Eltiron sidestepped just in time and brought his own weapon down on Badelian's helm. He heard the marshal's horn blowing far away, signaling the end of the match, but he had to avoid two more of Badelian's wild swings before the sound penetrated and Badelian lowered his sword. There was a wary expression in Badelian's eyes as he watched Eltiron; he hardly seemed to hear the marshal announcing Eltiron's victory.

As he left the field and started back toward the royal box, Eltiron wondered what Badelian had been trying to do. He did not doubt that the man had used some sort of spell in an attempt to win the match, and he was equally sure that Terrel had arranged the whole incident, but he did not understand why Terrel would go to such lengths to make him lose a match in the sword-games. Losing to Badelian would have been embarrassing, but it wasn't as if he could have killed Eltiron. Injuries at the sword-games were rarely serious; at worst, Badelian might have broken Eltiron's arm or shoulder, or perhaps a rib.

Eltiron paused, remembering the force behind Badelian's swings. He *had* intended to break something. Eltiron frowned. What could Badelian, or Terrel for that matter, hope to accomplish by breaking Eltiron's arm? It would be painful and inconvenient, of course, and the wedding might have to be postponed for a day or two, but Eltiron could not imagine how that would benefit Terrel. Particularly since Terrel was the one who had arranged the wedding in the first place. And how had Amberglas known or suspected that someone would use magic against Eltiron in the sword-games?

As he entered the royal box, Crystalorn leaned over and said, "That was wonderful! I thought he was going to get you with that last stroke; how did you manage to duck in time?"

Eltiron glanced quickly around the box. The only other occupant was one of Marreth's women, who was seated on the opposite side of the box, gracefully fanning herself. Eltiron took a seat beside Crystalorn, and in a low voice quickly outlined what had happened.

"What are you going to do about it?" Crystalorn said when he finished.

"Nothing. I don't have any proof that Terrel actually did anything, or Badelian, either. Besides, talking to Vandaris is more important."

"Why?"

"Terrel's persuaded Father to do something tonight," Eltiron said in a low voice. "I don't know what, but it involves Vandaris. I have to warn her."

"She hasn't been back here since the games started, and you'll never find her in the crowd. You'll have to catch her coming off the field. So what are you waiting for?"

Eltiron left. The afternoon wore on. Eltiron won another match before he was defeated. He was satisfied that he had made a good performance, though not by any means the best. Still, he was glad to stop and return his mail and stick-sword to Kaliarth; the chain and the padding beneath it were far too heavy to be comfortable on a hot day.

Several times, Eltiron saw Vandaris and Marreth in the circles below, but they were never pitted against each other. To Eltiron's surprise, Marreth won five matches before he was defeated; he was much faster than most of his opponents expected. Vandaris fought seven matches and finally lost to one of the Barinash guardsmen who had accompanied Crystalorn.

When Vandaris left the field after her last match, Eltiron was waiting. He forced his way through the crowd of spectators, courtiers, and well-wishers until he reached his aunt. "Vandi, I have to talk to you."

"You and half Morada's army of heroes," Vandaris said as she shrugged off her coat of chain. "Can't it wait?"

"No!"

Vandaris gave him a sharp look. "All right, then. This way." She and Eltiron worked their way away from the field to where the crowd was thinner, then started back toward the royal box. "Now," said Vandaris, "what is it?"

Eltiron glanced around quickly, then told her about the fragments of conversation he had overheard. "So I think Terrel's planning to have Father arrest you for treason at the feast tonight," he finished.

"Hah! Marreth knows better than to try that. And even that snake-tongued idiot Lassond should have more sense than to try the same trick twice."

"Maybe, but Terrel's been watching you for weeks, Vandi."

"You think he's the only one? Half the court's been eyeing me ever since I got in, wondering whether they're better off trying to curry favor with the King's sister or trying to ignore someone Marreth doesn't seem to like much." Vandaris grinned. "Unfortunately, I'm hard to ignore. I agree, though; Lassond's up to something. The question is, what is he planning and what can we do about it?"

"If Father *is* going to have you arrested—"

"Arlayne's crown, man, he'll have a harder time taking me than he had with Trevannon! Particularly since I'll be prepared for him."

"Well, but what if I'm wrong and Terrel's planning something else?"

"If the rivers ran with wine, you'd be too busy worrying about them turning to vinegar to drink anything. I can handle Lassond; he doesn't know nearly as much as he thinks he does. And Marreth's easy." Vandaris smiled wolfishly. "He never has been able to manage anything unexpected."

Vandaris refused to say any more in the short distance left before they reached the royal box, and once they rejoined the rest of the party there was no opportunity for private conversation. Marreth was already there, beaming down on the final rounds of the sword-games and calling for wine. He still wore his chain, ahd his face was flushed and sweaty from the heat and the unaccustomed exertion. Terrel stood at the King's elbow; he gave one long, measuring look in Vandaris's direction, then ignored her completely for the remainder of the games. Marreth alternated between scowling at Vandaris over his wine cup and boasting of his own performance in the games.

By the end of the afternoon, Eltiron was even more worried

than before. Terrel seemed to be in a remarkably good humor, which made Eltiron distrust him even more than usual. He was glad when the sword-games were over at last and he could return to the castle to prepare for the feast. He welcomed the chance to wash away the dust and sweat of the fight, but he did not intend to linger in his bath. He would dress quickly, then visit Vandaris to find out what her plans were. Eltiron threw open the door to his rooms and stopped short.

The castle tailor and his two assistants looked up from the piles of silk and silver occupying two of Eltiron's chairs. "Ah, it is Your Highness!" said the tailor, bowing. "It is good that you come so promptly! No, do not come closer until you have removed the dust; we must have a care for the silks! When you are finished we will proceed to the dressing!"

Eltiron groaned mentally. How could he have forgotten? The castle tailor would hardly trust anyone else to assist Eltiron into the garments he had spent so many days fitting, and he would not be satisfied with less than perfection. Eltiron would be lucky to get to the feast in time; he might as well forget about seeing anyone beforehand. With a sigh he nodded to the tailor and went into the next room to wash.

The bath refreshed him, and when it was finished he submitted with no outward protest to the tailor's ministrations. Being dressed took even longer than he had feared, and by the time the tailor and his men were finished, Eltiron was ready to explode. In spite of his frustration, he managed to thank them in a reasonably steady voice before he went down to the feast.

When he reached the hall, Eltiron let the doorkeeper announce him while he paused to look for Vandaris. The hall was packed with a glittering throng of Sevairn nobility, as well as ambassadors and representatives from the other six kingdoms. Most of them were standing; a few were seated at the long tables. At the far end of the room, the royal table stood on a raised platform. Marreth, his face flushed, sat in a gold-draped chair at the center of the table. To his left was a delicate, dark-haired woman wearing an elaborate headdress of silver filigree and diamonds.

Crystalorn sat on Marreth's right, and as soon as Eltiron saw her, he forgot about looking for Vandaris. Her hair was piled on top of her head in a heavy mass of waves that drew attention to the lines of the face below. She looked . . . she looked . . . Eltiron stopped trying to think of a description and made his way to the table. He sat down beside Crystalorn and said, "You look very nice," then mentally cursed himself for the stupidity of the remark.

"Oh, do you really like my dress?" Crystalorn said. "I wasn't sure it was quite right."

"What dress? Oh, of course. I mean, yes, I like it." Inwardly, Eltiron cringed. Morada's crown, did he have to sound like an idiot every time he opened his mouth?

Crystalorn giggled. "I see. Don't say anything else; you'll spoil it. Did you talk to Vandaris? What'd she say?"

"I told her, but I don't know whether she's going to do anything about it," Eltiron said, after checking to make sure Marreth was occupied with the "lady" on his left.

"She'll do something," Crystalorn said, grinning. "This evening's going to be more interesting than I expected."

Eltiron thought he would prefer a nice, boring dinner, but he didn't say so. He watched the doors, hoping to see Vandaris arrive, but she did not come. When Terrel and Salentor were finally announced, Eltiron began to wonder whether Vandaris would attend the feast at all. He saw Terrel seating himself beside Salentor and frowned. Chief Advisers were not usually given a place at the royal table for a wedding feast, though on less formal occasions they might join the royal family by the King's permission. Then he heard the doorkeeper call Vandaris's name and turned his head. He didn't recognize her at first; then he did and nearly gasped aloud.

Vandaris was wearing the most elegantly barbaric costume Eltiron had ever seen. Her hair had been curled and bound with gold net. Her dress was made of a deep red material that shimmered and flowed as she moved. The full sleeves ended in long cuffs made of gold. Two leather straps, worked in gold, crossed between her breasts, each supporting a curved dagger in a jeweled sheath. She wore a girdle of gold; the skirt below it was slit almost to the waist on either side, and her shoes were gold. She did not look at all like herself, and yet Eltiron could not imagine a formal dress that would suit her better.

She stood in the doorway for a moment as a rustle of astonishment swept through the hall, then moved forward toward the royal table as if she were completely oblivious to the sensation she was causing. Behind her, Tarilane entered almost unnoticed.

"That's *Vandaris?*" Crystalorn said as the two made their

way through the crowd. After a moment she added thoughtfully, "I like her dress; I wonder if she'd tell me where it came from?"

Eltiron was spared a reply; Vandaris had reached the table and was seating herself on his other side. "Vandi, what are you *doing?*" he whispered.

"Waiting for dinner," Vandaris said. "And it won't be long; looks like Marreth's getting ready to start making toasts."

Eltiron turned in time to see Marreth rise to his feet and lift his goblet. He did not even glance in Vandaris's direction, and Eltiron felt suddenly uneasy. Marreth wouldn't let Vandaris appear so dramatically without doing something. Eltiron was so worried he almost missed the traditional opening toasts of health to the bride and groom, but as the toasts went on, he began to relax. Perhaps Marreth was still in a good mood; perhaps he wouldn't do anything after all.

Marreth finished the customary toasts and paused. "And now, my lords, I have an announcement. Tonight we celebrate the wedding of my son, Prince Eltiron Kenerach, to the Princess Crystalorn Halaget of Barinash, but we have another cause for celebration as well. I give you a toast: To my beloved Lord Adviser, Terrel Lassond, and his promised bride—my sister, Vandaris!"

Chapter Fourteen

Jermain looked from Carachel to Ranlyn and back. Part of him wanted to shout that Ranlyn's accusation could not be true, that Carachel could not, would not, have planned such a thing, but another part held him silent. The charge was monstrous, but it explained too many things—Carachel's reluctance to tell Jermain much about the Matholych, his insistence on holding the Hoven-Thalar against all reasonable military practice, Elsane's visit ten days before. Jermain felt like a fool; why hadn't he seen, or at least suspected?

Silence hung over the camp. At last Carachel looked up; not at Ranlyn, at Jermain. His face was a mask, but his voice held a plea. "I do what I must."

"The wall between 'must' and 'will' is often hidden beneath the sand," Ranlyn said.

Carachel's eyes were still on Jermain. "What I do is the only way to keep destruction from the Seven Kingdoms; I swear it!"

"Do you truly expect me to agree to such a slaughter?" Jermain's voice was icy.

"Will you have the Matholych come again, and again a hundred years from now, and on forever? I can end this now! If I—"

He stopped suddenly, staring at Jermain's chest, and his face went white. Involuntarily, Jermain looked down. The medallion Amberglas had given him glinted back at him through the slash Laznyr's knife had made in his tunic. Jermain lifted it out from under the tunic. When he looked up, both Ranlyn and Carachel were watching the medallion.

Ranlyn wore an odd, intense expression that might have been recognition; Carachel looked stunned.

"Where did you get that?" Carachel demanded.

Startled by the irrelevance of the question, Jermain did not answer, and Carachel's face darkened. "So that is how you crossed the spell that guarded the dueling ring! You led them to me, you killed them so I could not use their power—you, whom I trusted." Carachel's voice trembled, and his eyes stared unseeing toward Jermain. "Which of the leaders of the Guild of Mages sent you? Halendarian? Suyil?"

"None of them sent me. I entered your service at your own request, and I am now leaving it."

"You swore an oath to me."

"And you lied to me." Jermain turned on his heel and started toward Ranlyn.

"No! I never lied to you. Never!"

Jermain looked back. "Then you withheld the truth to manipulate me into doing as you wished. Do you think I am a fool? It is as well that the Hoven-Thalar are beyond your control!"

"What do you mean?"

Jermain glanced at Ranlyn, but the nomad's face was expressionless. He turned back to face Carachel. "The Hoven-Thalar are traveling east, not north. You have no need of an army now, nor of my services to command it. When your army reaches Gramwood, there will be nothing for it to fight."

Carachel whirled to face Ranlyn. "You! I knew something was wrong in the south, I felt it days ago, and it is your doing!" He raised his right hand to point, and the serpent ring gleamed ominously.

"Would you seek to keep me from fulfilling the debt I owe my people?" Ranlyn said softly. "Then it is well indeed that it is not within your power to do so."

"I will stop the Matholych despite you!"

"Your will is written in sand," Ranlyn said calmly. "Whether it remains or vanishes lies with the wind that moves the sand. My people you can no longer touch, and no debt lies between us." He looked toward Jermain, as if Carachel were of no further importance. "My debt to truth has here been paid. There remains only the Lady of the Tower to seek before I return to my tent." He bowed, then turned and started walking toward the forest.

"No! I will have no more of your interference!" Carachel gestured and spoke three unfamiliar words.

Ranlyn stiffened and went white. He swayed slightly, but he did not fall or cry out. Carachel's lips tightened, and he clenched the fist that wore the serpent ring. Ranlyn jerked, then slowly collapsed, and Jermain could see that he was fighting for breath.

Jermain leaped forward and grabbed Carachel's outstretched arm. He heard Carachel shout, and something like a blow sent a wave of heat across his chest. He reeled backward and fell. Through the roaring in his ears, he heard Carachel cry out in surprise. He struggled to his knees and reached for his dagger. Another blow fell, momentarily blinding him. He rolled, hoping to avoid the next stroke; as he did, he thought he heard a faint, familiar voice say, "Dear me, how extremely difficult. Not that it's at all surprising, since—"

"Traitor!" Carachel's voice was a howl of rage. An explosion knocked Jermain to the ground, surrounding him with flames. He rolled again, shielding his eyes with his left arm. He smelled singed cloth and felt heat on all sides. Then something seared the center of his chest, and he heard Carachel scream. There was a sound like metal shrieking against stone, the flames died, and there was silence.

Jermain twisted, rolled, and came to his feet, dagger ready. Several paces in front of him Carachel lay unconscious, his breath coming in harsh gasps. Ranlyn lay a little to one side, and Jermain saw with relief that he was beginning to stir. Slowly, Jermain returned his knife to its sheath, then checked to see the extent of his own injuries.

He found none, and almost did not believe it; the memory of the pain was too vivid. The only sign of the brief battle with Carachel was the medallion, which was now a black and shapeless lump of metal instead of a silver disc. Jermain stared at it, wondering numbly how the medallion could be melted when the chain from which it hung was untouched. And this was the simple messenger's medallion he had been so glad to see instead of a magic amulet that might draw him into sorcery! He frowned suddenly. Had Amberglas actually told him the medallion was not magical, or had he simply assumed it?

"Jerayan." Ranlyn was on his feet; he looked pale, but otherwise unharmed. Jermain started forward, but the nomad raised a hand and he stopped in midstride.

Ranlyn's lips curved in a faint smile. "Again, it seems, I owe you a life." He studied Jermain briefly, then turned and knelt beside Carachel in a swirl of robes. A moment later, he rose again and came forward. "I owe you a life," he repeated and reached out. Automatically, Jermain extended his own hand. Ranlyn's fingers opened, and the serpent ring dropped into Jermain's palm.

"My debt is paid," Ranlyn said.

"I don't—" A shout cut Jermain off in midsentence. His head snapped around, and he saw three of Carachel's councillors coming through the trees, accompanied by half a dozen men-at-arms.

"Ranlyn!" Jermain jammed the ring into his belt pouch as he jerked his head toward the soldiers. The two men ran for the rear of Jermain's tent. A second shout told them they had been seen, but Jermain did not stop to find out whether the soldiers were coming after them. Even if the councillors did not order a pursuit, Carachel was certain to do so when he recovered.

Jermain rounded the end of the tent and jerked Blackflame's tether free. Thank Arlayne he had not had time to unsaddle the horse! Ranlyn went past and vanished among the trees as Jermain flung himself into the saddle. Blackflame tossed his head, then plunged after Ranlyn.

There was a confusion of small branches snapping, and a shout of dismay as Jermain passed the startled sentries. He saw no sign of Ranlyn, and he slowed Blackflame's headlong gallop. Behind him, he heard the sounds of the camp belatedly stirring to action. Then he caught a glimpse of a big-boned chestnut horse breaking out a screen of small trees just ahead, and he urged his horse forward once more. A moment later, Jermain and Ranlyn were riding side by side.

"Which way?" Jermain shouted.

"South." Ranlyn's voice was almost lost beneath the sound of the horses' hooves. Behind them, the noise of the camp faded as they drew away from it.

Jermain nodded and dropped back to let his friend lead. The Hoven-Thalar was by far the better horseman, and, in addition, Jermain had not been able to replace Blackflame's bridle. Though the horse was well trained and responsive, it required concentration to guide him using only knees and voice.

As soon as they were well away from the camp, Ranlyn

turned west. Jermain's surprise at this choice of direction
faded quickly. Their pursuers would expect the fugitives to
head south, or southeast, to join the rest of the Hoven-Thalar;
with luck, they might be confused long enough to give Jermain
and Ranlyn a good start, perhaps even long enough for the
fugitives to cross the border into Sevairn. Not that Sevairn was
much safer for Jermain than the vicinity of Carachel's army,
but at least the Border Guards along this part of the Sevairn
border were unlikely to be actively looking for him.

They crashed onward, more interested in speed than silence.
As the trees grew denser, the ride became a nightmarish echo
of his flight from the Border Guards almost a month before.
This time the immediate enemy was not their pursuers, but the
gradually deepening twilight. Travel at night would be almost
impossible in this forest, yet they could not afford to be too
close to Carachel's army when daylight came. There were
other similarities, though. Chief among them was the fact that
once again Jermain had been betrayed by a man he trusted,
one he had thought honorable and worthy of respect. By a
friend. He closed his mind to the cold knot of bitterness, and
concentrated on riding.

As the daylight grew dimmer, Ranlyn and Jermain slowed
their mounts, until finally they were moving no faster than a
walk. Ranlyn still led the way, and from the twists and turns
he was making, Jermain guessed that the nomad had some
goal in mind. He was, therefore, not surprised when, just
before it became too dark to travel safely, they reached a small
stream.

The two men dismounted. They stood in silence while the
horses drank, then Ranlyn said quietly into the darkness, "A
burden shared is less than half as heavy. Will you speak of
what troubles you?"

Jermain frowned. Was he so easy to read? "What 'troubles'
me is what might have happened. It's as well that you came
when you did."

"Ah." Ranlyn paused, then said softly, "I fear I have
brought grief upon you, friend of my blood. For that, I sor-
row."

"It is my fault, not yours! How could I have been so blind?
Carachel . . ."

"Do not blame yourself for having been deceived. A man
who can so greatly deceive himself must indeed be skilled in
lies."

"Carachel knows exactly what he is doing! Don't try to excuse me that way. Even his wife would condemn him if she could; she tried to make me listen and I refused."

"Perhaps he does know. Yet I have seen more of him than you realize, and I think he has for so long thought himself a man of virtue much misunderstood that he does not recognize what he has now become. And I think he longs for companionship; I saw grief in his face when he knew your rejection."

"You defend him? He would have destroyed the Hoven-Thalar completely!"

"Have I not made use of him in preserving my people, even as he would have used me in preserving his?" Ranlyn replied. "Yet I do not seek to justify him; I say only that he may once have been a man of goodness, and still thinks himself so."

"I do not believe it," Jermain said in a flat voice.

Ranlyn's head turned to study Jermain through the gloom, and Jermain's lips tightened. This subject was not of his choosing; he had no desire to speak of Carachel now, not to anyone, and to Ranlyn least of all.

But Ranlyn did not continue the conversation, as Jermain had expected. Instead, he inclined his head and held it briefly bowed, then turned and began unsaddling his horse. A little irritated, and unable to say why, Jermain did likewise.

They spent a cold, uncomfortable night beside the stream. As soon as it began to grow light, they saddled their horses and went on, riding in the stream itself to hide their trail from their pursuers. Blackflame wore a spare bridle from Ranlyn's pack; it made the ride considerably simpler for Jermain.

They rode at a steady pace, rather than trying to gallop through the water, and again Jermain was reminded of a recent journey. This time, the memory was of his trip north with Carachel and the fellowship they had shared during their morning rides, before Carachel had donned the serpent ring and cast his traveling spell. . . . Jermain thrust the memory of friendship out of his mind and nudged Blackflame to a faster walk. In a moment, he was beside Ranlyn.

"We have a problem," Jermain said without preamble, and in a few terse sentences described the way Carachel had compressed their journey. "And there's no way we can outride that," he finished.

"Nor is there need to," Ranlyn replied. "Be at ease; I have dealt with such as he in times past, and the wearers of the Ring of Two Serpents hold no power without their talismans. He shall cast no spells until he finds us and reclaims his ring; that is the chief limit of the power of the Servants of the Red Plague.''

Uneasily, Jermain looked down at his belt pouch, and another thought struck him. ''Then Carachel won't stop looking for us after a day or two. He'll keep after us until he gets it back.''

''Yes.''

''Well, at least he'll have a hard time catching us if he can't use magic. No one in that camp has a mount as good as these. And unless he has better trackers than I think he does, he'll have to be lucky even to find us in this forest.''

''I would not say so much. We carry the ring, and it calls to him. He will come for it if he can, but it leaves no easy trail for him to follow, only a pulling at the strings of the heart. We can avoid him for many days.''

''Wonderful,'' Jermain said sarcastically. ''I already have one King trying to kill me; I didn't need another. Especially not one who's a wizard as well. It's a strange debt-clearing you've given me, that brings danger at our heels, and not one I'd have chosen willingly.''

For the first time, Ranlyn looked disturbed. ''Are you not under the protection of the Lady of the Tower? It was her amulet that guarded you against the wizard; I am sure of it!''

''The Lady of the . . .'' Suddenly the pieces fell together in Jermain's mind, and he stared at Ranlyn in consternation. *''Amberglas?''*

Ranlyn nodded. ''Indeed yes. She has long been a friend to me and my clan.''

''Then Amberglas is the one who promised you safe passage through Fenegrik Swamp?'' Jermain found it difficult to reconcile the power such a promise implied with his memory of Amberglas.

''Have I not said it? She owed no debt to us, yet she pledged us her help against the Red Plague. The Hoven-Thalar debt to her is great.''

''I see.'' Jermain did not feel capable of a more complete response. He remembered his conversation with Amberglas about his travels among the nomads, and wondered if she, too, had tried to use him. But she had asked nothing of him, and if she had told him less than she might have, it was only prudent to keep such plans secret from a chance-met stranger. He smiled slightly to think of Amberglas as prudent.

Abruptly, Jermain frowned. He knew that Amberglas was not the scatter-wit she seemed, but it was all too easy to think more of her apparent vagueness than of the abilities she displayed less frequently. He would have to be careful not to underestimate her, even if it was unlikely that they would meet again. His frown deepened. His judgment seemed rather poorer than usual lately. He had been mistaken first about Amberglas, then Carachel. And about Eltiron before that.

Jermain shook his head angrily, trying to dismiss the unwelcome thoughts of Carachel and Eltiron. Ranlyn looked at him inquiringly, but he shook his head again and slowed Blackflame briefly, so that they returned to their position behind Ranlyn. Conversation was not what he wanted at the moment.

They left the stream at midmorning, riding up a flat shelf of stone that formed the northern bank. Jermain nodded his approval; there would be no hoofprints in the river bank to mark the place for Carachel's men. "That was a stroke of fortune," he said as they rode away from the stream.

"The gods of fortune look with greatest kindness on those who do not ask for their favors," Ranlyn replied.

"You knew that rock was there?"

"I knew," Ranlyn said. "I have had much occasion to travel in these lands of recent years."

"Do you know how close we are to the border?"

"Another day's ride by common measure; less for such mounts as ours. And we may easily shorten the time if we speed our going."

"Not so fast, my friend. The last time I tried to get into Sevairn, the Border Guards nearly killed me; I'm not anxious to repeat the experience."

"The swordbearer Vandaris seeks you. Would she not arrange safe passage?"

"She might try, but I'm not willing to bet either of our lives on her succeeding. Marreth is the one who's King, and only the King commands the Border Guard." Jermain saw puzzlement in Ranlyn's face, so he explained his encounter with the Border Guard in greater detail. "They had orders to kill me," he finished. "And I doubt that the orders have changed."

"If we must choose between the sandstorm and the nest of snakes, I would prefer the snakes," Ranlyn said. Jermain looked at him, startled. "A careful man may keep from wak-

ing snakes, and a quick man may slay them. The sandstorm is
a surer death,'' Ranlyn explained smoothly.

Jermain laughed. ''And the Border Guard are the snakes?
Well then, we had best plan how to keep from waking them. If
I recall correctly, there's a major guardpost just south of
here.''

They discussed the matter as they rode, and decided to turn
their route slightly northward, to avoid the guardpost. Jermain was a little surprised at the ease with which Ranlyn
agreed to the change. After all, the new path would take him
farther away from the Hoven-Thalar clans, which were presumably heading southeast.

Once the question of direction was settled, they urged their
horses to greater speed. Though they had seen no sign of
Carachel or any of his aides, Jermain did not doubt that the
wizard would follow them. Even if he did not, Jermain wanted
as much distance between themselves and Carachel as possible, and Ranlyn seemed to agree. For the rest of the day, they
alternated their horses' pace between a steady trot and a brisk
walk.

A little after nightfall, they reached the general area of the
border between Sevairn and Barinash. The precise boundaries
of the kingdoms were not well defined, particularly in such
well-forested regions, and the two men spent a nerve-racking
two hours picking their way through the dark forest, hoping
that neither the Barinash nor the Sevairn guards had chosen
this night for a long patrol.

They continued riding almost until the middle of the night.
When they were well past the part of the forest where border
patrols were likely, they stopped and tended to their tired
horses, then ate a meager dinner of their own from the store of
food in Ranlyn's bags. When they finished, Ranlyn insisted on
taking the first watch. After a few moments of fruitless argument, Jermain capitulated. He rolled himself in his cloak and
lay down near the horses; in a few minutes, he slept.

Chapter Fifteen

Eltiron sat stunned. Vandaris and Terrel, betrothed? If that was what Terrel had been talking to Marreth about, at least one of them must be mad. In theory, thê King had the power to give his sister in marriage to whomever he pleased, but Vandaris would never accept such an order from Marreth, particularly when Marreth had announced his intentions in such an arbitrary way. And why in Arlayne's name would Terrel want to marry Vandaris?

"I don't suppose you'd care to explain why you haven't consulted me about this," Vandaris said. Her tone was mild but managed to carry to the far end of the hall without difficulty. Eltiron swallowed, wishing he were somewhere else.

"It is the responsibility of a King to provide for the welfare of his house and family," Marreth said. He looked very pompous and pleased with himself. "It is also a King's prerogative to reward those who serve him well. This marriage will do both with a single stroke; our most noble and loyal Lord Terrel Lassond will be allied to the royal house through our beloved sister, Vandaris, which—"

"Horse liver. What's your real reason, frog-face?"

Marreth's composure deserted him. "You're a disgrace to the royal house of Sevairn. My house! Running around with mercenaries and stirring up trouble—I should have done this years ago! You need someone to keep you under control, and I haven't got time!"

"You mean, you couldn't do it if you tried," Vandaris retorted affably.

"You'll marry Terrel tomorrow!" Marreth shouted, ignoring the embarrassed stirrings of the nobles and ambassadors. "I have the right, and there's nothing you can do about it!"

Vandaris's laugh shocked Eltiron almost as much as Marreth's announcement had. He turned and saw light flash from the hilts of Vandaris's daggers as she leaned back in her chair. "You've really done it this time, Marreth," she said, shaking her head. "Too bad you didn't ask me about it before you made a fool of yourself in front of the whole court. You can't marry off someone who's already married."

A ripple of astonishment ran across the crowd and died. Marreth stared at Vandaris in confusion. "You? Married?"

"I sure didn't mean Lassond, beetle-brain."

"Impossible!" Marreth brought his hands down on the table with a crash. "When could you have gotten married?"

"Oh, it *could* have happened any time in the last twenty years or so. Actually, it was right after the campaign in Tindalen, about sixteen years ago."

"Some soldier or other, I suppose! Well, I'll have the marriage declared null, and you'll marry Terrel Lassond anyway!"

"Don't be stupid. You don't want to offend Lisaren Corriel."

"Ha! What do I care about a mercenary?"

"He's the Queen of Tindalen's brother. Besides, even a King can't declare a marriage null if it has issue." Vandaris smiled sweetly at Marreth's rapidly purpling face. "Tarilane, meet your uncle; he's not much, but he's the only one you've got, so make the best of him."

There was a brief silence while everyone assimilated this new revelation, then Marreth began cursing incoherently. Vandaris shook her head in mock sadness and reached for her wine goblet. Marreth, infuriated by her composure, bellowed and lunged toward her. He shoved Crystalorn out of his way, chair and all; plates scattered as he bounced off the edge of the table, and the dark-haired woman on his left screamed. Still shouting, Marreth reached for Eltiron, who was the only person still blocking his path to Vandaris.

Eltiron caught a glimpse of Marreth's face—red, strained, and twisted with rage. Another plate crashed to the floor as the King lurched against the table; then Marreth gasped and clutched at Eltiron's arm. Eltiron stared in shock as Marreth slid slowly to the floor, half under the table.

For an eternal instant, no one moved. Then Vandaris shoved her chair back and knelt beside her brother. Eltiron watched numbly as she felt at Marreth's neck for a pulse, shook her head, and closed the eyes that were staring unseeingly past Eltiron's left shoulder. She hesitated, then gently removed the golden circlet from Marreth's head and stood up. A whisper ran across the crowd like wind over a field of grass, dying suddenly as Vandaris held up the circlet.

"King Marreth Kenerach is dead," she said in an expressionless voice and looked at Eltiron.

Eltiron heard a low wail from the woman who had been Marreth's dinner partner. Terrel looked white and sick; everyone else seemed simply shocked. Vandaris set the circlet in the center of the table. "The King is dead," she repeated, still looking at Eltiron. "What orders do you have, Your Majesty?"

"I—" Eltiron swallowed hard. He rose awkwardly to his feet and almost tripped on Marreth's body. He swallowed again and tried not to think about where he was standing; phrasing a suitable response was difficult enough without that added distraction. "I regret the inconvenience to my guests, but under the circumstances I do not think this a good time or place for feasting. I will order the meal served in the Long Hall for those who wish it." He glanced at Vandaris, who nodded encouragingly. "For myself, I beg to be excused. Until I have conferred with my—my advisers, I can make no firm plans. I bid you good eve, my lords and ladies."

Eltiron bowed and sat down rather quickly, pushing his chair backward as he did, so that he was no longer sitting directly above the body. He wanted to change to another seat, but he was not sure his legs would hold him up long enough.

Vandaris remained standing. "You have heard His Majesty's commands. Let it be done." She swept a cold gaze across the room before she turned and stepped down from the platform. Tarilane hesitated, then slipped quietly from her chair and followed.

The nobles stirred, then began slowly moving toward the doors. Most of them pointedly avoided looking in the direction of the royal table; a few, bolder or less tactful, studied the tableau openly. Except for Marreth's dark-haired woman, who was weeping delicately into her slender hands, no one still remaining at the royal table moved. Eltiron thought of the

rumors that would be circulating in another hour and shuddered.

A hand touched his shoulder, and he turned. It was
Crystalorn. She seemed a little shaken, and she kept her eyes
turned determinedly away from Marreth's body as she asked,
"Well, now what happens?"

"I don't know," Eltiron admitted. He looked around. The
hall was nearly half-empty. "Where's Amberglas?"

"Isn't she here?" Crystalorn looked startled.

"I haven't seen her since the sword-games. I suppose I'd
better get someone to look for her; we may need her later."

There was a gentle cough behind him, and Eltiron turned.
The castle steward and four footmen stood there, stiffly erect,
as if they were waiting for something. Vandaris brought up the
rear; as Eltiron looked at her, she jerked her head toward
Marreth's body, which was still lying almost at Eltiron's feet.
Eltiron gulped and gestured to the steward to proceed. The
men bowed and stepped forward to lift the body.

"Hold!" cried a voice from the end of the table.

The footmen stopped. Eltiron's head jerked around. Terrel
stood posed dramatically at the far end of the table, with
Salentor behind him; he appeared to be completely recovered
from the initial shock of Marreth's death. As Eltiron looked at
them, the two men bowed.

"Your Majesty," Terrel said in a much calmer voice, "I
fear you are about to make a grave mistake, and I must advise
you against it. The body of His late Majesty should not be
given into the hands of the Lady Vandaris until a thorough investigation has been made."

"What do you mean?" Eltiron demanded. He glanced
quickly around the room and breathed an inconspicuous sigh
of relief. The hall was now nearly empty; even Marreth's
woman had stopped weeping and was moving slowly toward
the door. Whatever mischief Terrel had in mind, very few
besides the royal family would hear it.

"Why, only that His Majesty's demise under such circumstances as these may give rise to unwelcome speculation.
Lady Vandaris appears to have sufficient reason to wish King
Marreth's death. It might be best to assure that no further
questions can be asked."

"I think you're forgetting that you are—you were—my
father's adviser, not mine," Eltiron said coldly. "And I still

don't see what you're talking about.''

"His Majesty was clearly in good health; his participation in the sword-games this afternoon proves it. Such a sudden death, and such a public one, is certain to raise questions in people's minds. It seems . . . unnatural.''

"Yes, yes; and people are certain to be upset at such a time," Salentor put in. Terrel gave him a murderous look, and he stopped speaking.

"Just what are you implying, weasel-face?" Vandaris said, ignoring Salentor. "Poison?"

"I would never accuse a member of the royal family of such an unworthy weapon, Your Highness," Terrel said, bowing.

"That is one of the silliest things I've ever heard," Crystalorn broke in. "You wiggle around until someone else says it, then you say you'd never bring it up yourself and sound virtuous about it! You're as bad as Salentor.''

"Probably worse," Vandaris agreed, ignoring Salentor's somewhat garbled protest. She eyed Terrel critically as she fingered the hilt of one of her daggers. "If I were you, I'd be careful not to start any unfortunate rumors. It might be very dangerous.''

"Besides, I trust Vandaris," Eltiron said hastily. Much as he would have liked to see Vandaris demolish Terrel in duel, he did not relish the idea of drawing the ring on the floor of the banquet hall, and Vandaris might well demand it if Terrel kept on with his insinuations. There would be more than enough rumors running through the streets of Leshiya without adding stories of a duel between the late King's Chief Adviser and his sister.

Terrel bowed. "Then, Your Majesty, I sincerely hope your trust is not misplaced.''

"Do you really?" said a new voice from the rear of the hall. "I don't think I believe you at all, though of course it would be quite improper for you to say anything else, besides being most unwise. But then, a great many people don't seem to mind being unwise, which is most unfortunate for them, though not always for other people.''

"Amberglas! Where have you been?" Crystalorn said. "You won't believe what's been happening.''

"That's extremely unlikely. Of course, a great many things are—unlikely, I mean—snow on Midsummer's Eve, for instance, and green sunsets, and those extremely improbable headdresses people used to wear in Bar-Zienar, which must have been exceedingly awkward as well as uncomfortable."

As she spoke, Amberglas came forward to join them. She smiled in Eltiron's general direction; he thought she looked a little tired. She nodded absently at Vandaris, totally ignoring Terrel and Salentor, and looked at Marreth's body for a long moment. She turned back to Crystalorn and continued, "Not that this isn't quite as awkward, though not in precisely the same way, even if it does look nearly as odd. So it's very difficult to be certain until you've told me."

Crystalorn began giving Amberglas a summary of the events of the evening. Eltiron glanced back at Terrel and Salentor and almost laughed aloud at their bewildered expressions. Eltiron turned away so that they would not notice his amusement and nearly bumped into the castle steward, who was still waiting patiently beside Marreth's body with the footmen.

"May we continue, Your Majesty?" the steward said, bowing as if he had not noticed Eltiron's awkward recovery.

"Yes, of course," Eltiron said. He thought of adding instructions not to speak of Terrel's hints, but one look at the stiff little nod the steward bestowed on Terrel convinced him that such a warning would be unnecessary. He turned away as the impassive footmen lifted Marreth's body and carried it out of the hall. After a moment, he heard the doors close behind them with a soft thud, and he let out a long breath just as Crystalorn said, ". . . and then Lord Lassond started hinting that Vandaris poisoned King Marreth."

"I must beg to differ with your interpretation, Your Highness," Terrel put in smoothly. "I would not dream of doing such a thing."

Crystalorn looked at him. Amberglas smiled in his general direction, looking even vaguer than usual. "Then you must be Terrel Lassond, which certainly explains a number of things, though most of them aren't particularly useful. But then, a great many people aren't at all useful, so it's not in the least unusual, even if it's not precisely the same thing. Still, it does make for rather a busy evening. What exactly *did* you say?"

Terrel blinked. "I said only that His Majesty's sudden death might cause unpleasant rumors."

"I shouldn't be at all surprised," Amberglas said. "Though people do occasionally say more than they intend to, which frequently causes a great deal of difficulty for everyone. Like that extremely foolish King who accidentally ordered his daughter dyed blue, which wasn't at all what he'd meant, besides being quite awkward at court. But then, a great many things are unusually awkward at courts—eating dinner with people who dislike each other, for instance, and wearing formal clothes, and telling the truth, which makes it quite understandable that people misunderstood.''

Terrel looked at Amberglas with a wary expression, as if he were certain she had insulted him but couldn't untangle exactly how she had done it. Salentor looked from Terrel to Amberglas and back, then cleared his throat uncertainly. Vandaris chuckled, and Terrel turned to look at her speculatively. "I am amazed, Your Highness, that you can find humor at so sad a time.''

"Look, onion-brain—"

"Wait a minute," Eltiron interrupted. He looked at Amberglas. "What did you mean a moment ago, about telling the truth and people misunderstanding?''

"I said it was frequently an awkward thing to do at court," Amberglas said calmly. "Which might explain why Terrel did such an extremely poor job of it, though of course it might be just that he hasn't practiced very much.''

The others looked from Eltiron to Amberglas in astonishment; Eltiron ignored them. "Are you saying Terrel's right? Vandaris really did poison my father? That's impossible!''

"Not exactly, though I suppose you could look at it that way. Of course, there aren't many things that are completely impossible, though I believe a few exist. Touching one's chin to the back of one's neck, for instance, and picking up a hole, and giving orders to a cat. At least, one could give the orders, but it's very unlikely that the cat would follow them. Still, I doubt very much that Vandaris is the person who was poisoning King Marreth.''

There was a brief stunned silence; then Vandaris said, "You're sure he was poisoned, Amberglas? It looked more like too much wine and too much temper to me.''

"And I don't see how anyone could have done it," Crystalorn said. "I've been sitting next to him since he got here, and everyone at the table drank the same wine he did.''

"Just not as much," Vandaris muttered.

Terrel looked at Crystalorn and bowed slightly. "Barinash has always watched Sevairn with great interest.''

An angry flush rose in Crystalorn's face, and Eltiron felt his own temper fraying. Crystalorn was certainly not responsible for any of the ''border incidents'' that kept a constant friction between the two countries! Or was Terrel trying to imply that *Crystalorn* was the one who had poisoned? . . .

''Under the circumstances,'' Eltiron heard himself say coldly, ''I do not find it odd that the Princess of Barinash should wish to observe her prospective father-in-law closely. And I will remind you again, Lord Lassond, that you were my father's adviser, not mine. I think you had better leave us.''

Terrel's eyes flickered. ''As Your Majesty wishes.'' He bowed and turned to leave.

''Not so fast,'' Vandaris said. ''Eltiron, I hate to say it but you can't let him leave. If he starts telling people that Marreth died of poisoning . . .''

''He would be quite wrong,'' Amberglas said firmly. ''Of course, he might not mind being wrong, though people generally do, which I suppose could be rather unpleasant for you.''

''But Amberglas!'' Crystalorn's voice was sharp with irritation. ''You said just a minute ago that King Marreth was poisoned!''

''I didn't say he died of poison,'' Amberglas corrected her gently. ''I said he was being poisoned, which is not at all the same thing, though it would have been if he hadn't died of something else first. Of course, it wasn't exactly something else; he probably wouldn't have collapsed at all if someone hadn't been giving him herrilseed.''

Eltiron stared. Herrilseed was a rare poison with unique effects: a large dose killed quickly, painfully, and obviously, but a series of smaller doses was just as certain, and nearly undetectable until death came. In addition, such small doses could be given years apart and still have the same effects. Eltiron felt sick; he'd eaten the same things as Marreth. Had he been poisoned as well?

Vandaris gave a low whistle. ''Herrilseed! You're sure?''

''Quite sure. There was the odor of lilacs, for instance, which are quite out of season just now, though not by much, and that unpleasant blue tinge in his fingernails. And of course herrilseed does tend to make one's temper extremely uncertain, though I understand Marreth's temper wasn't particularly certain to begin with, so it may not matter.''

"It would certainly explain a lot," Vandaris said thoughtfully. "We'll have to have someone take a closer look at him. How long do you suppose it's been going on?"

"Probably two or three months, though of course it's very difficult to say for certain; herrilseed is so very unpredictable. That is, unless one knows exactly how strong it is and how much someone has been eating, which is quite difficult to do if one isn't the person who's been giving it to someone."

Terrel was watching Amberglas narrowly, and as she finished speaking he smiled. "And how long have you known of this, my lady? Or is that, too, an awkward thing to say to a citizen of the country which is the source of herrilseed?"

"Dear me, what an extremely odd idea," Amberglas said, tilting her head to one side and studying the air three feet in front of Terrel's head with mild curiosity. "Whatever made you think I am a citizen of Barinash?"

Terrel's eyes moved from Amberglas to Crystalorn, and then to Salentor. "It was a natural assumption, my lady," he said without looking back at Amberglas.

"How very interesting," Amberglas murmured. "And which one of you made that assumption?"

Terrel's attention came back to her with a jerk, but before he could respond Crystalorn frowned and said, "Well, if somebody really was poisoning King Marreth, I think you're the one who did it! Nobody thought of poison until you started accusing people of things."

"King Marreth was my friend and patron, Your Highness; I would never have done anything to harm him. Besides, if I had been poisoning the King it would be foolish indeed for me to mention poison when no one else was looking for it."

Crystalorn eyed him for a moment. "I'm not so sure. You have the slinkiest mind I've ever seen; I'll bet you could come up with a good reason."

Terrel's eyes narrowed, but as he started to speak a dull knock echoed through the hall. He stopped short as the doors swung open and Tarilane appeared, followed closely by the tall figure of Wendril Anareme, commander of Sevairn's armies. They came forward, and Wendril bowed. "Your Majesty, Your Highnesses, my lords and ladies."

"Took you long enough to get here," Vandaris said, looking at Tarilane.

"I had trouble finding her in the crowd," Tarilane said

crossly, "and then everyone we passed wanted to know what was happening in here."

"Well, now you can go find Lord Farris, Lord Reistron, and Lord Hensel," Vandaris said without sympathy. "And while you're looking for them, you might listen for anyone suggesting that Marreth's death wasn't natural. It'd be useful to know whether there are any rumors, and if so, who's spreading them. Oh, and do try to be a little more inconspicuous."

Tarilane scowled as she left, and Vandaris turned to talk to Wendril. Eltiron hardly noticed. He was too busy watching Terrel and Salentor watch Amberglas. If he could only get rid of Terrel, and Salentor along with him! But Vandaris was right; they would only cause trouble if they weren't watched. Eltiron frowned and looked at Wendril, and inspiration struck.

"Commander Anareme," he said, "you're just the person I need. Could you find one or two trustworthy men to escort Lord Lassond and Lord Parel to their rooms? For their own protection, of course; I don't want someone to mistakenly blame one of them for the unfortunate events this evening."

A ghost of a smile touched Wendril's lips as she bowed again. "Of course, Your Majesty." She went to the door and exchanged a word or two with the guards outside. A moment later she returned with two large guards, who politely but firmly escorted Terrel and Salentor from the hall.

Eltiron watched them go with feelings of profound relief. It was only when he looked back at his companions that he realized they were all staring at him. "I wanted to get rid of them," he said defensively.

"So did we, numb-wit," Vandaris said. "I wasn't criticizing; I was just surprised you picked that way of doing it."

"If you had a better idea, why didn't you do something?" Crystalorn said.

"Does it matter now?" Vandaris transferred her attention to Wendril. "There's one other thing, though; make sure those guards don't let either of those two out of their rooms until tomorrow morning."

Wendril raised an eyebrow. "Won't that start a lot of rumors?"

Vandaris shrugged. "Would you rather have rumors of poison running all over the city? We can decide what to do with them when we've had a chance to talk."

"Poison? But I thought—I mean, everyone knows that Darinhal's been warning Marreth about his heart for years; I thought it was obvious what happened."

"It's more complicated than that," Vandaris said. "Someone was giving Marreth herrilseed; I'll explain more when the Council is over."

"I would think you ought to discuss it with the lords Farris, Reistron, and Hensel as well."

"Not tonight; we'd have to give too many explanations. I'll tell Darinhal to take a close look at the body, and he can make the discovery. Then we'll have another Council and a formal announcement. We need all the time we can get."

Wendril inclined her head, then looked at Eltiron. It was a moment before he realized that she was waiting for his approval; then he nodded. Wendril went to the door to pass the orders on to her guards.

"I still think Terrel was the one poisoning Marreth," Crystalorn said as Wendril left.

"He has the temperament for it," Vandaris agreed. "But I doubt that he's behind this."

"Why?"

"The only reason Terrel Lassond has for doing anything is that it benefits Terrel Lassond. He wouldn't gain a thing by poisoning Marreth; he'd lose. He's not enough of an idiot to think Eltiron will let him run the kingdom the way Marreth did."

Wendril rejoined them, and a moment later Tarilane returned with the three lords. Vandaris immediately began enumerating the decisions to be made. By the time she finished, Eltiron was profoundly depressed. There seemed to be an enormous number of things to be done, most of them in an impossibly short time. Funeral arrangements had to be made as soon as possible, and plans for Eltiron's coronation. The wedding would have to be delayed; it simply could not be held until after the funeral, and Eltiron would probably want to wait until after the coronation. In the meantime, formal messages and apologies must be sent to the ambassadors and lords who had come so far for the wedding.

Then there was the matter of the army, which still had not departed for the southern part of the kingdom. The lords Farris and Hensel disagreed strongly over where the army

ought to go; Lord Reistron did not think it ought to leave
Leshiya at all until after the coronation. At first, Eltiron had
difficulty keeping his temper; by the time the discussion was
over, he was having difficulty staying awake.

At last the conference ended. A few of the most pressing
issues—notably the funeral arrangements and the postpone-
ment of the wedding—had been dealt with enough to allow
others to begin work. The remaining decisions had been put
off until a more formal meeting could be called. Eltiron
groaned inwardly, foreseeing more days spent in interminable
meetings. As soon as the conference was over, Vandaris
hauled Eltiron off to the Long Hall to make reassuring comments to whatever guests still remained. Not until the last of
the nobles had left was Eltiron able to go to his rooms and
consider all the implications of his sudden change in status.

The following day was even worse. Eltiron spent most of it
accepting condolences from the nobles of Sevairn and wondering when Darinhal would burst in with the news of Marreth's
poisoning. He saw little of Vandaris and nothing of Crystalorn or Amberglas. He would have liked to order everyone else
out of the room so he could talk to Vandaris or Crystalorn,
but these were the most important lords of Sevairn and he
could not justify insulting them just to serve his own whims.
Besides, that was exactly the sort of thing Marreth had done
all too often, and Eltiron did not want to start his reign by
behaving in the same arbitrary manner as his father.

The only good thing about the day was that he did not have
to deal with Terrel. Vandaris, it appeared, had slipped sleep-
ing drops into his morning meal, then put about the story that
Terrel was keeping to his rooms, overcome with grief for the
King. Eltiron did not think it was a terribly convincing story;
Vandaris cheerfully admitted that he was right.

"But it doesn't matter," she told him. "Lassond was Marreth's adviser; people expect advisers to change when there's a
new King. They won't believe he's grieving, but no one will be
surprised that he's keeping out of the way, either."

It was a relief not to have Terrel around, but Eltiron continued to worry about him during odd moments of the day.
Terrel could not be kept away from the court for much longer,
and when he finally did appear, he would have more to complain about than Marreth's poisoning. Something would have
to be done.

Unfortunately, all Eltiron's worrying did not give him any idea of what the something should be. By the time he returned to his rooms at the end of the day, he was too exhausted even to think clearly about the problem. His thoughts developed an uncomfortable tendency to focus on the memories of Marreth's red, strained face, of Vandaris's frozen calm, of the limp mound of the body as it was carried away. Finally, Eltiron gave up and went to bed, but it was a long time before he fell asleep at last.

Chapter Sixteen

Jermain awoke to darkness. He lay still for a moment, trying to identify the source of the uneasiness he felt, but he was unsuccessful. He sat up, and behind him Blackflame moved restlessly. Jermain sniffed; there was a faint smell of burning in the air. Feeling more uneasy than ever, he put out a hand toward the small pile of belongings that contained his dagger.

A dark shape at the foot of a tree stirred, and Ranlyn's voice, disembodied by the darkness, said, "Your time of watching is not yet."

Jermain stopped in midreach. "You've seen nothing?"

"No more than the common restlessness of a forest. Had it been otherwise, I would have roused you."

Feeling slightly foolish, Jermain sat back. It was true; nothing seemed unusual except the uneasy feeling that had receded but not yet vanished. After a moment, he shook himself. "I thought I smelled smoke."

"It comes from no fire of my making, nor have I seen another fire to be its source."

"Maybe I dreamed it. Look, it may not be my watch yet, but it can't be too much longer. I might as well take over now."

"As you will have it."

Jermain reached again for his dagger. His hand closed around the hilt, just above the sheath, and he was surprised into a cry of pain as the heat seared his palm. He dropped the dagger and clenched his other hand around his wrist, as if he could block the pain by squeezing hard enough.

Ranlyn was at his side almost before the dagger hit the ground. "What goes?"

"My dagger—when I picked it up, it burned my hand."

Ranlyn's head turned to look at the still-sheathed knife. He reached down and brushed the hilt with a fingertip, quick as a cat's tail twitching. He flicked it again, less carefully, then picked the dagger up. "There seems no evil to it now."

Gingerly, Jermain touched the hilt with his good hand. "You're right. But I don't see—"

Something flickered at the edge of his vision, and he broke off and looked down. His leather belt pouch now lay on top of the pile of odds and ends he had removed when he lay down. Smoke was curling from its surface in a thin stream that seemed to glow faintly yellow in the darkness.

Ranlyn's gaze followed Jermain's, and he went very still. Then he set the dagger carefully on the ground and groped behind him in the darkness until he found a short stick. He watched the smoke an instant longer before he reached out and prodded the pouch with the end of the stick.

The leather cracked and fell apart in small flakes, releasing a puff of smoke and a charred smell. Among the fragments of the pouch, the serpent ring glowed and flickered with a harsh, yellow light that made the serpents appear to move and twist about each other. The light was not bright, but it hurt Jermain's eyes. Heat radiated from the ring; it was like standing in front of a smith's forge.

"Debt of Kazaryl!" Ranlyn whispered. His face was drawn, and the strange light gave it a sick yellow tinge.

"What in—"

"That accounting must wait. For now, I ask your silence."

Jermain nodded. Ranlyn did not take his eyes from the ring, but after a moment he let out his breath in a long sigh. Slowly, he stretched his hand out above the ring and began murmuring in the language of the nomads, too rapidly for Jermain to follow. The ring's light began reluctantly to fade.

Then, with shocking suddenness, light flared again, brighter than before. Ranlyn cried out and fell backward, dragging Jermain with him. The two men sprawled on the ground, staring at a globe of light the size of a man's head that surrounded the ring. Within the globe, something like crimson smoke shifted and flowed, hiding the ring almost entirely except for occasional glimpses. But it looked too alive for smoke, and

Jermain felt chilled as he looked at it.

Ranlyn made a strangled noise. Jermain glanced at him just as light flared a second time, blindingly bright, then died completely. Jermain waited, motionless, while his eyes readjusted to the darkness. When nothing further happened, he looked across at Ranlyn. "What was that?"

"My debt to you is beyond speaking, and the debt I owe your people and my own is greater than the height of the sun. He who wore that ring is more powerful than I had guessed, to make use of a ring he does not wear."

"Carachel did that? I thought he couldn't reach us without the ring!"

"He was not reaching for us, but using the power of the ring for some other purpose. And that should be impossible to him, yet it was not."

"How do you know that? And when did you learn so much about magic?"

"I am no student of such sorcery as you of the north use. Yet my clan is one appointed from the earliest times to guard the path of the Red Plague and warn against its coming. So do we know some few ways of dealing with it and with the Servants of the Red Plague, and one of these I used against the ring. And even then I did not accomplish my purpose, but awoke the Red Plague instead. I have been too certain, and so brought danger on us both."

"That red smoke was this Red Plague?"

"A part of it only, and not clearly seen. But almost do I pity this sorcerer, if the Red Plague comes again to the call of his spells."

"As long as it ignores us, I'm not going to worry about him. And I thought you said it was your spell that brought that thing."

"Can a rock-lizard command the wind, or a sand mouse call the lightning? I do not know if the Red Plague sought my spell or if that wizard worked its waking for some purpose, but I am sure it yields control to neither of us. Should he use the ring again, and the Red Plague comes, we have no certainty of safety."

"Wonderful. Do you have any more good news?" Ranlyn shook his head, and Jermain sighed. "Well, now that it's happened, what do we do about it?"

"This storm is of my own making; therefore will I take the

danger it brings upon myself, and leave you to make your way where you will. For myself, I must take the ring to the Lady of the Tower, and if I reach her in safety I will give her my knowledge and abide by her advising.''

"You can't involve Amberglas in this!"

"She has given aid to my clan, and she seeks to halt the Red Plague. I owe her a debt of what knowledge I may give her. I have already made a mockery of my debt-clearing to you; do not ask me to abandon this as well.''

"You're right," Jermain said after a moment. "I wasn't thinking. But if you're taking that ring to Amberglas, I'm coming with you. I'm not leaving you to face Carachel alone.''

"No! Would you make my burden heavier still?"

"I don't think you have a choice. You gave me that ring as a debt-clearing; mistake or no, you can't take it back unless I let you. And I won't, unless I come with it.''

Ranlyn's head bowed, and for a long moment there was silence. Then he said in a low voice, "As you will. What I owe you now, only my death can repay.'' He rose and turned away. Jermain watched as Ranlyn wrapped himself in his cloak and lay down beside the horses, his back toward Jermain.

After a moment, Jermain picked up his dagger and strapped it on. His burned hand made it an awkward job, but at last he was satisfied that he could reach the knife easily with his good hand. Then he returned to his saddlebags to look for something to bind the burn. When the job was finished, he chose a tree and sat down. Eyeing the ring warily, he settled back to take his turn on watch.

Ranlyn was moody next morning. He did not speak except in response to direct questions, and Jermain did not press him. They ate and saddled the horses in silence, studiously ignoring the small pile of charred leather with the serpent ring at its center. At last, just before he mounted, Ranlyn retrieved the ring, first carefully wrapping his hands with cloth so that he would not touch it directly. He transferred the wrapping to the ring, then concealed it somewhere in the folds of his robes. Finally he mounted and turned to Jermain. "You are still of the same intention?''

"I'm coming with you.''

"Then we ride north to the tower." Ranlyn turned his horse's head.

"Wait!" Jermain sat frowning, mentally counting days.

Ranlyn looked at him. "I have told you I will do this."

"That's not the problem. I don't think we'll find Amberglas at her tower. She was leaving for Leshiya the last day I was there, to go to Princess Crystalorn's wedding, and I don't think she's had time to get back. She's probably still in Leshiya!"

"You are sure?"

"Count it up for yourself. I'd guess it's a week's trip at least to Leshiya from Amberglas's tower, and the wedding preparations would take at least three weeks, probably four. And it's only been three and a half weeks since I left the tower."

"It is possible. But it will take five or six days for us to reach the city, and if you are wrong we will have as much again before us."

"And if I'm right it would take us just as long to get from here to the tower and from there to Leshiya, and by then she probably *would* be gone. Do you think I *want* to go to Leshiya? I just want to get this over with."

"It is not certain," Ranlyn said after a moment. "But he who meddles with sorcery finds few things certain. We will ride for Leshiya." He glanced at Jermain. "This does not change your resolve?"

Jermain shrugged. "Carachel is more dangerous than Marreth. I still have a few friends in Leshiya, and you said Vandaris was looking for me. She may have made some arrangements. It's a risk, but what isn't?"

"Then let us begin." Ranlyn shifted slightly in his saddle, and his horse began to move.

They rode in silence for most of the day, stopping once to catch two squirrels to supplement Ranlyn's dwindling store of food. Jermain's burns did not affect his horsemanship, though they continued to pain him. By nightfall the two men were nearing the edge of the forest, and Ranlyn's mood improved considerably. Jermain began to relax, hoping that Ranlyn had at least accepted his presence as inevitable.

Neither of them mentioned the serpent ring until they made camp at last. Then, after a short discussion, Ranlyn drew it out of his robes and placed it on a rock beside their fire, where

it could be watched easily during the night. Neither Ranlyn
nor Jermain saw any further manifestations during their
watches, but when they started off again next morning,
Ranlyn refused to allow Jermain to carry the ring. Jermain
made only a token protest; he knew that however small
Ranlyn's knowledge of the ring might be, it was certainly
greater than his own. If something did begin to happen,
Ranlyn might have some idea what to do.

By midmorning they were out of the forest and traveling
north and west toward Leshiya. Though they kept a watchful
eye on their trail, they saw no signs of the pursuit they expected, and Jermain began to hope that they had managed to
gain a respectable lead. Near midday they passed a village and
stopped briefly to replenish their supplies. After that they
avoided towns as much as they could.

They camped that night in a field. The weather was fine,
and Jermain preferred not to take the small risk of being
recognized at an inn, while Ranlyn claimed to be more comfortable sleeping in the open. Once again, Ranlyn set the serpent ring where they could watch it, and twice during his
watch Jermain thought he saw it flicker, though he was not
certain enough to awaken Ranlyn. When he mentioned it next
morning, Ranlyn looked grave and set a faster pace for that
day's travel.

They made good time. Ranlyn elected to abandon the fields
in favor of one of the smaller roads, and riding became easier.
Near noon, Jermain saw the walls of the city of Felsdon near
the western horizon. He pointed them out to Ranlyn and said,
"We're doing better than I'd expected. If we keep this speed,
we'll be in Leshiya in less than three days."

He paused, squinting, then reined Blackflame in. A low
cloud of dust was rising south of the city, along the line of the
road he knew was there but could not see. Jermain could
almost make out the forms of the men and animals that raised
it, and the banners that rose above the dust were so familiar
that he did not need to see them clearly. "Ranlyn! Look
there!"

Ranlyn turned in the saddle, then nodded slowly. "It would
seem that the sister of your King has had her way; the army of
Sevairn moves south. It is as well we are no nearer. We can
avoid them without trouble."

"Yes. But I wish I knew how she did it," Jermain muttered.

He watched the shifting dust with mixed feelings. If Vandaris had persuaded Marreth to send the army south, she might well have found a way for Jermain to get safely into Leshiya. On the other hand, if Marreth had not changed the order of exile, the army could easily become a grave danger to Jermain, and its presence served as a painful reminder of his former achievements.

"Jerayan. You delay to little purpose." Ranlyn's voice pulled him away from his thoughts. Jermain glanced again at the distant column of the army, then shook Blackflame's reins and started forward once more.

For the rest of the day they rode in silence. At twilight they halted and made camp in a small wood by the side of the road. They cared for the horses, then gathered wood for a fire and sat down to eat. Ranlyn seemed moody and withdrawn, and finally Jermain asked him point-blank what was wrong.

"The web of my debts grows tangled," Ranlyn answered, "and it is difficult to balance the claims of deeds with those of duty. Yet no man is ever free of obligation, nor of the choice of paths it brings."

"I will release you from your debt to me."

"If a man stands at the sea's boundary and commands the water to vanish, will it do so? Twice now have you kept me from death at risk of your life: once when you offered water and your own blood to draw the skag-morrah away from me, and again when the Servant of the Red Plague would have denied my breath. Such obligation cannot be cleared in words."

Jermain shook his head, remembering the long, lizardlike creature he had found preparing to feed on a paralyzed nomad. "I'd have done as much for anyone I found in straits like that! I've seen what a skag-morrah leaves of its prey; I wouldn't abandon my worst enemy to that."

"That only makes my debt the greater."

"Doesn't my debt to you count for something? I owe you at least as many life-savings as you owe me. And you showed me the truth about Carachel."

A sudden smile lit Ranlyn's face. "The place where debts merge and balance is a problem never yet made clear. Where wise men debate to no conclusion, shall you and I solve matters? Yet some debts I have no desire to see ended, and the friendship I owe you is one of those."

"I'm glad to hear you speak so plainly," Jermain said with an answering smile. "Sometimes your explanations are . . . less than clear."

Ranlyn laughed. "You are a diplomat, in truth. But it grows late, and tomorrow brings more travel. Will you watch first, or I?"

"I'll take it this time."

Ranlyn nodded. He reached inside his robes and drew out the small package that contained the serpent ring, then paused, listening. Jermain looked at him questioningly; then he, too, heard the sounds of something approaching. Ranlyn thrust the package back into his robes and Jermain rose and loosened his dagger in its sheath.

A moment later, a horse and rider appeared among the trees, heading directly toward their fire. The horse moved as if exhausted; at the edge of the ring of firelight, it stopped and stood trembling while its rider dismounted. He was a short, dark-haired man who looked as if he had spent the past three days riding, with very little pause for sleep and none at all for grooming.

"Sirs, I beg your hospitality for myself and my animal," the man said with a smooth bow. "I am on an urgent errand for Sevairn's King."

Jermain's eyes widened in recognition, then narrowed. "Salentor Parel! And what 'urgent errand' could you have for the King of Sevairn?"

Chapter Seventeen

Eltiron was awakened by a loud pounding on his door and the sound of someone shouting, "Eltiron! Morada's sword, man, wake up! Eltiron!" He rolled to his side and sat up. "All right! I'm awake!" he shouted. "Just a minute!"

The pounding subsided. Eltiron struggled hastily into the first garments he found, then opened the door. Vandaris was pacing in the hallway, her boot heels ringing faintly on the stone floor. She looked up as Eltiron emerged. "Lassond's gone," she said without preliminary.

Eltiron stared for a long moment, then swallowed hard as pictures of the possible results began to whirl through his mind. "How?"

"I don't know exactly, but he had help. I'd guess that man-servant of his, and probably someone else as well. The guard was still unconscious when I left."

"And Salentor?"

"I sent Tarilane to check. She'll meet us back at Lassond's rooms."

"Tell me what happened," Eltiron said as they started down the hallway toward the wing of the castle that had housed Terrel Lassond.

The answer was, very little. Vandaris had been awakened by the Captain of the castle guard. The man assigned to relieve the guard at Terrel's door had arrived to find the door open and the man he was replacing unconscious on the floor. He reported to the Captain at once, and since Wendril Anareme had gone with the army, the Captain came to Vandaris. Vandaris had stopped only long enough to check the man's story before coming to awaken Eltiron.

By the time Vandaris finished her explanation, they had reached Terrel's rooms. Eltiron saw one of the castle guards sprawled in front of the open door; another knelt beside him. "Errin's Tomb, hasn't he come around yet?" Vandaris demanded.

"No, Your High—Captain Kenerach," the kneeling guard said. "Nothing seems to help. Captain Lorrach left to notify the gate guards and get a healer."

Eltiron heard the exchange with only half his mind as he stared uneasily into the dark interior of Terrel's rooms. Hadn't Tarilane said once that no one but Terrel and his servant ever went inside? Eltiron remembered the mysterious conversations he and Crystalorn had overheard, and shivered. Then his eyes widened and he turned to Vandaris with a jerk. "Vandi—"

"Vandi!" Tarilane's call came echoing down the hallway. A moment later Tarilane arrived, panting. "That Lord Salentor is gone, too. His guard's just like this one."

"Dragonfire and starshine, those worm-hearted weasels must own half the people in the castle! Tari, go find Captain Lorrach again, and tell him Parel's in it, too."

"No," Eltiron said before Tarilane could reply. "First go tell Amberglas, and ask her to meet us in the courtyard right away. You can find Captain Lorrach after that."

Tarilane looked at Eltiron, then at Vandaris. Vandaris raised an eyebrow, and Tarilane looked back at Eltiron and shrugged. "You're the King." Then she grinned and ran off down the hall.

Eltiron turned to Vandaris, who was watching him with a quizzical expression. "I'm sorry, Vandi, I didn't mean—"

"Sweet snakes, man, don't apologize! She's right; you are the King. But why wake Amberglas now, and why the courtyard?"

"Because of the Tower of Judgment," Eltiron said. "Remember, I told you I'd seen Terrel that day, and I thought he might—"

He was interrupted by a blistering oath from Vandaris. "I should have thought of that," she said when she finished cursing. "My brains must be going soft from too much court life. If Lassond's been dealing with a sorcerer, the first thing he'll do is report. Come on!" She gave a few brief instructions to the kneeling guard, then she and Eltiron hurried down the hall.

The courtyard was dark and quiet; the torches set beside the castle doors only emphasized the blackness beyond. Eltiron could see a light in the gatehouse, and the shadows of the sentries moving inside, but that was all. Even the moon had set, and the silhouette of the Tower of Judgment was barely visible against the stars.

"Doesn't look as if they've tried to get out of the castle yet," Vandaris said.

Eltiron jumped. Vandaris didn't seem to notice. "Wait here," she said and walked across the courtyard to the gatehouse, leaving Eltiron standing uneasily in the shadows beside the door.

Vandaris returned a few moments later. "The guard says it's been quiet; unless Lassond and Parel have grown wings, neither of them has tried to leave the castle yet. So let's check the tower."

Eltiron shifted uncomfortably. "Shouldn't we wait for Amberglas, or at least—"

Light flashed once from the top of the Tower of Judgment. Vandaris bit off an exclamation and sprinted for the tower door. Eltiron followed, feeling more uncomfortable than ever. As they approached the tower, he thought he saw a shadow slip away from the door. He started to call a warning to Vandaris, and then a bright crimson globe bloomed from the top of the Tower of Judgment and Eltiron was knocked to his knees by a sudden wave of pain.

Dimly, Eltiron heard a cry of agony from somewhere far above him, and the startled shouts of the sentries, but he could not concentrate on anything but his own pain. He felt as if he were being slowly flayed alive and turned inside out, or as if a hundred leeches were trying to eat him by sucking him out of tiny holes in his skin. He cried out, and something rose within him, hot and white and burning. Even alone, it would have been nearly as hard to bear as the pain that surrounded him; the two together made him feel as if he were being pulled apart. He cried out again, and the white flame grew and touched the pain outside him.

Light flared from the Tower of Judgment, so bright that it penetrated even the haze of pain enclosing Eltiron. And then

the pain and the light were gone, with a suddenness that made
Eltiron gasp, and he found himself kneeling just outside the
door of the tower. He drew a deep, shuddering breath and
realized that Vandaris was bending over him, a look of concern on her face. Behind her, two sentries stood with drawn
daggers and bewildered expressions.

Eltiron tried to speak, but it was a moment before he had
his breath back. "I'm all right now, I think," he said at last.

From the corner of his eye he saw the sentries relax slightly,
but the worried look did not leave Vandaris's face. "For how
long?" she demanded.

"How should I know?" Eltiron said as he climbed to his
feet. "I'm not even sure what happened!"

"It looked like the same sort of fit Marreth had, without the
temper. Blood of the Black Bull, if someone's been giving you
herrilseed as well—"

"Dear me, that *would* be awkward." Amberglas's voice
came from the direction of the castle. Eltiron turned to see her
coming toward them, apparently oblivious to the confusion of
soldiers and staff that was developing in the courtyard. "At
least, it would be awkward for some of the people here in
Leshiya; I expect it wouldn't matter in the slightest to the
Emperor of Hern. Whatever made you think of it?"

"We'll discuss it later," Vandaris said, nodding toward the
growing number of curious guards and servants who clustered
around them, murmuring and eyeing the Tower of Judgment
warily. "Right now I want to find out what was going on up
there."

Eltiron looked at the tower. "All right, then, let's go."

"You aren't coming. Dragon's teeth, you're the King; you
think you can just walk into a dangerous situation without a
reason?"

"Not at all," Amberglas said firmly as she moved forward.
"He isn't going to walk, he's going to climb, which is quite
different, besides being much safer than staying out here
where he can't really do much. Of course, there are a great
many people who don't do much and who are quite safe,
though perhaps a bit boring; still, I'm afraid Eltiron isn't one
of them, which is probably just as well since most people don't
like being bored."

Vandaris's eyes narrowed, then suddenly she laughed. "All
right, Amberglas. But we're taking a couple of guards with us,

just in case something else starts happening.''

"Of course." Amberglas smiled and moved toward the tower door. For a moment, Eltiron looked after her without moving. He was not sure he wanted to see whatever was waiting at the top of the tower. On the other hand, he also did not want to stand in the courtyard and simply wait for Vandaris to return or for the pain to come again. With some reluctance, Eltiron followed Amberglas toward the tower. Vandaris came behind him with two sentries carrying torches.

At the top landing of the tower they paused to catch their breath, then Vandaris pushed the door open. Nothing moved in the darkness outside. After a long moment, the two sentries raised their torches and stepped cautiously forward, sending uncomfortable shadows flickering across the tower-top ahead of them. They were halfway to the battlements when one of them made a choking sound. The guard turned and motioned; his face was a sick yellow in the torchlight. Vandaris hurried forward, then stopped short. "Morada's crown!" she said in a shaken voice.

Eltiron joined her and looked down. A dark shape sprawled bonelessly on the stones, barely recognizable as that of a man. Only the head and one hand were visible outside the loose folds of clothing, and they were dry and shrunken. The lips were pulled apart in a death's-head grin; the skin was stretched so tightly that it had split in places, revealing streaks of raw, red flesh and white bone. Eltiron looked hastily away, feeling sick.

"Dear me, how very unpleasant," Amberglas murmured.

"More than unpleasant, I'd say," Vandaris replied. She squatted beside the corpse, frowning, then looked at the sentries. "This isn't Lassond, unless he's taken to wearing servant's clothes. Keep looking."

The guards nodded without enthusiasm and began walking around the curve of the tower in opposite directions. Almost immediately, one of them shouted. Vandaris rose and walked over; Eltiron followed more slowly. The guard was standing over a second crumpled shape, this one huddled against the base of the tower battlements. Eltiron carefully did not look closely.

"That's Lassond," Vandaris said after a moment. "Blood and rust, he looks worse than the other one! What did this?"

"I believe it was the Matholych," Amberglas said calmly.

"There are very few other things that are quite so thorough about killing people, and most of them aren't at all likely to frequent towers at night. Not that it's a particularly likely thing for the Matholych to do, either, but—"

"The Matholych was here?" Eltiron interrupted. "You're sure? But how did it get here?"

"That exceedingly foolish person, Terrel, probably did something to bring it, though not, I expect, deliberately. Accidents are so very easy, particularly if one doesn't know exactly what one is doing, which is quite likely in this case, what with sorcery being so very unpopular in Sevairn. Still, it could be rather useful to know precisely what it was he did."

"*Lassond* was a sorcerer?" Vandaris shook her head. "I don't believe it!"

"I don't believe I said he was a sorcerer, though it's quite possible. Not, of course, that it's at all likely he was a particularly *good* sorcerer, or I doubt he'd have gotten into such a predicament." Amberglas looked in Eltiron's direction. "It's really quite fortunate you were here; it would have been so very inconvenient to have the Matholych in Leshiya. Rather like having a basilisk in one's cellar, which would be extremely awkward for practically anyone. I don't suppose you'd care to find out what he's holding?"

Vandaris gave Amberglas a startled glance, then bent forward. Eltiron looked down and swallowed hard. Vandaris was right; Terrel did look worse than the first body. He forced himself to watch as Vandaris gingerly pried the shrunken fingers apart, revealing an intricate web of gold wire with a large amber stone set in its center. It was the same medallion Eltiron had seen on the night he and Crystalorn had overheard Salentor and Terrel talking.

"How exceedingly unfortunate," Amberglas said. Eltiron looked at her and felt a slight sense of shock. Amberglas was gazing directly at the medallion, her eyes narrowed and her face intent.

"What is it?" Eltiron asked.

"That," said Amberglas without looking away from the medallion, "is an amulet for speaking across distances. It's a rather strong spell, and quite difficult to set up, though of course anyone can use the amulet once it's been made."

"Who in Arlayne's name would give something like that to

Lassond?'' Vandaris demanded. ''And who was he talking to with it?''

''Dear me, I thought you knew. It was made by a Black Sorcerer named Carachel; that's his mark on the front, just below the stone.''

''The Wizard-King of Tar-Alem?'' Eltiron said.

''Carachel is *not* a wizard,'' Amberglas said firmly. ''Though I believe a great many people think so, which is quite—''

''Blood-rot and shadowfire!'' Vandaris exploded. ''Do you mean that this lizard-livered, slime-hearted, toad-brained vulture in peacock's feathers was nothing but a Tar-Alem *spy*?''

Before Amberglas could reply, there was a groan from the far side of the tower. Vandaris's head jerked around and she motioned to the sentries. One of them gave her the torch he was holding and faded into the darkness, while the other started forward, sword in hand. Eltiron heard another groan, then a series of scuffling noises and a loud scream. A moment later the sentries returned, dragging a burly man in the bedraggled uniform of a Border Guard of Sevairn. His face was covered with small red blotches, and he was screaming in evident terror.

''Now what?'' Vandaris muttered.

''How very interesting,'' Amberglas said. ''It's Captain Morenar. At least, that's who it was a month ago, but perhaps he's changed since then; I don't believe it would have been at all bad for him.''

''You!'' The Border Guard stared wild-eyed at Amberglas. ''You brought the brown fog and made us walk, but I came back and got him out to call about you, only the red mist came, and it burns and burns and burns. . . .'' He collapsed, sobbing.

''Well, at least he's getting quieter.'' Vandaris looked at Amberglas. ''You know him?''

''Not really,'' Amberglas said. ''We met once, when he was chasing Jermain Trevannon in Barinash, which was not at all justified. Still, I really don't believe that's a particularly good reason to be rude. I sent him to the Dragoncrest Mountains.''

''He's the one who was trying to kill Jermain?'' Eltiron said, and the pieces came together in his mind. ''I knew Terrel was behind it!''

"Doesn't surprise me," Vandaris said. "And I'd bet he's the other one who helped Lassond escape. Not that it did either of them much good."

"Do you think—" Eltiron was interrupted by another loud scream from the prisoner.

"Carachel knows!" he shrieked. "Carachel knows about you now! I told the lord and the lord came here and told him, before the red thing came, before it came, before—"

"He's madder than Marreth," Vandaris said disgustedly. "Who stuck the bat in his skull?"

"I rather think the edge of the Matholych touched him, which would certainly account for his extremely odd behavior, though he didn't have that excuse the first time, and perhaps—"

Another scream from Morenar interrupted her. He lunged forward, breaking free of the guards, and reached for Amberglas. Just before he touched her, the sorceress made a brushing motion with her hands. Morenar went reeling backward in a shower of sparks, right into the arms of the guards.

Amberglas studied him absently for a moment, then made a small flicking gesture with her left hand. Eltiron felt a sudden cold sensation run down his back like ice water trickling from the point of a knife. Morenar, who had begun cursing incoherently, broke off in midword and sagged slowly to the stones of the tower-top.

The two sentries looked uneasily from their suddenly sleeping captive to Amberglas; their expressions held considerably more respect than they had earlier. Vandaris shook her head. "That's a relief. How long will he stay that way? And will he make any more sense when he wakes up?"

"Not a great deal, I'm afraid; it's rather difficult to do anything about the Matholych's damage, which is one of the things that makes having it around so very awkward. He'll wake up in the morning or whenever someone calls him."

"Good. Leave him there, then, and take a look around in case there's another one we've missed," Vandaris said to the sentries. "And if you find anything odd, don't touch it."

The sentries nodded and left. Vandaris looked down at Terrel's body once more and shuddered. "And we still have to do something about this. Is that thing he's wearing safe to touch?"

Amberglas leaned forward and touched the amulet lightly with one finger. Her expression became suddenly intent. "How *very* interesting," she murmured.

"What is it?" Eltiron asked.

"Black Sorcery," Amberglas said absently. "Or rather, using Black Sorcery in the Tower of Judgment, which of course is precisely what Terrel did when he used this amulet. I believe that's what summoned the Matholych, though of course it's difficult to be quite certain without trying it, which really wouldn't be at all advisable under the circumstances."

"If using sorcery in this tower summons the Matholych, why didn't it show up a few minutes ago when you put Morenar to sleep?" Vandaris demanded.

"I didn't say using sorcery summoned it. I said using Black Sorcery summoned it, which is quite different. I don't believe it's at all surprising that something like the Matholych would be attracted by Black Sorcery, and of course anything that eats magic would be quite interested in any of Galerinth's towers, what with all the magic in them, even if it is the wrong sort of magic to suit the Matholych. At least, I think it is; the Matholych is such an extremely odd creature that it's very difficult to be entirely sure."

"Will you take care of that amulet, then, Amberglas?" Eltiron said. "No one else in Leshiya knows much about magic, and I don't think I want anyone starting with that. Particularly not if it's likely to bring that—that *thing* back." For some reason, he found himself reluctant to name the Matholych aloud.

"I think that would be quite wise." Amberglas bent and retrieved Terrel's medallion, eyed it thoughtfully for a moment, and put it in the pocket of her gown just as the sentries returned.

As soon as Vandaris established that there was nothing else on the tower-top, she insisted that the sentries be left to take care of Morenar and the two corpses while Eltiron and Amberglas accompanied her back to the courtyard. "After all that fire and flash, people are going to start worrying if you don't show up again soon," she told Eltiron. By the time they reached the foot of the stairs it was clear that Vandaris was right; even through the heavy wood of the tower door Eltiron could hear the rising din of the crowd outside.

Vandaris put her hand on the door, then paused and looked at Eltiron. "You want to make the speech? They're sure to want one, and it'll look better from you."

"I—oh, all right," Eltiron said.

"Just tell them everything's fine and they should go back to bed; we'll make an announcement in the morning. It won't be bad."

Before Eltiron could reply, Vandaris shoved the door open and stepped out of the tower. The crowd quieted somewhat as she held up her hand and called loudly, "His Royal Majesty, King Eltiron Kenerach!"

Eltiron stepped forward to stand in front of the crowd. He had forgotten just how many guards and servants and courtiers lived in and around the palace, not to mention the additional numbers who had come to help with the wedding. He swallowed hard and started talking. It was not as difficult as he had expected, once he had begun. When he finished, Vandaris made some pointed remarks to the guards who were nearest the tower, and they began clearing the courtyard.

"Thank Viran that's done," Vandaris said. "Wait here a minute, Eltiron; I want to talk to the Captain at the gates."

Eltiron nodded, and Vandaris left. She returned a moment later, looking grim.

"Salentor Parel's gone."

"You're sure?"

"Nobody saw him, if that's what you mean, but I'll bet my best boots that he got away during the fire show on the Tower of Judgment. All the guards came rushing out here when the lights started, and one of them found the outer guardhouse door unlocked when he finally bothered to go back and check. I sent a message to the guards at the city gates to watch for him, but I don't think they have much chance of catching him; there are just too many strangers in Leshiya."

"But Salentor's the Barinash ambassador! How are we going to explain this?"

"Blame it on Lassond. He can't contradict us, and the sooner he's completely discredited, the better."

"I suppose so," Eltiron said dubiously, "but I don't think Crystalorn is going to like this much."

Eltiron was right; Crystalorn did not like it. Her reasons,

however, were not quite what he had expected—Crystalorn was incensed at being "left out" of the night's excitement. She refused to speak to him for most of the day, which lent color to Vandaris's "official explanations" but did very little for Eltiron's state of mind. To top matters off, Darinhal, the castle physician, chose that morning to announce his "discovery" of Marreth's poisoning. Eltiron had just enough presence of mind to blame that, too, on Terrel's sorcery.

Amberglas added to Eltiron's uneasiness by announcing that Terrel's rooms appeared to have some sort of protective spell around them, which was not at all the sort of thing one normally found in Sevairn, at least not in the past several hundred years, though it might, of course, have been quite normal before that. Eltiron listened long enough to learn that the spell had probably been set through Terrel's medallion, then immediately ordered the entire wing of the castle evacuated. He had no desire to let the Matholych turn any of his guests or staff into shriveled corpses if it should reappear. Only when the evacuation was underway did he turn back to Amberglas.

She did not appear at all put out by Eltiron's behavior; she simply informed him that it would take a great deal of time to remove the spell, unless of course he wanted everything inside Terrel's rooms to crumble into dust, which would almost certainly be dreadfully inconvenient for the castle housekeeper. Eltiron told her that he did not want Terrel's rooms or anything in them crumbling to dust, and he would appreciate it very much if she would remove the spell.

He left her staring absently at two candles, three gold buttons, a small bag of powdered herbs, and a brown striped kitten that had somehow found its way into the castle, and he found himself wondering just how Amberglas intended to use such an odd assortment of things to break the spell on Terrel's rooms. Shaking his head slightly, he went looking for Vandaris.

He found her in the courtyard with Tarilane, and she pounced on him at once, demanding his reasons for evacuating an entire wing of an extremely full castle. When Eltiron explained, she shook her head and agreed grudgingly that it was probably a good idea, but it would certainly complicate the preparations for Marreth's funeral the following day.

"Tomorrow?" Eltiron said. "But—"

"We can't wait forever, turtle-skull, and it will settle people down a bit. Besides, it's time you moved into the King's chambers."

"I don't think I want to, at least not until we find out how Father was being poisoned."

Vandaris looked startled. "You're right. And that reminds me; where's Crystalorn? Somebody has to search Parel's rooms, and since he was the Barinash ambassador it'll be better if she gives her consent. She *is* the Princess of Barinash, after all."

Eltiron did not feel ready for another confrontation with Crystalorn. Despite his slightly garbled protests, Vandaris dragged him off, with Tarilane trailing behind them. Fortunately, the prospect of searching Salentor Parel's quarters had a wonderful effect on Crystalorn's disposition, and she immediately apologized to Eltiron for her earlier temper.

When they reached Salentor's rooms there was a brief argument concerning whether he, too, had a protective spell on his belongings. Tarilane settled matters by walking inside while Eltiron and Crystalorn were both trying to talk at the same time. When nothing happened to her or to the contents of the rooms, the others joined her.

Vandaris began systematically working her way through Salentor's belongings. Eltiron, Crystalorn, and Tarilane stood and watched; Vandaris made it quite clear before she began that she was not anxious for their inexpert assistance.

"Parel was in even more of a hurry than I thought," she commented after a time. "He didn't take a single gold chain or jewel with him, as far as I can tell."

"Maybe he wasn't expecting to get out of here," Crystalorn suggested.

Vandaris was working at the lock on one of the desk drawers. "I'd still expect him to take time to—aha!" The drawer opened at last; she sorted quickly through the contents and pulled a small wooden box from the back. "This looks interesting!" She flipped the lid of the box open.

"Well, what is it?" Crystalorn said impatiently after a moment.

Vandaris turned and held the box out. It was half-full of a pale green dust. "Powdered herrilseed," Vandaris said in an expressionless voice.

Chapter Eighteen

For a long moment, Salentor stood staring at Jermain. Then he sagged against his horse in evident relief. "Trevannon! Then Carachel does know what's been happening."

Jermain hardly hesitated. "You doubted it?"

"I haven't been able to reach him directly for nearly four days." Salentor sat down heavily beside the fire. "But I certainly didn't expect him to send *you* to Sevairn."

"The decision was made at the last minute," Jermain replied carefully. Pretending to be still in Carachel's service could be an extremely dangerous game. On the other hand, the opportunity to untangle a little more of Carachel's web of intrigue was too good to pass by. He noticed that Ranlyn was maintaining an impassive silence and thanked Arlayne for the nomad's quick wits.

"I assume Carachel gave you a message for me," Salentor said in a tone very close to arrogance.

Jermain's eyes narrowed. "Certainly not. This matter was of far too much importance for us to wait for a message."

"But if you have no message—"

"I believe King Carachel is following a few days behind us. Presumably he will give you your *orders* when you see him. You can, of course, wait for him to arrive before you give your news, but I doubt he would be pleased."

Salentor wilted. "Of course, of course. Ah, how much do you know?"

"You are aware that Carachel has placed me in complete command of his armies?"

"He informed me of it some weeks ago," Salentor admitted reluctantly.

"Then I believe you may gauge the extent of his trust from that. As we left the camp in rather a hurry, however, it will be best if you make your tale as complete as possible. We know the broad outlines, of course, but there are doubtless many important details you can give us."

"It's all the fault of that woman the Princess insisted on bringing with us from Barinash!" Salentor burst out. "She managed this all, somehow!"

"If you are referring to Amberglas, my information is that she is a sorceress," Jermain said in bored tones.

Salentor looked at him, visibly startled. "Terrel did manage to warn you! What does Carachel intend to do about her?"

"That is for him to tell you, if he sees fit," Jermain said with an outward show of polite firmness. Inwardly, he was shaken. Carachel was in league with Terrel? How long had that been true? He smiled and said, "But perhaps you have some suggestion in the matter?"

Salentor reddened. "I am not the one who should deal with sorcerers."

"You deal with Carachel."

"Yes, and see what it's brought me! For eighteen years, I've helped him, since he first visited Barinash, and he thinks more of Terrel Lassond than— But that is hardly important now."

"I hadn't realized you had served Carachel so long," Jermain said mildly. He wondered briefly whether Salentor was always so clumsy or whether it was exhaustion and lack of sleep that made him so careless of what he was saying. "Then you've worked with him since before he became King of Tar-Alem."

"Yes, and he knew how to value a favor then! When he and the Queen were—" Salentor stopped short, as though he had just realized he was being indiscreet. He looked at Jermain uncertainly. "You will forget you heard that?"

"You need have no fear; I have no interest in old scandals," Jermain said. It sounded as though Carachel had tried to gain power in Barinash the same way he had eventually done in Tar-Alem—through the country's Queen. Of course, Annawan of Barinash had been King Urheld's wife, not his daughter, so the parallel was not exact.

"I admire your discretion." Salentor made an awkward half bow without rising.

"Thank you. But I fear I distract you from your tale. Perhaps you would begin with your arrival in Sevairn?"

"I thought Terrel had already reported all that," Salentor said suspiciously.

"Of course, but I would like to hear your version. I have no great reason to trust Terrel Lassond, for all he serves the same ruler as we."

Salentor looked at him sharply, and for a moment Jermain thought he had gone too far. Then Salentor began to speak, and in a matter of moments Jermain realized the reason for his reluctance. No matter how he tried to hide it, Salentor's performance in Leshiya was little short of incompetent. He had begun by trying to undermine Terrel's position with Carachel, but he had reckoned without Marreth's uncertain temperament and Terrel's deviousness. By the time he arrived in Leshiya, Terrel had already taken full credit for arranging the wedding that would bring Sevairn into alliance with Barinash and, through Barinash, with the Wizard-King of Tar-Alem. Salentor's efforts to regain Carachel's favor by persuading Marreth to send troops to join Carachel's army had backfired. Apparently, Marreth did not trust Salentor any more than Jermain did, and the fact that he was receiving similar counsel from his own advisers only made him more suspicious.

Foiled in his initial attempts, Salentor had begun prowling the back channels of the Sevairn court, looking for information. He had found a good deal of it, and he repeated nearly every piece of gossip in detail. Jermain listened carefully, though only three items were of any real interest to him: the rumors surrounding Eltiron's role in Jermain's exiling, the reports of Eltiron's sojourns in the Tower of Judgment with Amberglas, and the vague hints—hardly more than guesses—that Terrel Lassond was playing his own game in addition to Carachel's.

"You are certain of this?" Jermain said. "Carachel is unlikely to accept such accusations without proof."

"I didn't have time to get proof," Salentor said, turning red. "I only heard of it the day the King died, and that was when everything fell apart."

This time Jermain was not quite successful in hiding his

reaction. Marreth, dead? "I'm sure that confused matters," he said after a moment. Salentor looked at him suspiciously, and Jermain forced a bland smile. "But please continue."

"It was at the wedding festival, four days ago. Marreth was trying to outshine that sister of his in the sword-games, and Terrel spent most of the day clinging to him like a wet cloak. That made me suspicious, but I wasn't sure what it was about until the feast, when Marreth announced Terrel's betrothal to Vandaris."

"Vandaris consented to that?"

"Apparently Marreth didn't ask her; he and Terrel arranged it between themselves."

Jermain stared for a long moment, then bust into laughter as a picture of Terrel married to Vandaris rose irresistibly in his mind. "That would be a wedding to remember, certainly!"

"Maybe, but I doubt it was part of any plan of Carachel's to put Terrel Lassond in the line of succession to the throne of Sevairn!" Salentor snapped.

"Marriage to Vandaris would hardly do that; even if Marreth and Eltiron were both dead, she'd never let her husband rule in her place. Anyone who's met her could guess that."

"There are ways to arrange such things," Salentor said evasively. "Fortunately, it came to nothing because Vandaris is already married—at least she claims she is, and I'm certainly willing to believe her brat of a sword-squire is her daughter."

"Vandaris, married?" Jermain made no attempt to hide his surprise.

"I didn't think Terrel would have mentioned that," Salentor said with some satisfaction. "Her announcement was what set Marreth off, and when he collapsed so suddenly she took over and ordered everyone out. Terrel tried to stop her and nearly ruined everything, accusing her of poisoning Marreth."

"King Marreth was poisoned? Terrel said nothing of that!"

"*Terrel* said nothing? But it was Carachel who—" Salentor stopped, and his suspicious look returned. "I thought you said Carachel trusted you with his plans."

"What is spoken is but a shadow of the truth of the heart, and shadows dance to whatever flame is nearest." Ranlyn spoke for the first time, and Salentor jumped. Ranlyn leaned forward, and the firelight made his face a mask. "The one you speak of owes a debt of life and truth and honor to him who sits before you, and this is truth. Yet beware lest the truth be lost by your own understanding of it. For men see what they wish, but truth changes not for their desires."

Salentor looked at Ranlyn uncertainly. Jermain leaned forward and stared coldly at the former Barinash ambassador. "I think you had better go on, Salentor," he said in a tone of command. "Unless you wish to accuse me of something?"

Salentor's eyes jerked from Ranlyn to Jermain, and he swallowed hard. "No, of course not," he said hastily. He launched into a confused explanation, though he continued to dart distrustful looks at Jermain from time to time. Jermain gathered that Carachel had given Salentor some sort of drug to give to the King of Sevairn, that Salentor had been able to give Marreth only one of the doses he had been told to administer, and that Terrel had ruined everything with his accusations, which resulted in Amberglas discovering that someone had actually been giving Marreth poison.

"Not that *I* believed her; there was no way she could have known, and she said it had been going on for months, which is ridiculous. Besides, he obviously died of some sort of seizure. Then Terrel and I were hauled off to our rooms by the guards and confined without the slightest reason! Of course, I tried to get in touch with Carachel at once, but he didn't respond to the amulet at all."

Jermain frowned. Clearly, Carachel had provided his henchman with some spell, so that he could relay information such as Marreth's death. Slowly, Jermain nodded. Four nights before, he and Ranlyn had made their precipitous departure from Carachel's camp, taking with them the serpent ring and leaving the wizard in no condition to work magic. No wonder Salentor had gotten no reply!

"They kept us locked in all the next day," Salentor continued. "I would probably still be there if one of Terrel's men hadn't returned to Leshiya and helped us escape. He was the one who told us that Amberglas was a sorceress. He's a Border Guard, a Captain named Morenar."

"Morenar is one of *Terrel's* men?" Jermain said in surprise. "I thought his loyalty was to the King!"

"I'm sure Carachel thinks so, too," Salentor replied with satisfaction. "But it was quite clear from some of the things they said that Morenar's been following Terrel's orders first for some time. He wouldn't talk much about it, but I think he found out about Amberglas on one of his jobs for Terrel."

"I'm sure Carachel will be very interested to hear about that," Jermain said thoughtfully. So it was Terrel, not Marreth, who had been responsible for that attempt to kill him! Jermain looked at Salentor. "So Morenar helped you escape?"

"Yes, and we could have gotten away with no one the wiser if Terrel hadn't insisted on going up the Tower of Judgment to contact Carachel. He hadn't been able to do it from inside the castle, either."

"The Tower of Judgment? Why in Arlayne's name would he do that?"

"He *said* it was easier to work the spell from there. He went up with Morenar and some servant of his, and I stayed in the courtyard. Terrel was gone for some time, and then there was some sort of red light from the top of the tower, which of course attracted everyone's attention. I had to slip away in the confusion before I was noticed; I'm afraid the others didn't get away. That was two days ago; I've been riding south ever since, to make certain Carachel was warned."

Or rather because he'd had no choice left, Jermain thought. It occurred to him that two nights ago Carachel's ring had become hot, and he and Ranlyn had seen the Matholych in its glow. There was almost certainly a connection. Jermain leaned forward. "And have you attempted to reach Carachel again since you left Leshiya?"

"Uh, yes, I did try once or twice, but he never replied. The spell didn't seem to be working very well; I think the medallion may have been damaged."

"I am not surprised, after what you have been through," Jermain said diplomatically. Salentor's manner made him certain that the man was lying. "If there is some other problem, no doubt Carachel will explain in more detail when he arrives. For now, I suggest you rest; Ranlyn and I will split the watches tonight, as you are clearly exhausted."

Salentor nodded, apparently pleased by this consideration. Jermain smiled inwardly; he did not trust Salentor to stand watch. Salentor settled himself by the fire, and in a few moments was, to all appearances, fast asleep.

Ranlyn looked at Jermain. "And now what wish is yours?"

"None. You sleep; I'll take the first watch. Lord Parel has given me much to think on."

Ranlyn nodded, smiling slightly, and his eyes rested briefly on Salentor's recumbent form. Jermain needed no further hint to be certain that Ranlyn believed no more than he that Salentor slept. "Ponder well, then," Ranlyn said. He crossed to the shadows on the opposite side of the fire from Salentor, rolled himself in his cloak, and lay down.

Jermain felt a momentary twinge of conscience as he realized that Ranlyn still carried the serpent ring somewhere in the folds of his robes. Still, they certainly could not leave the package out where Salentor might see it. Finally Jermain put the matter out of his mind. He had more than enough to think about without worrying over what he could not change.

Salentor's information had shaken Jermain thoroughly. He coldly reviewed everything he had learned, acknowledging his mistakes and trying to fit more of the puzzle in place. It was a humbling exercise. Very few things, apparently, were as he had believed them to be. He seemed to have done Marreth an injustice, believing that it was the King who wished to be rid of a troublesome ex-adviser, and he had badly underestimated Terrel's influence and ability. From what Salentor had said, Terrel had been working for Carachel for nearly a year. It was therefore fairly likely that Carachel had been involved in Jermain's dismissal from the Sevairn court, though he probably had not ordered the subsequent attempt to kill him. For one thing, the Wizard-King had taken Jermain into his service barely five days after the attack, which was not the action of a man who wanted to be rid of him. Besides, it was fairly clear that Terrel had his own plans; murdering Jermain could easily be one of them.

Slowly, Jermain worked his way down a mental list of the notables of the Sevairn court, trying to decide which of them were in league with Terrel and Carachel and which were not. Several times he thought of Eltiron, but each time he shoved the thought away. It kept returning, and finally he grew uncomfortable enough to face it squarely. Had he misjudged Eltiron as he had so many others?"

Reluctantly, Jermain forced his memory back to his last day in Leshiya, the day of his trial and exile.

The Tower of Judgment loomed above him as the guards escorted him across the courtyard. There was no one else in sight, and Jermain felt a twinge of misgiving. Surely Marreth had realized by now how ridiculous the charges really were? But the courtyard would not be empty at this hour of the morning unless Marreth had ordered it, and such orders were given only when the most dangerous of criminals were being brought to trial.

His fears were confirmed when he reached the second floor of the tower. There were only three people waiting in the trial room: Marreth, Acrol Corteslan, and Terrel Lassond. It would be a private trial, then, the sort given when the accused was clearly guilty of treason. But how could Marreth truly believe that? Terrel might have fabricated some "proof" to support his claims, but Marreth was unlikely to accept it without support from some other quarter.

Jermain bowed deeply to the King. He wondered briefly why Eltiron was not present; as Prince, the boy had the right to attend even a private trial if he wished, and Jermain would have expected him to come, if only to show support for a friend. But perhaps Marreth had deliberately not informed his son of the time.

Marreth motioned, and the guards left. As the door closed behind them, he cleared his throat. "Let's get this over with. Jermain, you're charged with treason against the throne of Sevairn. I assume you deny it?"

"Yes, Your Majesty."

"All right." He turned to the two courtiers to start the debate. "Corteslan, Lassond, you were both at the Council meeting. What're your opinions?"

"There are many ways of interpreting Lord Trevannon's actions," Acrol began doubtfully. "And the Hoven-Thalar invasion is something that should certainly have been brought to Your Majesty's attention."

"Assuming, of course, that there will in fact be a Hoven-Thalar invasion," Terrel said. "No one else has heard a whisper of such a move."

"Well, yes, but—"

"And Lord Trevannon did refuse to say just how this news came to him, and to him only," Terrel went on smoothly. "But perhaps now he will explain?"

Jermain did not reply. Once the debate started, the accused was allowed to participate, but he would not play into Terrel's hands by trying to answer such an obviously slanted question. Better to remain silent.

"He certainly should have told Your Majesty how he knew of this supposed invasion," Acrol said, turning to Marreth.

"It seems a little convenient, does it not?" Terrel said. "Perhaps Lord Trevannon used his influence among the Hoven-Thalar to arrange—"

"What influence?" Jermain demanded. "Whoever told you that lied!"

"You accuse my son of lying?" Marreth rumbled.

"Prince Eltiron?" Jermain stared, stunned. Despite his youth, Eltiron was among the few members of the court that Jermain both liked and trusted unreservedly. Eltiron would not have joined in Terrel's accusations. Would he?

"I believe you'd already left the Council when the Prince mentioned it," Acrol said.

"And what, exactly, did His Royal Highness say?"

"He told us about your visits to the Hoven-Thalar caravan," Marreth answered. "And that spy you met there. So there's not much point in dragging this out any longer. Unless you have something to add?"

"Prince Eltiron's evidence was most helpful," Terrel murmured.

Anger swept over Jermain. So Eltiron had been spying on him! How else would he have learned of Jermain's trips to see Ranlyn? And he had not even had the honor to make his accusations to Jermain's face; he had waited until Jermain had left the Council before he spoke. It must have been Eltiron's support that had persuaded Marreth to take Terrel's accusations seriously.

Jermain looked at Marreth. He could see from the expression on the King's face that Marreth's mind was made up, but he tried to argue anyway. It did him no good. With brutal swiftness, the trial proceeded to conviction and sentencing, and Jermain was stripped of position, title, goods, and country. . . .

A stick fell in the center of the fire, sending up a shower of sparks and bringing Jermain's mind back to the present. He frowned, trying to sift the facts from his memories. Clearly, Eltiron was the one who had told the Council of Jermain's visits to the Hoven-Thalar; Marreth, Acrol, and Terrel had all said as much. But if Eltiron had been part of Terrel's plot to discredit Jermain, why hadn't he attended Jermain's trial?

The fire burned low while Jermain fought to separate the truth from his own assumptions. Finally he gave up. He could not say that Eltiron was blameless, but there was at least a slim chance that the Prince had not deliberately betrayed him. With that conclusion he would have to be content, at least until he had more information.

He rose stiffly and added wood to the fire, noting with surprise how much time had passed. When the fire was burning well once more, he shook Ranlyn awake and they exchanged places. He was more tired than he had realized, for despite his emotional turmoil, he slept almost at once.

A horse's shrill scream brought Jermain to his feet almost before he was fully awake. The scene before him drove every other thought from his mind. On the opposite side of the campfire's remains, Blackflame was rearing and pawing the air. In front of the angry horse, Salentor dodged and backed away to the full length of the reins he had wrapped around his left arm. As Blackflame descended, Salentor jerked viciously at the reins, causing the horse to stumble.

Jermain shouted and started forward, drawing his dagger as he ran. The cry distracted Salentor; he looked over his shoulder and saw Jermain just as Blackflame reared again. The reins tightened, jerking Salentor forward. He had time for one terrified scream before Blackflame's iron-shod hooves descended on his head and he collapsed to the ground. Blackflame stepped fastidiously away and stood waiting for Jermain.

Jermain inspected Salentor just closely enough to be sure he was dead, then unwound Blackflame's reins from Salentor's arm. The horse tossed his head and moved a little farther away, and Jermain looked around for Ranlyn. After a moment, he located a crumpled heap in the shadows near the dead fire, and he went over and knelt beside it. Ranlyn appeared to be alive and unharmed, but nothing Jermain did could wake him, and his skin was cold and damp. Finally, Jermain gave up. He spread his cloak over the unconscious nomad and went back to examine Salentor's body in hopes of finding some explanation for Ranlyn's condition.

The Barinash nobleman lay face down, one side of his head crushed by Blackflame's hooves. When Jermain turned him over, the first thing that caught his eye was the large gold medallion Salentor was wearing. Jermain reached for it, then paused. Even through the layer of dirt that covered it, he could see the stone at the medallion's center glowing faintly. He shoved the medallion to one side with a short stick from the stack of unused firewood and continued searching.

Nothing else was immediately obvious, but when he touched Salentor's belt pouch, he found that it was warm. Cautiously, he opened it and dumped its contents on the ground. He was hardly surprised to find the little package of cloth that contained the serpent ring among the rest of Salentor's odds and ends. A faint glow was visible through the wrapping. He cupped his hand above it without touching it and felt the heat radiating through the cloth; then he sat back, thinking.

The medallion was the basis of Salentor's spell for contacting Carachel. Somehow, Salentor must have used it to reach Carachel and learn of the true state of affairs between Jermain and the Wizard-King; that would explain how Salentor had found out about the serpent ring and why he'd been trying to escape with it. Carachel must have thrown a spell on Ranlyn, or Salentor would never have been able to take the ring from him. But surely Carachel would have cast his spell before if he could have done so; either he was much closer than Jermain and Ranlyn had thought, or . . .

Jermain looked from the cloth-wrapped serpent ring to the dirt-covered medallion. Both were still glowing; presumably both were necessary to whatever spell Carachel was using. And hadn't Salentor implied that damage to the medallion would keep it from working? Jermain picked up a rock, then looked back at Ranlyn and hesitated. What if destroying the medallion didn't break the spell, or made it worse? But he could think of nothing else to try, and he could not afford to wait long if Carachel was getting closer. He brought the rock down, then pounded on the medallion until the central stone was cracked and the gold was bent and twisted.

When he finished, he looked at the ruins of the medallion for a moment. There was no trace of a glow. He stretched a hand toward the package that held the serpent ring, and felt no warmth from it. Sure that he had accomplished something, but uncertain as to what, Jermain turned back to Ranlyn. This time he had no difficulty in rousing the nomad, and he explained quickly what had happened.

When he finished, Ranlyn shook his head. "I might have

guessed some ruse when he who lies dead there went privately to give his water back to the land. What he did was done then, for I have memory of little after it."

"It was Carachel's ring that knocked you out, then?"

"It was the ring."

"That thing's been nothing but trouble; for a wooden half-pence, I'd leave it sitting there."

Ranlyn looked at him with concern. "You would return it to its wearer, and with it the greater portion of his power? There is little wisdom in this."

"I know, I know; we don't have much choice. I just hope Amberglas will know what to do with it when we get to Leshiya."

"As you say. And the matter grows more urgent."

"That's obvious," Jermain said. "Salentor would have gotten away completely if he hadn't been stupid enough to try to steal Blackflame, and if Carachel is close enough to cast spells . . ."

"Distance can mean less to a sorcerer than to the wind. Yet while we have his ring, it is the only barrier we can depend on."

"Then we'd better make it as big a barrier as we can," Jermain said grimly. "Blackflame's saddled and the fire's out; I can check the rest of Salentor's gear while you get ready. Night travel has never been one of my favorite pastimes, but I think we have to try it."

Ranlyn nodded and the two men rose. Jermain dragged Salentor's body into the bushes while Ranlyn saddled his horse, and in a few minutes they were ready to leave. Jermain untied Salentor's horse and set it free, then swung into his saddle. Without looking back, the two men rode into the darkness, heading in the direction of Leshiya.

Chapter Nineteen

Eltiron stared at the box in Vandaris's hand. "I don't understand! Salentor couldn't have poisoned Father; Amberglas said it's been going on for months, and Salentor's only been in Leshiya for two and a half weeks or so."

"That doesn't mean anything, slow-top. He could have hired someone months ago to start the job, or he may just have been supplying it to someone else. One thing's sure, though; Salentor Parel was involved somehow. Herrilseed isn't exactly the sort of thing someone keeps around to cure headaches."

"Are you going to announce this to the court tonight?" Crystalorn asked. She looked a little white, and she seemed to be deliberately avoiding Eltiron's eyes.

"Storm and starfire, no!" Vandaris said. "Things are confused enough already. If we give away all our information, we'll never get this mess unraveled. Unless you want to tell them," she added, turning belatedly to Eltiron. "After all, they're your court."

"I don't think we should tell anyone but Amberglas right now," Eltiron said promptly, and was rewarded with an approving nod from Vandaris and a shaky smile from Crystalorn.

"Then let's see what else we can find." And Vandaris went back to her search. She found nothing else of interest, and finally she called a halt. She locked the room once more, then went with Tarilane to inform Amberglas of their discovery. Eltiron, after a brief and highly unsuccessful attempt to converse with Crystalorn, returned to his duties.

Marreth's funeral occupied most of the following day, due
in large measure to the number of speeches. Each of the other
six kingdoms had sent a representative to Sevairn for Eltiron's
wedding, and all of them had to be allowed to deliver their
condolences publicly. To do otherwise would be to risk offending both the ambassador and the ruler he represented. By
the time the last of them finished, Eltiron thought he was
beginning to understand why his father had been out of temper so frequently.

The day ended with a feast, but Eltiron did not enjoy it.
Crystalorn had been avoiding him all day, and he spent most
of the evening trying to find out what was bothering her. The
Princess of Barinash looked a little more flushed than the
warmth of the room would justify, and she seemed uncomfortable. Unfortunately, a formal banquet was a difficult
place to hold a private conversation even when both parties
were cooperating; when one of them appeared to be actively
attempting to prevent such a conversation, it became impossible. Crystalorn could not avoid Eltiron completely, since she
was seated beside him as his promised bride, but she could
keep up an animated conversation with the ambassador from
Vircheta on her other side.

Finally, Eltiron stopped trying to talk to Crystalorn and
concentrated on watching her. By the time he left the feast, he
was profoundly disturbed. It was not merely Crystalorn's
uneasiness; he had also noticed the sidelong looks and furtive
whispers of the lords and ladies of Sevairn when they glanced
in Crystalorn's direction. He wondered how they would have
behaved if they had known that the Barinash ambassador had
kept a box of herrilseed in his rooms. It was not a comforting
thought.

He was still worrying when Vandaris arrived the following
morning. She wasted no time, but went right to the point of
her visit. Lord Reistron had cornered her at the end of the
feast the night before. "He wants you to call off your marriage to Crystalorn," Vandaris said.

"I can't do that! We'd have the Barinash army on the border in less than a month if we insulted them so badly."

"Reistron doesn't think so. Besides, he's not suggesting
sending her home right away, just delaying the wedding a few
times until the situation becomes obvious to everyone."

Eltiron stared at Vandaris. "He told you that?"

"Not in so many words, but his meaning was clear enough. He's not the only one, either; everyone knows you didn't have much hand in picking your bride, and there are plenty of people who don't like the idea of an alliance with Barinash."

Eltiron looked at her a moment longer, then turned away and began pacing angrily up and down the room. He was nearly as annoyed with himself as with Reistron. He had never even thought about what effect Marreth's death and Salentor's flight might have on Crystalorn's position in Sevairn, and he'd seen little of her in the days preceding the funeral. No doubt that had been additional fuel for the gossips. And there had certainly been gossip; if Reistron was willing to approach Vandaris about canceling the wedding, half the court must be speculating about the possibility. Crystalorn herself must be aware of it; it would explain at least some of her behavior at the feast.

It occurred to him suddenly that he did not *want* the wedding to be canceled. But how was he ever going to explain that to Crystalorn, after he'd let this kind of rumor start? "Now what do I do?" he muttered.

"Think about it before you do anything," Vandaris said. "Even a snail-brain like Reistron gives good advice once in a while. If you intend to be a reasonably good King, you'll have to learn to tell when."

"You mean you think he's right?"

"I meant what I said, stone-skull, and not a featherweight more. I learned a long time ago not to give people advice about getting married. It's not worth the effort; they never listen anyway unless they figure it out for themselves. So stop thinking with your temper and start using your brain. You might start by considering who wanted Sevairn and Barinash allied, and why."

Eltiron frowned. Terrel was the one who had talked Marreth into the wedding, and from what Crystalorn had said, Salentor had persuaded her father to consent. Both advisers were involved somehow with Carachel, but why would Carachel favor an alliance between Sevairn and Barinash? Eltiron could think of nothing, but the idea that the Wizard-King of Tar-Alem might be interested in his marriage to Crystalorn made him profoundly uneasy.

His thoughts were interrupted by a perfunctory knock at the door. An instant later, Tarilane burst into the room. "Vandi!

We just— Oh, good morning, Your Majesty. Vandi, Amber-glas wants you to come to that Lord Terrel's rooms right away. She says she's found something important. At least, I think that's what she said.''

Vandaris was on her feet before Tarilane stopped speaking. Eltiron followed more slowly, considering. At the door he stopped and looked at Tarilane. "Would you find Princess Crystalorn and tell her, too?"

"But I—Oh, all right, Your Majesty."

"Don't worry; we'll see that nothing exciting happens before you get there," Vandaris said dryly.

Tarilane gave her a disgusted look and left. Vandaris turned to Eltiron and grinned. "Made your decision already, hmmm?"

"She ought to be there, that's all," Eltiron said. "Salentor was involved in Terrel's plotting somehow, and he might have had something to do with Father's death. Whatever Amber-glas has learned, Crystalorn has a right to know about it."

"Praiseworthy sentiments," Vandaris murmured, but her lips twitched as she turned and started down the corridor.

They reached Terrel's rooms before Crystalorn, but not by much. She and Tarilane arrived moments later, looking flushed and out of breath, just as Vandaris raised her hand to knock on the door. Crystalorn gave Eltiron a puzzled look, then the door swung open and they all went in. Eltiron was not sure whether to be glad or sorry that she had not said anything.

Inside Terrel's rooms, the air was dry and smelled of dust and unfamiliar herbs. Two small rugs by the door and a large bowl of faded flowers were the only spots of color; the walls were lined with brown books and small, oddly shaped boxes. On the other side of the room, Amberglas stood behind a long table, frowning faintly down at a small bone, a fist-sized rock, two boxes, a book bound in crumbling leather, a packet of letters, and what looked like a large map of the Seven Kingdoms. She looked up as they entered.

"Dear me, all of you at once. Not that I object, though with only one chair it may be a bit uncomfortable for some of you, since I expect you'll all want to hear about things. People generally do, even if the things aren't particularly interesting, and then of course when one starts explaining they become bored very quickly."

"Tarilane said you'd found something important?" Eltiron said, looking with uneasy curiosity at the odd collection of objects on the table.

"Several things, to be precise. Though some are only important to a Black Sorcerer, which is just as well, since Black Sorcerers are interested in such extremely unpleasant things. Or someone who wants to be a Black Sorcerer, which is not at all wise, though of course some people do, or there wouldn't be any. Black Sorcerers, I mean; there are a great many things that there would be a lot of no matter what people do. Or don't."

Vandaris scowled. "Lassond was a Black Sorcerer?"

"Not exactly, though of course it's very difficult to be certain. There isn't a great deal of difference between the sorts of things a Black Sorcerer keeps in drawers and the sorts of things someone who merely wants to be a Black Sorcerer keeps in drawers. On the other hand, most Black Sorcerers would have been much more thorough about the warding spells. Still, he was certainly trying."

"What was it you wanted to tell Vandaris?" Eltiron asked quickly when Amberglas stopped. He was as interested as the others in Terrel's dabblings in magic, but they could spend hours trying to get the details from Amberglas. If she had something important to tell them, it would be better to start with that and return to the discussion of Terrel later.

"The map, of course. And the letters, though they're quite old and not particularly useful, which is understandable since Carachel didn't have to send Terrel letters once he'd given him that amulet. But people frequently do things they don't have to do—climbing mountains to see what's at the top, for instance, and learning the two hundred names of that peculiar little man from Gramwood backward—so I suppose it isn't particularly surprising."

Vandaris studied the map for a moment, then looked up at Amberglas with a startled expression. "These are charts of troop movements!" She bent over the map once more in concentration. The others watched for a moment, then Crystalorn shook her head impatiently and said, "What are all the rest of these things for, Amberglas?"

"That usually depends a great deal on who's using them. Though of course there are some things they wouldn't be at all useful for doing. Weeding the garden, for example, or mending shoelaces, or deciding whether to wear green satin pants with a purple-and-orange tunic. Not that it ought to be a particularly difficult decision.''

"Well, what did Terrel use them for, then?" Crystalorn sounded as if she were nearing the end of her patience.

"Sorcery," Amberglas said calmly, touching the bone with the tip of her finger. "And learning sorcery." She touched the book, and a brown crumb clung to her fingertip for a moment as she drew it away. "This"—she indicated the rock—"I believe was used as a paperweight. And the two boxes are different kinds of herrilseed. Or rather, that's what they have in them; it would be a bit difficult to make a box out of herrilseed."

"Herrilseed!" Vandaris's head jerked up as Eltiron and Crystalorn stared at Amberglas. "Rust and dragons-breath, how many people in this idiot-infested castle were poisoning Marreth?"

"But that doesn't make sense!" Eltiron burst out. "Why would Terrel want to poison Father? He was Chief Adviser; Father almost always did whatever he said! And he must have known I wouldn't listen to him if I were King."

"Not exactly," Amberglas said. "Though I can see why you might think so; still, there's very little you could have done about it under the circumstances."

"Amberglas, what are you talking about?" Crystalorn demanded.

"The herrilseed, of course. There are a great many things one can do with herrilseed besides poisoning people, particularly if one is a Black Sorcerer. Making people hate things, for instance, or love them, or believe certain things and not others, or anything that generally involves controlling someone. Of course, one has to be rather good at Black Sorcery to manage some of the more complicated things, but the love spell is exceedingly easy, and even a beginner could manage quite a good control spell if he tried hard enough."

"What good does it do you to control somebody if you have to poison them first?" Crystalorn said.

"Very little, I should imagine, though it doesn't really matter since once one has enchanted the herrilseed it isn't nearly as dangerous, though of course it's never perfectly safe and it always has rather unpleasant side effects."

"Then why would anybody use it?"

"Most people wouldn't, but then most people aren't Black Sorcerers, which is really quite a good thing if one thinks about it. And of course, even if someone has been taking treated herrilseed, only a sorcerer can set the effects of the spell in motion, which is one of the things that makes treated herrilseed so very useful to that sort of person. Most control spells aren't at all specific about whose orders someone will follow, which perhaps explains why most sorcerers use herrilseed instead."

"You mean those are control spells?" Vandaris said, eyeing the two boxes dubiously. "No wonder Marreth was acting peculiar!"

"Actually, I believe the one on the left is a love spell, which is much easier to do. Terrel really should have stopped with that, but perhaps he was only practicing. And of course he may have felt he needed the control spell as well, since it would have been rather awkward to have Marreth in love with him."

Vandaris laughed. "That's certainly true. Still, love potions don't seem much in Lassond's style, unless—" She broke off, staring into space with a thunderstruck expression, then began cursing with considerable feeling.

"What is it?" Eltiron asked when she paused for breath.

"That weasel-hearted, scum-brained, dung-headed slime-rat was going to use that love potion on *me*! I should have killed him while I had the chance. Slowly."

"Well, he can't do anything now," Crystalorn said practically. "So why shout about it?"

"Don't you see? He wasn't just a spy; that slimy worm was going to make himself King of Sevairn the same way Carachel got to be King of Tar-Alem—marry into the royal family and get your wife to hand the kingdom over to you when she inherits! Of course, he'd have had to dispose of Marreth and Eltiron first, but I doubt whether that would have worried him much. And then he'd have a kingdom, and Carachel would have one of his own men in control here."

"I don't think it's at all likely," Amberglas said, blinking at the air just left of Vandaris. "Of course I may be wrong, but then Carachel did such a nice job on that other batch, if one can call that sort of thing nice, and I doubt that he would have sent Salentor to give it to Marreth if Terrel was already doing it, however poorly. It only takes a few doses, after all, and there's no need for the same person to put the spells on the herrilseed and the spells on the person who's been given it. He could have used Terrel's.''

"I don't care whose idea it was," Vandaris said. "I—"

"Wait a minute!" Crystalorn interrupted. "You mean Salentor was working for Carachel, too? And he really did poison King Marreth?"

"I don't think Carachel would have given herrilseed to him otherwise, particularly not with a control spell on it, though of course he may not have told Salentor what it did, which would have been much more sensible than anything else he's done that I know of, even if Salentor couldn't have controlled anyone. Not that Black Sorcerers are any more sensible than most other people, and of course, it didn't make any difference in the end.''

"What do you mean?" Eltiron asked.

"Dear me, didn't you realize? Salentor Parel wasn't giving herrilseed to Marreth, or at least, not *only* to Marreth, though it's very difficult to be certain, particularly with Terrel's spells confusing matters. There was too much missing from that box he had, you see; if Marreth had eaten all that in addition to what Terrel was giving him, he would have been quite dead long before he actually was. It's so very easy to give someone too much treated herrilseed, though of course that isn't precisely what happened to Marreth.''

"But then who *was* Salentor giving herrilseed to?" Eltiron said with a sudden sinking feeling.

"I'd say there were three likely possibilities," Vandaris answered slowly. "Crystalorn, me, and you. Assuming that Parel didn't use the herrilseed until he got to Leshiya.''

Eltiron swallowed hard and looked at Amberglas. "Is there any way to find out whether one of us has been given herrilseed?"

"There is nearly always a way to find out things, though frequently it takes far more time and trouble than it's worth, but not, of course, in this case. Except for Terrel, who really ought to be included since Salentor disliked him so very much, but of course it's quite impossible to tell anything about him at this point, so perhaps it doesn't matter.''

Vandaris looked thoughtful. "I suppose you're right; Lassond could have been getting stuck with his own spear. Pity no one thought of it sooner so we could have checked before he was buried.''

"But you can check us? When? How long will it take?"
Crystalorn said to Amberglas.

"Of course," Amberglas said rather vaguely. "I should
think it would take about an hour or so for each of you,
though one can't be completely certain until one is finished.
And then, of course, it usually doesn't matter."

"An hour? But you knew right away that King Marreth had
been poisoned!"

"Marreth," Amberglas said gently, "was already dead.
There are a number of spells which work much better on dead
persons than live ones, since they tend to be fatal if one isn't
dead, and of course there were quite a few traces of the spells
that had been used to control him, which almost any sorcerer
would notice immediately. It's one of the disadvantages of
using herrilseed, but of course there aren't many sorcerers in
Sevairn, so perhaps they felt it was worth the risk."

"Well, can you at least tell whether someone's put spells on
Eltiron or Vandaris or me?" Crystalorn said.

Amberglas's face went blank for a long moment, then she
nodded. "Yes, of course. Which is not to say whether anyone
will try, but at least there's nothing there now, which is quite
reassuring under the circumstances."

"I still don't understand what happened," Tarilane com-
plained. "Who was doing what to whom, and why?"

"Terrel and Salentor were both working for Carachel,"
Eltiron said slowly, trying to sort it out clearly in his own
mind. "Terrel was using herrilseed to control Father, but he
didn't tell Carachel that. Carachel sent his own batch of herrilseed with Salentor, who was supposed to use it on Father.
Salentor may have given some to Father, but he must have
used some on someone else, too." He shook his head in frustration. "I wish there was a way to be sure of all this! It's all
just guessing so far."

"People who don't expect to be caught frequently do things
which are quite foolish," Amberglas said absently. "Putting
salt in the honey jar, for instance, and stealing the crown
jewels of Bar-Zienar. And writing things down so that people
will know how clever they've been, which really shows the
exact opposite most of the time."

"You mean Terrel left something in those papers?" Eltiron
gestured toward the table.

"Not at all. But of course I haven't had time to check all the rest of them, what with dismantling the warding spell and so on, which really took far more time than it should have. So I'm afraid I don't know."

After a few more minutes, Eltiron ended the discussion by setting everyone to look through the rooms for documents of potential importance. The hunt went smoothly, and soon an untidy pile of letters, notes, and other papers began to grow at one end of the table. Eltiron was just beginning to sort through them when a loud crash, closely followed by a startled shout, sent him running into the small room that had served as Terrel's study. Vandaris was close behind him.

Crystalorn looked up, coughing, as they came in. She was squatting beside the remains of a tall, heavy cabinet which had apparently toppled over, filling the room with dust and revealing a large square hole in the wall behind it. "What happened?" Eltiron demanded.

"I was trying to move it and it fell over," Crystalorn said between coughs. "I'm afraid I ruined it; I'm sorry. But look what was behind it!"

"So Lassond spent his spare time chopping holes in the castle," Vandaris said. "Can't say I think much of the idea."

"But there's something inside! And it feels like magic."

"I don't see anything," Eltiron said, trying to peer over the debris. "Are you sure?"

"Of course I'm sure! Just look." Crystalorn leaned forward and reached for the hole. As her hand passed through the opening, there was a loud popping noise. An instant later, flames flared through the entire room, and Crystalorn screamed. Eltiron plunged forward into the burning room, trying to picture Crystalorn's position.

Heat washed over him and flames roared in his ears. He flung a hand out to where Crystalorn ought to be, and felt a moment's panic when he found nothing but the stone floor. He moved and almost immediately found an arm. She grabbed at him as he hauled her to her feet and started back toward the doorway. Just as they reached it, something dark and heavy dropped over his head. He fought it for a moment; then he heard Vandaris beside him shouting, "You're on fire! Stop fighting, crack-skull!"

Eltiron stopped resisting. Someone, presumably Vandaris, knocked him to the floor, where he was rolled and pounded on for a few confusing moments. Then he heard Vandaris say,

"There, that's finished it." The pounding ceased, and he was allowed to climb to his feet and look around.

He stood just outside the doorway to Terrel's study. The flames inside were already dying; with a slight shock, Eltiron realized how little time had passed. The heavy weight that had smothered his burning clothes was one of the rugs from just inside the door of the main room. Crystalorn stood beside him. A good part of her hair and eyebrows was gone. She was wrapped in the other rug, and water was dripping from her singed hair onto the withered flowers scattered around her feet. Eltiron's face must have shown his surprise; Crystalorn flushed slightly and said, "Tarilane dumped the flower bowl over me. You were—I mean, thank you. Very much. I think you saved my life."

Vandaris interrupted before Eltiron could reply. She insisted on examining them both for serious burns, but to Eltiron's relief she found only a few superficial injuries. Except for her hair, Crystalorn's condition was only slightly worse than Eltiron's; her dress's heavy material and voluminous skirts had kept most of the fire away from her, though the dress itself was ruined.

"Next time, don't be so quick about trying to get into places that have been hidden so well," Vandaris said to Crystalorn when the examination was over. "Particularly when magic's involved. You're luckier than you deserve."

Crystalorn nodded. "I know. And we've lost that book, whatever it was. I'm sorry."

"Not at all," said Amberglas. Eltiron and the others turned to find her standing in the doorway of Terrel's study. The hem of her skirt was dusted with ashes and her face wore a satisfied expression. In her hands was a bundle, wrapped in slightly blackened leather. "As I believe I mentioned, Terrel was *not* a particularly good sorcerer, which is extremely fortunate for us but quite inconvenient for him, or at least it would be if he were still here to be inconvenienced."

Further questioning produced a somewhat clearer explanation. The spell Terrel had used was usually intended to operate within an extremely limited area, such as the niche in the wall. Terrel, however, had not blocked the open side of the niche, so when the spell was triggered most of its force exploded outward into the room. This was fortunate for two reasons: it left the bundle within the niche nearly intact, and it dissipated the fire over a larger area, giving Eltiron and Crystalorn time to escape the burning study. When the flames died, Amberglas had simply gone in and removed the contents of the niche.

The leather-wrapped bundle proved to contain a sheaf of papers and small brown book. After some discussion, these and the rest of Terrel's papers were divided among Eltiron, Vandaris, Amberglas, and Crystalorn.

Eltiron devoted much of the following day to sorting through his portion. At midafternoon, Amberglas arrived to perform the promised tests for herrilseed poisoning. The tests were shorter than he had expected, but the results were not encouraging. Neither Vandaris nor Crystalorn had shown any signs of receiving herrilseed, treated or untreated, but Eltiron had apparently received at least one dose, and possibly more.

"Not enough to do any physical damage, though of course it's a bit inconvenient; still, you ought to be able to keep from being controlled, especially since you know about it now, which always makes that sort of thing much more difficult, provided of course that someone tries," Amberglas told him.

Eltiron did not find this particularly reassuring. To avoid brooding, he plunged back into his study of Terrel's papers, and by evening he had worked his way through the pile. Next morning, he sent for Amberglas, Crystalorn, and Vandaris to find out what they had discovered.

"Not much," Crystalorn said. "Most of what I read was boring official things. There were copies of a couple of notes to people in Sevairn, though." She gave Eltiron a sidelong look. "I don't think Terrel liked you much."

Vandaris snorted. "That's no news. Anything else?"

"Lots of bills for odd things, like lead gloves and snake-skins."

"Black Sorcery involves so many unpleasant things," Amberglas murmured. "Though one probably wouldn't consider them unpleasant if one were a Black Sorcerer."

"I had better luck, I think," Vandaris said. She proceeded to outline the deductions she had made from the letters and map regarding Carachel's strategy. Carachel had apparently intended to unite the Seven Kingdoms against the Hoven-Thalar, and had succeeded in persuading all but Navren and Sevairn. "So it may not have been necessary to send our army south after all," Vandaris finished.

"I don't think I would say that," Amberglas said thoughtfully. "Though doing the right thing for the wrong reason generally makes one feel so very silly, even if it is far better than doing the wrong thing for the right reasons, which seems to be far more common. Still, I suspect all those other armies will be quite unhappy when the Hoven-Thalar don't arrive, so it may very well be useful to have someone there to stop them."

Vandaris stared. "Don't arrive? Amberglas . . ."

"I rather thought you might think so," Amberglas said vaguely. "But it would have been much worse to let the Matholych eat them, particularly since they did ask, and quite politely. So I expect by now most of them are on the other side of Fenegrik Swamp, which is extremely sensible of them."

The ensuing silence was broken by a loud pounding on the door. "What is it?" Eltiron called. He felt somewhat annoyed; he'd specifically told the steward to see that this meeting was not interrupted.

But when the door opened, the steward himself was standing outside, panting slightly. "Your pardon, sire, but—Lord Jermain Trevannon has arrived, and desires to see you."

Chapter Twenty

At a normal pace, and traveling by day, the ride to Leshiya would have taken almost two and a half days. Jermain and Ranlyn made the trip in a day and a half by riding nights and increasing their speed enough to make significantly better time without letting the horses founder. They reached the city at midmorning, when the number of people outside the gates was large enough to make them inconspicuous; but despite the crowd, Jermain was recognized by one of the guards almost as soon as he entered the city.

The guard seemed unsurprised by Jermain's reappearance in Leshiya. A few moments of wary conversation revealed the reason: Eltiron had apparently issued a full pardon for Jermain as soon as he became King. Jermain relaxed a little, and when the guard offered to accompany them to the castle, he accepted.

The guard was a fountain of information about the recent odd events at the castle; he spent the entire ride cheerfully recounting various versions of the tale of Marreth's death, the sudden departure of the Sevairn army, the shocking revelation of Terrel's sorcery, the missing Barinash ambassador, and Marreth's funeral. Some of what he said confirmed the story Salentor had told them, but some was plainly the wildest of rumor. By the time they reached the castle, Jermain thought he had a fair idea what had been going on in Leshiya during the past week, though a few tantalizing gaps remained.

At the castle gates, the guard's announcement of Jermain's identity produced a gratifying stir, though Ranlyn's appearance raised a few eyebrows. Jermain knew several of the men,

223

and they spent a few minutes in conversation until the castle steward arrived to conduct Jermain and Ranlyn into the castle.

Inside, the steward ushered them to a small study and asked them to wait while the King was informed of their arrival.

"There is no need to disturb the King right away," Jermain said. Eltiron would hear of their presence soon enough; at the moment, Amberglas was the one he wanted to see. "For now, it will be enough if you ask the Lady Amberglas to join us; we have a message of some urgency for her."

"But it's the same thing," the steward said in some dismay. "That is, you do mean the Lady Amberglas who arrived with the Princess Crystalorn from Barinash? She's in council with the King."

"Then tell them both."

The steward started to reply, then stopped. "Yes, my lord," he said after a moment, and bowed and departed.

Jermain stared after him, wondering whether his instinctive response had been wise. He was still reluctant to face Eltiron; whether the new King of Sevairn had actually betrayed him or whether he had misjudged Eltiron's actions, the meeting was certain to be awkward. But since the night of Salentor's death he had known that he would have to see Eltiron again. Perhaps he had known even before, when he had prompted Ranlyn to turn toward Leshiya instead of Barinash. Putting it off would only make the encounter more difficult.

His broodings were interrupted by the return of the steward, who requested that they follow him. To Jermain's surprise, he brought them to Eltiron's chambers instead of to one of the small meeting rooms where Marreth had usually held his councils. The steward knocked, then opened the door. "Your Majesty, Lord Jermain Trevannon and his companion Ranlyn of the Hoven-Thalar," he announced, and stepped aside to let Jermain and Ranlyn pass.

Just inside the room, Jermain paused. He felt Ranlyn's presence beside him and dimly noticed the others waiting around the table, but his eyes and mind were focused on the man seated directly across from him. A corner of his mind noted that Eltiron had changed a good deal in the past seven months; he looked older and more sure of himself than the somewhat diffident boy Jermain remembered. He was thinner, too. "Your Majesty," Jermain said, bowing.

"Jermain," Eltiron said. He rose uncertainly to his feet, and for a moment his youth was evident. "Then one of the messengers found you?"

"No, Your Majesty." Jermain's tone was harsher than he intended; he saw Eltiron flinch. Then the young man lifted his chin and looked directly at Jermain, and Jermain found himself thinking of Eltiron for the first time as a King, not a boy.

"Then I can deliver my apology in person," Eltiron said, and Jermain stiffened. Eltiron faltered briefly, then went on, "From what Amberglas has told me, I know you believe I helped Terrel Lassond persuade my father to have you exiled. I cannot deny that my thoughtlessness contributed to his success, but it was not by my design. Terrel used my carelessness for his own ends. He is dead and there is no way I can prove what I say; I wouldn't be surprised if you refused to believe me. But I swear by Arlayne's crown that it is true."

For a long moment, Jermain could not reply. Then he shook his head and said in a voice that seemed suddenly rusty with disuse, "I believe you."

"A debt of truth is often difficult to see ended," Ranlyn said from behind Jermain. "And the burden grows like a dune beneath the winter wind when the truth told reveals the wrongs done by the teller. To be a witness to such courage is a privilege and an honor. I owe you a debt."

Eltiron looked briefly startled; then he bowed. "Both the honor and the debt are mine," he said formally, and Jermain wondered briefly where he had learned the proper reply.

"As soon as you stone-heads are finished being polite, I'd like to find out what brought Trevannon back if he didn't hear from any of our messengers," the woman seated beside Eltiron said, looking pointedly at Ranlyn.

"At least one of your messages reached me, Lady Vandaris," Jermain said, grinning. Marreth's sister had changed very little. "But since at that time I knew nothing of Marreth's death, I chose to be cautious."

"Caution is such an extremely useful thing," said a familiar voice from the end of the table. Jermain turned his head and saw Amberglas. She looked just as vague as he remembered, but there was something warm and welcoming in her manner that made him feel as though he were returning home.

The sorceress smiled in his general direction and went on, "Though of course it isn't always necessary. Rather like wearing shoes; one frequently doesn't need them at all, but what with things like thistles and pins and dogs and so on it's usually quite wise, and people generally like to be thought wise even if they aren't, very, which is a good thing for the cobblers under the circumstances. I expect that's why you're still standing there."

"Yes, please join us," said Crystalorn. She smiled at Jermain from her place beside Amberglas.

Jermain bowed again, feeling a bit light-headed, and looked at Eltiron, who motioned to the place beside Vandaris. Ranlyn remained standing for a moment; then, in a single motion, he went down on one knee before Amberglas. The sorceress tilted her head to one side and regarded the nomad with absent-minded curiosity as he began to speak.

"I have seen the power you gave to the good of my people," Ranlyn said. "And I say to you that I and all the clans of my people owe you a debt which is longer than the length of the wind. We owe you water for your refreshment and your pleasure. We owe you blood for your healing and your renewal. We owe you life for your service and your protection whenever you desire it. Your debts are ours; if you owe a debt of water, we will supply it; if you owe a debt of blood, we will give it; if you owe a debt of life, we will pay it whatever the cost to ourselves. This I swear, for myself and for the clans of the Hoven-Thalar, to be binding for all—"

"No," Amberglas said.

"Your pardon?" Ranlyn's face was impassive, but Jermain knew him well enough to hear the anger in his voice.

"I haven't the least objection to your making oaths and promises for yourself, though of course what you were suggesting does seem a bit extreme. But binding other people for all time is an exceedingly dangerous thing to do, particularly when they aren't there, no matter how justified it seems, and it frequently has rather unpleasant consequences for everyone. So I'd rather you didn't, though it's extremely good of you to offer."

"As you wish it. But for myself, my oath still stands."

"That's very kind of you, though not at all necessary. And I expect it will be quite inconvenient if every Hoven-Thalar I meet insists on repeating it; but then, I don't generally meet very many, so it may not matter. Hoven-Thalar, I mean; I meet quite a number of other sorts of people, and it would be far more inconvenient if all of them did that whenever I saw them, though I can't think why they should, since most of them don't see things quite the way the Hoven-Thalar do. So perhaps you had better sit down and explain."

Ranlyn rose to his feet and seated himself beside Jermain; when he began to speak again, the undercurrent of anger in his voice had been replaced by a trace of amusement. "Little enough is there to explain. In this time does the Red Plague come northward, and then the Hoven-Thalar must move or be destroyed, as the grass must bend or be broken by the wind. Yet it seemed we had less choice than the grass, for the only road open to us led north, and to move north would bring war. Therefore the clans went to the Lady of the Tower, and asked of her some way to avoid both war and the Red Plague alike. This has she provided, and so I and all who count themselves of the clans of the Hoven-Thalar stand in her debt."

"I believe I, too, owe Amberglas something," Jermain said into the silence that followed. "Though in my case it is only my life twice over, not my entire country."

"That is *quite* enough of that," Amberglas said, looking faintly irritated. "Unless of course you wish to be tiresome, which would be rather foolish and not at all like you. At least, I hope it wouldn't. You might try simply explaining what you've been doing instead."

Jermain grinned and plunged into the story of his past seven months. He stuck to a straightforward recounting of events, leaving out his emotional reactions to Eltiron's supposed betrayal. When he reached his meeting with Carachel, Vandaris and Eltiron exchanged frowns, but they did not interrupt until he told them of Salentor's appearance.

"Do you know where he is now?" Eltiron said, leaning forward.

"Trying to explain his life to the Judge of Souls," Jermain replied. "He was killed trying to steal Blackflame."

Eltiron's lips tightened briefly; then he sighed and shook his head. "I'm sorry, but not for his sake; there were some questions we wanted to ask him."

"I may have a few answers." Rapidly, Jermain summarized his conversation with Salentor and finished his narrative.

"That fills in a lot of gaps in our information," Vandaris commented. "I'd been wondering why that map in Lassond's room showed such strange troop movements. But if Carachel was trying to hold the Hoven-Thalar long enough for the Matholych to eat them, he'd have to keep everyone in the thing's path, whether it made sense as strategy or not.''

"You seem to know a good deal more than I'd expected, and I heard some rather odd rumors on my way through the city. What's been happening here?''

Jermain was looking at Vandaris as he spoke, but it was Eltiron who answered. Jermain shifted uneasily, then realized with a slight shock that the idea of talking to Eltiron was making him uncomfortable. He concentrated on listening, and after a moment found it easy to slip once more into the role of King's Adviser, weighing every word and every scrap of information.

Though he had guessed the general outline of the story Eltiron told, most of the details were unfamiliar. He was surprised to learn that Terrel had actually dabbled in sorcery. He noticed that Eltiron made a point of mentioning that the plans for his marriage to Crystalorn had not been changed by Marreth's death. For a moment he thought that Eltiron was remembering Jermain's long-standing opposition to an alliance between Sevairn and Barinash; then he saw Crystalorn listening intently and realized that Eltiron was being careful not to look in her direction. Jermain made a mental note of the interaction, and turned his attention back to Eltiron's story.

Eltiron continued by summarizing the investigation of Terrel's rooms. "That reminds me," Vandaris interrupted. "You never told us what you found in your batch of Lassond's papers. Anything interesting?''

"Jermain's already told you most of the things involving Carachel," Eltiron said. "Terrel had some things about his own plans, but I don't think they matter much anymore.''

"Maybe not, but I'd still like to know.''

"All right, then, listen.''

The papers Eltiron had taken included some old letters from Carachel to Terrel, some official documents that belonged in the castle archives, and a number of Terrel's private papers. These included proof of Terrel's treachery and Jermain's innocence, should it be needed. Terrel had been instructed by Carachel to remove Jermain and take his place; sending Morenar to murder him had been Terrel's own idea, because he'd feared that Jermain would become more useful to Carachel than he himself. Eltiron's marriage to Crystalorn was also part of Carachel's plan, though Terrel had apparently had some idea of marrying Crystalorn himself. Vandaris's reappearance had offered an easier way to power in Sevairn—marry her, poison Marreth, and blame Eltiron for the King's death, then use the herrilseed love potion to acquire the kingship formally. He'd had the covert support of a fair number of Sevairn nobles, though he had told none of them the full extent of his plans.

"And what did he think Carachel was going to do during all this?" Vandaris demanded. "For that matter, what was that snail-wit going to do about the Matholych? Or didn't Carachel tell him that part?"

"Carachel told him," Eltiron said, "but I don't think Terrel believed him. I think Terrel thought Carachel was just using the Matholych as an excuse to get control of the Seven Kingdoms, and that Carachel wouldn't care who was on the throne of Sevairn as long as the King did what he wanted."

"Dumb-brained lack-wit," Vandaris muttered. "If he didn't believe in the Matholych, why was he trying to learn sorcery?"

"Maybe he thought Carachel would approve, or maybe he wanted to take Carachel's place." Eltiron seemed to be thinking of something else; he glanced at Amberglas, then his eyes came back to Jermain. "There's only one more thing you should know, I think." He hesitated, then looked down at the table and went on with a rush. "Amberglas thought that Salentor must have used some of his herrilseed on one of us, and when she checked everyone yesterday . . . well, she was right. He gave it to me."

Jermain stared at Eltiron, stunned both by this calm announcement and by his own reaction to it; he'd thought whatever affection he'd had for Eltiron was dead. The news appeared to be a shock to Crystalorn and Vandaris as well; Crystalorn went white, and Vandaris glared ferociously at Eltiron and Amberglas. Eltiron glanced up and shrugged slightly, then returned to his contemplation of the tabletop.

"You realize that there's a good chance that Salentor told Carachel what he'd done, don't you?" Jermain said after a moment.

Vandaris snorted. "He'd have been the biggest fool in the Seven Kingdoms to do that."

"He was," Jermain replied. "But he almost certainly talked to Carachel that night at our camp, and he'd have been a bigger fool not to tell Carachel everything, once he realized how much he'd given away. And Carachel is following me to get his ring back. Isn't there anything that can be done about that poison?"

"I'm afraid not," Amberglas said. "That is, one could do a great many things about Eltiron's having been given herril-seed, but none of them would work very well, which is quite unfortunate just now."

"Then we'll have to do something about Carachel," Vandaris said. "He's the immediate problem, anyway; that Math-olych thing won't get here for another month at least."

"There is truth in what you say," Ranlyn said from beside Jermain. "Yet has the Red Plague reached out once already to touch one within your city."

"We can't do anything about it now," Vandaris retorted. "And Carachel's a lot more likely to get here in the next day or so than the Matholych is. Assuming that you're right about him chasing you instead of that red blob."

"One way or another, we'd have one less problem if he were," Jermain said moodily. Vandaris raised an eyebrow, and Jermain continued, "Carachel said he'd been gathering power to face the Matholych; and according to Ranlyn, the Matholych gets weaker as it eats power. If Carachel fights the thing, either he'll use up a lot of power winning, or he'll lose and the Matholych will eat him. Either way, the winner wouldn't be nearly as hard to deal with."

"Too bad we can't persuade him to do it, then."

"I don't quite think so," Amberglas said thoughtfully. "I'm afraid it seems a little too much like what Carachel was planning to do to the Hoven-Thalar, feeding them to the Matholych to make it weaker so he could win, you know, though of course there aren't nearly as many of him, which is quite fortunate for us even if it's not for him."

Jermain opened his mouth to reply, then shut it with a snap. Amberglas was right; what he had suggested was exactly what Carachel had planned to do.

"It matters less than runes drawn in sand," Ranlyn said. "The Servant of the Red Plague is not foolish, to attempt to face power without power of his own, and we hold the source of his power. So will he follow us, until the Ring of Two Serpents is once more in his keeping.''

"That's it!'' said Vandaris suddenly.

Everyone looked at her. "What's it?'' Eltiron said.

"If Carachel's power is in the ring, he can't do any harm as long as we keep him away from it. So we set a trap for him.

"And we use the ring as bait.''

Chapter Twenty-one

Eltiron did not participate in the lively discussion that followed Vandaris's suggestion. He listened with barely half his attention while Jermain, Vandaris, and Ranlyn argued about the advisability of the idea and the details of the trap, and as he listened he watched Jermain.

He had been prepared for the awkwardness of their meeting, and he had anticipated the difficulty of making at least a semi-public apology. He had not been ready for the hard lines around Jermain's mouth, or for the bitter tone in which he spoke of Carachel. He had not expected Jermain to avoid speaking to him and address most of his comments to Vandaris. He had not expected Jermain to be a stranger.

He shifted slightly, and tried to concentrate on the discussion. Ranlyn was saying something about a Hoven-Thalar spell that might be used to hold Carachel harmless.

"You're a magician?" Vandaris said skeptically when Ranlyn finished.

"No more than you, in things of every day. But the charms that hold the Red Plague will ofttimes hold its servants, and many such spells are in the keeping of my clan."

"It sounds as if it might work," Eltiron said. "But Carachel's the King of Tar-Alem; what will his army do when they find out he's a prisoner? And the other Kings won't like it much, either; it sets a bad precedent."

"When the other rulers of the Seven Kingdoms find out what Carachel's been trying to do, they'll be fighting for the privilege of chopping his head off," Vandaris said.

"And I doubt that Carachel's men are particularly loyal to

him," Jermain said. "They won't do anything immediately, and with a little encouragement they might even be persuaded to support Elsane. I don't believe she'd object to having her kingdom back."

"Do you really think this has a chance of succeeding?" Crystalorn burst out. "Carachel's a sorcerer!"

Jermain looked at her. "Do we have any other choice?"

"Nearly everything has *some* chance of succeeding," Amberglas said absently. "Of course, sometimes the chance isn't a particularly good one; but then, a great many highly unlikely things happen anyway. People accidentally growing blue roses, for example, or crossing the ice-fields of Mithum alone in the middle of winter, though I believe the woman who did that was a hero. Still, heroes are highly unlikely, though it's quite understandable when one thinks of the sorts of things they do, which may account for their being quite rare and so seldom around when they could be useful. Not that it's likely to matter much in this case."

"All right," Eltiron said. "If you think there's a chance it will work, we'll try Vandaris's idea. I think Jermain's right; we don't have much choice." He looked at Amberglas a little anxiously; he was not completely sure he had interpreted her speech correctly.

"Exactly," said Amberglas.

"Good." Vandaris sat back in her chair. "Now, anybody have any idea where the best place would be to set a trap for a wizard?"

"We'll want room enough to move," Jermain said. "Carachel's no fool; he won't come alone."

"He can't have more than a dozen men with him or we'd have heard; I've got men out looking for odd things and they wouldn't miss a group that size. There are enough guards here at the castle to take care of that many. We could set up this spell in the practice yards and put more guards behind the Tower of Judgment in case we need them."

"Won't Carachel know something's going on when he sees the guards?" Crystalorn objected.

"He'll know we were expecting him, my lady, but if he sees guards he won't be looking for a magical trap," Jermain answered. He looked across at Amberglas. "He probably knows you're a sorceress, so you'd better stay out of sight.

Will that cause any problem with the spell?''

"I shouldn't be at all surprised if you were right," Amberglas said. "And of course the tower is close enough for us to tell when we're needed, if we are."

"What do you mean, 'we'?" Vandaris said.

"King Eltiron and myself, of course. It really wouldn't be at all wise to have someone about who's been given herrilseed when a Black Sorcerer is going to be around, particularly if that someone is the King. But I doubt that Carachel will notice either of us inside the tower."

"She's right, Eltiron," Vandaris said after a moment.

Eltiron nodded slowly. He wasn't sure whether he should feel disappointed or relieved.

Jermain looked at Ranlyn. "Can you set your spell in the practice yards? And can you hide it so Carachel won't notice it?"

"What is the size of this place?" Ranlyn said. Jermain described the practice area, and Ranlyn nodded. "A spell-circle has little need of larger space, and the sand will cover it. It will not be found by the Servant of the Red Plague, for it bears no likeness to his magic, and once he steps within its boundaries he will have no means of leaving it without the Ring of Two Serpents. And that we hold."

"Fine," Crystalorn said. "But how are you going to get Carachel inside this spell-circle?"

"At its center will I hold the ring," Ranlyn replied calmly. "So will he enter it, to regain what he desires."

"No!" Jermain said. "It's too dangerous!"

"Someone has to," Vandaris said. "Carachel's sure to smell the meat rotting if he sees his ring just sitting in the middle of the courtyard."

"Then I'll do it!"

"No," Ranlyn said. "This task is mine, for the debt I owe to you and to the clans. So has it been from the first calling of the wind, and so shall it be."

Jermain glared for a moment at Ranlyn's impassive face. "I'll be there with you anyway."

"As you will have it."

"Then I'll have to join you," Vandaris said with a mock sigh. Eltiron looked at her in surprise, and she shrugged. "Morada's eyes, you think I'm going to miss all the fun?

Besides, it'll look better to have three of us waiting for him."

"I think I'd better just sit inside the Tower of Judgment with Eltiron and Amberglas," Crystalorn said. "I'm afraid I'm not very good with swords."

"Oh, no, you won't," Eltiron said without thinking.

"What!" Crystalorn glared at him.

"Because you're the Princess of Barinash," Eltiron said quickly. The thought of Crystalorn coming anywhere near such a dangerous confrontation made his blood run cold, but he could hardly explain that in front of Vandaris and Jermain.

"I hadn't thought of it, but you're right," Jermain said. "She should be on the other side of the castle with all her own guards and as many of ours as we can spare."

"But *why?*" Crystalorn asked. "If Eltiron and Amberglas will be safe in the Tower of Judgment . . ."

"They won't be safe," Jermain replied. "They'll just be out of sight. And Sevairn has enough potential problems with Barinash right now without adding your death or injury to the list."

Crystalorn looked from Jermain to Eltiron, then down at the table. Eltiron felt like a worm.

"Well, thank Viran that's settled," Vandaris said after a moment. She looked at Jermain. "Now, can we have a look at this ring that's causing so much trouble?"

Jermain hesitated, then reached into his belt pouch and pulled out a small, cloth-wrapped package. He unfolded the top layer of cloth, placed the whole thing on the table, and pulled away the remaining wrappings. With a small clink, the Ring of Two Serpents dropped onto the table in front of Eltiron. It *was* made of two serpents, one gold and one black iron, and it was glowing faintly.

"Dear me, how extremely interesting," Amberglas said into the tense silence that followed. Eltiron pulled his gaze away from the ring and saw her looking directly at it, her face intent. She leaned forward and brushed the tip of one forefinger across the ring once, very gently. She gave a small, satisfied nod, and then her expression went vague once more.

"What's he doing with it?" Jermain demanded.

"Looking for it, of course. I suppose he could depend solely on his bond with it, but that's really much slower and not at all necessary, though since his ring is leaking bits of the spell it would probably be much wiser."

"Can you tell how long we have before he gets here?" Vandaris asked.

Amberglas frowned slightly and touched the ring again. "About two hours, I think, though I believe he could do it in less if he tried."

Vandaris looked at Ranlyn. "Is that enough time for that spell of yours?"

"It is enough, though little will there be of excess."

"Then we'd better get started," Eltiron said, rising. The others followed his example, and in a few minutes they were all on their way to the practice area. Eltiron stayed long enough to be sure that things were going smoothly, then left to give the necessary orders to the castle guards. His duties kept him too busy to watch the spell-casting; he caught an occasional glimpse of Ranlyn drawing strange runes in the sand and then carefully erasing them, but that was all. As soon as the spell-circle was closed, Vandaris and Jermain began directing the guards to their places. Crystalorn tried to start another argument with Vandaris about watching the confrontation from the Tower of Judgment; Vandaris's response was to order one of the largest guards in the courtyard to escort the Princess back to the castle at once.

Crystalorn and the guard were hardly out of sight when a horn blew from the top of the castle wall, announcing that Carachel and his men had been sighted. Eltiron sprinted for the Tower of Judgment as the guards took up their positions across the end of the practice yard. He reached the doorway and glanced around to make sure Amberglas was already inside before he pulled it shut. Then he crossed to the window and peered cautiously out.

The guards stood, looking tense and uneasy, in their assigned places. Ranlyn was about twenty paces from the door of the tower, in the middle of the area where he and Amberglas had been working. His left hand was clenched around the cloth-wrapped serpent ring; his right held a long, slender knife. Jermain and Vandaris stood on either side of him, their right hands resting on the hilts of their swords. For what seemed like hours, nothing happened; then there was a shout from the gates of the castle. A tingle ran down Eltiron's arm where it rested on the stone below the window. As he snatched his hand away, six men rode into the courtyard.

The leader of the group, a grim-faced man on a bay stallion, pulled his horse to a halt when he saw the waiting castle guards. He turned his head, scanning the courtyard. His eyes narrowed as they fastened on Jermain, and his expression hardened. Eltiron saw Jermain's back stiffen very slightly, and he knew that the rider must be Carachel.

"I have come for my ring," the rider said.

"No." Jermain's voice rang with the same determination as Carachel's.

"The Matholych comes! Will you let it destroy the Seven Kingdoms again? Without the ring I have no chance of stopping it."

"And with it? Even with your ring, you would have had to give the Hoven-Thalar to the Matholych to weaken it before you attacked. What will you feed the Matholych this time? The armies of Gramwood and Mournwal and Barinash, perhaps?"

Carachel's lips twitched. "I do what I must."

There was a moment's silence as the implications of Carachel's statement sank in. Then Jermain muttered an oath and half drew his sword. He stepped forward and Ranlyn flung a hand across his path to stop him. Eltiron saw a scrap of cloth trailing from Ranlyn's clenched fist as Jermain halted.

"*You* have it, then!" Carachel's voice was low, but it held a note of triumph, and his eyes were fixed on Ranlyn.

"I hold it; such is my debt. And I will not return it to your keeping while I yet live."

Without taking his eyes off Ranlyn, Carachel dismounted. Three of his men did likewise; the other two shifted their positions so that their horses were between Carachel and the Leshiya Castle guards. The Leshiya soldiers started to move in; Jermain waved them back. "Leave him for me," he said, drawing his sword.

Carachel ignored them all. He stepped forward, then paused. Inside the Tower of Judgment Eltiron held his breath. The wizard took another step, then hesitated again, frowning. His gaze left Ranlyn and swept around the courtyard. He looked at Ranlyn again, and his eyes narrowed. Then he spoke a single word and gestured with his right hand.

A dome of bright blue light flared in the middle of the courtyard, blinding Eltiron for a moment. When his eyes cleared, the sand of the practice area was blackened in a wide circle that passed barely two paces in front of Carachel.

Eltiron groaned mentally; Carachel had almost been within their trap!

Carachel gestured again. Ranlyn shouted and fell to his knees. His dagger dropped to the ground, but his left hand remained stubbornly clenched around Carachel's ring. Eltiron thought he saw a wisp of smoke or steam seeping between his fingers. At the sound of the cry, Jermain's head turned in Ranlyn's direction; Eltiron caught one glimpse of his face, twisted with anger, and then Jermain lunged toward Carachel. One of Carachel's guards intercepted him. Vandaris leapt to his aid, the castle guards followed, and in moments the courtyard was full of battling figures.

Only Carachel and Ranlyn did not move. The wizard's frown deepened, and he repeated his gesture. Ranlyn cried out as his left arm jerked forward, dragging him with it. Eltiron heard a snapping sound, and Ranlyn fell forward, gasping, as a streak of gold light flew from his hand toward Carachel.

Carachel finished with the ring and looked up. "Enough!" He gestured, and the fighters all over the courtyard were suddenly motionless, frozen in place. Carachel's head tilted to one side as if he were listening to something far away, and his eyes almost closed. Then he nodded and gestured again.

Eltiron moved away from the window. He felt Amberglas's hand on his arm, but he shook it off and crossed to the door of the Tower of Judgment. He was too warm; he needed air. He pushed open the tower door and stepped outside.

The castle guards stood in a line facing Carachel's men; Ranlyn lay sprawled on the sand between them. Carachel stood at the end of the line; he smiled slightly as Eltiron came out of the tower. "You are King Eltiron? I am pleased to make your acquaintance, though I think the circumstances could have been better. You have nothing to fear from me; you, too, will do what you must."

Eltiron found himself nodding, and panic struck him. He tried to move, to scream, and could not. Carachel had cast the control spell on him, and he had not even noticed!

"You have nothing to fear," Carachel repeated, and Eltiron's panic drained away. A tiny part of his mind still knew what was happening, but he could not even summon the desire to fight the spell. Carachel smiled again. "Wait here until I am finished." He turned to Jermain. "I am sorry that we had to meet again in this way. I have no choice in what I do now; if I did I would spare you and your friends in spite of what you have done. But I need more power so that I can reach the southlands in time to face the Matholych, and I must take it from your deaths. I am sorry.''

He turned back to Ranlyn and raised his right hand, and sunlight glinted from the blade of the dagger he held.

Chapter Twenty-two

Jermain struggled against the spell as Carachel bent over Ranlyn's body; he managed to turn his head a finger's breadth, but that was all. He tensed, waiting for the blow, but Carachel did not strike. Instead, the wizard lowered his knife to the ground and began drawing something in the sand beside Ranlyn's head.

"I really don't think that's at all wise," Amberglas said from the doorway of the tower.

Carachel's head jerked in her direction, and he was suddenly very still. Then he rose to his feet in a single fluid motion and made a half bow. His eyes never left Amberglas. "Lady Amberglas, I assume?"

Amberglas inclined her head slightly, but did not speak. She stepped past Eltiron's motionless figure and stood waiting. Carachel studied her for a moment, then stepped over Ranlyn's unmoving form, so that the space between himself and Amberglas was empty.

"I await your challenge," he said.

"I don't believe it matters," Amberglas replied. "Unless of course you are trying to practice being patient, which is really quite difficult for most people in spite of having so many opportunities. Waiting for a Hundred-Year-Plant to flower, for instance, or sorting three bushels of mixed grains into separate piles. Though I really can't think of a good reason why someone would want to mix three bushels of grains together and then sort them again, which perhaps explains why it doesn't happen very often, except of course in stories. Still, it would be good practice."

"Pardon?" Carachel sounded startled. "I don't believe I understand you."

"I'm not at all surprised."

"Make your challenge, and let us be done with this delay."

"No."

Carachel stared. "What?"

"Dear me," Amberglas said. "I really thought I'd made it quite clear, but then there are people who prefer to have things explained several times even when it isn't necessary, so perhaps it's not surprising. I have no intention of challenging you."

There was a moment's silence; then Carachel laughed harshly. "What do you intend to do, then? If you wish to stop me, there is no other way."

"You are quite wrong," Amberglas said softly. Her eyes were very bright. "Of course, you seem to be wrong about a great many things, so it isn't at all unusual."

Carachel hesitated, then shook his head. "Whatever you can do, or think you can, it does not matter. But I do regret this, lady."

With a sudden shock, Jermain remembered the duel he had witnessed. That wizard had spent a long time on careful preparations, yet Carachel had defeated him with apparent ease. Amberglas had made no such preparations, as far as Jermain knew; despite her abilities, she might be just as easy for Carachel to beat. And that other wizard had preferred death to whatever he'd expected Carachel to do. Jermain wrenched desperately at the spell that held him, hoping that somehow he could free himself in time to help Amberglas. His sword-arm moved, sluggishly; it was not enough.

Carachel stretched out his hand and a stream of golden light poured toward Amberglas. A sword-length in front of her the light splattered into a starburst of sparks, and Jermain let his breath out in relief.

"Are you quite certain you don't wish to change your mind about all this?" Amberglas's wave encompassed Ranlyn, Eltiron, and the two rows of nearly motionless men on either side of the courtyard.

"I have no choice." Carachel sent another probe of light toward Amberglas, with the same result as the first.

"Everyone has choices," Amberglas said severely. She did not seem to notice Carachel's spells at all.

"Enough!" Carachel's shout rang from the walls of the courtyard. "If you will not begin this, I shall. I challenge you to the combat sorcerous for the wrongs you have done to me!"

Amberglas tilted her head and blinked at him. "Yes, I suppose that might seem like the logical thing to do next. To you, I mean; it seems rather silly to me."

"You still refuse to fight?"

"Not at all. I told you I didn't intend to challenge you; I didn't say anything at all about not fighting if you challenged me."

"Then let no man pass the circle until the combat is decided."

Carachel raised his arms in a commanding gesture. Jermain saw the serpent ring begin to glow, and with all his might he willed himself to step forward. His legs moved, but slowly, as if he were wading through the mud-holes of Fenegrik Swamp; then suddenly the spell gave way. He went sprawling forward, but managed at the last minute to turn the fall into a roll. He came up on one knee, sword ready, and stopped.

Carachel and Amberglas were facing each other inside a circle of light that separated them from the rest of the courtyard. As Jermain watched, Amberglas raised her hands as if to brush away a cobweb in front of her; the gesture looked almost absentminded, but as she finished, small flashes of lightning began darting from her hands to Carachel's. The serpent ring flashed once, and the lightning vanished. Carachel brought his hands down, and black fire leapt up around Amberglas. The sorceress looked at it with an expression of mild interest, and her hands began moving in a short, repetitive pattern.

A shout from his right jerked Jermain's attention away from the combat. He rose and spun just as one of Carachel's guards brought his sword down. Jermain's block did not deflect the blow quite far enough; the sword slid off his blade and bit into his left shoulder. An instant later one of the Leshiya guards spitted his attacker from behind.

More of the castle guards came running around the Tower of Judgment, and in a few minutes Carachel's guards were overpowered. Jermain sheathed his sword, then gripped his wounded shoulder to stop the bleeding; the pain made him gasp. He turned back toward the light encircling Carachel and

Amberglas in time to see Vandaris's sword bounce off the
glowing barrier. "Vandaris! What do you think you're
doing?"

Vandaris looked over her shoulder and shrugged. "Somebody had to try something. Doesn't look as if there's much
more we can do until they're finished, though. Back off, tin-
heads!" The last was directed toward the castle guards, who
had begun gathering around the edge of the glow to watch the
battle within. Carachel's ring shone white as he threw globes
of light in a steady stream; Amberglas's hands moved rapidly
in one complex pattern after another as she deflected or
blocked them all.

The guards began to move away from the barrier in response to Vandaris's tongue-lashing. Jermain hesitated, then
went over and knelt beside Ranlyn. The nomad was beginning
to stir; he moaned as Jermain rolled him onto his back. Jermain shuddered as he got a good look at the hand that had
held the serpent ring. On the inner surface, the flesh was
charred to the bone, and three fingers showed unnaturally
twisted lumps where they had been broken.

"Jerayan."

The hoarse whisper startled Jermain; then he saw that Ranlyn's eyes were open and staring at him. He nodded once, unable to speak.

"Jerayan, it is over and again have I failed."

"It's not over," Jermain said, and his gaze returned involuntarily to the circle of light. He noticed absently that the
circle seemed to be widening, but most of his attention was on
the whirling sparks and explosions within it.

Ranlyn's eyes followed Jermain's, and the nomad tensed.
"Their power is too closely matched," he said after a moment. "Give me your aid in rising."

"There's nothing you can do now," Jermain said, but he
helped Ranlyn to his feet. The two men joined Vandaris near
the edge of the dome, to wait for the end of the duel.

"Jermain!"

He turned his head and saw Eltiron, still standing near the
tower door. Reluctantly, he walked over. "What is it?"

"I wanted—Jermain, if Carachel wins, I want you to kill
me," Eltiron blurted. His face was white and his eyes never
left the battle within the glowing barrier.

"What?"

"You heard me. And keep your voice down; I don't want Vandaris to hear."

"Eltiron, you can't—"

"I have to. It's the herrilseed; Carachel *did* know about it. He isn't just controlling me; there's a link or something, too. Even through that." He waved at the barrier of light. "I can feel him every time he throws something at Amberglas. He told me to wait here until he was finished, and I— Jermain, just do it!"

For a moment, Jermain could not force himself to respond, and Eltiron misread his silence.

"It's not just me, Jermain. Sevairn doesn't need another puppet King. Vandi will do a better job of ruling than I would."

Jermain doubted it, but he nodded. He could not refuse the quiet determination in Eltiron's voice. He wondered briefly whether Eltiron had changed more than he had thought or whether he had simply never known the boy as well as he had believed. He tried to find something to say and failed.

He was just turning back toward the duel when a brilliant flash of light half blinded him. Eltiron cried out and staggered against him; Jermain took the shock on his injured shoulder and gasped. He twisted his head to look at Amberglas and Carachel, and almost immediately forgot both his shoulder and Eltiron.

The light surrounding the two mages was flickering, and with every flicker it grew dimmer. Jermain saw that the circle had widened again while he had been talking with Eltiron; one edge touched the wall of the Tower of Judgment ten paces from where Jermain and Eltiron stood. Amberglas and Carachel had paused in their spell-casting to watch the barrier. Outside it, the castle guards were backing away. Then, with another bright flash, the light vanished completely.

There was an instant of utter stillness; then Vandaris started for Carachel. She was checked in midstride by a cry from Ranlyn. "The Red Plague! See where it comes!"

Between the Tower of Judgment and the outer wall of the castle, a mist was rising out of nowhere. It shone with a redness that shifted and changed as the mist thickened—the red of roses, the red of burning, the red of dripping blood. As Jermain watched, it grew swiftly into a cloud twice the height of a man and began to spread.

                              *   *   *

Eltiron stared at the Matholych, feeling a sick horror that
was only partially his own. The thing was just opposite the
place where Carachel's circle had touched the Tower of Judgment, and Eltiron was certain that it was the contact between
the two that had drawn the Matholych to the tower once more.
Then Carachel shouted in defiance, and the golden aura surrounded him once more. Lightning leapt from the wizard's
hands, forming a crackling web around the red mist, and its
growth slowed. At the same instant, Amberglas made a chopping gesture and Eltiron saw the mist flinch away from her as
though it had been struck.

The combined attack halted the growth of the Matholych
but could not drive it back or force it to return to wherever it
had been. It hung in the air above the courtyard and seemed to
grow denser. Carachel's expression became more desperate;
Eltiron could feel the sorcerer's fear growing as he threw more
and more of his stolen power into the battle, without effect.
Carachel began groping for new sources of strength, and
Eltiron felt himself begin to weaken as the wizard drew on the
link that the control spell had formed between them.

"Eltiron." Amberglas's voice sounded strange and far
away. With an effort, Eltiron turned his head. Amberglas
made a quick throwing motion at the Matholych, then turned
and looked directly at Eltiron.

Eltiron felt a slight shock as their eyes met. He saw Amberglas smile and heard her say, "The tower, Eltiron. That is
your part in this. *Use it!*" Her fingers flicked briefly; then she
turned back to the battle.

Something like a wall in Eltiron's mind crumbled suddenly.
Power rose hot and white and burning within him. The pain
made it difficult to breathe; all that made it bearable was his
link with Carachel. The wizard was still pulling strength from
Eltiron, and he drew off enough of the burning energy to let
Eltiron endure the rest without screaming. The Matholych
drew back as Carachel turned the new power against it, and
the wizard's eyes blazed with triumph.

The Matholych swirled and shifted, seeking, and its hunger
made another kind of pain in Eltiron's mind. He wanted to
run, but he was bound in place, doubly bound by his link to
Carachel and his link with the Tower of Judgment. Through a
haze of pain, he realized that the tower was the source of the

burning force within him. Amberglas had opened his mind to it, but he did not know how to use the power it brought him. It was too painful; he could hardly think clearly. All he could do was serve as a channel for Carachel.

Suddenly Carachel cried out. The Matholych expanded swiftly, swelling into a huge cloud that stretched from the outer wall of the castle to the Tower of Judgment. Eltiron heard a terrible scream as one of the castle guards was engulfed by the unexpected growth. Then the Matholych brushed the tower, and the screams were his own. The pain lasted only an instant before the Matholych jerked away from the tower, but it was enough to drive Eltiron to his knees. He gasped with relief as it ended; the burning power of the Tower of Judgment still flowed through him, but it was almost bearable by comparison. He fought his way back to his feet.

Carachel stood only a few paces from the edge of the red mist, light streaming from both hands. Amberglas was farther back, her hands moving continuously, forming intricate designs in the air. The Matholych had drawn away from the Tower of Judgment, but it still touched the outer wall of the castle. Where it rested, the stone was being eaten away. From the top of the wall, Eltiron heard a scream of terror, and his heart froze.

Crystalorn! He could not see her, but he knew he had not mistaken her voice. Somehow, she must have slipped away from the guard and returned to watch the battle from the sentry walk atop the wall, where she could remain hidden. A large block of stone fell, and the top portion of the inner wall came with it. Through the resulting gap, Eltiron caught a glimpse of Crystalorn's white face as she tried to scramble away from the collapsing portion of the wall. Hopelessly, he cried out her name.

At Eltiron's cry, Carachel looked up from his battle with the Matholych for the first time. He froze for a single breath, and Eltiron felt the wizard's rage and his inexplicable fear for Crystalorn. Then Eltiron felt power rushing through him, and he was sucked along with it into Carachel's mind as the wizard threw all his power into a spell.

There was a moment of disorientation and impossible knowledge. From a strange double viewpoint, Eltiron saw Carachel raise his hands and point toward the crumbling wall; the stone froze in midfall, just long enough for Crystalorn to climb back to safety. Only then did the wizard turn back to the Matholych.

During his moment of neglect, Carachel had lost ground, and he had to retreat hastily to avoid being caught by the mist. Now he and Amberglas fought side by side, and still the Matholych expanded. Carachel backed up a step, then two, but Amberglas did not move. Carachel glanced at her, then slowly retreated again, and the Matholych moved forward to within arm's reach of the sorceress.

From the corner of his eye, Eltiron saw Ranlyn leap toward Carachel's back. Carachel pulled the knowledge from Eltiron's mind an instant too late. As the wizard started to turn, Ranlyn crashed into him, and the impact sent both men reeling into the red mist of the Matholych.

Red light exploded within the Matholych as the two men screamed and fell shriveled to the ground. The serpent ring flared intensely white and was gone, and the expansion of the Matholych ceased abruptly. Eltiron barely noticed. His mind was too full of Carachel's agony; the link that joined them had not yet broken, and he could feel all the wizard's fear, and his pain, and the knowledge of failure that was worse than pain. And then Carachel was dead, but the channel he had opened held.

The Matholych flowed down the link, dark and searing, and it pulled at Eltiron like thousands of hooks ripping at his flesh. The pain of the white power from the Tower of Judgment intensified, and Eltiron screamed aloud as the two forces met within him. They were too strong to bear, and too different; the clash between them was like ice water thrown on molten lead, exploding into burning droplets of intense pain that faded slowly into nothingness. They were too different . . . and suddenly, through the haze of pain, Eltiron knew.

The red mist was no living creature. It was power, raw power, collected over the centuries into a huge, mindless mass that had no purpose except to absorb more power. But the core of it, the beginning of it, shaped all the power it absorbed, and that core was the exact opposite of the power within the Tower of Judgment. The Matholych had begun as the power Galerinth had taken from the Tower of Judgment and the other towers he had built, the power he had feared would be used for evil.

The revelation hit Eltiron all at once, but he was too mired

in pain to use it. Then a bit of knowledge came out of
nowhere, and he shoved the Matholych back along the link,
out of his mind, and held it there. His head cleared, and he
realized that it was Carachel's information he had used, and
that the makeshift mental barrier would not last long. He
dismissed the thought and looked around, trying to decide
what to do.

The Matholych was a dense red pillar in the center of the
courtyard. Jermain stood, sword in hand, staring at it, and
Eltiron realized that it had been only a moment or two since
Ranlyn and Carachel had been swallowed by the red mist.
Amberglas stood in front of Jermain, calmly casting spell
after spell, though her face showed signs of strain. She seemed
to find it easier to hold the Matholych now, and Eltiron
remembered that the mist grew weaker as it absorbed magic.

He raised a hand, then hesitated, undecided. He thought he
knew enough, now, to force the Matholych back to the wastelands, but the ghost of Carachel's voice in his mind demanded
more. Banishing the Matholych was only a temporary solu-
tion, though it might last for years; the red mist would return
again and again unless, somehow, it could be destroyed.
Eltiron could think of only one way to do that—rejoining its
power to the towers where it had begun. And to do that he
would have to let both powers meet inside himself again.
Another man, a true sorcerer, might be able to find a different
means of accomplishing the joining, but Eltiron had only
borrowed knowledge to use, and this was the only way for
him.

The memory of the pain held him back. He stood motionless for a long moment, feeling afraid and very much
alone. He thought briefly and wistfully of Crystalorn; then he
took a deep breath and drew with all his strength on the white-
hot power of the Tower of Judgment.

His hands rose in a strange, half-familiar gesture as the
power flooded him, and through the rising pain he felt a series
of brief shocks as the power of the other towers linked with
the Tower of Judgment. He struggled to control them while he
groped for the remains of the channel Carachel had made in
his mind, the channel that led now to the Matholych. He
found it, and with the last of his willpower he opened it and
pulled the Matholych into himself.

Pain exploded in sharp, spinning bursts of agony, like

wheels of red-hot daggers. Mindless with agony, he tried to
make it stop, but it was too late. He had no control over the
forces he had unleashed. The two powers clashed and spun
and battered, exploded into searing shards that bored tunnels
through his mind, and slowly, too slowly, died.

The Matholych thinned and faded and vanished, and
Eltiron felt the magic the Matholych had stolen flowing
through the towers, back into the land from which it had
come. As it did, the towers began to disintegrate. He wanted
to shout a warning, but he had no strength left. His efforts
had left him drained, and he felt himself topple. The last thing
he saw before he lost consciousness were the stone blocks of
the Tower of Judgment, falling all around him.

Chapter Twenty-three

When the Tower of Judgment began to collapse, Jermain had just enough time to pull Amberglas out of the path of the falling stones. He ducked his head and covered it with his good arm until the sound of the collapse ceased, then looked up. A low mound of rubble and a cloud of dust were all that remained of the Tower of Judgment. Of Eltiron there was no sign.

Without giving the dust time to settle, Jermain started forward. Choking and cursing, he made his way across the pile toward the place where he had last seen Eltiron. He was dimly aware that there was not as much wreckage as there should have been, but he did not stop to think about it. He found the spot at last, and began to dig.

The huge stone blocks of the tower had crumbled into fragments; most of them were fist-sized, and the largest was perhaps twice the size of a man's head. His injured shoulder hampered his efforts, but Vandaris joined him almost immediately, followed by four of the castle guards, and after some digging they reached Eltiron. Jermain looked him over quickly with a soldier's impersonal expertise, then lifted him carefully out of the rubble and carried him to a clear patch of ground just beyond. As he laid Eltiron down, someone beside him said, "Is Eltiron—is he dead?"

Jermain looked up and saw Crystalorn watching him; her face was white and anxious, but he had no time for reassurances. "He's alive, barely," he said sharply. "Find a healer."

Crystalorn nodded and ran off. She returned with Darinhal, the castle physician, and with some relief Jermain turned the unconscious Eltiron over to him. He left Crystalorn trying to peer over the healer's shoulder without getting in his way, and walked slowly back toward the place where the Tower of Judgment had stood. The initial shock of events was beginning to wear off, but he still felt stunned by the speed with which everything had happened.

Vandaris was standing beside the rubble, directing a group of soldiers and servants who were busily clearing the stones away. When she saw Jermain approaching, she waved to them to continue and came to meet him. She looked sharply at his face, then asked, "Eltiron?"

"Alive. Darinhal's with him. What's all this?"

"There were at least four people inside the tower when it came down," Vandaris replied.

"Four!" Jermain stared at the mound of stones. "I don't think you have much chance of finding them alive."

"Someone has to try. Besides, it keeps people from asking questions I don't have answers for."

Jermain looked at the remains of the tower again and shuddered. "Vandaris, what could have done this?"

"That's one of the questions I was hoping no one would ask yet. But as long as you have, let's see if we can get an answer."

Without waiting for Jermain to reply, Vandaris turned and walked toward the castle wall. Jermain followed. The section of wall that the Matholych had touched was broken apart, and Jermain saw Amberglas sitting on one of the stone blocks. She looked up as they approached, and Jermain was appalled by the lines of exhaustion in her face.

"All right, Amberglas, what happened?" Vandaris demanded, waving at the remains of the Tower of Judgment.

"I won't know until I've talked to King Eltiron. I believe he was responsible."

"*Eltiron* did that?"

Amberglas nodded tiredly. Vandaris studied her for a moment, then shook her head. "You need rest, and you'll be no help here until you get it. You'd better go inside; I'll send someone if you're needed."

Amberglas nodded again. She rose with difficulty and started toward the main part of the castle. Vandaris watched her with a frown until a shout from one of the men on the rubble-heap distracted her.

Jermain and Vandaris went over to see what the problem was; when they arrived, the white-faced guard simply pointed to the patch of rubble he had been clearing. There were two figures still partly buried beneath the stones, their skins dry and so badly shrunken that there were long, red streaks where they had split open. One of the figures was face down, and a ring of flesh on the third finger of its outflung hand was charred and blackened.

"Ranlyn," Jermain murmured, "and Carachel."

"What should I *do* with 'em?" the guard asked.

"Find someone with a stronger stomach than yours and have him bury them," Vandaris said.

The guard gulped and nodded. Vandaris turned away, but Jermain remained standing beside the bodies. He made a silent farewell to the man who had been his friend, and tried not to think of the man who had become his enemy. He felt numb and drained. For the first time in years, he did not know where he would go now or what he would do next. He did not care.

Jermain slept for the rest of the day, except when one of the healers stopped in his rooms to change the bandages on his shoulder. The following morning, one of them told him he should stay in bed for another day. His thoughts had an uncomfortable tendency to run over the less pleasant scenes of the previous day again and again, and he blamed himself for Ranlyn's death. He had no doubt of Ranlyn's reasons; the nomad had decided that Amberglas alone could handle the Matholych if it were weakened sufficiently, and the obvious way to weaken it was to feed it power. Carachel's power. But if Jermain had not suggested throwing Carachel to the Matholych, Ranlyn might not have done it.

By midafternoon Jermain could stand it no longer, and he insisted on getting up. It was not so much that he felt well as that he had to get out of the room. His first act was to check on Eltiron. To his surprise, a young girl was standing by the King's chamber door, refusing admittance to everyone.

"Nobody gets in," she informed him. "His Majesty isn't ready for visitors yet, or that's what the healer said."

"Then Eltiron will live?"

"Far as I know." She looked curiously at the sling he wore around his left arm and her eyes narrowed. "Who're you?

Were you in that fight with the wizard and that pink thing yesterday?''

"I was. My name's Jermain Trevannon."

"Oh! Vandi wants to see you. I'm Tarilane," the girl added as an afterthought.

So this was Vandaris's daughter! Jermain studied her for a moment. Too soon to say how she'd turn out, but he doubted that she'd ever be very tall. And she was younger than he'd expected. With Vandaris training her, though, she had an excellent chance of becoming a first-class swordswoman. Jermain bowed. "Thank you for the information, Your Highness."

"What? Oh, because Vandi's my mother. You'd better not let her hear you call me that, though; she doesn't like it."

"I see. Where will I find her?"

"She's down in the Great Hall with Crystalorn—I mean, with the Princess Crystalorn." Tarilane leaned forward confidentially. "She's not in a very good mood."

"Oh?"

"About a dozen lords came to see her this morning, and she had to be polite to them."

Jermain could not suppress a chuckle. "I think I understand."

"And that's not all." Tarilane grinned suddenly, giving her a strong resemblance to a delighted imp. "After the lords left, Crystalorn tried to show her how to use one of those magic fire-starting sticks Amberglas made, and it exploded."

"Very disconcerting. Was anyone hurt?"

"Of course not; it was mostly just sparks. Amberglas says it's because Eltiron, I mean King Eltiron, let the magic out of the pink thing. She says it's going to be a lot easier to work magic in Sevairn and Mournwal and Gramwood now, and maybe in all of the Seven Kingdoms. She promised to teach me how to do it when I'm finished learning swordcraft from Vandi."

"I wish you well with it. Now I had better go to Vandaris, before she becomes even more, ah, irritable." Jermain bowed again, and took his leave. The discussion made him uncomfortably aware of how many changes there had been in Leshiya in the past months, and how many more could be expected in the near future. He tried to imagine Sevairn full of people like Amberglas and Carachel, and shuddered. Then he shrugged the thought away and went to find Vandaris.

"Trevannon! About time you got here," Vandaris greeted him as he entered the hall. She was seated behind a long table littered with papers; Crystalorn occupied the chair next to her. "You in any shape to work yet?"

"It depends on the work," Jermain replied, indicating his sling. "It'll be a while before I'm ready for swordplay again."

"Did I say anything about swords, turtle-wit? I need some advice about people, and you know a lot more about Sevairn's nobles than I do, even if you haven't been around for a while."

"If I can help, I will." Jermain found Vandaris's manner more irritating than usual, but anything was better than lying in his room, staring at the ceiling and thinking of Ranlyn and Carachel. "What is it you want?"

Vandaris shoved some of the litter aside and picked up a thin stack of papers that had been underneath them. "This used to be Terrel Lassond's; it's his list of nobles he thought would support him. I need to know which ones knew what they were doing and which ones were just being stupid. Particularly stupid, that is; if you try to point out every idiot at court we'll be here for weeks."

"And you're willing to trust my judgment?" After the mistakes he'd made recently, Jermain wasn't sure that he wanted anyone relying on him. Especially not for something like this.

Vandaris gave him a sharp look, then shook her head. "I said I wanted advice, not decrees. Eltiron will have to make the final decisions about who'll stay at court and who won't. But it'll be easier if he has some idea who the real traitors and potential traitors are."

"All right, then." Jermain took the list and sat down across from Vandaris. He skimmed it rapidly, then went through it a second time more slowly. On this third pass, he read name by name, marking as he went and occasionally stopping to consider for a long time before he went on to the next name.

When he finished, he had divided the list into three parts: those he was sure had cooperated wholeheartedly with Terrel, those he was equally sure had merely been dupes, and a smaller group of which he was uncertain. Then he and Vandaris discussed each of the names on the "doubtful" list, while Crystalorn listened intently.

Finally they finished, and Vandaris rose. "That's everything? All right, let's see if Eltiron's in good enough shape to look at it yet."

They made their way to Eltiron's chambers, where Tarilane informed them that the castle physician had just left. He had left a message for Vandaris, saying that she could see the King for a few minutes but was not to tire him. Vandaris snorted and knocked on the chamber door.

To Jermain's surprise, it was Amberglas who answered. She appeared to be almost completely recovered from her exertions of the previous day; the only signs of the experience were the fine lines at the corners of her eyes which Jermain was sure had not been there before. She tilted her head to one side and blinked at them for a moment.

"Very good. I thought perhaps you would be getting here soon. Come in; Eltiron's been asking for you." She stood aside, and they went in.

Eltiron was sitting in a large chair by the window. His right arm was splinted, he had a number of nasty-looking bruises and a black eye, and he looked exhausted, but he looked up and grinned as they approached. "Vandi! I've been waiting for you. I didn't think Darinhal would be able to keep you out much longer."

Eltiron regretted his impulsive greeting almost as soon as it was uttered. Amberglas had succeeded in reducing the throbbing in his head, but she had not been able to dismiss it entirely, and even the mild effort of calling out sent a stabbing pain up the back of his skull.

"What makes you think Darinhal could keep me out at all?" Vandaris demanded as she strode inside and swung herself into a chair next to Eltiron. Jermain, Crystalorn, and Amberglas followed more slowly as she went on, "Or did all that rock scramble your brains?"

Despite his aches, Eltiron grinned again, but he was more careful about speaking when he answered. "Not so you'd notice, although Amberglas and Darinhal both keep telling me I'm lucky to be alive."

"I'm not surprised. How bad's the damage?"

"The arm is broken, and so are two of my ribs; Darinhal's got my chest wrapped so tight in bandages that I can hardly

breathe. Plus assorted bruises and a headache you wouldn't
believe even if I could describe it.''

"Better than I'd expected," his aunt said without sympathy. "The only reason I can think of that your brains weren't
mashed is that three quarters of the Tower of Judgment seems
to have disappeared on the way down. You wouldn't happen
to know anything about that, would you?"

"Not exactly," Eltiron said uncomfortably. "The towers
couldn't seem to hold all of the Matholych, but I don't know
why."

"Towers? The only one that fell was the Tower of Judgment," Jermain said. "The rest of the castle towers are intact."

"There were seven towers, one in each of the Seven Kingdoms somewhere," Eltiron explained. "Amberglas says a wizard named Galerinth built them, but they only had half the
magic they should have had, so they didn't work properly.
The Matholych was the other half of their power."

"I thought the Matholych was a creature or a disease or
something," Crystalorn objected. "How could it be part of a
bunch of towers?"

"It wasn't," Amberglas said. "Which is precisely the problem. Not that it's at all surprising; things like that happen
quite frequently when one believes one knows more about
magic than one actually does, which is far more common than
it ought to be."

She looked directly at Eltiron as she finished speaking, and
he found himself wondering how much she knew or had
guessed. He had not mentioned the link he had felt with Carachel's mind, nor had he spoken of the knowledge of magic and
sorcery that had come to him through it. Most of what he had
learned had faded quickly from his conscious mind, and he
could not have said whether his nightmares the previous evening had come from the encounter with the Matholych, from
the few remaining scraps of Carachel's memories, or simply
from having been hit on the head by a large number of rocks.

"Of course not," Amberglas said, and Eltiron realized that
he had missed someone's question. "The power was still
shaped by Galerinth's spell, but only by the wrong half of it,
which is why it was so very much the opposite of the towers in
most ways."

"So the Matholych could move, and the towers couldn't,"
Vandaris said. "And the towers had solid forms, and the

Matholych was just a red cloud. But why did it kill people?
And why in Arlayne's name did it keep coming north?"

"It came north because of the towers. I believe it wanted to
get back where it belonged, if something that isn't really alive
can want things, which I suppose might be possible even
though it doesn't happen very often. The rest was really just
an extremely unpleasant side effect."

"A side effect? Dragonfire and starflowers, that thing ate
halfway through the outer wall of the castle in less than a
minute! And you say that's a *side effect*?"

"Exactly. Galerinth was trying to make the towers totally
good, you see, and not being totally good himself he wound
up with an exceedingly peculiar mixture. Though I'm afraid
the Matholych didn't precisely *eat* through the wall."

"It certainly looked to me as though it were eating!"
Crystalorn said, shuddering.

"What a thing looks like is frequently quite different from
what it is. Those odd little insects that look like dry twigs, for
instance, and very bad pastry that's been covered in whipped
cream, and the crown jewels of Mournwal."

"The crown jewels of Mournwal?"

"About half of them are paste. At least, they were the last
time I saw them, but that was rather a long while ago, so I suppose a few more of them might have been replaced by now. I
can think of a great many better ways of paying for one's
government, but then, perhaps whoever is the King of Mournwal just now doesn't have a great deal of imagination."

"They're *paste?*" Crystalorn sounded outraged.

"I believe I did say they weren't what they seemed," Amberglas said gently.

"About the Matholych," Vandaris prompted.

"Yes, of course. You see, Galerinth apparently had exces-
sively grand ideas, which isn't at all surprising, because if he
hadn't been that sort of person, he wouldn't have tried to cast
that spell in the first place, and everyone would have been
spared a great deal of trouble and inconvenience. I believe he
wanted to use the towers to control all the magic in the Seven
Kingdoms."

"I don't think I see how that explains what the Matholych
was doing," Jermain said.

"It was the other half of the spell on the towers," Amberglas said patiently. "But I'm afraid they were quite out of balance in a great many ways, so of course the towers didn't do enough and the Matholych did far too much. I rather doubt that Galerinth expected the Matholych to be quite so active about soaking up magic, though he really ought to have realized that destroying things and killing people can generate a good deal of power, which of course his spell would have to deal with somehow if it were going to control *all* the power in the Seven Kingdoms. But unfortunately, he didn't."

"I still don't understand why the towers collapsed," Eltiron said.

"Dear me, I thought that was quite obvious. The Matholych had been sucking up power for years, and so of course it grew bigger, though I believe it took rather a long time to assimilate everything it took in, which is perfectly reasonable since the spell wasn't designed for that sort of thing in the first place. So it was entirely too much for the towers to absorb all at once like that, and the whole spell came apart, which is really the best thing that could have happened under the circumstances."

"How long have you known all this?" Crystalorn asked suspiciously.

"If you are referring to the details of the spell on the towers, I've known most of it since yesterday, though of course I've studied them for years and it was quite evident that they had *some* connection with the Matholych even if it wasn't clear precisely what it was. Spells are so much easier to understand when one can watch them being put together or taken apart."

An unpleasant thought crossed Eltiron's mind, and he looked at Amberglas. "You lived in one of them, didn't you?"

Amberglas nodded absently. Eltiron said, "I'm sorry."

"That's quite all right," Amberglas said vaguely. "There wasn't anything particularly interesting about it, except of course itself, and one can say that about nearly everything, whether it's magic or not."

Crystalorn looked from Amberglas to Eltiron and frowned. "Well, if Amberglas's tower is gone, what are you going to do about it?"

Eltiron winced as the rising note in her voice stimulated his headache again. "There isn't much I *can* do! I can't put it

back up again; I'm no sorcerer." He did not feel like bringing
up the bits of knowledge he'd acquired from Carachel.

"But—"

"King Eltiron is quite right," Amberglas interrupted
firmly. "And besides, there are a great many other places I
haven't tried living in yet. The capital of Navren, for instance,
or that odd little seaport in northern Vircheta that changes its
name every few years for no particular reason. Though I expect I will start with Sevairn, since it's much more convenient
at the moment."

"I'm glad you'll be staying," Eltiron said. "I may need a
sorceress around when the rulers of Vircheta and Mournwal
and Tar-Alem and the other kingdoms start asking why their
towers collapsed. Most of them weren't exactly in out-of-the-
way places."

"You don't have to worry about those flea-brains," Vandaris broke in, grinning.

"What makes you say that?"

"I've heard the talk going around Leshiya. By the time the
Kings hear it, I doubt that any of them will want to offend the
Wizard-King of Sevairn."

"*What?*"

"You heard me, granite-ears."

"But I can't—I mean, I'm not—" Eltiron broke off, took a
breath that made his ribs ache, and tried again. "*Carachel* was
the Wizard-King! I don't want his title!" He saw Crystalorn
frown in puzzlement and Jermain nod slowly in understanding. Then Vandaris shook her head.

"You don't have any choice. People think you're a wizard,
so Wizard-King is what they'll call you. If you forbid it, they'll
just do it behind your back and make up stories about the
things you do in secret."

"Vandaris is right, I'm afraid," Jermain said. "Carachel
never titled himself Wizard-King; others did that for him."

"I suppose so, but I don't have to like it," Eltiron grum-
bled.

Jermain nodded again, and Eltiron looked at him for a moment. "What are your plans now, Jermain?"

"I have none, Your Majesty."

"Then would you resume your position in Leshiya as King's
Adviser?"

Jermain hesitated. "I'll . . . think about it," he said at last.

Eltiron started to reply, then looked at Jermain and stopped. They had not spoken privately since Jermain's return, and this was not a good time or place for whatever else needed to be said between them. But he had made a beginning, and perhaps that was all he could expect for now.

There was a moment's silence, then Vandaris looked at Crystalorn. "There's one thing still bothering me about that fight yesterday. Why did Carachel let himself be distracted like that? He risked his neck to save yours, and from all I've heard, that's just not like him."

"I don't care whether it was like him or not," Crystalorn said. "I could feel the Matholych coming after me, and I knew I couldn't get away in time, and then I felt Carachel throw his spell. I don't know why he did it, but I'm glad he did!"

Vandaris did not look away. "It still seems odd to me."

"It *was* odd," Eltiron broke in. He had to get Vandaris off this subject. "But since Carachel is dead, we don't have any way to know his reasons."

"That may not be precisely correct," Amberglas said. "But I really wouldn't recommend that anyone try learning Black Sorcery just to ask Carachel questions which it's extremely unlikely he'd remember the answers to anyway, particularly since I very much doubt it would make any difference now."

Vandaris shrugged. "All right, then, let it be."

If Vandaris had not been watching him, and if the bandages around his chest had not been so tight, Eltiron would have breathed a sigh of relief. He knew why Carachel had helped Crystalorn. He had known since the impossible moment of oneness when the sorcerer had drawn on all his power to save her, and had drawn Eltiron into his mind along with it. Crystalorn was Carachel's daughter; Carachel had been unshakably certain of it. That was why Crystalorn had been able to feel Carachel's magic, and the Matholych, and the magic of the Tower of Judgment earlier. How Carachel had seduced the Queen of Barinash, and how he had kept his secret so long, Eltiron neither knew nor wanted to know. His only real concern was to make sure the secret remained a secret, for Crystalorn's sake.

He saw Vandaris watching him closely, and for a moment he was afraid that she had somehow guessed the direction of his thoughts. Then she said, "Fire and ice storms, you look exhausted as a day-old corpse! Here's the list we came to give you; Trevannon's marked the nobles he thinks knew what they were doing when they supported Terrel Lassond. We can discuss it tomorrow or the day after, when you've had time to go through it."

She dropped a folded paper on the table beside Eltiron, then turned to Jermain and Crystalorn. "Come on, we've done enough damage for one day."

Jermain glanced at Eltiron and rose; Crystalorn followed. "A moment, please," Eltiron said. "I would like the Princess Crystalorn to remain." He looked at Crystalorn and added, "That is, if you'd be willing to."

Crystalorn turned and looked at him uncertainly. Vandaris shot him a sharp look, then grinned and took Jermain's good arm and hauled him along with her, out of the room. Amberglas surveyed first Eltiron and then Crystalorn with an absentminded air that nearly made Eltiron laugh. She nodded once and turned toward the door.

"Amberglas?" Crystalorn said hesitantly.

"It's certainly possible," Amberglas said vaguely. "Though I'd really recommend you settle it yourselves, and of course the sooner it's taken care of the easier it's likely to be for you to stop fretting about it. So I believe I shall leave anyway." She turned and departed; the door closed softly behind her.

"Please, sit down," Eltiron said. Now that he had the opportunity he'd been waiting for, he did not know how to begin. How did one tell a person one wanted to marry her? Particularly if one was already betrothed to her? His head hurt, his ribs ached, and he was beginning to think this had not been as good an idea as it had seemed.

Crystalorn sat down and looked at him for a moment. "You want to talk to me about the wedding, don't you?"

"I—yes, I do. Since so much has happened."

"Well?"

"I thought we could have the wedding and the coronation at the same time. That is, if—if you wanted to. Marry me, I mean." This wasn't coming out at all the way Eltiron had thought it would. He groped for the right words, then suddenly abandoned the effort and blurted, "I do want to marry you, I don't care what the Sevairn nobles say. But if you don't want to marry me, we'll think of something so it won't matter.''

"I don't think that'll be necessary," Crystalorn said, studying him. "But I think we'd better wait a month or so, until you look a little more like a King and a little less like something the dogs chewed over."

Eltiron looked blankly at her for a moment before her words penetrated. "You really want to marry me? After the way you've been avoiding me, I was afraid . . ."

"So was I. I kept hearing people talk about how King Marreth ordered you to get married and picked the bride and everything, and I thought you'd want to get out of it once he was dead."

"Not after I'd met you."

"How could I know that? You never said anything."

"There never seemed to be time."

Crystalorn looked at him. "I think I'm going to have to teach you a couple of things about being a King. You don't have to wait until there's time for things if you don't want to."

Eltiron laughed; the resulting pain in his ribs made him wince. Crystalorn saw it and frowned. "Vandaris was right; you do look tired," she said. "Maybe I'd better go."

"I'd rather you didn't, but I suppose Darinhal will make a fuss if you stay."

Crystalorn grinned suddenly. "He's not the only one. This court has more gossips than all of Navren and Gramwood put together! I can hardly wait to see what they do when they find out I'm going to be Queen of Sevairn after all. But I'd better leave anyway."

She looked at him, then leaned forward suddenly and kissed him, warm and gentle. He caught her hand in his good one as she straightened up to leave. "You'll come back tomorrow."

"Of course. *If* you're well enough." She smiled, slipped her hand out of his, and left.

He looked after her, feeling happier than he could remember being in a long time. Briefly, he wondered whether he should have told her that Carachel was her father. If anyone had the right to know, she did. But it didn't really matter; he would have time to think about it later. They had the rest of their lives.

Now that he thought of it, there were a few other things he ought to deal with as the King of Sevairn—the armies Carachel had gathered in Gramwood, for one. Perhaps if Sevairn offered to help Elsane regain her title as Queen of Tar-Alem, she would disband them. He would have to talk to Jermain about that. And there was Vandaris . . . How long could he persuade her to stay this time? He might need her support if he decided to make any changes among the nobility of Sevairn. And Amberglas . . . He was still planning when he fell asleep.